AN HEIR FOR THE BILLIONAIRE

BY
KAT CANTRELL

MILLS
BOON

First Published in Great Britain 2016
By Mills & Boon, an imprint of HarperCollins*Publishers*
1 London Bridge Street, London, SE1 9GF

© 2016 Harlequin Books S.A.

Special thanks and acknowledgement are given to Kat Cantrell
for her contribution to the Dynasties: The Newports series

ISBN: 978-0-263-91872-4

51-0816

Our policy is to use papers that are natural, renewable and recyclable products and made from wood grown in sustainable forests. The logging and manufacturing processes conform to the legal environmental regulations of the country of origin.

Printed and bound in Spain

Kat Cantrell read her first Mills & Boon novel in third grade and has been scribbling in notebooks since then. She writes smart, sexy books with a side of sass. She's a former Mills & Boon So You Think You Can Write winner and an RWA Golden Heart® Award finalist. Kat, her husband and their two boys live in north Texas.

One

If there was any poetic justice in the world, Sutton Lazarus Winchester had gotten his.

Nora sagged back against the wall of the sterile hospital room, unable to process the inescapable fact that her seemingly infallible father was indeed dying of inoperable lung cancer. She should feel relieved. His tyrannical reign was nearly over. The man who couldn't be bothered to walk her down the aisle at her own wedding lay pale and gaunt in a hospital bed, as if a bit of his spirit had already fled for hell in advance of the rest.

The relief didn't come. Nora had traveled home to Chicago with the barest hope she might find a way to reconcile with her father in his last days. And now that she was here, the sheer difficulty of that task nearly overwhelmed her.

"I had to see it for myself," Nora murmured to her sisters, Eve and Gracie, who flanked her as she faced down their father. None of them had gotten too close to the bed in case Sutton had more gusto than he seemed to have. Right now he appeared to be asleep but that didn't matter.

Like a snake, he waited until you were within striking distance and then sank his fangs into the tenderest place he could find, injecting poison and pain until it suited him to stop. It was how he'd always operated, and Nora had no doubt he'd find a way to do it from the grave.

"We all did," Eve murmured back. "The doctor wasn't too happy with me when I asked her to allow another doctor to review the oncology reports. But I had to make sure."

Methodical to her core, Eve never missed dotting an *i* or crossing a *t*. As the oldest Winchester sister, she'd always been large and in charge and seldom let anything stand in her way.

"Wanted to see the death sentence with your own two eyes, hmm?" Nora said without malice.

Sutton had terrorized all three of his daughters, but Nora was the only one who'd grown so sick of the constant drama surrounding her father that she'd moved halfway across the country to Colorado, effectively— and gratefully—turning her back on the money, the glitter and the heartbreak of the lifestyle she'd been born into.

Eve glowered. "Wanted to make sure it wasn't manufactured. I wouldn't put it past that Newport scum to have paid off a doctor to produce a false report."

"Do you really think Carson could find someone willing to do that?" Gracie asked, and it was clear she had no ill will toward the man the sisters had recently learned was their half brother.

The total opposite of Eve, Gracie always saw the best

in people. Nora's younger sister had such a big heart, even in the midst of the huge scandal caused by the recent revelation that during one of his past affairs, Sutton had fathered a son—none other than his business rival Carson Newport.

Now that Nora had seen her father, she could turn her attention to Carson, who was her second order of business while in Chicago. Oh, Nora didn't give two figs about Sutton's money and whether Carson Newport had a legal claim to any of it. Eve and Grace could fight that battle. But the man was her brother. She *was* curious about him. And she didn't appreciate the idea of her sisters losing out on their inheritance; it meant something to them, even if it came down to nothing more than a just reward for the years of being Sutton Winchester's daughters.

"I wouldn't put anything past him. There are a lot of unethical things people will gladly do for money, including doctors. And especially Newport," Eve responded, tossing her honey-blond hair over her shoulder impatiently. It was longer than Nora remembered, but then, they hadn't seen each other in quite a while. Not since before Sean had died.

The grief over her husband's untimely death, never far from the surface, bubbled up; coupled with the shock at seeing the larger-than-life head of the Winchester real estate empire laid out in a stark white hospital bed, it was too much.

One, two, three… Nora kept counting until she reached ten. That was all the time she was allowed to feel sorry for herself. Sean was gone. Nora wasn't and she had adult things to handle that wouldn't get done if she spent all her time curled up in a ball of grief as she had after the grim-faced army liaison had brought her the news that Sean had been killed in Afghanistan.

He'd never gotten to meet their son. It was the cruelest travesty in a litany of truly terrible circumstances. But Nora still had that tiny piece of her husband alive and present in their little boy, and no gun-toting terrorist could ever take that away.

A woman with thick-framed glasses and hair swept up in a no-nonsense bun appeared at Sutton's bedside, the tablet in her hand and white lab coat indicating she had medical business at hand. She checked a few things on her tablet and then glanced at the knot of Winchester women.

"I'm Dr. Wilde. We haven't met." The doctor rounded the bed to shake Nora's hand. "You must be the nonlocal sister."

"Nora O'Malley," she affirmed. She'd shed the Winchester name as fast as she could after she and Sean tied the knot, and it would take an act of Congress to get her to ever change it to anything else. "So it's true? My father is dying and there's nothing you can do?"

Dr. Wilde bowed her head for a moment, her discreet diamond earrings sparkling in the light. "As much as I hate to admit defeat, yes. It's true. I couldn't operate, due to the tumor's location, and then the cancer spread too fast to employ chemotherapy. He probably has another five months, tops. I'm sorry."

Five months. It was way too fast. How could she find the will to forgive her father for not loving her in such a short period of time?

"Don't be," Nora insisted, even as the doctor's prognosis hit her sideways. "It's his own fault. We all told him to stop smoking but he thought that deal he'd made with the devil would keep him alive forever, I guess."

She'd known that's what the doctor would say. But it was so different to hear it from her mouth personally. That was partly the reason she'd forced herself to get on a plane to Chicago, though traveling with a two-year-old had been exhausting.

And now it was shockingly final. Sutton would be dead by New Year's Day.

Sutton's personal assistant, Valerie Smith, poked her head in the door, not one ash-blond hair out of place. "Is your father awake yet?" she asked. "I was going to bring Declan in if you wanted."

Third order of business: to finally let her father meet his grandson.

It had been a difficult decision. The poison that Sutton managed to infuse into everybody around him couldn't be allowed to affect her son. But his grandfather was dying. Nora had hoped that on his deathbed, her father might have an epiphany about his character, his choices, his closed heart—*something* that would allow all of them to make peace with Sutton's passing and go on.

"No, he's still asleep." Nora couldn't help but feel grateful for the reprieve. She'd steeled herself for this moment of reckoning but nothing magical had happened to the disappointment and hurt inside upon seeing her father in person. "But I'll take Declan so you can have a break."

Valerie had offered to take the cranky and bored two-year-old to the cafeteria in search of Jell-O or saltine crackers, the only two things he wanted. He refused to eat the fruit snacks and banana chips Nora had shoved in her carry-on bag—the only two things he'd wanted when she'd been packing back home. Reason was not in the wheelhouse of a toddler, so holding out the packages and telling him that was the snack he'd picked hadn't worked.

The little boy popped into the room and Nora's heart lurched, as it always did when she caught sight of his curly mop of red hair. He looked like Sean, of course, and it was both a blessing and a curse to have the visual reminder of what she'd lost. "Hey, Butterbean. Did you find some Jell-O?"

Nora extracted herself from her sisters with a hand to Gracie's arm and a smile for Eve, guilt crowding into her chest that she'd opted to take the out of caring for her son instead of sitting here with her family. They'd all been by Sutton's side from the beginning, supporting each other, showing solidarity to outsiders, but Nora just…couldn't.

Declan nodded. "Jell-O."

It came out sounding more like *je-whoa*, but Nora had never had any trouble interpreting Declan-speak. The shiny machines of the hospital room caught his attention and he weaved toward the nearest one, finger outstretched. Nora scooped him up and kissed his head. "Not so fast, Mr. Curious. Have I told you the story about the cat?"

"Cat." Declan made a sound like one, except it was more of a yowl than a traditional meow. He was so funny and precious and her heart ached that his father wasn't here to see how he'd grown, how fast he learned things, how he slept with one foot stuck out from the covers— just like Sean had.

As quickly as she could, Nora bustled her son out of the hospital room before anyone saw the tear that had slipped down her face. Sean had died nearly two years ago. She should be ready to move past it. Ready to date again, find someone to ease her loneliness. But she couldn't imagine being with someone other than Sean, who had been the love of her life, the man who had thoroughly captured her heart the moment she'd met him at a football game during her junior year of college.

Seeking a quiet place to regroup, Nora spied an alcove with two chairs away from the main hospital corridor. She and Declan settled into the chairs, or she did. He sat in the opposing one for a grand total of four seconds before he squirmed to the ground and scooted around like his pants were on fire. Nora laughed.

"Problem with your diaper there, Butterbean?"

That had been Sean's nickname for the boy the moment he'd seen the ultrasound pictures she'd held up to the camera during one of their Skype calls. She'd kept the name, even after he was born, because Declan still resembled a bean when swaddled in the brown blanket Sean's mother had bought for her grandson.

Of course, Nora didn't do much swaddling these days, not with an active two-year-old.

Declan didn't answer, too preoccupied with his task of cleaning the hospital floor with his butt. Thirty more seconds and she'd use hand sanitizer on every inch of exposed skin, before he got around to sticking a random body part in his mouth. Midwest Regional was a highly acclaimed hospital, but sick people came through these halls all the time. A mother couldn't be too careful.

"Ms. Winchester?" A young hospital worker in plain clothes stopped near Declan. Her name badge read Amanda.

"O'Malley," Nora corrected. "But yes, formerly Winchester."

And she didn't choke on it. There might be hope for her yet to work through all her anger and disillusionment with her father.

The worker smiled. "There's a private room set up for the family if you'd like me to show it to you."

"Oh, yes. Of course."

How could she have missed that Sutton's wealth and influence had extended even to the hospital? It had been a long time since Nora had lived the life of a socialite, and even longer since she'd wanted to. But the lure of a private place, away from the crowded hospital, called to her.

Amanda punched in the code on the keypad outside the room and then promised to write it down for her. Nora pushed open the door and nearly gasped, but not over the sumptuously appointed room. Her mother's house had far more antique rugs and dark, heavy furniture than this place. No, her attention was firmly on the long table lining the wall that held enough food for four Winchester families. The empty bags under the table sported the logo for Iguazu, a new, trendy Argentinian fusion restaurant so hot that Nora had even heard of it back home in Colorado. A couple of uniformed delivery people were still setting up the warming mechanisms for the silver serving trays, so the food had obviously just arrived.

"What is all this?" Nora asked Amanda.

"Someone sent it for the family. Oh—" Amanda rummaged in her pocket "—there's a note for you."

Intrigued, Nora accepted the envelope and scooped up Declan with her other arm as he eyed the blue flame under the rolltop chafing dishes. "Thank you."

Amanda wrote down the keypad code on a sticky note and cheerfully waved as she exited behind the delivery people. Nora sat in one of the overstuffed wingback chairs and wedged Declan in tight so he couldn't squirm away, then ripped open the envelope.

The typed note was short and to the point: *Good food can make anything more bearable.*

In closing, the note contained only a simple statement—*Cordially Yours*. No signature.

Nora's eyes narrowed as she read over the phrase again. It tickled the edges of her memory and then came to her all at once. It was a phrase that had been a bit of a joke between Nora and a friend—Reid Chamberlain.

Wow. That was a name Nora hadn't thought about in years. Reid, his brother, Nash, and his sister, Sophia, had gone to the same private schools as the Winchester girls, practically since birth. Reid and Nora were the same age and had often been in the same class. Their parents ran in the elite circles of Chicago society, so it was only natural that they'd seen each other socially, and at boring grown-up events. What else was there for kids to do but bond?

It would have made more sense for Nora to become friends with Sophia, but it hadn't happened that way. Reid had always been the object of her fascination.

They'd spent a good bit of time getting into trouble together, playing make-believe in the cupboards of each other's kitchens until the servants chased them out, or getting up a game of hide-and-seek across the expansive Chamberlain estate grounds with their siblings. She'd loved it when they hid in the branches of the same tree, giggling quietly behind their hands when Nash or Gracie stood directly below, frustrated over not being able to find them. For a while, she'd had a bit of a crush on Reid.

But that had been before he grew into his looks and body, both of which put him firmly in the sights of every teenaged socialite-in-training in the greater Chicago area, shoving Nora to the back of the pack. Then Reid had started running with a crowd that worshipped at the altar of money, prestige and fast cars. She didn't blame him. Ninety-nine percent of the people in her life subscribed to the philosophy of *whoever has the most toys at the end wins.* They'd grown apart. It happened.

Last she'd heard, Reid Chamberlain had only increased his wealth and prestige through a series of brilliant moves in the hotel industry. He dominated the Chicago market along with a host of other cities.

Surely Reid wasn't the one who'd sent the smorgasbord. They hadn't talked in years and the joke involving *cordially yours* hadn't been a code of any sort, just something they'd said to each other when they mimicked how grown-ups talked when trying to impress other grown-ups. Lots of people could use the phrase on a regular basis.

Nora texted Eve and in a few moments, the rest of the Winchesters barreled into the private room to see the anonymous gift for themselves. Since she hadn't eaten in forever, Nora fixed a plate for Declan with a few French fries, his favorite and likely the only thing from the table he'd eat, and then took full advantage of the generosity of their unknown benefactor for herself. The dishes held layers and layers of steaming, mouth-watering food: Argentinian asado-style steak thick with chimichurri sauce, a tray of empanadas, a variety of grilled vegetables and cheeses.

Nora took a bit of everything, intending to go back for more of the dishes she liked the best. Eve and Gracie followed suit as they chatted about the identity of their anonymous friend, but even after a round of seconds, the spread looked like it had barely been touched.

"This food is delicious," Nora commented. "But it won't last long and there's so much of it. We should share it with the staff."

"That's a great idea," Gracie said enthusiastically. "They all work so hard. I wonder how often any of them get to eat at a place like Iguazu, where you have to know someone to get a table. I've only been there once and that took some doing. I'll mention it to Amanda so she can spread the word."

You needed an "in" to eat at Iguazu? Nora's intrigue meter shot into the red. Who would have sent food to the Winchester family from such an exclusive place? One of Sutton's associates? People tolerated Sutton because he was powerful, and sure, lots of them had sent impersonal gifts over the years, but rarely did anyone go out of their way to do something difficult or thoughtful. Even more impressed with the gesture, Nora fingered the note in her pocket.

Nurses, doctors and hospital staff streamed into the room in short order, exclaiming over the feast and thanking the Winchester women for their generosity. Crowd noise increased as people found seats and socialized. Nora's temples started to pound as the long day of travel caught up with her.

On the other side of the room, Declan had climbed into Gracie's lap, and she laughed as he stole French fries off her plate, apparently not having stuffed his little face enough with those his mother had given him. Declan was in good hands with his aunt, providing Nora with the perfect opportunity to grab a few minutes to herself.

Nora caught Gracie's eye and nodded to the door, then held up her palm with her fingers spread, mouthing, "Five minutes?"

Gracie smiled and waved her off.

Gratefully, Nora ducked out and went to the ladies' room to splash some water on her face. Belatedly, she realized there was probably a private bathroom in the area she'd just left. It had been a while since Nora had lived in her family's wealthy orbit. She'd never really embraced the privileged lifestyle anyway, even choosing to go to the University of Michigan, a public college, much to her mother's chagrin. But that was where she'd met Sean, so she'd considered it fate.

Out of nowhere, Reid popped into her head again. He'd gone to Yale, if she recalled correctly. Not that she'd spent a lot of time keeping track of him, but the private high school they'd attended had been small enough that everyone knew everyone else's business.

As she fingered the note in her pocket again, Nora's curiosity got the best of her. What if Reid had sent the catered spread? She should thank him. Gracie and Eve had known Reid, of course, but they'd never been close with any of the Chamberlain siblings, not as Nora had.

But why would Reid have done something so nice without signing the note? Suddenly, she had to know if her childhood friend had been behind the gesture. If for no other reason than to satisfy her curiosity.

Nora was nothing if not resourceful. After all, she'd walked away from her family's money and lived a simple life in Colorado on the monthly Dependent Indemnity Compensation payment that the government sent Nora as a surviving spouse of a military serviceman killed in the line of duty. Creativity came with the territory.

She pulled out her phone and tapped up the restaurant's website, then called. A cultured female voice answered. "Iguazu. How may I help you?"

"This is… Ms. O'Malley from Mr. Chamberlain's office." Nora crossed her fingers. She hated lying, but the ends justified this little white one. "Mr. Chamberlain would like confirmation that the food he ordered to be delivered to the Winchester family at Midwest Regional was delivered."

"Absolutely, let me verify."

Music piped through the speakers as Nora was put on hold. She grinned. That had been way too easy.

The music cut off as the Iguazu employee came back on the line. "Ms. O'Malley? Yes, the food was delivered and as specified, the note given directly to Nora Winchester. Please let Mr. Chamberlain know we're pleased he's chosen Iguazu for his catering needs and we look forward to his next event."

Somehow Nora squeaked out a "Thank you," though how she'd spoken when her tongue had gone completely numb, she'd never know.

Reid had not only sent the food, he'd specified that *she* should receive the note? Why? The signature *had* been some kind of code. One he'd clearly thought would mean something to her. And it did. She'd been besieged by memories of an easier time, before Sean, before she'd really understood what an SOB her father was.

Reid had wanted her to figure it out. She had to know why.

After the long trip and the blow of seeing her father so ill in that hospital bed, yet not feeling the rush of forgiveness she'd hoped for, Nora should have *wanted* to go home and shut out the world. But she'd been doing that for two years and all it had gotten her was a severe case of loneliness and a crushing sense of vulnerability.

Very little had happened lately that she'd had any control over. Her life had been spinning without her permission and all she'd been able to do was hang on. It was time to do something affirmative. Something decisive. Like thank an old friend for his kindness.

Two

On the way to Reid Chamberlain's downtown Chicago office, Nora pulled up a few articles about him on her phone. If she was going to beard the man in his den, she should at least know a few things about who he'd become over the years.

Gracie had volunteered to take Declan back to the Winchester estate, where Nora would be staying while in Chicago, and then insisted on calling for a car to take Nora on her mysterious errand. Being secretive wasn't second nature to Nora, but she didn't want to bring up Reid, at least not until she knew the purpose behind his kind gesture.

Especially when all of the articles she'd managed to find about Reid pointed to a very different person from what she'd expected. There were almost no pictures of him, save one very grainy shot that showed Reid rushing from a dark car to the covered doorway of one of his hotels. He'd turned his face from the camera, so the angle showed only his profile, but even that little bit clearly conveyed his annoyance at the photographer.

The caption underneath read "Reclusive billionaire Reid Chamberlain."

Reclusive? *Reid?* He'd been the life of the party as long as Nora could remember. Heck, that was the reason they'd grown apart—he'd become so popular, his time was in constant demand.

Doubly intrigued, Nora glanced up as the car slowed to a stop and the uniformed driver slid out to open the back door for her to exit. She got out and found herself standing in front of the brand-new Metropol Hotel in the heart of downtown Chicago.

A study in glass and steel, the hotel towered over her, reaching to the heavens. *Good grief.* This was Reid's office? She'd read that Nash Chamberlain had designed the Metropol, and it was nothing short of breathtaking, rising several dozen stories high and twisting every so often. The architectural know-how required to design it must have been great, indeed.

Impressed, Nora swept through the door opened by a uniformed attendant and approached the concierge, glad she'd opted for heels and a classic summer-weight pantsuit today. The concierge glanced up with a ready smile. Her mind went blank. Lying to the woman from Iguazu had been one thing, but this man was right in front of her, staring at her expectantly. She should have thought this through.

What if Reid wasn't here? Or hadn't really wanted her to seek him out? She'd only assumed he'd meant for her to figure it out. He might actually be mad that she'd tracked him down.

So what if he was mad. This trek had been about

something greater than a mere thank-you. *Taking control here.* Nora squared her shoulders. No apologies.

"I'm here to see Mr. Chamberlain. Tell him Nora O... Winchester is here." And she didn't even choke on the name. "Nora Winchester. He'll see me right away."

Wow. *Brazen* should be her middle name. The articles had called Reid reclusive and she'd waltzed right in to demand that he admit her without question? This was a dumb idea.

The concierge nodded. "Of course, Ms. Winchester. He's expecting you."

Nora picked her jaw up off the floor for the second time that day. "Thank you."

The concierge tapped a bell and a young man in a discreet rust-colored uniform that mirrored the hotel's accents appeared by Nora's side before she could fully process that Reid was *expecting her.*

"William will show you to the elevators and ensure that you reach Mr. Chamberlain's office," the concierge said.

Meekly, she followed the bellhop to the elevator bank, her heels sinking into the plush carpet that covered the rich dark hardwood floors. When they got on the elevator, the bellhop swiped a badge over the reader above the buttons and pushed one for the forty-seventh floor.

"Forty-seven and forty-eight are secure floors," William explained with a smile. "Only VIPs get to see Mr. Chamberlain. It's been quite a while since we've had one."

VIPs only. And Nora Winchester was one. What would have happened if she'd introduced herself as Nora O'Malley? Would the concierge have politely booted her out the door?

Nervous all at once, she discreetly checked her hair

and makeup in the mirrored paneling of the elevator. She'd twisted her blond hair up in a chignon this morning before her flight, and several loose strands had corkscrewed around her face. Not a bad look.

Silly. What did it matter how she looked? Reid had thrown her all off-kilter by telling his staff to expect her.

The elevator dinged and within moments William was ushering her into a reception area populated by a stately woman with steel-colored hair, who closed her laptop instantly as Nora entered.

"You must be Ms. Winchester," she said. "Mr. Chamberlain asked for you to be shown right in."

Far too quickly, the receptionist steered her through a set of glass doors and to an open entryway at the end of the hall, then discreetly melted away.

The man behind the wide glass desk glanced up the moment Nora walked across the threshold of his office.

Time fell off a cliff as their eyes locked.

Nora forgot to breathe as Reid Chamberlain's presence electrified every nerve in her body. And then he stood without a word, crossing to her. The closer he came, the more magnetic the pull became. He was all man now—powerful in his dark gray suit, a bit rakish with his brown hair grown out long enough to curl a bit on top, and sinfully beautiful, with a face that became that much more devastating due to a five o'clock shadow that darkened his jaw.

And then he was so close she could see the gold flecks in his brown eyes. A dark, mysterious scent wafted from him, something citrusy but mixed with an exotic spice that wholly fit him. She had a feeling she'd be smelling it in her sleep that night.

"Hi, Nora."

Reid extended his hand. For a moment, she thought

he was reaching for her, to hug her, or…something. But instead, he closed the door and leaned into it, his arm brushing her shoulder.

The *snick* of the door nearly made her jump out of her skin, but she kept herself from reacting. Barely. Did he have something in mind that was so intimate and private that it wasn't fit for prying eyes?

Her pulse jumped into her throat. "Hi, Reid."

He crossed his arms and contemplated her. "You got the note."

"Yes." Impulsively, she put out her palm, intending to touch Reid on the arm to express her thanks.

But at the last minute, something in his expression stopped her. Something dangerous, with an edge she didn't understand, but wanted to. Touching him suddenly held all kinds of nonverbal implications, maybe even an invitation she wasn't sure she meant to extend.

Goodness. How had a simple thank-you become so… *charged*? She let her hand drop to her side and his gaze followed it, marking the action.

"What can I do for you?" he asked simply.

He was not the same boy she remembered. She could see hints of his teenage self in the way he held his body, and small things such as the length of his lashes were the same, but his gaze had grown hard and opaque. It was almost as if he'd grown an extra layer between himself and the rest of the world and no one was allowed to breach it. One of the things she'd always liked about Reid Chamberlain was his smile. And that was noticeably absent.

The man was—according to the news articles—reclusive, and wealthier than King Solomon, Croesus and Bill Gates put together. But it didn't seem to have made him happy.

What could he do for her, indeed? Probably not much. But maybe she could do something for him. "You can smile for me, Reid. It might actually break this awkward tension."

Against all odds, the corners of Reid's mouth twitched. He fought to suppress the smile because he didn't want to encourage Nora Winchester into thinking she could command him into doing her will five minutes into their renewed acquaintance.

Besides, Reid didn't smile. That was for people who had a lightness of spirit that allowed for such a thing. He didn't. Normally. Nora had barreled into his office and the moment he'd seen her, it was like a throwback to another time and place—before all the shadows had seeped into his soul.

Which sounded overly dramatic, even to himself. That was why he never thought about his own miserable existence and instead worked eighteen hours a day so he could fall into bed exhausted at the end of it. When you slept like the dead, you didn't dream. You didn't lie awake questioning all the choices you'd made and cursing the genetics that prevented you from doing a simple thing like becoming a father to your orphaned niece and nephew.

Nora's presence shouldn't have changed anything. But it had. She'd breathed life into his office that hadn't been there a moment ago and he was having a hard time knowing what to do with it.

It was troubling enough that she'd tracked him down in the first place. And more troubling still that he'd been anticipating her arrival in a way that he hadn't *anticipated* anything in a long while.

"Smiling is for politicians and people with agendas," he finally said.

The air remained thick with tension and something else he wasn't in a hurry to dispel—awareness. On both sides. Nora was just as intrigued by him as he was by her. Reid was nothing if not well versed in reading his opposition. And in his world, everyone was the opposition, even Nora Winchester, a woman he hadn't spoken to in nearly fifteen years and who'd apparently interpreted his note as an invitation to invade his privacy.

He should be annoyed. He wasn't. That made Nora dangerous and unpredictable. Unexpectedly, it added to her intrigue. The heavy pull between them tingled along his muscles, heating him to the point of discomfort. He hadn't been this affected by a woman's presence since he was a teenager.

"Oh, really. And you don't have an agenda?" Nora crossed her arms in an exaggerated pose he suspected was designed to mimic his. "What was with the note, then?"

"It's polite to include a note with a gift," he replied as he fought a smile for the second time. He hadn't expected to like the grown-up version of Nora as much as he did. What was he supposed to do with her?

When his admin had called Iguazu to check on the delivery, imagine his surprise to learn that a mystery woman from "his office" had already called. A quick check-in with the hospital told him that Nora had indeed received his note. It hadn't taken much to guess she'd figured out that he'd sent the catering and would be along to see him in short order. He'd been right.

"Uh-huh. And is it customary to use a private joke in said note and then pretend you didn't intend for me to figure out you sent it?"

Her wide, beautiful mouth tipped up at the corners and communicated far more than her words did. She was toying with him. Maybe even *flirting*. Women didn't flirt with him as a rule. Usually they were much more direct, wrangling introductions from mutual acquaintances and issuing invitations into their beds before he'd learned their last names.

He'd taken a few of them up on it. He wasn't a monk. But he'd never held a conversation with one or called one again. Not since the day when his father had killed more than half of his family, including himself.

Nora was a first. In more ways than one. His body's awareness dialed up a notch. She was close enough to touch but he didn't reach out. Not yet. Not until he got a much better handle on his reaction to her. And maybe not even then. Nora certainly hadn't dropped by to be seduced by the CEO of Chamberlain Group. But that didn't automatically mean she'd be averse to the idea. It just meant he needed a clearer sense of the lay of the land before he made a move on a childhood friend.

"Are you…*accusing* me of deliberately trying to get your attention with a throwaway signature line on a note?" Reid hadn't enjoyed interaction with a woman this much in so long, he couldn't even *say* how long.

Her gaze narrowed. "Are you denying it?"

Cordially Yours. He hadn't uttered that phrase in over a decade. How had she remembered that joke? Or maybe a better question was: why had he put it in the note?

Maybe he'd intended for this to go down exactly as it had.

When he'd heard about Sutton Winchester's terminal diagnosis, Reid's first thought had been of Nora. They hadn't spoken in a long time, but she'd played an important role in his youth, namely that of a confidante for a boy trying to navigate a difficult relationship with his parents. He remembered Nora Winchester fondly and had never even said thank you for the years of distraction she'd provided, both at school and at parties.

The gift had been about balancing the scales. Reid didn't like owing anyone anything.

He certainly hadn't sent the food for Winchester's benefit. The old man could—and most definitely would—rot in hell before Reid would lift a finger to help him. The man had more shady business deals and crooked politicians in his back pocket than a shark had teeth. Reid wouldn't soon forget how Chamberlain Group had been on the receiving end of a personal screw-over, courtesy of Sutton Winchester.

"The food was for old time's sake. Nothing more." Nor should he pretend it was anything more. "Let's just say I wasn't expecting a personal thank-you for the catering, and leave it at that."

She laughed and it slid down his spine, unleashing a torrent of memories. Nora *was* an old friend, and for a man who didn't have many, it suddenly meant something to him that he had a history with this woman. A positive history. She'd known his sister, Sophia, and that alone made her different from anyone else in his life except Nash.

Yeah, letting her walk away untouched wasn't happening. Reid had long ago accepted his selfish nature and he wanted more of Nora's laugh.

"Obviously you *were* expecting me." Nora's gaze raked over his body as she called him on it. "Your staff couldn't have been clearer that they'd been waiting for me to arrive. How did you guess I'd be coming by?"

"Oddly enough, you tipped me off. My admin called

Iguazu and learned that Ms. O'Malley from my office had already inquired after the status of the delivery."

Guilt clouded Nora's gaze and she shifted her eyes to the right, staring at a spot near his shoulder. "Well, you didn't sign the note. How else was I supposed to figure out if you were the one behind the nice gesture?"

"I don't make nice gestures," he corrected her. "And you weren't supposed to figure it out. Is Ms. O'Malley a fake name you use often to perform nefarious deeds?"

He couldn't resist teasing her when it was so obvious she hadn't a deceptive bone in her body. Flirting, teasing and smiling—or nearly doing so anyway—were all things he hadn't indulged in for a very long time, and all things he'd like to continue doing.

But only with Nora. All at once, he was glad she'd tracked him down.

"Yes," she informed him pertly. "It's a name I use often for all my deeds. I got married."

Genuine disappointment lanced through his gut. Where had that come from? Had he really been entertaining a notion of backing Nora up against the door and taking that wide mouth under his seriously enough that learning she was married would affect him so greatly?

Ridiculous. He shouldn't be thinking of her that way at all. She was an old friend who would soon walk out of his life, never to be heard from again. It was better that way. It hardly mattered whether she'd gotten married. Of course she had. A woman as stunningly beautiful and intrinsically kind as Nora Winchester wouldn't stay single.

Some of the sensual tension faded a bit. But not all. Nora's smile did interesting things to him and he didn't think he could put a halt to it if he tried.

"Belated congratulations," he offered smoothly. "I hadn't heard."

"You wouldn't have. Sean was stationed out of Fort Carson in Colorado. We got married on base, much to my mother's dismay. It was a small ceremony and it happened nearly seven years ago." She waved it off. "Ancient history. I'm a widow now, anyway."

"I'm sorry for your loss." The phrase came automatically, as he did still have a modicum of manners despite not spending much time in polite company.

But Nora—a *widow*? Dumbfounded, he zeroed in on Nora's face, seeking…something, but he had no idea what. She'd said it so matter-of-factly, as if she'd grieved and moved on. How had she done that? If it was so easy, Reid would have done the same.

The specters of Sophia and his mother still haunted him, which didn't mix well with polite company, and he doubted he'd ever be able to toss off the information that they'd passed as calmly as Nora had just informed him that her husband had died.

Death was a painful piece of his past that shouldn't be the thing he had in common with Nora. The loss of his mother and sister *should* be the reason he showed Nora the door. Nonetheless, it instantly bonded them in a way that their shared history hadn't. He wanted to explore that more. See what this breath of fresh air might do to chase away the dark, oily shadows inside, even for a few moments.

"Thank you," she said with a nod. "For the condolences and the food. I want to thank you properly, though. Maybe spend some time catching up. I'd like to hear what you've been up to. Let me take you to dinner."

That bordered on the worst idea ever conceived. He cultivated a reputation for being a loner with practiced ease, and didn't want to expose their new rapport to prying eyes. And there would be plenty if he took a woman to dinner in a small town like Chicago.

"I don't go out in public. Why don't you come back for dinner here? I live in the penthouse, one floor up. My private chef is the best in the business."

No, *that* was the worst idea ever conceived. Nora, behind closed doors. Laughing, flirting... It didn't take much to imagine where that would lead. He'd have her in his arms before the main course, hoping to find the secrets deep in Nora's soul. Especially the one that led to moving past tragedy and pain.

But the invitation was already out and he wasn't sorry he'd issued it. Though he might be before the evening was out. No one had ever crossed the threshold of his home except very select staff members who were well paid to keep their mouths shut about their boss's private domain.

That didn't stop the rampant speculation about what went on in his "lair," as he'd been told it was called. Some went so far as to guess that all sorts of illicit activity went on behind closed doors, as if he'd built some kind of pleasure den and had lured innocent young girls into his debauchery.

The truth was much darker. Racked with guilt over not being able to save his mother and Sophia, he wasn't fit for public consumption and the best way to avoid people was to stay home.

The distance he maintained between himself and the rest of the world was what kept him sane. Other people didn't get that part of his soul was missing, never to be recovered. The hole inside had been filled with a blackness he couldn't exorcise and sometimes, it bubbled up to the surface like thick, dark oil that coated everything in its path. Other people didn't understand that. And he didn't want to explain it to them.

"You don't go out in public?" Curiosity lit up her gaze. "I read that you were reclusive. I thought they were exaggerating. You being all shut up away from other people doesn't jibe with the person I once knew."

"Things change," he countered roughly. "I have a lot of money and power. People generally want a piece of both. It's easier to stay away from the masses."

His standard answer. Everyone bought it.

"Sounds very lonely." Somehow, she'd moved closer, though he hadn't thought they were all that far apart in the first place. Her wide smile warmed him in places he'd forgotten existed. Places better left out of this equation.

"Expedient." He cleared his throat. "I run a billion-dollar empire here. Not much time for socializing."

"Yet your first instinct was an invitation to dinner. Seems like you're reaching out to me."

Their gazes caught. Held. A wealth of unspoken messages zipped between them but hell if he knew what was being said. What he wanted to say.

"It's just dinner," he countered and he could tell by her expression that she didn't believe the lie any more than he did. They both knew it would be more. Maybe just a rekindling of their friendship, which felt necessary all of a sudden. Nora was someone from before his life had turned into the twisted semblance of normal that it had become.

"Oh, come on, Reid." She laughed again. "We're both adults now. After the note and the rather obvious way you shut the door half a second after I walked through it, I think it's permissible to call it a date."

He glanced at the closed office door and just as he

was about to explain that he valued his privacy—nothing more—he discovered his mouth had already curved up in a ghost of a smile, totally against his will. "A date, then."

Yet another first. Reid Chamberlain didn't date. At least not since his father had murdered the most important people in Reid's life—and Reid had been forced to reconcile that he shared a genetic bond with a monster.

Three

The dress Nora had chosen for her date with Reid—or rather the dress Eve and Gracie had bullied her into wearing—should've been be illegal.

Actually, if she moved the wrong way, it would be.

The plunging neckline hit a point well below her breasts and the fabric clung to every curve Nora had forgotten she had. Simple and black, it was more than a cocktail dress. It was a dress that said: *I'm here for what comes after dinner.*

Nora was not okay with that message. Or maybe she was. *No.* She wasn't.

"I can't wear this," she mumbled again.

"You can and you are," Eve countered. Again. "I've only worn it one time. No one will recognize it."

As if committing a fashion faux pas was the most troublesome aspect of this situation.

Part of the problem was that Nora liked the way she

looked in the dress. The other part of the problem was that Nora didn't have the luxury of sticking around for what came after dinner, if she even had a mind to be available for...*that*. She had Declan. Her son made everything ten times more complicated, even what should have been a simple dinner with an old friend.

A friend whose very gaze had touched places inside her that she hadn't known existed. Until now, she hadn't realized how very good it felt to be the object of a man's interest. Sean had loved her and of course had paid attention to her, but this was something else. Something with a tinge of wicked. Purely sexual. It was exhilarating and frightening at the same time.

She practiced walking in front of the full-length mirror affixed to the closet in the master suite of her father's guesthouse. Yep. If she stumbled, her bare nipples would peek out with a big ole hello. So she wouldn't stumble.

Eve fastened a jewel-encrusted drop necklace around Nora's neck. "Perfect. It draws attention exactly where it should. To your neckline."

"It's like a big arrow that points to my boobs." Nora tried to shorten the chain but Eve took the necklace out of her hands and let the stone fall back into place in the valley between her breasts.

"Yes. This is not a date with a guy you met at church," Eve advised her. "Reid Chamberlain has a well-earned reputation. He doesn't invite women into his private domain. What few he's spent time with are very hush-hush about it, and it doesn't take a rocket scientist to figure out that he's giving these women a ride worth keeping their mouths shut over. You are beautiful and have something to offer. Make him aware of it and then make him work for it."

Gracie nodded as Nora swallowed. "It's not like that. We're old friends."

Eve took a flatiron from the vanity to their right and fussed a bit more with Nora's hair. "Yeah, well, I've known Reid a long time and he's never asked me to dinner."

Eve and Reid hadn't been friends, though.

Nora's history with Reid gave her one up on all these other women whom he *hadn't* asked on a date. When Nora had labeled it as such, she'd hoped that would dispel some of the confusion. It was always better to call a spade a spade, and it was clear—to her at least—that there was something simmering between herself and Reid. And dinner was A Date, she had no doubt.

Nora didn't date. She hadn't dated anyone since she'd met Sean nearly ten years ago. The only reason she had even agreed to this one was because Reid was a friend. It afforded her a measure of comfort to think about jumping back into the pool with someone she knew. Someone she'd always had a crush on.

Except the way he looked at her... She shivered. There was a lot more than friendship in his dark, enigmatic gaze. Tonight was a chance to finally see what it was like to be with Reid and not think of him as "just" a friend. The real question was whether she'd act on the undercurrents or chicken out. Nora hadn't had sex in over two years. What if she'd forgotten how?

"Reid is not some mysterious guy with a shady reputation," Nora insisted, but it was mostly to convince herself.

He *was* different. She'd definitely noticed that earlier today. Darker, more layered. But she'd gotten the distinct impression he needed to connect with someone—*her*. Perhaps for the same reason she'd agreed to the date in the first place. They had a history. Being in his presence today had brought back some good memories. No reason that couldn't continue.

"Nora, honey, you've been away from Chicago for a long time." Eve wrangled the same lock of hair until she got it the way she wanted it. "Trust me, I've crossed paths with him a few times now that I'm taking a more active role in the inner workings of Elite. He was short with me, all business. He's like that with everyone. Except you, I guess."

"He runs a billion-dollar company," Nora said faintly. "You of all people should know that means you can't be Mr. Pushover, especially not in meetings."

Gracie shook her head and added, "Just be careful. The girl who does my nails is convinced he pays off the women he dates. Word is that he's got some very unusual…tastes. Things he prefers in the bedroom. Things that are not fit to be discussed among polite company. That's why they never talk about it. They're well paid to keep quiet and probably don't want anyone to know they participated."

"That's just speculation," Nora scoffed as her pulse jumped.

What kind of things? Unfortunately, she had a good enough imagination and some of what she envisioned couldn't be unseen. It was a delicious panorama of poses, featuring Reid Chamberlain in splendorous, naked glory. Not that she'd ever seen him without clothes, but Reid was devastating and gorgeous in a suit. It wasn't a stretch to assume he'd look good out of one, too. Throw in this new dark and mysterious side? It only added to his appeal. And heightened her nerves.

"Besides, it's dinner between old friends," Nora continued, her voice growing stronger as her resolve solidified. Whatever his predilections were in the bedroom, she'd probably never find out. "That's all. I'm a mom. We don't incite men's fantasies."

And she had to keep Declan forefront in her thoughts. There were no grown-up sleepovers in her future, not when she had a two-year-old who still woke up calling for mama in the middle of the night. This was a thank-you dinner, nothing more. An escape from her father's scary health problems and the scandal of the inheritance drama.

Eve's brows quirked as she spun Nora to face the mirror. "Honey, that body is every inch a man's fantasy, and by the way, you're a strong, entertaining woman. A man can and will be as attracted to what's up here—" she tapped Nora's temple "—as by what's down here."

All three Winchester sisters followed Eve's gesture as she indicated Nora's torso. Even Nora couldn't argue that the dress did highlight her curves. Nor could she argue that any man who was worth her time would be attracted to her brain.

"Regardless, I'll be home by ten," Nora promised. "Ten thirty at the latest."

She kissed Declan and left him in Gracie's capable hands. They settled in to watch cartoons, waving to Nora as she left, nervous as ever.

On the way over to the Metropol, Nora sat ramrod straight in her seat, too edgy to relax. The driver didn't try to talk to her, which was a blessing.

Her imagination went into overdrive again. If Reid did have unusual tastes…did that automatically mean she'd say no? The thought of being a bit more adventurous than normal with someone she trusted got her a little hot and bothered. Because of course Reid was still Reid. There was nothing anyone could say to convince her that he'd turned into a monster who incited women into submitting to his twisted sexual practices.

Besides, her heart belonged to Sean. Anything that took place with Reid could be left behind once she went home to Colorado. It was freeing to not have the slightest worry about what might happen in the future.

When the concierge snapped for a bellboy to escort her to the penthouse—a different bellboy from last time—she forgot to breathe for a moment as the elevator doors slid shut. This was a one-way ticket to something she had no idea if she was *really* ready for.

You're being silly. You have no idea if the rumors are true. No idea if Reid even planned to do anything more than eat dinner. Also? He wasn't going to hold her prisoner. If she didn't like where the evening was headed, all she had to do was leave.

Of course, there was always the possibility that she would be on board with more than dinner. Maybe. The jury was still out.

The elevator doors parted, leading to a small alcove with a dazzling white marble floor. She stepped out and faced a closed unmarked door directly opposite the elevator.

"Have a good night, ma'am." With a silent swoosh of the elevator doors, the bellhop disappeared and then there was nothing left to do but knock.

Except the door opened before she could. Reid stood on the other side, wearing a different suit from earlier. This one had more closely cut lines and a darker hue and showcased his broad shoulders in a way she couldn't quite ignore. His jaw was shadowed with stubble that lent his handsome face a dangerous edge. Or perhaps she was imagining the edge after her conversation with Grace and Eve.

"Hi, Reid." Her voice came out all breathless and excited, turning the short phrase into something else entirely.

His gaze slowly traveled down her length, stopping every so often as if he'd run across something worthy of further examination. She felt the heat rise in her exposed chest but she refused to cover herself by crossing her arms. Still, her muscles flexed to do exactly that three times in a row.

"That dress was worth waiting for," he finally said, his voice as smooth as it had been earlier.

"Waiting for?" She scowled to cover her excitement. Two seconds in and he was already starting the seduction part of the evening, was he? "I wasn't late. I'm right on time."

His dark eyes took on a tinge of amusement, but his smile still hadn't returned. "By my count, I've been waiting fifteen years."

Oh, my. She fell into the possibilities of that statement with a big splat. Had he harbored secret feelings for her way back, as she had for him?

That couldn't be what he meant. He hadn't exactly been sitting around pining over her. "What are you talking about? You forgot I existed the second you turned sixteen and your parents gave you that Porsche for your birthday."

He crossed his arms and leaned on the door frame. "Would you like to continue this argument over a drink, or stay in the hall?"

"You haven't invited me in yet."

"I was busy."

He gave her another sweeping once-over that pulled at her core. And still, he didn't step aside to allow her to enter his private domain.

She could not get a handle on him, and only part of that stemmed from her sisters' warnings swirling around in the back of her mind. He'd invited her here, yet didn't seem to know what to do with her. Maybe she should help him out.

"Well, I'm thirsty," she informed him with a touch of frost. "So I choose the drink over the hall. You must not entertain much or you'd have already poured me a glass of wine."

A ghost of a smile played at his lips. "Forgive me, then. I *don't* entertain often and my manners are atrocious. Please come in, Ms. O'Malley."

With that, he stepped aside and swept his hand out. Clearly, she was supposed to take it. So she did.

The moment their flesh connected, awareness sizzled across her skin, raising goose bumps. A bit overwhelmed, she let him lead her into his penthouse.

With a whisper, the door shut behind her, closing her off from the world. And then she saw Chicago lit for the night beyond the glass wall at the edge of Reid's enormous living room.

"Oh," she gasped and his hand tightened on hers. "That's an amazing view."

Neon and stars, glass and steel, as far as the eye could see. The world was still out there, but they were insulated from it up here, high above the masses.

"I totally agree," he said quietly and she glanced at him.

His gaze, hot and heavy, was locked on her. Unblinking. Unsettling.

"You're not even looking." And then she realized what he meant and heat flushed her nearly exposed breasts again. "Um, didn't you promise me a drink?"

"I did. Come with me."

Apparently loath to let go of her hand, he led her to a wet bar where an uncorked bottle of wine stood next to two wineglasses. From that vantage point, she could see into the dining room, where a long table was set for two.

"Your servants have been busy," she commented as he finally dropped her hand to pour the red wine, filling each glass far past the line she'd have said would be an acceptable amount for a lightweight drinker such as herself.

But then, Reid didn't really know that about her.

"I gave my servants the night off." He handed her a glass and when she took it, he held his up in a quick toast. "To old friends."

She nodded and tossed back a healthy swallow. How she got the wine down her throat was beyond her; he hadn't taken his eyes off her once since she'd walked through the door and her self-consciousness was so thick you could cut it with a knife.

They were alone in this penthouse where no one could enter unless they had a special key for the elevator. Blessedly, deliciously *alone*. Should she be frightened? She wasn't.

Reid had gone to some trouble in anticipation of her arrival. The ambiance was sensual, edgy and quite delicious. All hard things to come by as a widowed single mom. Maybe she was far more wicked than she should be, but Reid made her feel beautiful and desirable and she wasn't going to apologize for liking it.

"Tell me something," she said impulsively, suddenly interested in picking up the thread of their conversation from the hallway. "You said you'd been waiting fifteen years for me to show up. What did you mean?"

He cocked his head, tossing a few curls into disarray, and she liked that he wasn't one of those men who used a ton of hair products. She could slide her fingers through his hair easily.

The thought warmed her further. That would be bold, indeed, if she just reached out and touched him. But that didn't mean she couldn't—or wouldn't—do it.

"Our friendship means something to me. I…didn't ever tell you that."

"Oh." A bit thunderstruck, she stared at him as the lines around his mouth grew deeper, expressing more than what his words had. Was he disappointed that he'd never told her for some reason? "That's okay, Reid. We developed other friendships and went on."

"You did. I didn't."

His cryptic words perplexed her. "You mean you didn't make other friends? But you were always with the popular crowd, piling into each other's cars after school and leaving dances or football games together to go someplace more exciting. Or at least that's always how I imagined it."

Reid shrugged slightly. "I passed the time with them. That's all."

Things weren't as they appeared back when they'd been in high school? Her heart turned over with a squish. "Sounds like you were a recluse in training, even then."

If things weren't as they appeared back then, what's to say the same wasn't true now?

His expression darkened. "In a way. I've never had much luck connecting with people."

"Except me."

Bold. But she didn't take it back. They'd been dancing around each other and she wanted to get on with the evening, whatever that entailed.

Their gazes met and he watched her as he sipped his wine, neither confirming nor denying the statement.

Go bold or go home. It was her new mantra, one she wanted to embrace all at once.

"Is that why you invited me to dinner?" she asked with a small smile. "Because you're lonely?"

"There's a difference between being lonely and desiring to be alone," Reid countered.

"That doesn't really answer my question, now does it?"

Nora was so close, Reid could easily count the individual strands of hair—honey wheat, warm sand, a few shoots of platinum—draped over her shoulder. He suspected it would be cool to the touch if he slid a strand through his fingers.

Dinner had been a mistake.

He'd wrongly thought that he and Nora would catch up, talk a bit about the past, that it would be an innocent opportunity to reminisce about an easier time. Before his world had crashed around his feet. He'd craved that with blinding necessity.

Instead, he'd spent the ten minutes she'd been in his penthouse trying desperately to keep his hands occupied so he didn't pull her into his arms to see if she tasted as good as she smelled. To see exactly what was under that black dress that showcased a body he hadn't remembered being so difficult to ignore.

You didn't seduce an old friend the moment she crossed your threshold. It was uncivilized and smacked of the kind of thing a man with his reputation would do. He'd done his share of perpetuating the myths surrounding his wickedness, mostly because it amused him.

Nora deserved better.

The problem was he had no interest in eating. At all. He'd developed an intense fixation with the hollow between Nora's breasts, which were scarcely contained by the bits of fabric that composed her dress.

You didn't stare at an old friend's rack, no matter how clearly she was inviting you to.

There were probably some other rules he should be reciting to himself right about now, but hell if he could remember what they were.

It had been too long since he'd had a woman in his bed; that was the problem. Nora Winchester O'Malley shouldn't be the one inciting him to break that fast. If he wanted to make the evening about catching up with an old friend, that was in his power to do.

"You're right," he allowed with a nod. "I didn't answer the question. I invited you to dinner because I wanted to thank you for being a good friend to me. The scales were unbalanced."

"Oh." Disappointment shadowed her gaze but she blinked and it was gone. "So dinner was motivated by the need to say thank you. For both of us, it seems."

"It seems."

That should have dispelled the sensual, tight awareness between them. That had been his intent. But she smiled and it lit up her face, inviting him in, warming up the places inside that had been cold since the plane crash that had changed everything.

"I feel properly thanked. Do you?" she asked.

"For what?" he nearly growled as he fought to stop himself from yanking her into his arms.

"For the food, silly." Her hands fisted on her hips. "That's the whole reason I asked you to dinner, remember?"

Yes, he did. They were two old friends. Nothing more. He had to remember that her labeling it a date might not mean the same thing to her as it did to him.

"Everyone has been properly thanked." He drained his wineglass and scouted for the bottle. The bite of the aged red centered him again. "Are you ready to eat?"

"Depends what you've got on the menu."

His gaze collided with hers and yes, she'd meant that exactly the way it sounded. Her smile slipped away as they stared at each other, evaluating, measuring, seeking. Perhaps he'd been going about this evening all wrong and the best course of action was to let their sizzling attraction explode.

But he couldn't help but think that if that happened, he'd miss out on the very thing he'd craved—friendship.

Four

Somehow, Reid dialed back his crushing desire and escorted Nora into the dining room. Maybe eating would take the edge off well enough to figure out what he wanted from this evening. And how to get it.

Since the servants had the night off, he played the proper host and served the gazpacho his chef had prepared earlier that day.

"This looks amazing, Reid," Nora commented and dug in.

A woman with a healthy appetite. Reid watched her eat out of the corner of his eye, which wasn't hard since she was sitting kitty-corner to him at the long teakwood table that he'd picked up on a trip to Bangalore.

The hard part was reminding his body that they'd moved on to dinner. It didn't seem to have gotten the message. Friendship or seduction? He had to pick a direction. Soon.

"I trust it's sufficient?" he asked without a trace of irony as Nora spooned the last bite into her candy-pink mouth. Not only had she actually eaten, she'd done it without mussing her lipstick.

That was talent. Of course, now his gaze couldn't seem to unfasten from her mouth as she nodded enthusiastically.

"So great. I'm jealous of your private chef." She sighed dramatically. "I wish I had one. I have to cook for myself, which I don't mind. But some days, it sure would be nice to pass that off to someone else."

"Why don't you hire someone?" he suggested. "It's truly worth it in the end to have control over the fat and sodium content of what goes into your body."

"When did you become a health nut?"

"When I realized I wasn't going to live forever and that every bad thing I put in my mouth would speed me on my way to the grave."

It was a throwaway comment that any man in his thirties might make, but he actually meant it. When you spent a lot of time alone, you needed a hobby. His was his health. He read as many articles and opinion pieces about longevity as he could, tailoring his workouts and eating habits around tried-and-true practices. At one point, he'd even hired a personal dietician but fired him soon after Reid had realized he knew more than the "professional."

Staying healthy was a small tribute to his late mother and sister. They'd had their lives cut short, so Reid had decided he'd live as long as he could. And he wanted to be in the best shape possible for that.

"Good point. I wish it was as simple as you make it sound." She smiled wistfully. "But my bank account doesn't allow for things like private chefs."

He did a double take. "Did something happen to your father's fortune?"

Surely not. The scandal of Carson Newport's parentage wouldn't have reached the epic proportions that it had if Sutton were broke. Word was that Newport wanted as much of Winchester's estate as he could get his hands on. Though they'd crossed paths a few times, Newport wasn't someone Reid spoke to about private matters, so he could only speculate. But he didn't think Newport was in it for the money. Vengeance, more likely. Which was a shame. Winchester had it coming, but that meant Nora would be caught up in the drama, as well.

Perhaps Newport had already gotten his mitts on Nora's share?

But she shook her head. "Oh, no. Dad's money is well intact. I just don't have any of it. Walking away from Chicago meant walking away from everything. Including my trust fund."

Reid blinked. "Really? You renounced your inheritance?"

"Really. I don't want a dime of that money. It's tainted with the blood of all the people my dad has hurt over the years anyway. Plus, money is the root of all evil, right?" She shrugged one shoulder philosophically. "I've been much happier without it."

"*Love* of money is the root of all evil," Reid automatically corrected. Nearly everyone got that quote wrong. "It's a warning against allowing money to control you. Allowing it to make you into a terrible person in order to get more."

"Is that a dig at my dad?"

It had actually been a dig at his own father, not hers. Reid contemplated her before responding truthfully. "No. But it applies."

Sutton Winchester was cut from the same cloth as John Chamberlain, no doubt. Nora's father just hadn't had the courtesy to rid the world of his evil presence the way Reid's father had. Not yet anyway.

"Oh, have you dealt with my dad, then?"

Her slight smile said she knew exactly how much of a bastard her father was, but that didn't mean she deserved the full brunt of Reid's honest opinion of the man. Whether this evening consisted of two friends reconnecting or two friends connecting in a whole new way remained to be seen, but he imagined bad-mouthing Nora's father wouldn't benefit either scenario.

"Let's just say that we've got a solid truce and as long as he stays in his corner, I stay in mine."

That was a mild and very politically correct way to put it. Because when it came to business, Winchester fought dirty. His misdeeds had included paying off a judge to rule against a Chamberlain Group rezoning request, planting a spy at a relatively high level in Reid's organization and—the pièce de résistance—attempting to poison Chamberlain Group's reputation in the media with false allegations about Reid's ties to the mob. Winchester had gall. Reid had patience, influence and money—he'd won in the end.

"Well, I'm sure my father is the poster child for what happens to people who love money more than their own family," she said without hesitation. "It's part of the reason I left. I got tired of living the life of a socialite, doing nothing more meaningful than being photographed in the latest fashion or showing up at a charity event. Money doesn't buy anything worthwhile."

He topped off both wineglasses and served the main course, cold lamb and pasta, then picked up the thread of the conversation. "When used correctly, money is a tool that makes life better."

"Doesn't seem to have done that for you," she pointed out, tilting her wineglass toward him in emphasis. "You shut yourself up in this billion-dollar prison. I've been in your presence twice now, and I have yet to see any evidence that money has made you happy."

What would she say if he agreed with her? If he said that money had done nothing but give his father the power to rip away Reid's soul? First by never being any kind of a father figure and then by taking his family with him on his journey to judgment day. The elder Chamberlain had picked his three-million-dollar Eclipse 550 as his weapon of choice, crashing the small jet deliberately and killing his wife and daughter.

Reid hadn't been on board. He'd been too busy chasing that next dollar.

Scary how alike he and his father were. You could run, but you couldn't hide from genetics. That's why Reid hadn't hesitated to say no when Nash came looking for someone to take in Sophia's twins. Reid wasn't father material. Reid was barely human material.

Money hadn't insulated him from heartache; it only afforded him the means to create what Nora called a prison. To him, it was a refuge.

"I like being alone," he finally said. "Having more money than the Bank of Switzerland allows me the luxury of kicking people out of my presence whenever I deem it necessary."

"Is that a warning?" Her smile bloomed instantly, zapping him in the gut. "Play nice or you'll see the backside of the door lickety-split?"

No, that wasn't what was on his mind, especially not when she treated him to the full force of her smile. Because now he was wondering what that mouth would feel like under his. She had to be a hell of a kisser—among other things.

"It's a fact," he said hoarsely as his throat went dry. "Take it as you will. Though in all fairness, few people ever cross the threshold in the first place, so all bets are off as to how quickly I might show you the way out."

"Hmm." Her gaze warmed as she perused him with an undisguised once-over, which raised the tension a painful notch. "So you're saying this is a bit of a unique experience?"

"Extremely."

She wasn't eating now. Neither was he. He was busy trying to keep his hands in his lap; even reaching for a fork might end up becoming a reason to abandon dinner entirely for a shot at experiencing Nora's kiss for himself.

"I've heard quite the opposite." She leaned an elbow on the table, drawing closer to him and wafting the scent of vanilla and strawberries in his direction.

That nearly pushed him over the edge. Other women smelled like thinly veiled invitations to carnal pleasures. Nora smelled like something he hadn't experienced in a very long time—innocence. He wanted her in a way he hadn't wanted anything he could recall in his life.

"Really?" he murmured. "What have you heard?"

Lies, exaggerations and wishful thinking, if it was any of the crap he knew was being passed around regarding his sex life. If she'd come here expecting an introduction to the forbidden side of pleasure, she'd leave disappointed.

"Nothing that I believed."

Her guileless blue eyes found his, warming him in a totally different way from anything she'd done thus far. "Really?"

She shrugged. "I know you. Those who are spreading rumors don't."

And perhaps that was true. They'd been friends, confidants and sometimes partners in crime. She seemed to still get him in a way no one else ever had. It thickened their connection and he liked that there was more here than just physical attraction. Liked how her innocence and strength of spirit promised to heighten their unique experiences.

All at once, he found himself in the middle of a paradox. The question here wasn't whether this evening would end in friendship or seduction, but how in the hell he'd gotten to a place where he wanted both.

Nora couldn't get over the jumpy, fluttery sensation in her stomach that Reid's intense stare produced.

Otherwise, she'd eat the exceptional lamb and pasta he'd placed in front of her instead of indulging in a third glass of wine that was probably going to get her into trouble before too long.

Because all she could think about was kissing Reid until he smiled.

He had hidden depths that he wasn't sharing with her. She could sense there was so much more behind his enigmatic brown eyes, so much pain she hoped to banish. She wanted to make him happy again. Was it so bad to be imagining that she could?

As he picked up his wineglass, she noted he hadn't eaten much, either. Too caught up in the conversation or just not hungry? Swirling the red wine, he watched it settle and then glanced at her, his gaze hot and full of something she wanted to explore. But she didn't know how to get to the next level.

"You might well be the only person in the world qualified to say you know me," he finally said, his voice huskier than normal, as if he had a catch in his throat the wine couldn't quite wash down.

She tried to laugh it off but the shock of his words wouldn't let her. "I was expecting you to argue with me. You know, say something along the lines of 'that was a long time ago.'"

"It was," he acknowledged with a tip of his head. "But not so long ago that I've forgotten how much I enjoyed our friendship. We never pulled punches with each other. I could always be honest with you about everything. We had something real that I foolishly let slip away."

Wow. That nearly knocked her flat. She'd moved on, but that didn't mean she hadn't mourned the loss of their friendship.

"It was a long time ago," she repeated inanely. "We can let bygones be bygones."

"You give me a lot of grace." He stood and held out his hand. "Since I'd like to continue the tradition of being honest, I've lost interest in eating. Come with me."

Nora's pulse rate shot into the stratosphere. Was this the part where he planned to take her up on the invitation of her dress? The part where she got to find out what came after dinner?

Only one way to find out. She reached out and clasped his hand, allowing him to draw her to her feet. Awareness bled through her, tightening her breasts and heating her from the inside out. Her knees shook a bit, causing her stilettos to wobble in the deep pile of the runner that led from the dining room to the living room, where the breathtaking view of the Chicago skyline was eclipsed only by the sheer beauty of the man lightly caressing her knuckle with his thumb.

He stopped near the window and dropped her hand

in favor of placing his palms on her shoulders. Then he positioned her directly in front of him so she faced the city. Their reflections blurred the neon lines of the buildings. She watched as he bent his head toward her neck.

"I like the picture you make," he murmured in her ear. "You and the vibrant city together."

His breath fanned across her sensitized skin, raising goose bumps and heat in an impossible mix of responses. But she couldn't have controlled her reaction if she'd tried. Okay, part of the excitement came from feeling safe, from feeling that she could trust Reid. But it also came from having those handy images from earlier pop back into her head. The X-rated ones.

His heat burned her back but she must have forgotten all the warnings she'd ever heard about staying away from fire because all she wanted to do was press backward into it. Let the power of attraction and desire sweep her away into an experience she suddenly wanted more than her next breath.

"I like you in that picture, too," she informed him. "In the spirit of being honest, I'm thinking about what that picture might look like if you kissed me."

The subtlest shift of his body toward hers was the only outward sign he gave that he'd heard what she said. Then she felt his fingers in her hair, lifting it away from her back, to be replaced with his lips at the hollow of her shoulder.

The shock of his kiss buckled her knees and she threw her hands up to steady herself against the window with a moan she couldn't bite back. She watched his reflection in the glass as he worked his way up the column of her throat, nibbling at her skin. She let her head list to the side to give him better access, but couldn't stop watching their reflections.

It was stimulating. Unreal. Unique.

He flattened his palms against her arms, sliding them upward until they covered her hands, pinning them against the glass. His torso aligned with her back and his hips nestled against her backside, nudging his thick erection into place at the small of her back.

Oh, my. That hard length spoke of his intent. If she wasn't ready for this, now would be the time to say so.

Her mouth opened. And then closed.

Didn't she deserve a night of passion with a man who made her feel alive for the first time in a long time? There was no shame in two people coming together like this, as long as everyone understood it was a fling, and nothing more. Her heart was permanently closed, but that didn't mean her body was, too.

Or was she trying to talk herself into something because she'd decided it was time to move on and had chosen Reid as the barometer of her success or failure? After all, who'd established that this was a fling? No one. They'd just had a conversation about their connection, their prior friendship and Reid's admission that he'd let her slip away, only to regret it.

"Reid," she breathed and he answered the plea with a firm full-body press that she felt all the way to her core.

One of his hands raced down her arm, tangled in her hair to cup the back of her head, turning it. And then his lips found hers. The kiss overwhelmed her, sucking her down a rabbit hole of pleasure even as her fingers curled against the glass, scrabbling for purchase against the slick surface.

There was none to be had. Reid took her deeper still, so she was even more off balance. He slowly drew her head backward as he added his tongue to the mix, licking in and out of her mouth in a sensuous rhythm that she responded to instantly, meeting him in the middle in a clash.

Obviously he didn't want to talk.

The kiss raged on as they tasted each other. The glass under her palms kept her upright, but barely, as Reid shoved a knee between her legs, his thigh rubbing near the place that needed his touch the most. The angle wasn't good enough. She arched her back, thrusting her hips backward, seeking relief for that sweet ache.

Cool air swept along her backside and she realized he'd hiked her dress up to her waist. His palm smoothed down the globe of her rear and she found enough of her brain was still functioning to be thankful Eve had talked her into a thong. The heat of his hand against her bare skin made her quake. Coupled with the friction of his thigh, she nearly came apart then.

"So responsive," he murmured, his lips moving against her collarbone as his hands explored her uncovered lower half. Helpless, she let him as sensations knifed through her.

His hand slid around to caress her abdomen and then lower and lower still, toying with the waistband of her panties until his fingers disappeared inside to cup her intimately.

She gasped as one finger slid between her folds, exactly where the flame burned the hottest.

This was all upside down and backward—literally. When making love to a woman, you started at the top and worked your way down. And you faced each other.

Reid had completely redefined seduction. She couldn't stop herself from reacting heavily to it, especially as she watched herself being pleasured in the reflection from the window. This must be what they meant when they whispered of his unusual tastes. She was an instant slave to it.

As he relentlessly drove her higher, she spiraled her hips against his hand and moaned his name. Her lids drifted shut for a brief moment until he drew off one shoulder of her dress, peeling it away from her breast. Her nipple hardened as it popped into view and he pushed her forward until it touched the glass. The shock of the cold surface against her heated flesh, coupled with his hand between her legs... It was too much.

She crested and cried out as the powerful orgasm overtook her. She would have collapsed if he hadn't snaked a hand around her waist, holding her tight against him, giving her a ringside seat to watch her half-naked reflection as she came, his fingers still deep inside her.

It was the single most erotic encounter of her admittedly tame life and she wanted more, with a fierceness she didn't recognize.

"That was amazing," he murmured in her ear as she settled. He withdrew and finally turned her in his arms to back her up against the window again.

"I think that's supposed to be my line." Breathlessly, she blinked up at him, suddenly shy now that they were facing each other. She'd just had the orgasm of her life, almost fully clothed, and he barely seemed ruffled. What had started as a ploy to get a smile out of him had swiftly become something else, something she'd been helpless to stop.

Now she wanted to return the favor. Without waiting for his okay, she curved her fingers around his jaw and pulled him down into a scorching kiss.

He met her and then some, the kiss spiraling into the stratosphere as they picked up where they'd left off a moment ago. She let her hands wander down his chest and found his waistband, then yanked his shirt from his pants so she could burrow underneath. The smooth skin of his back felt like heaven under her palms and she touched him to her heart's content.

Reid groaned into her mouth, even as he deepened the kiss, changing the angle, tongue hot and hard against hers.

Beep. The sound registered…somehow…and she pulled back from his drugging kiss. "Was that my phone?"

Reid blinked. "Mine is on silent."

Of course it was. He'd clearly set aside this evening to focus on her, but she wasn't in the position where she could do the same. Declan could be hurt or sick. Dismayed, she stared at Reid as reality came rushing back. "I'm sorry. I have to check that."

She stepped out of his arms, nearly weeping with need, not the least of which was a desire to make him feel as good as he'd done for her.

Scouting around for her clutch—which she hadn't seen in who knew how long—she finally found it at the wet bar, leaning up against the granite backsplash. She fished her phone from the depths and her heart plunged into her stomach as she saw Grace's name on the screen.

Nora had been letting her carnal side come out to play while something bad had happened to her son. A single mom shouldn't be dating, not while her kid was still so young. It was unforgivable. But then she read the text message and breathed a sigh of relief.

"Sorry," she called over her shoulder. "Declan is staying in an unfamiliar place and my sister just wanted me to know that he went down for the night without any fuss."

Thank God. Her pulse still thundered in her throat as she tapped back a quick message to Grace, noting it was nearly ten o'clock, the hour she'd said she'd be home. Grace had probably thought her timing was impeccable, that Nora was no doubt already in the car on her way back.

Good thing they'd been interrupted. This craziness with Reid—it wasn't her. She had responsibilities that she'd forgotten instantly the moment he'd touched her.

She slipped her phone back into her clutch and stood. When she faced Reid again, something had shifted in the atmosphere.

"Who's Declan?" he asked smoothly, his expression frozen into a mask she didn't recognize.

The hot, exciting man of a few moments ago had vanished. The one in its place had a hard, merciless outer shell that warned her to back off.

"Declan is my son. He's two."

Reid's expression didn't waver as a shadow fell over it. "You failed to mention that you were a mother. Deliberately?"

"What, like I was trying to hide it?" She laughed self-consciously. Hadn't she mentioned Declan? He was the light of her life. But then she and Reid hadn't really talked, not the way two old friends did who were catching up on each other's lives. "It never came up. I was married for almost five years before Sean died. We had a son together. It's relatively normal."

"Dinner was a mistake." Reid swiftly crossed to her and put an impersonal hand under her elbow, guiding her toward the door. His touch nearly made her weep—because it was so different from the way he'd touched her moments ago.

Stung, she pulled her arm free. "What's wrong with

you, Reid? I'm suddenly no longer attractive because I have a kid?"

"Yes."

He offered no further explanation as Nora stared at him, her mouth hanging open. "That's a pretty ridiculous statement. Lots of women who are very attractive have children."

"I'm not dating any of them," he countered. "Nor am I dating you. Kids are a deal-breaker."

"I didn't know we had a deal." She crossed her arms over her midsection, very much fearing she was about to throw up. "I thought we were reconnecting while I was in town. I never expected this to go any further than one or two nights, tops. What does my son have to do with that?"

Everything, apparently, but Reid had said his piece. His mouth was a firm, grim line as he extended his hand, indicating the door she was supposed to be disappearing through. The connection she'd felt, the attraction and good memories of the past, all of it fled instantly. Nora suddenly felt both cheap and ripped off at the same time.

Her Achilles' heel—vulnerability—nearly overwhelmed her. But she didn't have to take what he was dishing out. She was in charge of her destiny. This shadowy, unfathomable stranger wasn't the man she'd known once upon a time.

"Nice. I guess your reputation *is* quite overblown." She whirled and marched toward the door before he caught glimpse of the hurt that was surely spreading over her face. "Don't worry. I won't tell anyone you're too obnoxious to sleep with," she called over her shoulder, slamming the door behind her.

Five

All of Reid's employees gave him a wide berth for two days.

Which was relatively normal, but usually it was out of respect for his preference to be alone. Lately, it was to avoid his wrath as he found fault with everyone in his path.

For the fourth time since his morning coffee, Reid was confronted with yet another example of ineptitude as he exited the elevator on the forty-seventh floor. The meeting he'd just attended across town had been full of pompous blowhards who wouldn't know compromise if it bit them in their butts. Traffic had been impossible and now this—the sign in the vestibule, the one that was supposed to greet visitors, had fallen over. And not even the right way. The front lay facedown on the short pile carpet, its blank backside displaying a whole lot of nothing in the direction of the ceiling.

He stormed through the door into the reception area of Metropol's administrative office. "Mrs. Grant."

His admin glanced up from her computer. "Mr. Chamberlain."

He rolled his eyes. Mrs. Grant was the only person he'd ever allow to speak to him with that kind of snarkiness and that was only because she was irreplaceable. "Call building maintenance. The welcome sign has fallen over. And while you're on the phone with them, ask them whether they like their paychecks. It's inexcusable to have a hotel with this shoddy of an appearance. Guests can stay in a lot of hotels that aren't mine. We want them… What are you looking at?"

Mrs. Grant stared at him as if he'd grown another head. "Are you finished?"

"Just getting started," he shot back.

She tsked. "Not with maintenance, you're not. Unless you'd like to run this hotel all by yourself?"

"What are you talking about? The Metropol has a maintenance crew that employs a hundred people—"

"And those numbers will dwindle down to one surly CEO if you keep it up," she interrupted mildly. "We've already had two resignations today alone. I'm not calling maintenance, so you can forget all that bluster and nonsense. Watch and learn."

Mrs. Grant stood and skirted him, jerking her head toward the vestibule. Was everyone determined to extract their pound of his flesh? After that disappointing meeting that had been a colossal waste of his time, all he wanted to do was go to his office, where he could decompress by himself.

She pushed open the frosted glass door and held it open, refusing to budge until he followed her. With a long-suffering sigh, he did.

Pointedly, she widened her eyes as she bent over and righted the sign. "See? No maintenance crew required, Mr. Chamberlain. No small children were harmed in the fixing of this problem."

Small children. It wasn't a dig, as Mrs. Grant had no idea what had transpired between Reid and Nora two days ago. But it felt like a strong reproach of his behavior all the same.

He didn't like it. He'd been doing his level best to forget about Nora Winchester—or Nora O'Malley, or whatever she called herself these days—and the reminders were not welcome.

"You're right," he acknowledged gruffly. "I could have resolved that one myself, but the rest of the issues—"

"Are a normal part of doing business." She crossed her arms over her nondescript suit and eyed him. "What's wrong with you lately? Something's bothering you."

How did she know that? Suspicious, he eyed her back. "I have no idea what you're referring to."

"Save it, dear. You and I both know that you're a pussycat under that grumpy exterior. Someone got you all worked up and you're going to have to fix it before too long. Even you can't do it all yourself."

Want to bet?

He almost said it out loud. But that wouldn't make Mrs. Grant any less right.

He deflated under the sympathetic gaze of his admin. "Sorry. I've been a bit beastly, I admit."

"Why don't you take the rest of the day off?" she suggested. "It's nearly five anyway. I know you like to work monstrously long hours, but I promise your empire will not collapse if you leave the helm a couple of hours early."

Working long hours prevented his mind from wandering. That's when the grief crept up on him, whacking him the hardest—when he wasn't prepared.

He nodded, but only because the idea of getting out from under Mrs. Grant's all-too-shrewd gaze had a lot of appeal. "Have a good night, then."

She would handle his email and take calls on his behalf. Such was the benefit of having an admin who was so well trained; he could disappear for a few hours and she'd steer the ship in the right direction.

But when he walked in through the door of his penthouse, he caught the faintest scent of vanilla and strawberries, and the memory of Nora in his arms, as she'd looked while reflected in the window, exploded in his mind. The image of her—hot, unrestrained, pleasured—appeared as if by magic in the glass, multiplying exponentially across all the panes until she surrounded him.

Yeah, he couldn't blame his bad mood on anything except the disappointment of really connecting with Nora the other night only to find out the truth about her: she had a kid. It was fine. He preferred being alone anyway. A woman would only complicate his life to the nth degree and he didn't need that.

Grimly, he turned his back on the floor-to-ceiling windows and sought out a bottle of fifty-year-old Dalmore. The scotch burned down his throat but even the heavy scent of toffee and alcohol couldn't overpower the memories of the woman he'd nearly bedded two nights ago.

Nearly bedded, but hadn't, thanks to the fortuitous interruption that had revealed Nora's lies.

Oh, she'd had no problem mentioning she'd been married. A widow, he could deal with. A mom, he could not. And she hadn't bothered to inform him that she had a kid in tow. He couldn't handle kids, couldn't handle the guilt of not having the ability to care for one. If he'd wanted to find out how crappy of a father he'd be, he'd have taken Sophia's twins when offered the chance, thank you very much.

The scotch had done the opposite of what he'd hoped. Instead of dulling his thoughts, it sharpened them as they drifted to Phoebe and Jude. His niece and nephew were fraternal twins, but they looked a lot alike. Because they resembled Sophia.

His mood fell off a cliff.

Sick of his own company, and tired of battling the pile of remorse on his shoulders, which weighed more every day, he yanked his phone out and called Nash. His brother answered on the first ring.

"Reid. Is everything okay?"

Worry tinged Nash's voice, thickening the ever-present guilt swirling around in Reid's gut along with the scotch. Guilt that he hadn't saved his sister and mother. Guilt because Nash had stepped up where Reid had failed. Guilt over how hurt Nora had looked after Reid had unceremoniously shoved her out the door. And then he still had some guilt left over for how he'd treated his staff these past few days.

"Yeah. Does something have to be wrong for me to call?"

Nash didn't hesitate. "Uh, usually. But if this is just a random drive-by call, that's okay. How are you?"

Lonely.

Reid cursed to himself. Where the hell had that come from? Nora was not right about that. He liked being alone. Except he'd enjoyed her company. She'd made the darkness inside…bearable. More than bearable. She'd eased it. Especially when she'd kissed him, when she'd opened up, inviting him into her warmth. Disappointment about Nora's pint-sized complication didn't begin to describe it.

"I'm fine," Reid lied. "How are the twins?"

"They're three. It's an extension of the terrible twos, which apparently lasts until they're eighteen." Nash's chuckle rumbled across the line. "Gina has been threatening to put them in military school, but of course they've latched onto the idea like it's some big game. 'Will we learn how to shoot guns?' they asked. Both of them."

"Phoebe, too?" Reid fell onto the sofa that faced the view of the Sears Tower, propping the phone up against his shoulder so he could retrieve his drink from the coffee table. "That seems odd for a girl."

Nash's shrug was nearly audible over the line. "Last week, she wanted to be a ninja. Lest you forget, Sophia never cared about quote-unquote 'girl stuff.' Phoebe wants to do whatever Jude is doing. You should visit. See them for yourself."

He should. They were his blood, too, same as Sophia. But he couldn't. The twins were one more huge reminder of how he hadn't been able to be what those kids needed. How he couldn't be a father because he lacked…*something*. There was a big, gaping hole where the ability to nurture and care about other human beings should be, a hole formed by genetic predisposition and further hollowed out when the family he loved had been ripped away. No way would Reid ever care about someone again. Not to that degree.

He couldn't risk it. Not with Sophia's kids, not with Nora's. Not even with Nora herself.

"Chamberlain Group is in a transition stage, so it would be difficult to get away," he explained even as his gut churned over the fabrication. Chamberlain Group always came first, regardless of what was happening internally at his company. It was safer that way. He controlled what happened and that would never change.

"Yeah, that's what you always say." Nash spoke to someone else in the room, his voice muffled as if he'd covered the speaker with his hand. Then, more clearly, he said, "Gina says hi and wants to know if you're seeing anyone."

"What? Why would she ask that?" Reid scrambled for an explanation as to how his brother's wife would have heard about Reid's date with Nora. Had Nora told a bunch of people? Surely she wouldn't be so indiscreet. "I'm not seeing anyone and the media likes to exaggerate stories of my love life anyway. Has Gina heard something? Tell me who's talking about my—"

"Relax. She didn't hear anything in the media. I would have told you so, as I know how much you value your privacy. Gina has a friend she thought you might like and wanted to introduce you since you're not seeing someone. That's all."

Reid's conscience kicked in as he envisioned having dinner with this new woman the way he'd had dinner with Nora. A different woman would sit in that chair kitty-corner to his at the big table. A different woman would drink from his wineglass, peering up at him over the rim.

No. Those memories belonged to Nora. He never brought women home in the first place and now Nora was stamped all over his penthouse. Irrevocably. This was why being alone was better.

"That's nice. Tell her thank you, but no. I'm pretty busy right now."

"So you *are* seeing someone." Nash laughed. "I

thought your protests a minute ago were a little too ve-
hement for a simple question. Who is she?"

"I'm not." Reid sighed. Who was he kidding? He'd
been in such a bad mood because he didn't like how
things had ended. Because he'd secretly wished for a
different outcome and couldn't see a way around the
cold, hard facts. "But only because it turned out she
has a kid."

"Still sticking to that stupid rule I see. You have no
idea what you're missing out on. Kids are great and
if you like this woman, you should spend more time
with her and her child before drawing such a hard line.
What's the worst that could happen? You find out you
can't stand children and you tell her it's not working out.
But at least you tried."

"It's not that simple."

But it could have been. If he hadn't been so brutally final about motherhood being a deal breaker. If he
hadn't freaked out as he had. Things had gotten intense
and maybe he'd been looking for a way to break it up
before something happened that he couldn't take back.

No kids was his rule. But he'd wielded it like a blunt
instrument, desperate to reel back an encounter that had
exploded into something much more than he'd expected
it to be.

His guilty conscience roared to the forefront. If nothing else, he owed Nora an apology. The way he'd acted
was inexcusable, especially given that neither of them
was looking for anything permanent. Nora had even
said one, two nights tops, and she didn't live in Chicago. He'd drawn a line that didn't matter in the long
run because her kid wasn't a factor if they didn't even
live in the same city.

"Why not?" Nash asked.

"I said some things that I probably shouldn't have. She probably wouldn't even take my call."

"So don't call her," Nash advised. "Go to her with as many flowers as you can carry, tell her you're sorry you're such a jackass and then make it up to her."

Reid bit back a self-deprecating laugh. "Really? That works?"

"Gina's nodding her head so hard, it's about to fly off."

His bad mood eased a little. "Thanks. I'll try it."

Nora made him feel alive. He wanted more of that, and if he handled the apology right, maybe he could have it. What was the worst thing that could happen?

Sutton Winchester was awake.

Nora liked it better when her father was asleep. Then she could pretend the reconciliation she'd secretly hoped for when she'd decided to come back to Chicago might actually happen. When he was coherent and could speak? Forget it.

After her father had demanded to meet Declan—a first for them both—she'd patiently waited for something akin to grandfatherly love to surface. And of course she'd gotten exactly what she should have expected: a comment about how her son looked nothing like a Winchester, which was somehow the fault of her marrying someone with strong Irish genes. Then came a scolding over the fact that she hadn't cashed the six-figure check Sutton had sent her so she could educate his grandson properly. Apparently private schools offered the only acceptable education for a Winchester. And so on.

Having her hopes dashed was exhausting. And after the debacle with Reid, Nora was sick of being disappointed. Since taking control of a bad situation had become her new mantra, she'd walked out of her father's hospital room without another word, taking Declan with her.

Medical personnel dressed in scrubs rushed by on both sides as she caught her breath in the hall. Not wanting to be in the way, Nora ducked into an alcove. From this vantage point, she glimpsed a similar alcove down the way and a familiar face popped into her field of vision.

Eve. And she wasn't alone. A man occupied the alcove with her. He had his back to Nora so she couldn't be certain of his identity, but his longish blond hair and authoritative stature gave her a big clue that it was either Brooks or Graham Newport, one of Carson's twin half brothers. Nora had met them all briefly yesterday for the first time and hadn't spent enough time with the brothers to tell them apart yet.

Her sister's expression made it clear they were having a heated conversation. Intrigued, Nora watched them for a few moments. She had zero prayer of hearing what they were saying since a good fifty yards and a sea of people separated them. But their body language told an interesting story: namely, that the two were far more comfortable with each other than Nora would have guessed. Their torsos and hips nearly met at least three times in the tight alcove and neither of them seemed inclined to shift away.

What in the world? Was Eve playing coy with one of the Newport twins to get dirt on Carson? Her sister had been furious over the inheritance grab Carson had initiated. Maybe she was trying to influence whichever brother she'd cornered into getting Carson to back off. That had to be it. The sparks between the two must be her imagination.

Declan tugged on Nora's skirt and held up his chubby arms, silently asking to be picked up in his little-boy language. She complied and hugged him close. This was all that mattered. The most important thing in her universe sat encased in her arms and she'd fight to shield Declan from the evils of the world as long as she could. Men like her father would corrupt him, and men like Reid would hurt him.

So she'd keep doing this alone. Nothing had changed. Then why had dinner with Reid felt like the beginning of something different, only to have it all crash down around her?

"Sorry Grandpa turned out to be such a mean man," she murmured into his neck. "We'll figure out how to be the better person here. Somehow."

"Home," Declan told her.

"Yeah, soon," Nora promised, her heart aching at the thought of the empty house waiting for them both back in Silver Falls.

All she'd wanted from her night with Reid was companionship. A few moments of being treated like a woman again instead of a mom and widow. Over the years, he'd obviously become someone else, someone she didn't like, and she mourned the loss of her starry-eyed childhood vision of him the most.

When she stepped out of the alcove, Gracie appeared from around the corner.

"Oh, there you are," she called and halted. A harried nurse nearly plowed into her, so they both shuffled to the edge of the corridor. "I was looking for you to see if you wanted to watch a movie with me and Eve tonight. This bedside vigil is killing me. I could use a girls' night."

"Yes, absolutely." It sounded heavenly all at once, not to have to face a long evening alone. "Come to the guesthouse so I can put Declan to bed and we'll watch something there."

"Sure, that sounds great." Gracie glanced around the brightly lit hallway. "Have you seen Eve? I texted her but she hasn't responded."

"I'm here." Breathless, Eve skidded to a stop near Nora, the color in her cheeks high. "I was…um, on a conference call. What's up?"

Nora's brows lifted involuntarily at her sister's bald-faced lie, but she didn't call her on it. Instead, she tucked the information—both the cover-up and the fact that her sister had been cozying up with a member of the enemy camp—into her back pocket in case she needed it later. "Gracie and I were just organizing a movie night. You in?"

"Great, great." Eve nodded, but her gaze shifted over Nora's shoulder, obviously distracted by something. Or someone. "Eight o'clock?"

They all agreed on the time and Nora slipped away from the hospital with the excuse that Declan needed to take a nap. Which was true but Nora really needed to regroup after dealing with her father's domineering attitude.

Once she arrived at the guesthouse, Nora found herself too restless to lie down, though her body screamed with fatigue. She thought about how she should find a job when she got home. It had been nearly two years since Sean died and her dream of being a stay-at-home mom to a brood of children had died along with her husband. Before she'd married Sean, she'd dabbled in web design, but hadn't built up a freelance business worth hanging on to. Gracie was the Winchester sister with all the natural design skill, which she put to use in the fashion industry. Nora had just enough to get by. So maybe something else would present itself.

The day dragged and Nora was looking forward to movie night more than she'd have anticipated. She and her sisters had always been close before she'd left for Colorado, but they'd drifted apart as their circle of friends changed and the distance made it too difficult to spend quality time together. It was nice to pick up the threads of their relationship as if no time at all had passed.

Dinner was a somber affair for two and Declan picked at his food more so than usual.

"Eat your carrots," Nora said and nodded at the fruit snack pack she'd placed out of reach but within his line of sight as incentive. "Dessert is only for boys who finish their dinner."

"No. Now." Declan's stubborn little lip came out, signifying his Irish temper had started a slow simmer, threatening to boil over if he didn't get his way.

"Carrots. Then fruit snacks."

Nora forked her own microwavable mush into her mouth. The box might have been labeled Asian Noodles with Chicken but it sure didn't taste like much. Reid's nonchalant mention of a private chef drifted into her head. *As if.* That was just one more reason why it was better for them to have parted ways. The man had too much money and it had shaded his view of mere mortals. Not everyone got to hire staff to cater to their every whim.

If Nora had wanted to be a slave to the all-mighty dollar, she'd have taken Sutton Winchester's dirty money and lived high on the hog without a thought of the stipend the military sent her every month. To do so felt like a betrayal of Sean's sacrifice for his country. That money was hers, sent from beyond the grave by the man she'd loved.

Even though Declan exhibited more drama than a group of high school cheerleaders at prom, the carrots ultimately disappeared into her baby's mouth. Fruit snacks finally in hand, Declan calmed down. Later, he even took a bath without objection, then went straight down in his crib, leaving Nora tired but victorious.

Movie night could officially begin.

Except when she emerged from the back of the guest-house where the bedrooms lay, she saw her phone was flashing. She had a message. It was from Eve. Have to cancel tonight.

What in the world? She texted her sister back: Hot date?

The return message came back so fast, Nora wondered if her sister had been sitting on her phone: No, of course not! Why would you think that? That's ridiculous. Gracie and I decided to stay at the hospital with Dad.

At the hospital…where whichever Newport twin she'd been having such a heated conversation with had last been spotted. Nora sent a follow-up message: Seems like the scenery there is pretty good. Sure you don't have extra motivation to stick around? Maybe in the form of a MAN?

No.

Well. That was a clipped response if she'd ever heard one, and Eve's caginess only increased Nora's curiosity. But she let it slide, too disappointed in the lost movie night to worry about it for the time being.

But why Gracie had also canceled—that remained a mystery. One Nora would like to solve. Experience told her she had a long night ahead of her, heavy with reflection and loneliness. This was when she missed having a significant other the most. She should be used to it by now, especially since she'd pretty much decided that she'd be single the rest of her life. How could she possibly ever let herself fall in love again? She couldn't. So she'd be alone by default.

Mostly, she was okay with it. But not on a night when she'd expected to have company.

Nora tapped up Grace's contact info, intending to send her a message to ask what was up, when the speaker near the front door beeped. George, her father's gatekeeper, called out, stating she had a visitor.

Relieved, Nora couldn't press the intercom button fast enough. "Yes, I'm expecting someone."

Gracie wasn't canceling after all. Eve must have been using Grace as a cover and forgotten to actually get their stories straight before their youngest sister bailed on her. Too bad. Maybe Grace had the dirt on Eve's shenanigans.

Whatever the case, Nora was happy she wasn't going to spend the evening alone. Again.

Nora swung the door open, smile in place. But it instantly slipped.

Reid Chamberlain stood on her doorstep, holding a red tricycle in one hand and what had to be five dozen of the most amazingly full and beautiful flowers she'd ever seen.

Nora blinked but the image didn't change. "What are you doing here?"

"Apologizing."

Their gazes met and he pulled her into the moment, just as he'd done the first time in his office. And the second time at his door. *Mesmerizing.* That was the only word she could come up with for his mahogany-brown eyes. A sharp, quick memory of the last time she'd seen him, of what his hands had done to her body, weakened her knees.

She straightened them, refusing to be affected. Reid was mercurial, talking about connections and friendship in one breath and then turning into an implacable wall the next. This man wanted nothing to do with her son and therefore, he wanted nothing to do with her. He was moody and morose and far too complex. She'd let him hurt Declan over her dead body.

Reid held out the tricycle. "This is for your son. If you'll accept it. No strings attached."

The fact that he'd offered that first, before the flowers, knocked away a chunk of Nora's ire, quite against her will. She took it from his outstretched hand, but she had to use both of hers. The tricycle was much heavier than it appeared and he'd been holding it one-handed. "Thank you. He'll love it and he needs activities to keep him occupied. This was a nice gesture."

"I don't make nice gestures," he reminded her. She realized that she had no idea what motivated him, what governed his thoughts, why he shifted moods like quicksilver.

She set the shiny red tricycle inside the house, just to the left of the door where it was out of the way.

"That's right." Crossing her arms over her chest to ease the ache caused by the sound of his smooth voice, she eyed him. "You must want something. What is it?"

Her body hadn't gotten the message that Reid Chamberlain wasn't on the menu, apparently.

"For you to forgive me. I behaved badly the other night. I'm sorry."

A hint of the smile she'd once craved played at his lips as he stood there waiting for her response.

"For which part? The orgasm or for kicking me out?"

The ghost smile vanished. "I would never apologize for pleasuring you. It was an experience I'll never forget. One of the best I've ever had."

Oh, my. His gaze sharpened on hers and heat arced between them as she flooded with longing. "But we didn't even get to you. We were interrupted."

As if either of them needed the reminder.

"Make no mistake. It was just as good for me as it was for you. I'd do it again, anytime, anyplace."

She shuddered. She excited him and he'd enjoyed watching her as he touched her, aroused her, awakened her. It shouldn't be so stimulating. Not when they still had so much unsaid between them.

"I don't understand why you're here," she said faintly. "You said you didn't date women with kids."

"I'm making an exception if you'll let me."

His gaze bored into hers, communicating far more than his words did. He wanted her and was willing to break his rules. Only for her. She was ashamed that her soul latched onto the lovely thought so quickly.

She had to clarify what was and wasn't happening. Before things got out of hand. Again.

"Well, I'm not making any exceptions. Not when it comes to my son. I need to understand your intentions."

She needed to understand *Reid*.

He held out the flowers and waited until she took them. Merciful heaven, they were beautiful and smelled divine. She kind of wanted to throw them on the bed and roll around in them. Maybe with Reid—*after* he assured her he'd gotten over his aversion to moms. Declan was a part of her and Reid couldn't separate her from her son even if he tried. Nor would she let him.

"I intend to apologize," he repeated. "I can also explain why I don't date women with children. And why I'm standing on your doorstep, despite that. If more comes out of the evening, that's your choice."

Her heart tumbled a little at his sincerity. In a life where she mourned the loss of choices, being given one tipped the scales.

"Come in, then. But in the interest of full disclosure, my son is here. Asleep. But very much in the house and prone to waking up in need of a drink, crackers, his frog blanket, a missing stuffed animal and quite possibly a book that he'll have to have right that minute. Sometimes all of the above."

"I'll consider myself warned."

To his credit, Reid didn't hesitate to cross the threshold when she opened the door wider in invitation. He glanced around the lavishly appointed guesthouse with apparent appreciation for the priceless art on the walls and rare marble-inlaid floor. But he didn't comment and instead turned to face her in the foyer, which suddenly got a lot smaller despite the twenty-foot ceilings.

"Your son's name—it's Declan?" he asked out of the blue. "I want to refer to him appropriately."

"Yes." As an afterthought, she added, "O'Malley." But only because Reid had her all tripped up and sideways by making such a sweet effort.

"I remember. His father was killed in the line of duty."

Since the sudden lump in her throat wasn't conducive to talking, Nora nodded. She couldn't for the life of her recall telling him that.

"That's a legacy your boy should never forget." Reid

pursed his lips. "I have some things I want to talk to you about. Do you mind if we sit down?"

"That sounds so somber." She tried to laugh it off but his expression didn't change. It almost made her wish they could slide back into the place they'd been a minute ago, when the atmosphere grew heavy with implication and attraction the longer they stared at each other. "Should I open a bottle of wine?"

He inclined his head. "Sure. A little liquid courage couldn't hurt."

"Feeling shy?" she teased, a little desperate to get things back on even ground as she crossed to the wine refrigerator behind the small bar in the great room. "Surely we're past that stage at this point."

"The wine is for you."

There came that ghost of a smile again and it did funny things to her insides. What would happen if he really let go? Did she want to find out? The last time they'd been in close proximity, she'd ended up hurt and confused. She didn't want to give Reid an opening to do that again. But after his apology and comments about Declan and his father, maybe she could trust him.

She popped the cork on the wine that she'd planned to share with Grace and Eve. At least she wasn't alone anymore. But whether that turned out to be a good thing or not remained to be seen.

Six

Reid accepted the wineglass from Nora's outstretched hand and downed a healthy sip. Despite what he'd told her, the wine was for him, too. The darkest period of his life wasn't an easy thing to spell out, but he owed her an explanation and he planned to give it to her.

Except he'd never talked to anyone about this stuff. Sure, lots of women had tried to dig into his moods and tendency to be a loner, usually with disastrous results—for them. He was more than happy to let them be disappointed. No one got to see inside him.

But for the first time, here he was about to spill his guts to a woman he'd hurt and then driven away. She should've been furious and full of righteous indignation, not settling in next to him on the leather sofa, her T-shirt stretching nicely over her gorgeous breasts.

When she'd arrived at his penthouse the other day in that little black dress, he'd had a hard time unsticking his tongue from the roof of his mouth. He'd have said that version of Nora was his favorite. He'd have been wrong.

Dressed for a night at home, Nora had a tantalizing, comfortable air about her that invited him to get cozy. He ached to take her up on that invitation. The woman vibrated with sensual, fresh energy 24/7, and he couldn't look away. Nor did he want to.

"Also in the interest of disclosure," Nora said before he could open his mouth, "I appreciate that you're leaving the direction of the evening up to me. I've become a bit of a control freak in the last little while and like to know that I'm driving the bus."

And instantly, that bit of information jump-started his libido again. He didn't mind a woman in control one iota and his imagination exploded with ideas designed to help her get there.

Starting with her on top of him—fully naked, because that was a bridge he'd yet to cross—head thrown back as she used her fingers to pleasure them both to her heart's content. Nora had painted her half-inch-long nails a whimsical purple and he couldn't stop imagining them wrapped around his erection. That picture wasn't going to work, at least not if he hoped to be honest with her instead of using sex as an excuse to avoid intimacy. Until now, that had been his usual go-to method.

"Noted." He cleared his throat. "I appreciate that the theme of the night is full disclosure. In that vein, I admit, I was upset about what I considered an omission on your part about your son."

Her brows came together as she processed that. "I didn't not tell you on purpose. It just never came up and honestly, it never occurred to me that it would be an issue. Lots of people in their thirties have kids. Personally, I'd find it more surprising to learn that a married couple didn't have kids. Wait." She reached out and placed a hand on his arm, her expression turning grave. "You *do* know how babies are made, right?"

A smile raced across his face before he could catch it and she lit up instantly. Which both aroused him and made him uncomfortable because he still didn't know if they were headed toward a reconciliation that might include sex.

He'd be happy if she accepted his apology and they acted like friends, just talking for a little while. Because he wanted that, too.

"You so rarely smile, Reid." Her hand didn't move from his arm and warmth bled through him as she talked. "I've missed it. That's one of your best features and I've always liked your smile. Do it more often."

"I would have sworn I'd permanently lost my smile." The fact that she'd dredged up something from his depths that he'd assumed was gone forever somehow made all of this easier. And harder. "I came to deliver flowers, a gift for Declan and an explanation. Smiles weren't included in the deal."

"Then I'll consider it a bonus." She sipped her wine, watching him over the rim. "What is the deal, then? You're going to give me your song and dance about how you like your freedom and a kid would only cramp your style and then what? We pick up where we left off in your penthouse?"

"Is that what you think this is about?"

She blinked but it was the only outward reaction she gave. "Of course. I'm a big girl. I can take it if kids are not your thing, as long as you're honest about it. I don't have stars in my eyes about some rosy future between us. We're hot for each other, and given the preview of what sex is going to be like between us, why dither around?"

"Because," he growled, "it's *not* like that. I'm not… There's nothing wrong with kids. It's me."

His throat tightened up so fast he couldn't breathe. A sip of wine didn't help.

"Hey."

She squeezed his arm and waited until he glanced at her before she continued.

"If it's not like that, I'm sorry." She peered up at him from under her lashes and the sincerity in her hazel eyes sucked him under. "Tell me what it's like, then. If you want to."

He wanted to. But how did you explain something so deeply flawed about yourself to another person? Nora might be the kindest person on the planet, but she wouldn't easily accept what he had to tell her. And he couldn't stand the thought of that light in her eyes being snuffed when she found out just how messed up he truly was.

No. He actually *didn't* want to tell her. He'd operated out of pure selfishness for so long, he scarcely knew how to put someone else first. But Nora deserved to know the truth.

"You heard about Sophia?" he choked out. He might as well start at the beginning.

Nora's hand froze on his arm. "No."

"She died." Blunt. There was no other way to say it. Death was always blunt. And brutal. "About two years ago. My whole family was involved in a plane crash. I was the only one not on board."

"Oh, Reid." Her eyes filled with unshed tears. "I hadn't heard. I'm so sorry."

"Nash survived. Barely."

That hardly covered the emotional angst Nash had battled when he'd awoken in the hospital, in pain and facing months of recovery, only to realize he was the sole survivor. Guilt had burdened his brother for a while. But he'd eventually gotten over it. Reid never had.

"But no one else did?" Nora asked softly and her stricken expression said she already knew the answer.

"No. Everyone is gone. Sophia had two children who weren't on board, either. Twins, a boy and a girl. Her ex-husband isn't in the picture, so her kids were essentially homeless."

Nora shook her head as the tears finally cascaded down her cheeks. "How awful for them. How old were they when it happened?"

"Babies."

His throat closed. Tiny, helpless babies, only a year old. And he'd ignored them in their most desperate hour. Never mind the turmoil he'd been thrown into while mourning the loss of his mother and sister—but not his father. The investigators at the scene had told him that the black box had recorded John Chamberlain confessing a multitude of sins and a desire to take his family to the grave with him.

Nora slid her hand down his arm, then threaded her fingers through his and clasped them tightly. He stared at their joined hands and something welled in his chest, squeezing it pleasantly. Providing wordless comfort that he didn't deserve.

He yanked his hand free before he came to rely too much on her warmth. He owed her the unvarnished truth and he wasn't close to done. "Nash and I fought about what to do. We were both single men with demanding careers. What did we know about raising kids? I... Well, we agreed we didn't want them to go to strangers, but the whole idea of becoming a father didn't sit well with me."

That was way too kind a way of putting it.

"Of course it didn't!" Nora's staunch support rang out in her tone. "You'd just lost your family, and grief is a terrible place to be in when trying to make decisions. I know. Trust me."

"No." Bleakly, he met her gaze and forced out the words that would destroy that fragile, brave sympathy in Nora's expression. "You don't know. You can't possibly understand. I abandoned them. I didn't want to be a father. I'm not loving and nurturing, nor do I have any desire to learn. My company is my life. I chose that over my sister's children and forced Nash's hand."

Nora's expression didn't change. It should have. She should have been scowling at him and blasting him with ugly words about what a horrible person he was. Because *that* would be the unvarnished truth.

Instead, she smiled as two more tears splashed down her cheeks. *Smiled*, and the smile held more understanding and grace than he could fully comprehend. Combined with her tears, it wrenched something open inside him and tears he almost couldn't contain pricked at his own eyelids.

Mortified, he blinked them back. Sorrow had no place here; he had no right to feel anything other than condemned. This was a recitation of his sins, plain and simple.

"What happened after that?" she murmured softly.

"Nash took them in," he admitted hoarsely. "He was the bigger man. I...couldn't. I'm selfish. I work eighty or ninety hours a week because my empire makes sense to me. That's why I wasn't on board the plane. I was in a meeting that I couldn't miss."

He should have been on that plane. Nash had insisted he'd tried to overpower their father with no success, but if both of them had been there, things might have turned out differently.

"Guilt is a killer," she said simply, and that nearly put him on his knees.

How had she zeroed in on that? She saw too much, understood too much. *She* was too much.

"Reid. Look at me," she commanded, and God help him, he did.

She took his wineglass and placed it next to hers on the low coffee table near the sofa. Slowly, she cupped his jaw in both of her hands and brought his lips to hers for a sweet, unending kiss that had nothing to do with sex. It was absolution.

And he didn't want it.

But he couldn't stop the freight train of his pulse as her goodness and light filled the cold places inside. Greedily, he soaked it up even as his own arms came up to encompass her, drawing her closer.

She broke off the kiss and touched his cheek with hers. "It's okay," she murmured. "I'm not going anywhere."

"You should," he said roughly even as he tightened his arms. "You should be kicking me out as unceremoniously as I did you the other night."

"Why? Because you made a decision you regret?" She tsked. "Who hasn't?"

It wasn't the same. But oh, dear God, he wanted it to be. Wanted to latch onto the simplicity of what she was trying to convey. That kind of liberty wasn't available to him. "You're making this out to be something it's not."

"Stop arguing with me!" She drew back and *now* she was scowling. "You listen to me. You are not a bad person because you didn't want to take in Sophia's children. Kids are a huge responsibility and more people should think about their capacity for parenthood before jumping into it. You want to know something? I think it's honorable that you don't let things go too far with a woman when she has a child."

Dumbfounded, he stared at her as his hands fell to the couch on either side of her. "What?"

"You heard me," she shot back fiercely. "A mom has more to think about than herself. You got that and immediately shut things down between us, even though I was all about the moment. It was nothing but fun and games to me. *You* were the bigger person in that scenario."

He shook his head but it didn't erase the spin she'd put on his actions. "That's—"

True. Yeah, he'd been selfishly thinking of himself the other night but in the end, he had found the force of will to step away, even though it had been the last thing he wanted to do. And that was the only honorable thing he'd done. "You're not listening to what I'm saying. I turned my back on my blood, on my sister. It's unforgivable."

She waved it off as if he'd admitted to taking the last cookie. "Are they being beaten at Nash's house? Starved?"

"No. He hired a great nanny and then fell in love with her. Gina is the best mom to those kids." Which was totally not the point. "I would have botched it."

"See?" She threw up her hands. "It all turned out like it should have. Some people call that fate. You, on the other hand, have moped around about it far too long."

"Moped?" Reid Chamberlain had a reputation for being dark and brooding. Reclusive and mysterious. He did not *mope*.

Her wide smile lessened a little of the sting. That mouth… He was a huge fan of it. Some guys called themselves leg men and Reid had always thought that sort of attitude was so limiting when a woman had many attributes worth praising. But he got it now. When she smiled, he felt it in his gut. He was officially a mouth man.

"Well," she murmured, smoothing a finger over one of his knuckles. "Maybe *moping* isn't the right word but you're doing something. Carrying around a lot of guilt over the plane crash and what came after, I guess. Would Sophia be angry with you for how it turned out? If she was standing in front of you right now, would she punch you in the face and tell you that you're a crappy brother?"

"Maybe." When Nora's brows snapped together in frustration, he shrugged. "Maybe not. I think she'd approve of Gina. It doesn't make me any better of a person."

It also didn't make him any less selfish or any more of the kind of guy who could be a dad. A woman like Nora wasn't for him for a lot of reasons. She deserved better. She'd skipped right over that piece of the puzzle and nothing she said could change that.

"You can't think like that."

"Like what? That it's my fault?" He shook his head with a dark, unamused chuckle. "But it is. I could have done something. I could have saved Sophia and my mom. If only I'd been there instead of at the Metropol."

What had been his passion had become his refuge. The place he hid from his crimes. The world seemed to be spinning on without him, so obviously he'd made a good decision for once to remove himself from polite society.

Sympathy flooded Nora's gaze, weighted her touch as she squeezed his fingers. "Or you could have died along with them. Also fate. Because if you had, you wouldn't be here now. With me."

Something shifted in the atmosphere as they stared at each other.

"No. I wouldn't be." But he wasn't so sure that was a good thing. While he'd hoped she'd accept his apology and then perhaps they could move on to more intimate activities, he hadn't expected that she'd uncover all his raw places with her understanding and pointed questions. "I should go."

"Don't you dare run away." Her grip tightened on his hand, pinning it to the leather cushion. "We're just getting started. I'm happy you're here, in case that wasn't abundantly clear. I don't get out much. I haven't been on a date since before Sean was deployed over two years ago. I'm enjoying this."

"You're...enjoying this? Which part? When I made you cry or when I admitted how I put my company ahead of my family? I'm a selfish workaholic who can never be a father, which means you should kick me out before I hurt you, too."

A noise of disgust burst from her throat. "Stop it. You say that like working a lot automatically makes you a bad father. Declan's dad was stationed overseas. How often do you think they would have seen each other? But we had a plan to make it work. That's what you do when you have kids. You improvise. Compromise. Figure things out. Because they're so worth it."

Nora's face had taken on a sharp, sweet expression as she talked about her son. *That's* what was missing, what Reid's DNA had skipped over when building his soul. Reid had never felt that way about Sophia's children. They were cute, sure. But he didn't love them unconditionally, the way Nora obviously felt about Declan. Sacrifice wasn't in his tool kit.

"I'm not father material," he said.

She needed to understand this before anything else happened between them. She could spin his decisions in a way that made it seem like forgiveness might be possible, but there was no happily-ever-after where he filled in the holes of her and Declan's lives.

"You underestimate yourself," she countered. "When it matters, you find a way to be more than you ever thought you could."

"Chamberlain Group comes first," he said flatly. Brutally. "I have no desire to be a father and so I didn't become one, nor do I plan to ever do so. That's why I don't date women with children. Where could it possibly go?"

Nora's mouth flattened. "You might as well say you don't date women *without* children, either, because all of them might someday want to have one, so you're out from the get-go."

That was one of his worst fears. "Fair enough. Then it might be better to describe my current state by saying I don't typically date anyone."

"Except me."

He nodded. "You are the exception in more ways than one."

"That seems quite implausible given your *reputation*. It may not be one hundred percent true but the rumors have to start somewhere." She couldn't have infused more innuendo into the statement if she'd tried. If he didn't miss his guess, the whole idea intrigued her.

Normally, the subject of his prowess in the bedroom pissed him off because it almost always came from uninformed gossipmongers who latched onto a titillating topic in hopes of spicing up their own boring lives.

With Nora, it might well be an opportunity to push the boundaries with a willing partner whom he already knew how to play like a well-tuned piano. The whole idea intrigued *him*, as well. Against all reason.

"Make no mistake." He caught her chin with his palm and guided it upward in order to meet her gaze. She didn't balk, staring him down without blinking, making him think that her spirit might be his favorite thing about her. "I have plenty of sex. A few hours of pleasure now and again is one of life's basic necessities. But I always make sure my lovers know the score and I rarely come back for seconds."

A saucy smile bloomed on her face. "So you being here tonight. Is that considered seconds?"

"Yes. And thirds."

Heat gathered in her expression as she absorbed that. Awareness built on itself, stretching the moment into a charged encounter that shouldn't have aroused him as much as it did. At least not so fast. But his body reacted of its own accord. He had a hell of an erection even as his pulse raced double time.

"I'll consider myself schooled on the score, then," she murmured. "Full disclosure. I'm not looking for anything more than a few hours of pleasure. I'm going back to Colorado soon and I won't be coming back to Chicago. Tonight, you need me. I need you. There's nothing more complicated about us than that."

So it seemed as if he'd freaked out over nothing. And now he felt like whacking himself in the head with a hammer. He'd missed out on the culmination of his dinner with Nora the other night over his own stupidity. A hot, willing woman had surrendered herself to wherever the mood took them and he'd *kicked her out*.

Being alone suited him. Mostly. Tonight it felt right to be with Nora.

* * *

When Nora had expressed a desire to better understand this complex man, she'd never dreamed she'd get her wish in such a deep and irrevocable fashion. The pain radiating from his beautiful brown eyes… It was almost too much for her to bear. Too much for her to internalize.

Because she identified with it far more easily than she wanted.

"You need me?" he repeated.

So much.

"Yes." The answer floated from her throat on a whisper. "You're not the only one who's still dealing with loss."

Wordlessly, he held out his hand and she took it. The contact sang through her, vibrating along all her nerve endings. The moment stretched as they shared a near-spiritual sense of unity. *Connection.* It had been present almost from the first but she hadn't recognized it for what it was: two souls finding each other, finding what they'd both so desperately sought. Someone to ease the pain and loneliness.

It was so much more than reconnecting with an old friend. Because neither of them was the same person as before. That was okay. Tonight, they had connected on a whole new level.

The way Reid was looking at her was…*delicious.* Nora let the feeling flow all the way down into her core, where it burst open in a heated shower of desire.

She should have been ashamed. She'd never dreamed she'd be the kind of woman who could indulge in a wicked encounter with a man she had no intention of marrying, no desire to fall in love with and no plans to even see again. But she'd not only already done that the other night, her body was gearing up to do it again.

Except when Reid reached out, cupping her cheek with one hand, his touch blew that lie to pieces. This wasn't a one-night stand with an anonymous man. It was *Reid*. As she absorbed his heat, the hugeness of what he'd shared settled over her. *She needed him*—to salve her own loneliness, to feel alive. To connect with him on a higher level than just over mutual pain.

She wanted to connect through mutual pleasure. And afterward, to know they'd helped each other heal in some small way. They had no future together, but what they experienced tonight might change their individual futures. Oh, she genuinely hoped it would.

Reid's curls begged for her fingers so she reached out to sink her fingers into them all the way to the knuckle. The moment she touched him, he came alive, reaching back, yanking her into his arms. Their lips met hungrily, without hesitation. His essence spilled into her as he kissed her. Filling her. Beating back the weight of life as together, they experienced something good and wonderful.

They both deserved the peace to be found only in each other's arms.

Except, in her mind, the pleasure scale remained completely unbalanced. She owed him one unbelievable, mind-blowing orgasm, the kind he'd dream about for several nights to come.

Masterfully, he gripped her jaw and shifted her to take the kiss deeper. His powerful, thrilling tongue worked its way farther into her mouth to claim hers, taste it. Heat engulfed her, radiating along her skin, diving under it to boil her blood. Her pulse hammered as his hand snaked under her T-shirt to fan across her bare back.

She was drowning in him, in the sensations of his

hands on her flesh, his lips on hers. Who was doing the giving here?

Before he stole her ability to think completely, she pulled away and threw one leg over his lap to straddle him and...*oh*. His hard length nudged her core and he gazed at her without speaking, his eyes hot and heavy-lidded with desire. For her.

"Better," she murmured.

His hands settled at her waist and he pulled, grinding her harder against his erection. Sparks burst at the contact point and her head tipped back automatically.

"It's getting there," he growled, and fused his lips to her throat.

First he nibbled, then sucked hard on the tender skin at her neck. There would be marks in the morning. Good. She wanted this man's brand on her body. A physical reminder that they'd shared something.

But she wasn't ready to surrender to him, to the sensations she knew were in store for her at his hands. Somehow, she pulled his mouth from the hollow of her neck and forcefully manacled his wrists, pinning them to the couch on either side of his shoulders.

"You. Be still."

His brows rose. "Because why?"

"The other night, I was the star of the show. You were behind me and I couldn't see you in the window. This time, it's your turn. "

Intrigue filled his expression. "I'm dying to find out what that means. And how you're going to stop me from touching you as much as I please."

Challenge accepted.

Seven

Nora contemplated the man at her complete mercy. Of course, that state of affairs would last only as long as it amused him to allow such a thing. She had no illusions about whether or not he could break free of her hands if he wanted to.

But he wouldn't.

"You're going to do exactly as I say and like it," she instructed, rolling her hips forward to notch his erection deeper into her recesses. Exactly where she wanted it most. "I've had precious few things I can control in my life lately. If I say you don't get to touch me, you'll obey because you want me to be happy."

"Yes," he murmured, his voice thick with passion that made her shiver. "I do want you to be happy. What would you like me to do, then?"

It was a total turn-on to have his agreement, to have complete control over a man's body, especially one as powerful and commanding as Reid Chamberlain's. Especially one she'd dreamed about as a teenager. Of course, her harmless young fantasies had included a kiss under the mistletoe hanging from the center arch at her parents' house one Christmas. Or holding hands at a football game.

Having permission to do whatever she wanted to a man who had grown up to be sinfully gorgeous and masculine, one who had gained a reputation for unusual tastes, was a far cry from that.

It should frighten her. It didn't.

"Let me undress you," she said.

Bold, decisive. She liked it.

He held out his hands in surrender, one to each side, and she watched him as she worked on the first button. It popped free and she traced a line down his torso to the next one, delighting in the feel of his crisp chest hair against her fingertip.

His eyelids shuttered as she touched him, and that was a turn-on, too. She'd barely gotten started and she'd already pleased him. And there was more where that came from.

She spread his shirt wide, drinking in the curves and valleys of his well-defined chest, sucking in her murmur of appreciation because it sounded childish to be so impressed by a man's physique. But he was gorgeous, muscled and bronzed, as if he'd spent hours honing his body strictly for her viewing pleasure.

"I like it when you look at me," he told her unnecessarily. She could feel the evidence between her legs as his hips strained forward, seeking her hungrily.

What else might he like? She had precious little experience with men other than the one she'd been married to. Sure, they'd had a good relationship in the bedroom, but this was different.

Reid was different. And that meant she could be different, too. This was her chance to be as experimental as she wished, with no fear of judgment. No worries about where their relationship was going, whether he'd be good for Declan, none of that. Because this was one night only.

There were no rules.

It was freeing and exciting.

Pulling him forward by his shirt, she dived into a kiss with gusto.

Instantly, his hard lips softened under hers as he surrendered to her completely, allowing her to explore to her heart's content. She traced the line of his closed mouth, forcing her tongue inside, opening him wide so she could taste him. Wine and man melded together, delicious and tempting at the same time.

More. She deepened the kiss, drawing a groan from him that vibrated against her breasts. Her nipples hardened under her bra, aching to be free of the confines of her clothes. *Not yet.* This initial round was about Reid and his pleasure. Not hers.

Going on instinct alone, she broke off the kiss and yanked his shirt free from his arms, then slid to the floor between his legs. He watched her as she unbuckled his belt, and the unbanked fire raging in his gaze turned her fingers numb. Somehow she got the leather strap untangled and pulled, then worked on the button and zipper holding his pants closed.

His erection strained against the fabric and she accidentally grazed it with her fingernails. He sucked in a strangled breath, and that's when her nerves completely disappeared.

This was his turn. She had the power to make him come and she planned to.

Slowly, she drew down the zipper and then hooked the waistband of his briefs with her forefingers to slide them down just a bit, just enough. His erection sprang free, gorgeous and thick, and so close to her mouth she couldn't resist a small taste.

It pulsed under her tongue. She wrapped one hand around the base to hold him still as she took the rest between her lips. Groaning, he slid a hand to the back of her neck, holding her head in place, which thrilled her. She shut her eyes, concentrating on the flesh filling her mouth as she sucked.

His hips bucked, driving him deeper, and she worked him relentlessly, shamelessly, until he froze and uttered a guttural expletive, then came in a glorious, salty burst that left her quite pleased with herself.

She cleaned up, giving him a few minutes to collect himself, and then she settled back into a spot near him on the couch. "That was amazing."

His brown eyes filled with amusement. "I think that's my line."

Still no smile. She'd have to work on that. "Let me know when you're rested up. I've got a few more things on the agenda."

"I'm done."

Lightning quick, he hauled her into his arms and devoured her whole from the inside out with nothing more than a kiss. Lips burning against hers, his tongue demanded entry. Heat skidded across her skin as he swirled into her mouth, flesh on flesh. Relentlessly, he deepened the kiss again and again, winding his fingers through her hair to slowly draw her head backward until she was helplessly caught in his powerful embrace.

His mouth raced down her throat and cool air caressed her bare skin an instant before she realized he'd yanked her shirt and bra strap down to reveal one shoulder. The bite of his teeth as they sank into her flesh made her flinch, but then he rested the palm of his hand against her shoulder blade, soothing her as he held her in place, pleasuring her with his whole mouth.

And it was pleasurable. She had never thought her shoulder could be an erogenous zone, but she wouldn't make that mistake again. Moaning, she leaned into his lips as his tongue laved over the spot where he'd nibbled, which still smarted a bit. It was an intense experience. Unique. Much like watching herself come the other night.

The memory blasted through her, dampening the juncture between her legs. Desperate for relief, she rolled her hips against the crease of her jeans but it wasn't enough.

Reid paused long enough to notice her discomfort and with a wicked gleam in his eye, he sat back. "Don't forget, your wish is my command."

How *could* she have forgotten? If she wanted him to touch her, all she had to do was say so. With two fingers, she flicked open the button of her jeans and unzipped them. Wiggling free of her panties at the same time, she lay back on the couch. "I want that mouth on me. Here."

She rested a hand on her mound. His trademark ghost of a smile curved his lips as he swept her with a heated glance.

Wordlessly, he put a hand on each knee and pushed, opening her up. And then…she bucked as his tongue connected with her center. A thick wave of pleasure radiated outward to engulf her whole body.

Those gorgeous lips nibbled at her flesh at the same

moment he plunged his fingers into her core. Again. Deeper. He twisted his fingers inside her. Sucked at her. Higher and higher she soared as his talented mouth treated her to the hottest experience of her life.

When she came, she thrust her hips upward against his mouth and he bit down. Lightly, but enough that she felt it. The combination of sensations ripped through her, and she cried out as her vision dimmed.

Reid's fingers drew out the orgasm, draining her. Filling her. His mouth on her was the sweetest paradox. They were fully connected, yet not. She wanted more.

"Take me to your bed," he demanded hoarsely before she'd fully recovered. "I need to be inside you."

She needed that, too. *Now.*

Urgency Reid didn't recognize coiled low in his belly as he scooped up the still-quivering woman from the couch and carried her across the room. He followed Nora's breathless directions until he found the bed. Gently, he laid her out on the coverlet, fished two condoms from his back pocket and stripped.

She watched him, her gaze sensual and expectant.

With reverence, he sat her up so he could remove her T-shirt. They had a bad habit of getting way too hot, way too fast, and clothes seemed to be the least of their concerns.

No more. He wanted to see her. The creamy swell of her breasts fell loose as he unhooked her bra and he couldn't stop himself from thumbing one nipple. It felt like silk. He fondled the other one in kind and she arched her back, moaning as he circled them, squeezing gently.

"Reid," she gasped.

"Yes? Something you want?"

"You."

Nonsensical sounds poured from her throat as he sucked a pert, hard nipple into his mouth. Heaven. He rolled the tip along the ridges of his teeth. She liked it when he got a little rough, as evidenced yet again when she shifted against his lips, shoving her nipple deeper into his mouth. He liked obliging her. Her responses to the slightest bite…unbelievable.

He couldn't wait to see what else she'd like.

On a whim, he flipped her over and drew her up on her knees, shoulders down against the coverlet, her legs spread wide to reveal all her secrets.

"I want to see you," he murmured and knelt between her thighs to trace his tongue along the crease he'd so thoroughly acquainted himself with mere moments ago. But then he'd been focused on pleasuring her. This perusal was purely for his own benefit.

And it was hot. So hot, his erection flared to life again. Faster than he'd have anticipated.

Her hips rocked, pressing her folds against his mouth, and he indulged her by driving his tongue straight into her wet center. She filled his taste buds and he fingered her bud until her head was thrashing against the coverlet.

Nora was so wet for him. It was the most arousing taste he'd ever had.

"Reid, please," she sobbed, and as he was about to lose his mind anyway, he rolled on a condom and gripped her hips.

She was so gorgeous spread out like this. Her backside was legendary, lush. He watched as his tip nudged her entrance from behind and then he sank into her slick, tight center. Instantly, she accepted him to the hilt and she gasped as he held her in place, savoring the feel. Slowly, he withdrew and plunged in again, and the angle was amazing.

She was amazing.

Something snapped in his chest and spilled warmth all over him. But it wasn't the heat of lust. It was something else, and his frozen, dark places evaporated as if they'd never existed. There was only Nora.

Watching them joined like this… The image heightened the urgency of his lovemaking. He couldn't hold back and didn't have to. She met his hard, quick thrusts and then some. They came together again and again until they both cried out in tandem. As she closed around him like a snug fist, he emptied himself.

He snaked an arm around her chest and rolled, taking them both to the mattress, her hot body spooned tight against his.

He didn't let go. Might never let go. His torso heaved against her spine. Spent, he lay there unable to move, unable to collect his scattered thoughts.

How did they top *that*?

Of course, the beauty of it was that they didn't have to. He could leave and never call her again. A few hours of pleasure had been delivered, as specified.

He didn't pull away, jam his legs into his pants and scout for the exit as he had so many times in the past. Instead, he pressed his lips to Nora's temple and pulled her closer, still inside her and not the slightest bit interested in changing that. He should be. He should leave. She snuggled deeper underneath his arm, and he couldn't have pulled away if his life depended on it.

"I have another bottle of wine," she murmured. "And several chick flicks bookmarked on Netflix. Wanna watch *Bridget Jones's Diary* with me?"

"Sure." That was a mistake. What the hell was he doing agreeing to stick around?

"Really?" She half rolled and eyed him over her

shoulder as if he'd started speaking Swahili. "*Bridget Jones* isn't the kind of thing men usually go for."

He cursed. She'd expected him to leave, too. They weren't a couple who lay around post-sex and had wine, falling asleep in each other's arms. She'd probably just offered out of courtesy.

Smooth, Chamberlain. "Maybe I should take a rain check. Early meeting."

Her face fell. "Oh. I was looking forward to it. Grace and Eve canceled on me and, well… Never mind. We agreed this was—"

Capturing her wide, unsmiling mouth, he kissed her nonsense away. "Forget I mentioned anything about a rain check. I'll get the wine. You get the movie."

"Okay. Let me check on Declan. Back in a flash."

And that was how he found himself wrapped up in Nora, sitting up against pillows in her bed, watching a movie about a British woman played by an actress he'd swear wasn't British. But Nora laughed every so often, and it thrummed through his torso in a thoroughly pleasant way. He'd do it again in a heartbeat.

When the credits rolled, Nora glanced up at him. "This is the best date I've ever had."

At her sweet admission, something unfolded inside him, and he didn't know what to do with it. This had been a date? He had precious little to compare it with, but she'd been married, which meant she'd probably gone on a lot of dates with the guy she'd eventually tied the knot with. What had Reid done that was so much better?

"You need to get out more."

"Or less." She snuggled up against his chest and his arms tightened involuntarily. "I'm not a fan of crowds. Staying in like this is perfect. It's exactly what I needed."

It suited him, as well. She fit him far better than he'd

have guessed. The sex had been off the charts. No holds barred. Meaningful, when it shouldn't have been.

But that didn't change facts. The evening had been the best date of his life, too.

Too bad they weren't dating. "I should go."

She sat up. "You keep saying that. And then not doing it. In case there's any confusion, I'd be more than happy if you stayed the night."

As in *all night*? His throat pinched with something that felt a lot like panic. "That's not really my thing."

"Trust me, it's not my typical thing, either. But..." She trailed off, looking so frustrated and forlorn that he couldn't stand it.

Tipping her chin up, he forced her to meet his gaze. "What is it?"

"I just don't want to be alone. Not after the spectacular evening we've had so far." She crossed her arms over her stomach, vulnerability practically bleeding from her pores. "Stay."

"I'm not going anywhere."

The instant he said it, he wished he could take it back. What the hell was wrong with him? It was as if his brain and his vocal cords had never met. They certainly weren't on the same page.

But then she smiled and he forgot why it was a bad idea to stay. She didn't want to be alone and for the first time in a long time, neither did he. At least until she fell asleep. Then he could dash for the door without her being the wiser.

He pulled her back into his arms, content to just be with her, for now. Who could blame him, when the scent of vanilla and strawberries and sex lingered in the air? She was just as sweet dozing against his chest as she had been against his tongue when he pleasured her. He almost hated to leave. But he had to. That way, there would be no morning after, no opportunity for regret, for what-ifs, for *maybe we should think about a second date...*

Just one night. And it was over.

Reid turned off the TV and settled Nora's head against the pillow as he eased out from under her. She shifted, drawing her palm up to rest a cheek on it, but she didn't wake. He pulled the covers up over her naked form, hiding the faint marks on her shoulder and neck.

What they'd done behind closed doors was private. And he liked that he'd left her with something of a reminder that would fade into memory, just like their night together.

Which was over, he reminded himself yet again. Why was he still standing here soaking up the gorgeous vision of Nora sleeping in her bed, replete from his lovemaking? Because he wanted to curl up next to her again. Wake up with her in the morning and do it all over again.

That wasn't the deal. Nor was the deal open to alteration. It wasn't as though he'd had to talk her into one night only. She'd been the one to insist on that, which fit him to a T.

Reid went out into the living room and found his pants, underwear and shirt, but his belt was nowhere to be seen. Glancing back toward the hall that led to Nora's bedroom, he risked turning on the light in hopes of locating it.

"Mmmair. Mmmair."

What the hell was that? Reid's hand froze on the light switch he'd just flipped.

He whipped around. A tiny redheaded boy dressed in pajamas with a picture of a dinosaur on the chest stood in the dead center of the living room. Looking at him.

Reid's pulse jumped. "Um, hi."

Declan. Obviously. Reid did a mental sweep for the information he'd gleaned from Nora about her son. He liked books and blankets and was…how old? Two? Wasn't the kid too little to be wandering around in an unfamiliar house at night? By himself?

"Mmmair."

"Hey, buddy. You go on back to bed. Nothing to see here."

Not one muscle in the boy's body moved. Now what? Reid edged toward the door, eyeing it. Couldn't he still just leave? An ocean of Oriental carpet stretched between him and freedom. One small twist of the doorknob and he could—

"Mmmair."

Reid sighed. He'd be frustrated by the lack of communication, but Nora had probably drilled "Stranger Danger" into her son's head so well that he wasn't about to talk to some unfamiliar man who happened to be present in the living room at—Reid glanced at the clock on the mantel—1:45 a.m.

That's when Reid noticed the boy had tears welling up in his eyes. He cursed and then nearly bit off his tongue. You weren't supposed to talk like that around kids.

"What's wrong… Declan?"

Maybe if he called him by name, it would ease some of the tension, most of which seemed to be in Reid's legs, weighing them down. Rooting him to the spot. He couldn't leave, not now. Not in the middle of whatever crisis was going on with Nora's son. Besides, Reid couldn't walk out the door until he could be sure Declan wouldn't follow him outside or turn on the oven or order an X-rated movie with the universal remote lying on the couch.

The door was so close, and yet so far.

"Mmmair. Mmmair," Declan insisted, the tears spilling down his little face.

Nora. Nora could fix this. The kid obviously needed his mom, who could interpret this foreign, little-boy language with practiced ease.

But she was asleep. If Reid woke her up, there would be a whole…thing about whether he was going to stay the night. He couldn't do that, no matter how much he inexplicably wanted to. It wasn't fair to anyone.

Reid glanced at the door and then back at the hallway where Declan had come from. "Let's find your room, okay? We can handle that."

Wonder of wonders, Declan nodded. But he didn't move. Cautiously, Reid approached him the way he would a feral dog: hand outstretched, lots of eye contact and soothing noises.

The kid watched him unflinchingly. The moment Reid got within two feet, Declan's little arms stretched out and latched onto Reid's leg. Tight. Like a barnacle.

Oh, hell no. Reid groaned. What was he supposed to do now?

"Come on, kid. Give me a break," he muttered, wondering if it was okay to pry him off.

But he might hurt Declan. He had literally never touched a child in his life. Okay, well, not as an adult. He'd punched Nash plenty of times when they were growing up. But that was different. They'd been pretty close to the same size at the time.

Reid shook his leg. Gently. Declan did not magically detach.

"Declan." Reid waited until he looked up, and then spoke to him as he would anyone else who was being unreasonable. "You have to let go or I won't be able to walk."

Actually, that wasn't entirely true, as Reid discovered when he dragged his leg toward the hall—and Declan moved with him. So that was the secret. Reid shuffled. Declan shuffled. Eventually they got halfway down the hall, where Reid paused to get his bearings.

Which one was the kid's room? Nora's was at the end of the hall, as Reid well knew, but he'd failed to do an inventory of the rest of the house since it had never occurred to him that he'd be scouting for a place to deposit a two-year-old with stickier arms than an octopus.

Faint light spilled from one of the open doors. That seemed like a good candidate.

Reid did a few more shuffle-drag steps and peered inside the room. A white crib sat against one wall, with an antique writing desk against the adjacent wall. The floor was covered with a patchwork quilt sporting blobby animal shapes, and a night-light glowed from one of the plugs.

It looked as if the room had been repurposed for the little boy, but he didn't immediately untangle himself and toddle inside the way Reid had hoped.

"Here's your room, Declan," Reid whispered, ever mindful of Nora's open door not too far down the hall.

Declan tightened his arms. *Okay, then.* Looked like he was all in. Reid dragged Declan into the room and closed the door. "We'll just have us some men time, then."

Reid eased down onto the quilt. The moment his butt hit the ground, Declan's did, too, and he finally released his death grip. And he wasn't crying. So it was a win all the way around.

"Maybe we can get back in bed?" Reid suggested casually, eyeing the crib. How did one maneuver such a contraption? Clearly Declan had gotten out of it. Did he know how to get back in by himself?

This would be one of those times when it would be beneficial to have a manual. Reid fished his phone from his pocket and googled "How to put a baby in a crib."

Holy crap. An ungodly number of results appeared on the screen. But as he scrolled through them, most seemed to be about keeping the kid there once you got him into the thing.

"Yeah, already figured out that was a problem," he told his phone sarcastically as he thumbed past "15 Tips to Help Your Child Sleep through the Night."

Declan crawled over and peered at the screen with his head cocked, and then promptly plopped into Reid's lap, as if they'd done this a hundred times.

Reid groaned. The boy had put all his weight right on Reid's ankle bone. No problem. He could stand it. Probably. The seconds ticked by as together, they knocked out this task of reading useless articles debating the benefits of laying a baby on his back, stomach or side.

Nora's son wasn't even in the bed yet. How to position him on the mattress didn't matter a hell of a lot at this point in time.

Reid's leg started tingling. There was no helping it. He had to shift the child's weight. Dropping his phone, he gingerly gripped Declan's upper arms and pulled up, resituating his own legs, the boy's legs, and trying whatever else could be done with what felt like a fifty-pound sack of potatoes in his grip.

And then somehow, the boy half squirmed, half rolled and ended up cradled in Reid's arms. Huh. He'd have sworn Declan was too big to fit like this, but there you go. It seemed like a good next step would be standing and maybe he could ease the boy into his crib.

Should have thought of that, moron. What a simple solution.

Reid stood. Apparently he owed his personal trainer an apology for cursing the man out for the last three months over that exercise designed to hone his glutes. Reid hated that exercise. But it had worked.

He carried Declan to the crib and eased him onto the mattress. Maybe Reid should have actually paid attention to the article on the pros and cons of putting a baby on his stomach or back because hell if he knew whether this was the right way to do it.

Declan rolled and stood up, hands gripping the side of the crib. "Mmmair."

And...never mind. Reid sighed. "Seriously? Come on, lie back down. Please."

"Mmmair."

"What does that even mean?" Frustrated, Reid scowled at Declan. "Is that the name of your stuffed animal or something?"

Declan threw a leg over the side of the crib, clearly intent on repeating his escape.

"Oh, no. Not that again." Reid pushed back on Declan's leg and pointed to the mattress. "We're in the bed. We're not getting out until morning."

Which would be here much sooner than Reid would like, at this rate. If he didn't get this sorted out, he and Nora would be having a lovely conversation over coffee about how Reid had been the go-to substitute daddy during the night.

Ice coated Reid's lungs and they refused to fill with air. He wasn't father material. He'd told Nora this. And this situation was a case in point. Maybe Reid should just pretend he'd never heard Declan and get out while the getting was still good.

Declan stuck two fingers in his mouth. "Mmmair."

For whatever reason, the word sounded different than the other nine hundred times the boy had uttered it. Different enough that it was suddenly a word that had meaning. Reid frowned. "Did you have a nightmare?"

Two tears flung loose from Declan's face as he nodded. Progress. Except now everything was so much worse. A *nightmare*. As Reid had experienced his fair share of those, he fully sympathized. Poor kid. Only a heartless bastard would walk away after that kind of brave confession.

And while Reid would have labeled himself exactly that every day of the week and twice on Sunday...that little tear-filled face stabbed at something inside and there was no other recourse than to work through his reluctance. But what was Reid supposed to do?

Before he could think twice, Reid scooped the kid from his prison and stretched out on the floor, situating Declan near him on the patchwork quilt. His elbow landed somewhere in the middle of an elephant as he propped his head up on his hand.

Somehow, the words to a long-forgotten song filtered through his head. A song his mother had sung to him when he was young. Soon Reid found himself singing and stroking Declan's back. The way his own mom had done.

His throat seized up, cutting off the song midhum.

God, he missed his mother. She'd had her flaws but she'd loved Reid unconditionally and he'd forgotten what that felt like. Here on the floor with no one else but a near-mute little boy as his only witness, he let the memories flow and didn't check his monumental grief as he normally did.

Acute sadness welled up in him. It was almost too

much to bear. He had to get out of here before he became a blubbery mess. Besides, memories of his mother came part and parcel with memories of his father...which reminded Reid all over again what lurked in his DNA.

Darkness. Maybe even a deeper brand than Reid had already experienced. What if *becoming* a father brought out the worst traits of his bloodline and he found out too late? He should leave for that reason alone. No one under this roof deserved to be subjected to the murderous, suicidal tendencies that had lurked in his father's soul and surely lurked in Reid's, too.

But he forced himself to lie there with Declan until the boy fell still, his lashes flat against his cheeks and his chest rising and falling rhythmically. Surely the boy could sleep here on the floor, right? There was no way Reid could put him back in that crib, not with how clearly Declan had expressed his preference to be out of it. He'd probably wake up and climb back out again anyway.

Now he could leave with a clear conscience.

As Reid ducked out the door, he breathed deeply for the first time in what felt like a million years. It had been pure beginner's luck and only his intense desire to let Nora sleep had motivated him to succeed. No way could Reid ever deal with something like that again. It was way too intense.

Eight

What in the world?

Nora pushed open the door of Declan's room. It had been wide open when she checked on him last night before watching the movie with Reid. She always left it open so she could hear him if he called for her in the middle of the night.

Declan lay on the floor in the middle of his quilt, head pillowed on one chubby arm. Asleep.

Hands on her hips, her pulse hammering in her throat, Nora watched her son sleep. He'd started climbing out of his crib at home a couple of weeks ago but then he'd stopped and she'd—wrongly—assumed he'd had his fun doing it, then lost interest.

Guess not. He must have closed the door but how he'd done so without waking her up was baffling. It wasn't as though he could reach the doorknob, so he'd have to have pushed it shut. But she hadn't heard it, and her razor-sharp hearing had never failed her.

Good thing he hadn't come into her room last night.

Her cheeks warmed. Yeah, some of that might have traumatized Declan for life. And wouldn't that have been a disaster if Declan had run into Reid. One sight of her pint-size wonder would have sent Reid screaming for the hills.

No matter. Reid must have left well before Declan had performed his Houdini act. And that was perfect. Exactly as she'd expected. Their one night was over and she had several great memories to keep her warm for a good long while. Yeah, the sex had been *wow* and then some. No surprise there. But the way he'd made her feel…treasured. Beautiful. Exciting. That had been totally unexpected. Wonderful. Reid Chamberlain was so much more than a talented lover.

And if she'd been a little sad when she woke up and realized Reid had already left—without saying good-bye—no one had to know. She'd take that secret to the grave. She shouldn't have asked him to stay in the first place and she appreciated that Reid had figured out a way to let her save face, but not give in. Waking up together would have opened up their relationship to further speculation and there was nothing to speculate about.

Declan's eyes blinked open. "Daadee."

"What's that?"

Her son had added a new word to his vocabulary apparently. She loved the discovery process, where she got a chance to learn more about what went on in his head and communicate with this amazing little creature she'd been gifted with.

"Daadee."

"Daddy? Oh, honey." Nora shut her eyes for a blink. That was the one word she'd dreaded him learning. "Your daddy is in heaven. It's just you and me now."

A travesty. And what she wouldn't give for it to be different. But it was the cold, hard truth. If she'd loved Sean a little less or wasn't so worried about Declan being hurt by future loss, she might consider dating a nice man who could eventually fill that daddy-shaped hole in her son's heart.

After all, Declan would know Sean only from pictures. He'd never be held by his father or play baseball with his dad cheering on the sidelines. Nora had no doubt there were men out there who could love a kid who wasn't their blood. She just didn't have any interest in opening herself or her kid up for anything less than a sure thing. Which didn't exist. The odds favored an eventual breakup, more loss, more tragedy. Something other than a happily-ever-after—because that was Nora's reality.

"Daadee," Declan repeated and pointed at the door.

"Sorry, Butterbean. There's no daddy on the other side of that door."

Declan took it upon himself to make sure, doing a thorough search of the whole guesthouse, while Nora followed him, perplexed by his dogged determination. It rubbed at her the wrong way. Something had to have jump-started all of this.

Had Declan caught a glimpse of Reid last night and let his little-boy imagination go wild? Surely not. But then Nora hadn't ever brought a man around Declan. What if he had seen his mother kissing a man? Maybe he'd latched onto the idea of having a daddy of his own.

Nora's heart nearly squeezed out of her chest as Declan gave up his mysterious quest, finally plopping down on the Oriental carpet in front of the TV with a frustrated scowl. He refused to eat breakfast, refused the stuffed animals Nora tried to entertain him with, refused to watch any of his favorite shows. It was like trying to deal with a brick wall.

By 10:00 a.m., Nora was ready to pull her hair out. Her sisters had called from the hospital twice, wondering where Nora was. She'd intended to go by this morning but all the daddy talk had sidetracked her time frame.

"Okay, Butterbean. Enough with the theatrics. We're going to see Grandpa and you're going to be on your best behavior." Which was a little like telling the wind where to blow. Fruitless.

Somehow she got Mr. Impossible into the town car Eve had sent and buckled him into the car seat. Declan clutched a baggie of banana chips in lieu of breakfast, but it was food, so Nora considered it a victory.

The Chicago skyline unfolded outside the window and she was a little ashamed her eye shot straight to the twisted tower near the north end—the Metropol. Reid was inside the building somewhere. Was he thinking about their night together, remembering how amazing it was?

If so, that made two of them.

She shouldn't be thinking about him at all. He'd made it clear there was no future for them. If there was anyone more ill-suited to being that nice man who could fill the holes in her life, it was Reid Chamberlain.

Holes in *Declan's* life, she'd meant. Her own life had no holes. It was full of motherhood and dealing with her father's health problems. While she would go home eventually, she might have fudged the time frame with Reid a little bit, making it sound like she'd be jetting off in a few days, when she'd really planned to be in Chicago for the foreseeable future.

Her father was dying. She'd never forgive herself if she left without reconciling with him.

When Nora entered her father's hospital room, his eyes shifted toward her but otherwise, he didn't move.

"Hi, Dad."

Gaunt and pale, her father looked twenty years older than the picture she carried of him in her head. Cancer had aged him and it was a visual reminder that it would eventually kill him. Grief sloshed through Nora's stomach over the years of pain this man had caused. She'd missed out on having a loving father. Her son would, too, a commonality she mourned, but she'd had no control over the circumstances of Sean's death.

Sutton had made his own choices that prevented Nora's childhood from being the one she'd imagined other children getting to have. And some of those choices would prevent her son from knowing his grandfather. Some widows had supportive fathers who stepped into the gaping hole where their husbands used to be. Nora wasn't one of them.

"Nora." Her father's voice had degenerated into a gravelly growl, but it still carried a sense of authority. "You're late."

There were so many things she wanted to say in response to that, but none of them were conducive to reconciliation. So she smiled instead because that was what she did best: pretend everything was fine.

She chatted *at* her dad, not with him, because letting him get a word in edgewise gave him too much of an opening to say something horrible, mean or manipulative. Or all three. She told him about the modest house she lived in and the small town of Silver Falls that she'd moved to after Sean died because she couldn't stand living in Colorado Springs anymore, where the memories were sharpest.

Declan climbed up on Nora's lap to peer at his grand-father. "Pa."

"You may call me Grandfather," Sutton informed the boy, his brows snapping together. "Or you may refrain from addressing me."

Apparently, when correcting someone, her father had plenty of energy.

"For crying out loud, Dad. Declan is barely two." Nora stood, hauling Declan up against her hip, which got harder every day since Declan grew like a weed. "Since both of us lack the ability to meet your exacting standards, we'll do you the courtesy of removing our-selves from your presence."

Shaking so hard she feared she'd drop Declan, Nora fled the hospital room, nearly plowing into Eve outside the door.

"Where are you going?" she asked with a frown. "You've only been here for an hour."

"Don't start."

But Nora felt guilty and wondered if she'd been too hasty in dashing out of her father's hospital room. Ei-ther she wanted to reconcile—which meant accepting her father as is, poisonous personality and all—or she had to wash her hands of him.

Neither option made her feel like bursting into song Rodgers and Hammerstein–style right there in hospital corridor. She sighed.

"Okay, yeah." Nora set Declan down to give her arms a rest. She'd need her strength if she planned to continue arm wrestling with her father. "I know. We don't have long with Dad. I get it."

She marched back into the room and gritted her teeth. She lasted ninety-two minutes this time, which felt like an eternity. To Declan, too, apparently, as he had upended a tray of medical equipment, turned off the room's lights—twice—and called the nurse's station. The tittering women on the other end of the speaker didn't help. They thought talking to Declan was a riot and encouraged him to keep pushing the button as much as he liked.

Sutton, in a rare act of mercy, managed to fall asleep in the middle of the hubbub.

"I need to…" *Jump off a tall building.* Nora pinched the bridge of her nose. "Use the ladies' room. Be right back."

Eve distracted Declan by opening and closing her mirrored compact, nodding at Nora over her shoulder. "Who's that boy in there? Oh! Where did he go?"

Seeing how Declan instantly loved the game of peek-aboo, Nora decided to veer off in the opposite direction from the ladies' room and instead sought out some much-needed coffee. The lack of sleep the night before had started wearing on her.

But the reason for it—that made it all worthwhile.

Exhaustion must have had her seeing things because she could swear the cause of it had just stepped off the elevator with a stuffed horse the size of Declan under his arm.

Reid's gaze met hers across the corridor. And a slow smile spread across his face.

Her knees went weak. Oh, no. Reid had gotten under her skin when she wasn't looking.

"What are you doing here?" she whispered furiously as Reid caught up with her in the hall. Weak knees and hospital visits weren't part of the deal. Her resistance was down and there was nothing good that could come of this.

Reid pulled Nora out of the middle of the corridor and

into an alcove that afforded them a measure of privacy.
"I was concerned about your father."

"Sure you were."

The irony of having recently seen Eve and one of the
Newport brothers squashed into a similar alcove wasn't
lost on Nora. If anyone who knew her happened by, the
speculation would be rampant because this little space
was scarcely big enough for one person, let alone two.

Which meant that Reid's arms obviously would fit
only if he slipped them around Nora's waist. Since that
was where she secretly wanted them, that worked for
her, too.

His beautiful face still wore a hint of that amazing
ghostly smile, and his wholly masculine scent, much
stronger here in closer confines, nearly made her weep.

Somehow, her head tipped up and she landed in the
middle of a sweet kiss that seemed to surprise Reid as
much as it did her.

He simply held her close as the connection they'd
shared last night lit up like an electrical circuit had been
completed by the act of joining lips. All the angst and
disappointment and hurt from the last few hours at her
father's bedside melted away. The difficult morning with
a stubborn two-year-old vanished instantly.

And the darkness she sometimes sensed inside
Reid—that was gone, too.

This was precisely what she'd needed. *Reid.* Only
him. He energized her, enlivened all her nerve endings with a tingle that she couldn't pretend was anything other than the thrill of his presence. Despite all
the promises she'd elicited, from him and from herself,
he'd come anyway.

It meant something to her. What, she couldn't say yet.
Especially since he wasn't supposed to be here. Espe-

cially since they were all wrong for each other. Especially since she suddenly couldn't let go of him.

But he didn't deepen the kiss the way she half expected. She appreciated his discretion. They were within sight of her father's hospital room.

When Reid broke off the kiss—far too soon, in her opinion—he nuzzled her ear and she found about a hundred reasons to like that, too.

"No, really," he insisted and his breath warmed her neck. "Sutton is a fixture of Chicago business. Everyone is aware of his health situation and anyone with a pulse would be concerned. I wanted to check on him. And you. See how you were holding up."

"I'm fine."

His brows rose. "Try that on someone who didn't just spend hours learning how to read your subtle nuances, sweetheart. You can give me the real answer."

Something crumbled inside her under the dual spotlights of his brown eyes. "He's a beast, what do you expect? Cancer didn't magically make him into a nice person or a better father."

"Shh." Reid tightened his grip on her and one hand came up to cradle the back of her head as he pressed it to his shoulder.

And that's when she realized she was shaking. Of course he'd misinterpreted that as her needing comfort. But now that she was here, his shoulder was strong and she didn't mind leaning on it. It hid the fact that a couple of tears had worked their way loose and his dark suit jacket absorbed them easily.

"You were gone this morning."

Why had she brought that up? He'd left for really good reasons. None of which she could recall at this moment, but there were some.

"Yeah."

"But you came to the hospital. You don't like being in public."

"No."

His fingers tangled in her hair, stroking across her scalp, comforting her. These one-word responses weren't cutting it. Not when the ground was sliding away at her feet and she couldn't catch it. "You came for me. Why?"

He pulled back enough to capture her jaw with his hands, holding her face up so he could look into her eyes. "You know why. We're not finished. I want to see you, even if it's just for a few more days until you leave. Don't tell me to go."

No way. Her will wasn't that strong. Not with that kind of an admission. So she'd have to push him to leave on his own. "We agreed, Reid. One night. You said it yourself. Where could this possibly lead?"

He blinked and when he opened his eyes, she saw a vulnerability she didn't recognize in their depths. "We did agree. But the problem is, I don't think I can stick to it. I thought we were working through our attraction and that would be that. I've been useless at work for hours. I can't stop thinking about you. Can't we find a way to spend a few days together and *then* answer the question about where this is going to go?"

She was already shaking her head. "Reid, we've been through this. But maybe I wasn't clear enough. I have a son. He has to be at the root of all my decisions. I don't have a few days to play hooky with you while we run around like teenagers having sex in elevators."

"Well, that wasn't what I had in mind at all. But it is now."

She felt the heat rise in her cheeks. "You know what I mean."

"Yeah, but you don't know what I mean."

The corners of his mouth lifted in his ghost of a smile again. But she'd just basically told him to get lost, after he'd pleaded with her not to. Why was he forcing her to be the one making all the hard choices here? It shouldn't be like that.

"It doesn't matter what you meant. I'm a mom. You've got zero interest in kids." Nora had zero interest in finding someone permanent, even if he wanted a dozen kids. "We might as well be from different planets."

"Even if I meant I wanted to spend time with Declan, too?" Reid picked up the stuffed horse, which Nora had forgotten he'd dropped to the floor of the alcove because she was too busy leaning on his strong shoulders. Which she shouldn't have done. It was confusing her.

He was confusing her. "What are you talking about? You want to spend time with me *and* my son?"

Reid nodded as if this was the answer to all their problems. "I'm not trying to turn you into someone who's not a mom. Let me take both of you to Lincoln Park Zoo. They have giraffes. Declan might like to see them."

Oh, no. Declan couldn't be allowed to latch onto Reid as the answer to his "Daadee" quest. After the heartbreaking scene this morning, she couldn't afford to even introduce them to each other. There was no telling what her son would do with it.

"He would like that." What was wrong with her? *Say no. Right now.*

Except Reid's face transformed as he treated her to his rare megawatt smile and she forgot her own name and how to breathe.

The problem was *she* would like to spend more time with Reid, especially after he'd gone to such lengths to ask. Especially after he'd so sweetly included Declan.

Even if it was just for a couple of days, an extension of their one night. She could handle that. Probably.

"Tomorrow, then? We'll make a day of it. I'll take you both to lunch."

She nodded, though she'd have sworn she'd been about to tell him she had plans. *Oh, goodness.* What had she just agreed to?

Nora should have told Reid to take a hike when he'd accosted her at the hospital yesterday. He still didn't understand why she hadn't. It would have saved them both the trouble of ending it later on, because he knew good and well they were living on borrowed time.

No one, least of all Reid, had any illusions about what this was: he was dragging out their one night because he was too selfish to let Nora fade into memory. So selfish that he'd manipulated her into an actual date that included her son.

She should have said no.

Instead, she'd agreed to his impulsive invitation. It was insanity. And felt like the smartest thing he'd ever conceived. The best of both worlds. No one expected him to sign up for Fatherhood Duties and he got to breathe in the scent of vanilla and strawberries while easing the tension and fatigue on Nora's face.

Surreptitiously, he watched Nora as she directed his driver in how to install the car seat the man had carefully placed in the rearmost seat of Reid's limousine. It should look odd, or refuse to fit right. Obviously his driver either had experience at this sort of thing or the gods had blessed this zoo trip—because the seat went in like a charm and Nora got Declan into it with no fuss.

Which was good. Reid wiped his clammy hands on his khaki slacks. Nerves? Really?

· But it made a whacked-out sort of sense that foreboding was prickling along the back of his neck. After all, he rarely went out in public. And he'd already tempted the fates by going to the hospital yesterday. Thus far, he'd escaped any sort of media attention, but the odds of that continuing, when he'd be very visible at a huge tourist attraction such as Lincoln Park Zoo, were zilch. The press would work itself into a fever pitch over this and expose Nora to the joys of Chicago's fascination with its "most mysterious bachelor," as well.

He should have thought this through a bit more.

Except then Nora settled in next to him against the creamy leather seat and brushed his thigh with hers. He pushed the negatives to the back of his mind. *What's done is done.* If the media clued in to the fact that he had invited a woman and her son on a date, so be it.

Nora handed Declan a chunky book. He took it immediately and turned it over a couple of times with a little noise of satisfaction. Could the kid read already? Somehow Reid had the impression kids learned to read when they were like five or six. Maybe Declan was one of those Mozart-genius types who would become a prodigy.

Fascinated, Reid watched as Declan stuck the corner of the book in his mouth. Ah. So he didn't actually *read* it. The book was more of a chew toy. Honestly, Reid would have batted the cardboard out of the kid's mouth with an admonishment that books were for looking at, not eating. Which showed what he knew.

"Thank you," Nora murmured to Reid.

He glanced at her, though he kind of didn't want to miss a minute of observing Nora's son so he could keep demystifying little-boy things. "We haven't even gotten to the zoo yet. Maybe Declan will hate it. You should save your thanks for later."

Nora's warm hazel eyes caught and held his, refusing to let him weasel out of her gratitude. "You gave me an alternative to sitting at the hospital, where I'm forced to watch my father die bit by bit. Anything else will be a great time by comparison, unless the giraffes try to eat us."

Reid couldn't help the smile that flashed over his face. He'd been doing a lot of that lately and couldn't seem to find a reason to stop. "Well, there are some rules on this outing."

She pursed her wide, sexy lips. "Oh, really? Rules like make sure you know where your field trip buddy is at all times?"

As if he needed a rule for that. There was no danger of losing track of her. When she did stuff like that with her mouth, she got his full attention. A Victoria's Secret model could strut by in the tiniest lingerie the company made and he'd never notice.

"Yep. That's the first rule," he replied anyway. He slipped his hand in hers and threaded their fingers together. "So we're going to hold hands the whole time just to be sure we don't lose each other."

Her touch burned his palm, heightening the awareness inside the limo. Reminding him that handholding was the extent of the intimacy available to them when a pint-size audience sat a few feet away. How did people with kids ever find time alone?

"Might be hard to push the stroller if we're holding hands," she informed him pertly. "Can't wait to see how you navigate that."

"I run a billion-dollar hotel conglomerate," he countered. "I can push a stroller and keep up with my field trip buddy at the same time."

He hoped. Actually, he'd forgotten all about the

wheeled contraption his driver had loaded into the limo's trunk. But this had been his idea; he'd figure it out.

And somewhere along the way, maybe he'd figure out what he'd hoped to accomplish with this zoo outing. He'd only been trying to take Nash's advice. No one was extending marriage proposals—nor was anyone confused about whether one was forthcoming at some point in the future. It wasn't. Reid and Nora were spending time together without any pressure, without any expectations, until one or both of them decided they were done.

Until then, it gave him a chance to be in her orbit, a place he'd discovered suited him, and also afforded Reid an opportunity to be around Declan without the white-knuckle panic that had accompanied their first interaction. If this trip to the zoo turned out to be a disaster, then Reid could in good conscience tell Nora it wasn't working out…as Nash had said.

But Reid fully intended to give it the college try, especially if he could somehow find a way to get Declan asleep and contained so he could strip Nora naked later on. The zoo trip had been designed to grease those wheels and he wasn't ashamed to admit it.

"Rule number two is everyone has to have fun," Reid advised her. "So be warned. Anyone who doesn't have fun is banished to the car."

"I'd like to know how you plan to gauge that," she said with a laugh. "Do you have a fun meter in your pocket?"

"Why so many questions?" He squeezed her hand. "You don't trust me?"

Her gaze lit on his and grew heavy with implication. With awareness. With a hundred other things that he should do something to stop. But couldn't.

"I would trust you with my life, Reid. But you'll forgive me if I'm a little skeptical about all of this. Every conversation we've ever had has included your no-kids disclaimer. So yeah, I'm hesitant to embrace the zoo wholeheartedly."

That stung more than Reid would have expected, given that it was true. But it wasn't the whole picture. "I'm...trying something new. Because you're worth it."

Her gaze warmed. "You have no idea what that does to me, do you?"

"What, telling you how special you are?" He shook his head, a little off balance at the direction of the conversation. How had things veered into the realm of significant so quickly? "I hope it makes you ready for fun because that's rule number two, if you recall. Rule number three—"

"You're not changing the subject." She rubbed a thumb over his knuckle in apparent apology for cutting him off. "Humor me. I've been on my own for a long time and then was plunged into my father's health drama. Unwillingly. You're distracting me from both, with style. I appreciate it. This is the second-best date I've ever had."

He wanted to brush it off, to deflect all the *significance* because she had it all wrong. She was the one distracting *him*, treating *him* to an escape from his everyday world where the black swirl of tragedy colored everything. But to say so would only add to the implications, which were already far too deep to ignore.

He shifted uncomfortably but didn't let go of her hand because he liked the feel of it in his. "You're far too easy to impress. Not only has this date not even started yet, I haven't begun to treat you to the date you deserve."

"Well, I can't wait for the follow-up, then. My calendar is suddenly very clear."

"Mine, too," he lied. Or rather it wouldn't be a lie

once he told Mrs. Grant to call everyone he'd ever met and tell them he was busy for the next year.

An overreaction. But warranted. The things Nora made him feel... He never wanted it to end. He was so tired of not feeling. Of being forced to bear his burdens alone. Granted, he'd brought it upon himself, but only because no one else understood. Nor did he want to burden anyone else. Nora blew all of that away.

It would suck when this ended, as it surely would, despite his wishes to the contrary.

Reid's driver pulled up to the entrance of the Lincoln Park Zoo and scurried around to the back to unload Declan's stroller, unfolding it with ease on the sidewalk. Reid waited for Nora to unbuckle the little boy from the car seat and then he helped them both out of the limo. Once Declan was seated, they rolled toward the entrance, Reid pushing the stroller, and he fully appreciated that Nora didn't make one crack about how it actually took two hands to maneuver.

Nine

The third time Declan said, "Jraff," Nora almost burst into tears.

His vocabulary had exploded the last few days. It was miraculous, considering he'd been a slow starter in the speech department. Apparently a trip to the zoo had unleashed the kid's vocal cords.

Reid strolled ahead with Declan, pointing to the black howler monkeys that Nora recalled from trips to the zoo in her youth. Of course, her father had never taken her to the zoo. Not that she was casting Reid in the father role in this scenario. But he was a man and Declan was a child. It wasn't a stretch to think how nice it was to have someone around with strong, masculine arms to push the million-pound stroller that only got heavier as the day wore on.

For goodness' sake, it wasn't just nice. She'd been doing this single-mom thing from day one and it sucked. Only she hadn't realized how hard it had been to be the sole parent until there was someone else around to pick up some of the burden. Was it so bad to wallow in it for a minute?

Reid had already done more with Declan in this one excursion than Sutton had done with Nora in the whole of her life. Her gratefulness knew no bounds. What had started out as reconnecting with an old friend had become something else. Something she hadn't seen coming. *What* that was, she couldn't say. Or rather didn't want to say. Especially when Reid laughed—*laughed*—at something Declan said.

The darkness she'd sensed in Reid from the first moment hadn't returned. It was powerful to think she might have had something to do with that.

She realized he was getting too far ahead of her. How had that happened? This was her day of fun, too, but she'd been too busy soaking in the gorgeous sight of a man pushing her baby in a stroller. The same man who had rescued her from a day of withering away at her father's bedside. Rescued her from the guilt of not trying harder to forgive.

Nora caught up and ignored the flutter in her chest when Reid glanced down at her, his brown eyes full of mirth.

"What's so funny?" she asked.

"Declan would like the monkey to henceforth be named George." Reid ruffled Declan's head as the boy craned his neck to see the people behind him. "He's rather insistent, too."

Nora smiled. "That's the name of the monkey in one of his books. Curious George. Declan can be a bit stubborn when he latches onto something. I have no idea where he gets that from."

They pushed through a knot of people outside the

primate house and Reid lit up as he saw the sign for a nearby enclosure. "Zebras. We have to go."

He took off and, breathlessly, she followed. The day was every bit as fun as Reid had commanded it to be but not because she'd done anything special to follow his rules. Reid made it that way. His phone had stayed in his pocket except for a brief thirty seconds at the tail end of lunch when he scrolled through it, but then it disappeared again. Up until that point, she hadn't even realized he'd brought it.

His sole focus had been on Declan. Surprisingly. She'd half thought he'd invented this zoo trip as a way to butter her up so she'd say yes when he tried to charm his way into her bed again. If so, she would have been happy to tip him off that no zoo was required for that. Their whole relationship centered on what happened in the bedroom...and sometimes the living room. But that didn't change facts. They were sleeping together but that was it. All she'd let it be.

Which made this whole excursion that much more mystifying.

When they finally fell into the limo, exhausted and happy at the end of a long day, Reid captured her hand again and held it tight. "Navy Pier. Tomorrow. Don't make me beg."

"What?" She stared at him, trying to make the words fit the agenda she'd swear he had, but couldn't figure out. "You want to take us to an amusement park? Tomorrow? You have work."

I have another long day at the hospital. All at once, she didn't want to go back there, not on the heels of the alternative Reid had supplied her with.

"I do not have work. Oh, I mean, I do. The hotel industry doesn't sleep, no pun intended." He flashed that gorgeous smile he seemed to pass out rather freely now, and yet it still affected her exactly as it had in the hospital corridor yesterday—as if she'd been hit in the solar plexus by a freight train. "But I don't have anything that can't wait," he continued. "You're leaving soon. I'll catch up later."

Guilt coated the back of Nora's throat. She definitely wasn't staying in Chicago. Nothing could convince her to come back to this hellhole permanently, not even the death of the man who'd made it so miserable for her. But as she'd been using her imminent departure as an excuse to push away any hint of this thing between her and Reid blossoming into something more, she should correct his assumptions.

"My schedule is pretty open-ended. I wasn't sure what was happening with Dad, so I didn't buy a return plane ticket in case…well, I ended up having to help organize a funeral." Quickly, she rushed on. "So there's no hammer going down anytime soon. You certainly don't have to take off work to entertain us."

"Nora." Reid tipped up her chin so she met his gaze squarely. "I'm not entertaining you, like you need a tour guide for the city you grew up in. Don't be so silly. I'm spending time with you and Declan because I want to."

Oh. His sincerity convinced her and since there was nothing she wanted to do less than sit at the hospital, she found herself nodding. "Then we'd love it. Right, Declan?"

He nodded drowsily, his forehead resting against the padded car seat lip. He fell asleep on the way back to her father's guesthouse and in another surprising move, Reid insisted on carrying the sleeping toddler into his room, placing him gently on the crib mattress with ease.

"You'd think you'd done that a million times," Nora

said with a laugh as soon as Reid shut the door to Declan's room.

"I might have googled it," he admitted with a chagrined expression. "I guess some people are born with
the parenting gene, but I have to depend on technology
to figure out how to get a kid into a crib."

"No one is born with the parenting gene. We all have
to struggle through it and figure things out." Her heart
tightened, wringing out some emotions she'd have sworn
were dead and buried.

He'd done research on how to put a baby to bed? Reid
didn't want to have anything to do with kids. Why, in
all that was holy, would he have done that—unless he'd
planned to be in a position to need the information?
Something had changed fundamentally and she scrambled to wrap her mind around it.

"And now for my follow-up," he murmured and swept
Nora up in his arms, Rhett Butler–style.

Breathless, Nora clung to his neck, but that was
strictly to steady herself. There was no danger of Reid
dropping her as he carried her to her bedroom without
one hitch in his stride. He kicked the door behind them
and placed her on the bedspread. The sudden heat in his
gaze left no room for misinterpreting what he'd meant
by "follow-up."

"Did you google 'getting a mom into bed,' too?" she
asked with raised eyebrows, her hands fisting against
the bed in search of something to hold on to as the look
in his eye told her she was in for a wild ride.

"That's one I didn't have to research."

In a flash, he stripped off his khaki pants and button-
down shirt, treating her to the best sight of the day—
Reid in all his naked splendor. She sucked in a breath
as everything went liquid inside.

Just as quickly, he got her out of her clothes and rolled her into his arms, murmuring against her neck. They'd had some pretty inventive sex thus far, and Nora geared herself up for something that could rightly be called a "follow-up."

But in another surprise after a long day of them, Reid seemed intent on something different still: slow, languorous lovemaking.

She fell into the sensations, savoring them as he kissed her long and deep, touched her everywhere with a kind of reverence. When he finally pushed into her with a maddeningly unhurried glide that threatened to drive her off the edge, the perfection of it squeezed a tear loose from her.

A *tear*. It was only sex, for crying out loud. But when she focused on Reid as he withdrew, then repeated his torturous reentry, he caught her gaze. That smile spilled over his face, transforming him from the inside out.

Transforming *her*. This wasn't old friends becoming something more. It was a spiritual joining of two people, and she couldn't hold back any longer. Her heart exploded with so many unnameable things at the same moment as her body did. Things she needed to shut down—*immediately*. But couldn't. She was lost to this man.

Reid tensed with a low groan, experiencing his own release on the heels of hers, then gathered her close as if he'd never let go.

But he had to. Eventually. Nothing lasted forever and Nora was tired of losing things. It was better to never grab onto them in the first place.

Reid knocked on the door of the Winchester guesthouse for the third time in three days.

It was a habit he'd been trying to think of a reason to break and had failed miserably. He liked Nora. She always had a quick smile, her wry sense of humor matched his and she'd learned exactly how to use that wide mouth to drive him to the brink.

Sometimes, he let her push him over the edge because it was just that amazing when she took it upon herself to pleasure him. He always made it up to her later, though, usually twice. If he played his cards right, hopefully that would be on the agenda later tonight after they made an appearance at this pesky Foundation for Education fundraiser he'd agreed to attend.

Since he was on the board—because doing charitable works for kids should assuage his guilt over his niece and nephew, and yet, did not—he felt obligated to go. And for some reason he'd yet to fathom, Nora had agreed to be his plus-one. She shouldn't have. A public appearance together at a black-tie event was sure to get the tongues of Chicago wagging. But he could imagine only Nora at his side. Which had also become a bit of a habit that he couldn't figure out how to break.

When Nora swung open the door, Reid nearly forgot how to breathe.

"Wow." That was all that he could squeeze out around the sudden lump in his throat.

"It's okay?" she asked.

She spun around, sending the floor-length skirt of her dress flowing. It was the color of deep sapphire, strapless, with little folds of fabric over her breasts that highlighted one of her best features. She'd put her hair up in a loose bun, leaving tendrils to fall around her face. A glittery collar of blue stones that matched her dress circled her throat, winking in the low light of the setting sun.

But that sparkle paled in comparison with the woman.

"No," he murmured, not quite trusting his voice. "It's the opposite of okay unless you want to skip this black-tie shindig and go lock ourselves in your bedroom for a few hours. If that was your goal—bingo."

She laughed and waved over her shoulder at her sister Grace, who was just visible beyond the foyer playing with Declan on his patchwork quilt. "We're off. Back by ten."

"As if," Grace called. "I brought an overnight bag. Don't even bother acting like you didn't see it. I'm here till morning. Don't waste the opportunity."

Well, then. Grace might have just moved into the number one spot as Reid's favorite relative of Nora's. Or maybe she shared that spot with Declan. Imagine Reid's surprise as he'd developed a fondness for the kid over the last few days.

Of course the boy still scared the bejesus out of him with his fragile little body and inability to communicate in something other than short words and phrases that were impossible to decipher. Reid spent half his time in Declan's presence making sure he didn't do something wrong, which was stressful and frustrating. But the other half of the time, the kid was amazing. Funny, inquisitive, fearless.

Nora shut the door and it was just the two of them on the front steps. Reid swallowed as the reality hit him. This wasn't an excursion to the zoo or to Navy Pier that he could blow off as spending time with an old friend and her son if anyone questioned him. Or that he could justify to himself as nothing special. This was a real date in public with Nora Winchester O'Malley on his arm. The paparazzi would be there in full force as the whole point of the fundraiser was to get publicity for the foundation. There was nowhere to hide. No excuses.

He was dating Nora. And vice versa.

Maybe going public wouldn't be as invasive as he was envisioning.

That hope smashed into little pieces as the limo snaked toward the entrance of the Field Museum. The number of people in the throng of onlookers, most armed with cameras sporting telephoto lenses, was truly frightening.

"Sure you're ready for this?" he asked Nora.

"Not really, no," she admitted. "I practiced my dance steps all day but I'm relatively hopeless. I'm probably not going to enhance your reputation any."

"Ha. That's a lie. You enhance my reputation just by being on my arm," he shot back. "And I was talking about being ready for a public splash."

He hated the idea of their privacy being invaded, their lives raked over by strangers who had never spoken two words to either of them. There would be photos flung across the internet far and wide with ridiculous captions like Reclusive Billionaire Corrupts Chicago Real Estate Mogul's Daughter.

So far, they'd managed to avoid attention but that wouldn't last forever. In fact, judging by the frenzy of the crowd as his driver pulled to the curb, parked and came around to let them out, they'd just become very visible in the public eye.

"Oh. Yeah, I'm sorry, but you're the one who's mainly affected by that. I'll go home and no one will even remember my name." She waved it off. "That was part of the draw in vacating Chicago, after all. I also removed myself from the limelight. The socialite scene wears on you. I don't miss it."

What would it be like to just walk away? That was a scenario he'd never considered—but should have. All at once, it sounded heavenly. What better way to avoid all the gossip and speculation and people he didn't want to be around than to go somewhere else?

Of course, he couldn't run his empire unless he was in the middle of it. Other people might be able to handle working remotely, but not Reid. He breathed his hotels like air and liked it.

But the idea of chucking it all stuck with him as he helped Nora from the limo and hooked her hand on his arm to tread the red carpet lining the roped-off area leading to the entrance. Flashes bathed them as a hundred photographs were snapped in under a minute. Reid was grateful when they finally made it inside the museum. All the street noise was cut off instantly.

Faint strains of Mozart piped through the great hall from hidden speakers. Two dozen tables with white cloths and tea lights had been strewn about the cavernous space; one corner housed an elephant statue and a grand piano. A couple hundred of Chicago's elite worked the room, wheeling and dealing. More money would change hands under this roof than on the whole Magnificent Mile the weekend before Christmas.

"Eve's here somewhere," Nora commented as she craned her neck to scan the crowds. "She made me promise to say hi so she could see how the dress turned out. She had it sent over."

"There she is." Reid nodded as he spied Nora's willowy sister. "Dancing with Graham Newport."

Very cozily, as a matter of fact. The dance floor had been set up a good hundred yards from the entrance, but even at that distance, Reid could see the possessive slant to Newport's hold on Eve Winchester. Surprising, given the drama going on with the Winchester fortune, that Eve would fraternize with a Newport, but she didn't seem terribly put off by the proximity of her dance partner. They were so close, you couldn't wedge a sheet of paper between them.

It looked as if Nora wasn't the only Winchester sister making a public confession about her love life this evening.

"Huh." Nora zeroed in on her sister, a speculative look in her eye. "There's something going on there, which she has thus far refused to admit to. She's being very cagey about it, but there's no way she can shrug it off now."

"Especially not if we go dance near them." Which suited Reid's purposes as well, since he had a strong need to get Nora into his arms. The scent of vanilla and strawberries was particularly alluring this evening and it had been driving him nuts since the moment they got into the limo. "Assuming you want to dance?"

Nora's wide smile answered that question.

"Sure that's Graham?" she asked as Reid took her hand to lead her to the dance floor. "I don't know the twins well enough to tell them apart."

"I do," Reid said curtly, without explanation.

He'd crossed paths with the brothers more than once; they got around. That one was Graham for sure. He had a reserved demeanor about him you couldn't miss, a wait-and-see approach that was the opposite of his brother's. Brooks had a hot head and a quick mouth that sometimes got him into trouble as he leaped without looking more often than not.

Which made it all the more perplexing that Graham

was the one making time with a Winchester sister. If there was some nefarious intent behind their interaction, Reid would have put money on Brooks being involved.

Then everything else slid away as he swept Nora into his arms and held her close.

"This is the first time we've danced," he murmured. "I like it."

"Me, too." She peered up through those matchless hazel eyes, which had gone a bit soft and warm, and everything good in the world was right here. In his grasp.

Not for the first time, his gut knotted. She would leave soon. He did *not* like that. This thing between them wasn't burning itself out and he was in a bit of a quandary over the next steps. Mostly because he didn't see any miracles popping up that would fix all the roadblocks between them.

Neither of them had any business thinking of next steps.

He was going to have to say goodbye. Soon. He flat out didn't know how he was going to do it. Usually, that was the easiest word in the English language to utter. It should have been the easiest here, too, especially given Nora's permanent plus-one.

But goodbye wasn't happening tonight. Grace had given them a pass on what time they returned, which didn't even have to be until morning. Reid intended to take full advantage of it.

Eve and Graham finally noticed Reid and Nora dancing near them, though how they'd yanked their attention away from each other was beyond him. The couple sprang apart as if they'd been caught spray painting graffiti on the Cloud Gate sculpture in Millennium Park.

"Oh, hey, Nora," Eve called and crossed her arms,

then uncrossed them to let them dangle at her sides. "I didn't know you'd arrived yet."

"Yeah, you seemed pretty busy." Nora nodded at her sister's dance partner. "Hi, Graham. Nice to see you again, especially outside of the hospital."

There was a hint of frost in Nora's voice that Reid didn't recognize. He was glad it wasn't directed at him as her warmth was one of the things he craved in the middle of the night, when he woke up, alone and freezing, after a particularly vivid nightmare about Sophia and his mom.

Eve blushed, which seemed out of place on a no-nonsense, confident woman. Even as a kid, she'd been authoritative and decisive, with a take-no-prisoners approach. He'd always admired that.

Another couple nearly collided with the now-stationary group in the center of the dance floor.

"Well, I'm headed to the bar," Eve said brightly. "Thanks for the dance, Graham."

Reid nodded to Eve and Newport as they edged away, clearly uncomfortable with the audience. But as Reid was still dancing with Nora and loath to stop, he didn't worry about the dynamics of whatever was going on with Eve and Newport.

He just wanted to soak up as much Nora as he could and worry later about the screeching halt to their relationship, which loomed on the horizon.

At dinner, he and Nora predictably ended up at a table with Eve and Graham, as well as Brooks and his date, a bombshell model from Hungary who spoke little English. Brooks and Graham scarcely noticed her lack of conversation once they got going on what appeared to be a hot topic—their opinions about Nora's father, his money and the half brother they shared with the Winchester sisters.

The rib eye and lobster weren't bad, so Reid ate his dinner and stayed out of it until Brooks mentioned that he'd called an old friend who was a lawyer to help with his case against Sutton.

Nora flushed and laid down her fork. "You called a lawyer to fight my father? What on earth for?"

"Because Winchester's up to something. When the paternity test came back negative for us, he admitted he wasn't our father but then clammed up. He knows who our father is. I need him to spill his guts," Brooks explained. "And Carson has a stake in ironing out details, too, since he's an heir. An impartial lawyer can only help both situations. We can't be too careful."

"Carson is not an 'heir,'" Eve insisted with exaggerated air quotes and a hearty scowl. "He's nowhere in Dad's will and Winchester blood doesn't automatically earn Carson the right to anything."

Nora's mouth turned down and it was clear the conversation was upsetting her. Reid squeezed her hand under the table as everyone else forgot about eating in favor of jumping into the argument full steam.

"We say differently," Graham retorted. "Our friend Josh Calhoun is stopping by here on his way home to Iowa. He's a legal expert who should be able to shed some insight and then we'll see what's what. You can't block us from getting what's rightfully ours."

"What about what's rightfully *ours*?" Eve glowered at the man she'd just been dancing with so cozily. "Carson didn't have the pleasure of growing up as a Winchester. Our dad's estate belongs to those of us who suffered for years at his hands."

Brooks nearly came out of his seat. "You don't think

Carson's suffered over Winchester's selfishness? That SOB knew he'd fathered a kid and never bothered to claim him."

"He's lucky," Eve shot back. "Some days, I wish I'd never been claimed. But trust me when I tell you that the billions Carson thinks he's due belong to me, Grace and Nora. Period."

"Stop it!" Nora pushed back from the table and stood as the other diners at nearby tables began to murmur about the drama. "Fighting like this doesn't solve anything. We can't stop you from getting additional legal help, so you boys do what you think you need to do. But leave me out of it. It's only money and I don't want any of it."

With that, Nora spun and fled the hall. Reid nodded to the other stunned guests and followed her. He found her in the lobby, huddled in a corner. When he gathered her up in his arms, his stomach clenched as the tears running down her cheeks caught the light.

But then she clung to him and gave a soft little sigh that thrummed through him, winnowing under his skin, making everything better just because they were together. A dangerous fullness in his chest spread and it felt so good, he couldn't find a reason to stop it.

"I hate to ask, but would you mind if we left?" Her voice was muffled against his shoulder. "I know my family is ruining your party, but—"

"No one's ruining anything," he broke in. "If you want to leave, we're leaving."

He was the last person to argue with the idea of getting the hell out of Dodge, especially when the flip side meant that he got to have Nora all to himself. This surely wasn't his scene and if anyone didn't like that he'd left early, they could make an appointment during business hours for some time in the next century to complain about it.

"Thanks." She took a deep, shuddery breath and flashed a watery smile. "You've developed a habit of rescuing me from bad situations. I've kind of grown fond of it."

"I'm happy to be your knight in shining armor," he said gruffly, as the gratitude radiating from her eyes added to the already heavy moment. There were things going on here that couldn't be ignored. But they were not things he felt equipped to deal with.

Because at the end of the day, anything other than saying goodbye could only be described as selfish, selfish and even more selfish.

But as the night was still young and he'd never claimed to be a saint, he took full advantage of Grace's pass and ferried Nora back to his penthouse. They made love in his bed, and he surprised himself by asking Nora if she'd stay. Which he desperately wanted all at once. He'd been breaking all his rules left and right. What was one more? Especially when he felt the end of their relationship snapping at his heels like a rabid dog.

But she shook her head. "I've never slept apart from Declan. I'm sure I'll have to eventually but I'm not rushing it."

Reid let her go through an act of sheer will. He slept alone in his bed after all, his rules still intact, but not by his own choice.

But the morning news brought a healthy reminder of the situation.

Front and center in his newsfeed was a photograph of Nora on his arm as they exited his limo. But the caption didn't include the usual sexual innuendo, or allude to his playboy reputation and his status as a recluse. Instead, it asked a question that shocked him to the core: Is Chicago's Most Eligible Bachelor off the Market?

Had everyone clued in that he was falling for Nora before he had?

Ten

The days after the fundraiser dragged miserably. Nora didn't hear from Reid other than a slew of funny text messages at odd hours. While she appreciated that Reid was clearly thinking about her as much as she was thinking about him, she felt his absence keenly. More than she would have anticipated.

Declan played his game of searching for "Daadee" at least once a day and it killed her every time. She found herself daydreaming of a life free of complications, heartbreak and terminal diagnoses. Of course Reid had to get back to work and she had to get back to the reason she'd come to Chicago, though.

She'd done her duty by her father and gone to the hospital every day, even though it meant wading through hordes of media mongers who had begun following her constantly. Apparently, the scandal regarding Carson's parentage coupled with the photograph of Nora on

Reid's arm at the fundraiser had thrust her back into the limelight, the last place she wanted to be, the place she'd fled to Colorado to escape.

"I'm going to get some coffee," she announced to Sutton's personal assistant after a particularly long afternoon when her father had been awake more than usual.

It wore on her to listen to the endless lectures about how she should be raising Declan and her father's imperious demands that she move back to Chicago and "act like a Winchester."

Her counterargument—that she was an O'Malley and therefore not subject to patriarchal tyranny—hadn't gone over well.

Valerie nodded to acknowledge Nora's announcement. "Eve's been in the lounge for an hour. You might want to check on her to see if she's okay."

"Sure."

Nora sighed as she punched in the code for the family lounge area and pushed open the door. The smell of freshly brewed coffee nearly made her weep. She'd been dragging lately, sleeping fitfully and waking in a bleary-eyed stupor. It wasn't like her and she'd chalk it up to being back in Chicago to anyone who asked. But she had a feeling it was deeper than that and had Reid's name written all over it, which she did *not* want to examine.

The feelings she'd been ignoring seemed like a betrayal of Sean, and she wasn't dealing with that well. Nor did ignoring them make them go away.

Eve sat in a wingback chair near the window, staring out at the hospital parking lot as she nursed her own cup of coffee.

"On the lookout for loverboy?" Nora said by way of greeting.

Eve's head whipped around and the scowl on her face could have peeled the paint off the walls. "What's that supposed to mean?"

"Wow. I should call Grace and tell her she lucked out in volunteering to stay with Declan at the house instead of subjecting herself to the bad moods around here. But then, if she's drinking the same Kool-Aid, I'll just get my head bitten off."

"Maybe you should look in the mirror for the reason people are particularly touchy today," Eve advised her with a smirk. "You're rubbing everyone the wrong way. What's the matter? Reid finally stop calling? It was bound to happen. Women bounce off him like he's a trampoline. No one gets his attention for long."

"Hey. Leave Reid out of this." Was that what had happened? Their relationship had run its course? Sadness crowded into her chest all at once. She'd kind of thought they'd have a few more days together at least.

Somehow, the fact that Eve had clued in on it before Nora had made it worse. Her sister had obviously seen Reid's dating habits up close and personal since they ran into each other at least a few times a year. But it didn't matter. Nothing had happened that Nora hadn't already been preparing herself for. Things were going to end eventually. Why not now?

"Besides, it's not like that," Nora said a little more forcefully. "We're just old friends. Nothing more."

"Sure. That's why you're in a crabby mood."

"I'm not in a crabby mood! You're the one who's being weird about your love life."

Eve flinched and then tried to cover it by nonchalantly sipping her coffee. "I don't know what you mean."

Nora latched onto her sister's deflection with a bit of desperation. "Want me to spell it out? G-R-A-H—"

"There's nothing going on between me and Graham Newport," Eve shot back furiously, but not before Nora noted a heaping ton of guilt in her gaze. "I danced with him one time at a stupid fundraiser. Sue me. I'm not the one whose photograph is burning up the gossip sites as we speak."

Nora laughed but it sounded forced. Because it was. "That's old news. You're mistaken if you think anyone cares about a photograph of me and Reid."

Silently, Eve picked up her phone, tapped it a few times and scrolled through the plethora of hits on Nora's name, some as recent as a few moments ago. *Ridiculous.*

Nora's pulse jumped into her throat as she read page after page of perfect strangers commenting on her love life, including theories on whether she was into kinky sex or just put up with it for a shot at landing someone as mysterious and reclusive as Reid. There were also guesses as to whether Nora might next appear with an engagement ring on her finger.

She shook her head. "People need something better to do with their lives than speculate on something as inane as whether Reid is off the market. Besides, as you just pointed out, he's probably already forgotten about me. There isn't much to gossip about."

Nora crossed to get that much-needed cup of coffee and was shocked to see her hands were shaking.

If Reid did find some time in his schedule to see her again, she'd say no. She had to. She had no desire to expose Declan to this level of scrutiny, and that was surely next if the media chose to pick up on her status as a single mom. They'd have a field day with captions about whether Reid had hung up his handcuffs in favor of a baby carriage.

Actually, she'd be hard-pressed to say which idea was more ludicrous—Reid's reputation as a man with unusual tastes, or Reid as a father.

When her phone beeped, she almost didn't pull it from her pocket. She wasn't in the mood for another random text message from Reid with a noncommittal joke about chickens crossing the road.

But that wasn't the message.

I'm downstairs. I need to see you.

Yes. She needed that, too. So desperately. Thank goodness he was here. Her fingers flew to respond: Where?

In my car. Come down? I don't want to give anyone a chance to photograph us.

Brilliant, brilliant man. A smile spread across her face before she could catch it and then she was halfway out the door before she remembered to tell Eve to go back to their father's room. "I've got to go. Can you go sit with Dad?"

Nora shut the door on her sister's groan and hightailed it to the elevator. Once the doors slid closed, common sense wormed its way to the forefront. This wasn't a chance to get hot and heavy in his limo, though that was probably exactly what was on his mind. And hers.

Dang it. She'd have to take the high road and inform him it was over. They couldn't keep doing this. Disappointment settled low in her belly, but once again, she had to take control of the situation before it got out of hand. She still had the final word about what went on in her life.

When she got outside, she dived into the limo, head down and face shielded from the lenses of the paparazzi who seemed like a permanent fixture at the entrance to Midwest Regional these days. The moment the door closed, Reid swept her into his arms before she could squeak out a protest. And then her brain drained out the moment his lips touched hers.

Oh, yes. She'd missed him, missed his taste, missed his hands in her hair. And she couldn't pull away. She just needed one more second. Which turned into two and then three…and his hands drifted to her waist, where his clever fingers sought her bare skin.

Through some force of will, she surfaced and slapped a palm on his chest to push him back.

"Wait," she commanded breathlessly even as she curled her fingers into the soft cloth of his shirt, almost dragging him back to finish what he'd started. "I have a few things to say before my clothes end up on the other seat."

Reid smirked. "You're going to do a striptease? All right, if you insist. Carry on."

She bit back a laugh. How did he make her laugh so easily as she was about to embark on a difficult conversation? "I meant before *you* start taking them off. We have to talk."

"I know." He threw up a hand, a chagrined expression on his face. "I'm sorry I've been incommunicado but I had some things I needed to handle. I should have called."

She waved it off as if it was no big deal and all was forgiven. Really, that should be the case. The disappointment and heartsick moments at 3:00 a.m. were her fault, not his. "It's fine. It was a good breaking point for us anyway. The gossipmongers have been out in full force, as I'm sure you're aware. That's what I wanted to discuss. We shouldn't see each other anymore."

"I thought so, too," he admitted. "I tried to stay away. I really did. It didn't work for me."

Oh, it *so* hadn't worked for her, either. But that wasn't the point. "Well, we'll have to try harder. Between the media breathing down my neck and my dad—"

All at once, the horrific day came crashing down on her and broke her voice into pieces.

Instantly, Reid gathered her up in his strong arms and she let him because…well, there was really no excuse except she needed someone to care and he did. It was in his touch, in the soft words he murmured into her hair. The tears she'd been fighting didn't seem so weak after all. A few squeezed out, falling onto his gorgeous suit.

She was crying all over Reid Chamberlain and he wasn't pulling away. The way he should. *Good.* She was so tired of being an adult. She'd done about all the adult stuff she could handle for the day. His fingers slid across the back of her neck, cradling her against him, and it was the most peace she'd felt in days.

"What happened with your father?" he asked and the concern in his tone nearly undid her.

If nothing else, Reid was her friend and she had precious few of those. "The usual Sutton Winchester stuff. I guess I'm just particularly affected by it today."

"Because I haven't been around," he finished for her and guilt laced his flat statement. "You can say it. I left you high and dry and didn't call. But I'm here now. Let me take care of you."

With a really spectacular orgasm? She didn't know whether to laugh or cry some more. Mostly because it sounded like the best plan she'd ever heard in her life.

"That's not your job, though I appreciate the sentiment. I've been taking care of myself for a really long time."

He pulled back and pierced her with his brown eyes, which were still swimming with concern. But he didn't let go of her and she started to wonder if he ever would.

"You need to get away from all of this. I'm not kidding. You're letting your father get to you. You don't owe him anything and this bedside vigil is killing you. Why are you still here catering to your family's demand that you come back to Chicago?"

"Because—" All at once, she didn't have an answer. Why *was* she still here? Certainly not for her father, who wasn't going to turn into someone new so she could magically forgive him, as Reid had just painfully helped her remember. Oh, goodness. Had she been waiting for Reid to come around? "Because…"

Gently, he smiled. "Why don't you go home?"

Home. The word permeated her mind. Yes, that's where she wanted to go. "I can't go home. My dad is dying. My family—"

"Will be fine. You said he has until New Year's. That's months away. It's not like sticking around is going to cure his cancer, Nora." His fingers caressed her neck, warming her, and she was a little ashamed she leaned into his touch. "You said you didn't have a return plane ticket. Let me take you home. I have a private jet that's just sitting around."

She swallowed the *yes*. Now was not the time to crumble under the premise that Reid was—once again— rescuing her from her life. The fantasy world he'd drawn her into needed to be over. "That's not necessary. I can fly commercial."

"But you don't have to. Let me take care of you," he

insisted. "I want to. Let me. If not for you, then for Declan."

She hadn't seen that trump card coming. Her will melted away as if she'd left it in the rain. The lovely thought of not having to fly in a crowded plane with a two-year-old grabbed onto her and wouldn't let go.

She could go home, get away from the media's fixation on her relationship with Reid, remove Declan from the reach of their sharp claws—and avoid the hospital, where nothing in the form of reconciliation seemed to be happening.

How could she pass up what was simply an act of kindness from an old friend?

"What if my dad needs me?" Even she heard the feebleness in that argument, and Reid didn't let her get away with it.

He snorted. "Sutton needs a swift kick in the rear. And that's all I'll say about that. If anyone needs you, they know how to use the phone. Get away for a while and then come back, if that's your concern."

"You make it sound so easy." She smiled to take away the sting. "Some of us don't have access to a private plane to jet around whenever the whim strikes us."

"Then I'll stay until you're ready to come back," he replied nonchalantly.

"What do you mean, stay? As in *stay*? In Colorado?" Her voice had just entered the decibel range where only dogs could hear her, but *really*? "Reid, that's crazy."

And exactly what she wanted. Oh, yes, she did. Crazy, wonderful togetherness. Not an empty bed and even emptier heart.

"No crazier than trying to live my life here in Chicago with the media firestorm going on. I hate that you're affected by it, too. Besides, I told you. Staying away wasn't working for me. This affords us an opportunity to spend time together without all these eyes on us. So we're solving all our problems at once."

"But we're not… That is, you and I—" She couldn't even put a label on what she and Reid were. How did they get to a place where they were talking about continuing their relationship instead of ending it? A place where she *wanted* to talk about it?

"Stop thinking so hard, Nora." Without taking his eyes off her, he took her hand in his and held it to his lips. "Escape with me. Just for a little while. Let's be crazy and indulgent and ignore the outside world. Fall into the moment. Neither of us do that enough."

The beauty of his suggestion wrapped itself around her like a web, ensnaring her firmly. Real life had beaten her down so much that she'd forgotten how to seize the moment. Reid understood that and was offering her a chance to learn again.

Do not say yes. Do not say yes. But then…why shouldn't she?

He wasn't proposing. He wasn't saying he was staying forever. It was an extension of their wild, wonderful affair far away from those who were trying to turn it into something else. She could put off saying goodbye to the man who had become far more important than he should have.

"Okay. Take me home."

She'd have to deal with saying goodbye soon. But not today. And hopefully the fallout wouldn't include any broken hearts. Well, she'd just make sure of it.

When Reid woke, the smell of vanilla and strawberries clued him in that the cocoon he'd fallen into while in Colorado hadn't vanished while he slept.

His eyes blinked open and sure enough, Nora lay firmly encased in his arms, exactly where she'd been last night. Naked, lush, beautiful. He couldn't recall the last time he'd slept with a woman until morning. He liked it.

Kissing her awake had become as necessary as breathing and he didn't hesitate to indulge. That's what this little foray into craziness was about after all. Doing what felt right. Ignoring the voices in his head that said he was letting this woman hook him far deeper than he had any right to allow.

As he turned her head to take her mouth, she responded instantly, her body coming alive against his, sensation rushing along his skin as her backside drew flush with his raging erection. His hands flew to her breasts. He was desperate to touch, desperate to enflame her in kind.

She tilted her hips backward, adjusting herself against him. Groaning with the effort to stop from sliding right into her, as he ached to do, he half rolled over to blindly fumble for the condoms he'd hidden in her dresser the moment they'd arrived yesterday.

Finally, finally, he sank into the heaven of Nora's body. She took him deep and then deeper still as they moved in tandem, driving each other to the peak of bliss and back down the other side. The release was so much more than physical. He had no way to describe the way she filled him so there was no room for the misery that had lived inside him for so long.

How he'd convinced her to let him follow her to her home in Silver Falls, Colorado, he'd never know. All he knew was that he couldn't stand being away from her. He wanted to explore these new feelings for her that were so big and so important he could barely articulate them. So he'd shot for the stars and had been richly re-warded. So far.

They'd only just started down this seize-the-moment path and he liked not knowing what came next.

Eventually, they rolled from bed and got dressed, then saw to breakfast, which they ate sitting around the distressed pine table in Nora's kitchen. Her whole house was quaint, with a farmhouse style that absolutely fit her. He just hated that she was living here alone, without the benefit of her father's money to make her life easier.

Good thing he was here and could fill in the gaps.

As Reid finished his coffee and scrolled through the morning's headlines on his iPad, Nora ate cereal and chatted. Declan sat in his high chair, his gaze fastened firmly on Reid as if evaluating this new element in his environment. Once he focused his attention on the breakfast his mom had given him, she stood and announced she had about a million loads of laundry.

It was all very domestic. He liked that, too. He'd never had anything like this experience, which suddenly felt like a shame. There'd been a huge hole in his life that he'd only just discovered.

"Need some help?" he asked.

She snickered. "Do you even know what a washing machine looks like?"

"Sure, I've seen them lots of times," he returned easily. "In TV commercials. How hard can it be?"

"It would be a much bigger help if you sat here with Declan and made sure that he doesn't tip his high chair over." Nora tugged on one of Declan's red curls affectionately. "He's becoming quite the climber, aren't you, Butterbean?"

"Bean," Declan echoed and shoved a few more dry cheerios in his mouth.

"You can get him down when he's finished eating, right?" Nora called over her shoulder as she headed toward the bedrooms.

Reid and Declan eyed each other. "It's you and me, sport."

Declan nodded. "Daadee."

Reid blinked. "Uh…"

Clearly, this was not one of those times when the kid lacked communication skills. How had he never realized that Declan might draw some conclusions about Reid's presence in his life and interpret all of this in his own way?

"No, I'm not your dad. Though he was a great man. He fought for our freedom in a very dark place and wasn't able to come home."

For some reason, that choked Reid up. It was a raw deal for Nora and her son, but she'd handled the challenges of becoming a widow with grace. She'd created an amazing house that was every inch a home, with crayon scribbles posted on the refrigerator and toys strewn around the living room.

Despite the darkness of her circumstances, she hadn't let it affect her. It was amazing. He wanted to learn from her example.

"Daadee," Declan repeated, and pointed at Reid.

Reid shook his head. "No, bud. Just because we hung out that night doesn't mean I can do it again. I'm really good at telling other people what to do but they're adults and paid to listen. I—"

He broke off because it wasn't as if Declan could understand how difficult this whole subject was for Reid.

Especially when he didn't understand it himself. He stared at the redheaded pint-size human in the high chair less than two feet from Reid's chair. The kid had wormed his way into Reid's limited circle of people he cared about, and that made all of this worse. Declan and Nora needed someone with far more to offer than a brooding loner who was marking the days until he could return to his lair and shut himself away from the world again.

Except the concept didn't seem as appealing as it had in the past.

Reid's penthouse didn't have the same feel as Nora's house. His style leaned toward sharp, modern, stark. He would have insisted that he preferred it right up until the time he walked through Nora's door and felt the difference between the two.

At Nora's house, her warmth emanated from the very walls. He wanted to soak it up as long as possible. As long as she'd let him. There was nothing in his penthouse or his work at Chamberlain Group that could compare with having a lover and a friend rolled into one. As Nora had often said, money didn't buy happiness and he got that in a way he never had before.

Nora bustled back into the kitchen. "First load is in the machine and it's not even nine o'clock. That's a personal record."

Her sunny smile felt like a reward that he eagerly accepted.

Nora's phone beeped and they both glanced at it where it lay on the long island that separated the kitchen from the dining area. She frowned. "It's Eve."

She picked up the phone and thumbed up the message, then shook her head and made a little noise of disgust. "She says my dad wants to talk to me and would I please Skype her. That's just like him. It's not like he can pick up the phone himself. He's got to make it as difficult as possible on everyone else."

"So don't do it," Reid advised and Declan threw a Cheerio on the floor as his vote in the matter.

"Then he'll just take it out on Eve and Grace. That's how he operates." Her mouth tightened. "Better to get it over with, which I honestly think is part of his strategy."

She retrieved her small, off-brand laptop from the built-in desk near the kitchen and set it on the table to boot it up. Eve answered a few seconds after Nora clicked Call, and her sister appeared in the chat window.

"Thanks, Nora. Here's Dad." Eve shifted her own laptop to aim the video lens toward Sutton.

Sutton Winchester's gaunt face filled the screen. *Wow.* Reid had known the man was sick. Dying. But his appearance had so degenerated, it was a bit of a shock. He was pretty sure her father couldn't see him sitting near Nora because of the angle of her laptop, but Nora could, so he kept his alarm to himself. She knew her father didn't have long. She didn't need Reid to add to her burden.

"Nora." Sutton's imperious voice rang out in the small breakfast nook. "I'm very disappointed you've chosen to abandon your family in this time of need."

Reid bit his tongue. Emotional blackmail? The man had nerve.

Nora scowled. "Is that why you called, Dad? We've been over this. I told you I'd come back if there was a real emergency, but I have myself and my son to take care of. That's the most important thing right now."

Sutton coughed, prolonging the fit past the point where Reid had any concern left. It was clear Winchester was milking it.

When he'd recovered, Sutton glared at Nora. "And where exactly does the Spawn of Satan fit into that, may I ask?" This was the nickname her father had used for Reid ever since discovering that she was spending time with him.

"His name is Reid and you can leave him out of this conversation." Nora's gaze shifted toward Reid, as he stood, crossing behind Nora's chair to rest a hand on her shoulder.

"You rang?" he commented to Winchester mildly.

Reid would be the first in line to agree with the moniker Spawn of Satan. His own father was no doubt in hell trying to dethrone the devil as they spoke. But the fine, pinched lines around Nora's mouth were not okay. Just because she was related to this cruel, miserable man didn't mean Reid would stand by and allow her to be abused.

"Chamberlain," Winchester fairly barked. "Since warnings to my daughter have gone unheeded, I'll appeal to your sense of honor, whatever little of it you may have. Stay away from Nora. Your bad blood will only lead to pain and suffering. If she won't give you the boot, take it upon yourself to remove yourself from her house."

"Dad, that's enough!" Nora was fairly bristling under Reid's palm. "You have no idea what you're talking about. How dare you intrude on my life and then make demands of a man who's shown me nothing but kindness?"

Kindness? That was laying it on a bit thick but just as Reid was about to tell the old man to go to hell, Winchester cleared his throat. "You're obviously not thinking this through, Nora. You have a son to be concerned with. You do not want him to be negatively affected by your poor choices, do you?"

"The only poor choice I've made lately is making this call," Nora retorted darkly. "And asking this is probably the second one, but I have to know. What, exactly, do you think is going to happen to Declan by being exposed to Reid?"

Nothing good could come of that question, but now that she'd asked, Reid was interested in the answer, too. Not because he had any respect for Winchester's opinion, but simply because Reid had already arrived at the conclusion that he was bad news for mom and son. It couldn't hurt to solidify that fact in both his and Nora's minds.

That the answer came via her father stuck in his craw, though.

"The man is ruthless," Winchester announced as if Reid wasn't standing right there listening. "In his business dealings and his personal relationships, such as they are. Hasn't anyone explained his distasteful reputation to you? He's corrupt, soulless and cold. A man like him cannot be around my grandson. I forbid it."

Hearing it spelled out like that without a filter, without any pulled punches, was brutal. But it didn't make it any less true. He wasn't father material and Winchester saw it as clearly as Reid did.

"Reid," Nora said without turning around. "Tell my father Declan's favorite animal."

"Giraffe." Or at least it was now. He slept with the stuffed giraffe Reid had bought him at the zoo and carried it around as if he'd been gifted with the Hope Diamond.

"What time does he go to bed?"

"Eight o'clock. If you mean for the night. He also takes a nap after lunch." As Reid well knew since he'd taken complete advantage of the all-adult alone time on more than one occasion.

Nora cocked her head at her father, staring him down as she addressed Reid. "What did he eat for breakfast?"

"Cheerios." This was a fun game, especially since Winchester's complexion got grayer and grayer the longer Nora kept it up.

"Now it's your turn, Dad." Nora folded her hands. "If you can answer at least one of those questions about me from when I was two, I'll take your advice about Reid. Wait, I'll make it even easier. Answer it about me, Eve *or* Grace. Go ahead. Wow me."

Winchester sputtered as Reid's mouth flipped up into an appreciative smile that he didn't bother to hide. God, she was amazing.

"That's what I thought," Nora concluded. "You know how Reid answered those questions so easily? Because he spends time with Declan. He makes an effort. He's already a better father figure to my son than you ever were to me. And you're *my* blood. This conversation is over."

Nora clicked the lid shut to her laptop and put her head down on it.

Reid lightly massaged her shoulders in hopes it would be comforting and tried to unstick his tongue from the roof of his mouth. A *father figure*? That was… What was that? He had no context for the definition of the term, what she'd meant when she'd said it and whether the fifty-pound weight on his chest had landed there because the concept scared him or because it didn't.

After all, he did care about Declan. The kid had grown on him when he wasn't looking. He was funny, innocent and a piece of Nora. What wasn't to like?

Regardless, as far as all those things she'd asked him were concerned, his ability to answer didn't give him any special skill to do something as huge as be a father. Yet Nora seemed to think so or she wouldn't have made that point so well to her own father. Confusion clogged his throat.

"Sorry," she mumbled. "You shouldn't have been subjected to that. I—"

"No problem." This conversation needed some spin control before more things came out of her mouth that tilted his world. "You were brilliant, by the way."

Declan kicked his legs against the plastic footrest of his high chair and said, "Daadee."

And Reid didn't know what he was supposed to do with that, either.

Eleven

That afternoon, Reid tried to shake off the weirdness of the Skype conversation with Sutton Winchester and talked Nora into letting him rent them a sailboat for a spin around Chatfield Reservoir. Nora's small town of Silver Falls lay to the southwest of Denver, right at the foothills of the Rockies, and made for amazing views.

The skyline of Chicago had its own beauty but Reid appreciated the diversity of the vistas here, including the gorgeous blonde at his side as they boarded the fifty-foot cruising sailboat that he'd chartered for their fun afternoon. The captain welcomed them aboard and went over a few safety precautions while Declan explored the small seating area designed for the guests. The captain handed them all orange life vests and Nora actually got Declan to stand still for four seconds while she strapped him into his. A full crew scurried about the deck, making the sails ready for departure.

The wind kicked up and blew through Nora's hair as they headed out toward the center of the reservoir. It streamed out behind her and she laughed as Declan put his face up to the breeze like a dog sticking his head out the window.

This was the perfect distraction from the heaviness that had weighed Reid down all day. Not that Nora had noticed his reticence, or if she had, she'd elected not to say anything. Maybe she'd been thinking about the conversation, too, wondering if she should take back what she'd told her father. But she hadn't. Probably because she didn't realize that Reid had faulty genetics that prevented him from being the father figure she'd described.

Declan wandered over to the edge of the boat and gripped the railing, watching the water rush by with a happy smile. It jabbed Reid right in the stomach. What a rush to put that kind of expression on a kid's face. The poor guy had it tough with losing his dad and having a sick grandpa. If any of the excursions Reid had planned made his life a little easier, that was fair compensation for how much warmth Declan and Nora had brought to him.

Nora leaned in toward Reid, her eye still on her son. "Thanks for this. It's nice."

He smiled back in response. "Thank you for what you said to your dad."

"You're welcome. You aren't going to argue with me about what I said? I've been waiting for you to bring it up all day."

The seat cushion under Reid's butt grew uncomfortable and he sought a different position. But no amount of fidgeting changed the fact that she was right. He had been avoiding the subject. "You didn't have to say that about me just to get your dad off your back."

"I didn't. It's true." Her hand drifted over to clutch his. "You've been an amazing influence on Declan and he likes you. I know you think you're not father material, but it's obvious to me that you are."

Reid went cold. This was the part where he had to come clean with her. Where he had to be so very clear that answering a few questions about breakfast cereal didn't erase the Chamberlain genes from his makeup. "It's not that I hate the idea of being around kids. Declan is great. It's that I…have a lot of internal stuff to overcome."

"Don't we all?" She dismissed his comment with a wave of her hand. "Besides, I've told you before, I think it's admirable that you stop and think about these things before jumping into the deep end. That's part of what makes you father material, Reid. Because you care so much about doing the right thing. My dad never did. You're already better just in that one respect."

Reid opened his mouth to categorically deny every last word she'd said. And couldn't do it. Because all at once, he got her point. He did care about Declan. And Nora. How had that happened? He'd have sworn he didn't have the ability to nurture and love, that tragedy had ripped that away from him. Apparently, he'd been wrong. What else had he been wrong about?

He cleared his throat. "Thanks. I'm sorry your father is such a piece of work."

There was so much more he wanted to say but he couldn't get the swirl of emotion in his chest to stop long enough for him to form coherent speech.

"You'd think it would be easier to hate him. But I can't." Nora caught her lip between her front teeth, worrying it as she glanced at Reid. "He's still my father despite all the crappy stuff he's done over the years. Despite the horrible mandates he threw around this morning about you. He's my dad and I still love him. Am I insane?"

"No." He yanked Nora into his arms, simply holding her, because the break in her voice had echoed through the hollow cavity inside his chest and he needed her warmth just then.

He needed *her*.

She'd just described the very essence of unconditional love, something he scarcely understood, but wanted to. Nora had opened up a whole world of possibilities by breathing life into Reid's stale world. By shedding light on all the darkness of his existence. By presenting new ways to view old, set-in-stone beliefs.

If Sutton Winchester had been a horrible excuse for a human being and yet still had managed to retain his daughter's love, perhaps the fatherhood bar wasn't as high as Reid had always assumed it was. Hadn't he been successful at everything he'd ever tried? Why had he always categorically dismissed his weaknesses as bad DNA? Nora had overcome her genetics. She was a great mom. Surely if he tried, he could do leagues better than her father. Or his own.

And if that was true, maybe it wasn't a sin of the highest order to imagine that he'd found something in Nora Winchester O'Malley that was worth hanging on to with both hands—a family. He wanted that.

"I'm glad you're here," she said and pulled back a bit from his embrace. Not all the way, which was fortunate, because he'd just yank her back. "I really didn't expect anything to come out of tracking you down that day after you sent the catering. But I've been carrying this load by myself for so long that I've forgotten how much I need someone to turn to when it gets rough."

Yes, exactly. Her thoughts so eloquently and perfectly mirrored his, it was almost spooky. Or maybe it was just fate.

Hope filled him to the brim and he cleared his throat to tell Nora that something miraculous was happening. Something that afforded them an opportunity to write a different ending to their affair. Grief and darkness had held him back from caring about anyone for so long... and he was sick of being alone. He had an opportunity to be there for Nora and Declan, to perhaps atone for what he'd failed to do for Sophia and his mother.

But at that moment, the winds shifted, billowing the sails backward. The boat lurched as if it had hit a brick wall.

Declan slipped.

Reid watched it happen in slow motion as if time had literally slowed down, allowing him to internalize every second of the little boy's feet sliding out from under him. Declan fell to the deck, his forehead slamming against the wood paneling with a sickening thud. His red curls lay still as the wind died down.

Nora cried out and wobbled to her feet, throwing herself toward the boy. Her hands rushed over her son, checking his crumpled, unmoving form.

Reid's heart jammed into his throat. *No air.* He couldn't move. His hands went numb and useless. He shoved himself off the bench anyway, rushing after Nora to do...something. Anything.

The captain shouted to the crew and the boat settled into the wind. One of the crewmembers knelt by Declan and spoke to Nora, gently checking the boy's pulse.

The crewmember motioned Reid out of the way, so he crouched on the opposite side to smooth a hand over Nora's back because he needed to do something and this was the best spot to monitor the situation. Someone had to make sure Declan was being taken care of and it should be Reid since he was responsible for the injury.

Blood smeared Declan's forehead. The crewmember asked Nora's permission to hold a bandage on it, explaining the risks of concussion as tears streamed down Nora's face unchecked.

Reid's gut clenched. This was all his fault. Declan was too young to be out on a boat this size. A real father would have known that. Would have known what to do when his kid was hurt. But Reid didn't because he wasn't Declan's father. Nor should he be.

Sutton Winchester could see Reid's unsuitability a mile away. Like recognized like in the end. Perhaps Nora had completely missed the point of her father's warning. Instead of resisting it, she should have realized her father had in fact only been looking out for her because he'd be gone soon and unable to do so any longer. In a way, it was a complete reversal of Winchester's typical method of operation.

And the old man's point hadn't been lost on Reid. If Nora wouldn't listen to reason, then Reid had to be the one to do the right thing. The thing he'd known would be the end result of this affair all along—he had to extract himself from Nora and Declan's world before he hurt them even more. Because he loved them both.

The boat butted up against the dock. An ambulance sat idling nearby and two EMTs in dark blue uniforms stood on the dock waiting until the boat was secured. The instant the ropes held, they clambered on board and went to work evaluating Declan.

Nora's gaze never left her son. As well it shouldn't. Though Reid felt her slipping away even as he made conscious effort to let her go. In reality, she'd never been his and he'd never had any kind of claim on her. So whatever connection he'd become so aware of, so dependent on, couldn't continue.

The EMTs explained that only family could ride in the ambulance to the hospital and Nora nodded, finally glancing at Reid as if she'd just realized he was there. The look on her face—ravaged, tear-stained—gutted him. He'd done that to her, caused her pain and worry for her son by being so clueless about safety.

He had reasons why he didn't know more about kids. But they weren't good ones. And definitely not excuses. When you didn't know something and it was important to learn, you learned. Why hadn't he done that?

Because he'd been trying to turn his brief affair with Nora into something meaningful to assuage his own loneliness. He was nothing if not self-serving.

It was time to change that.

"I'm sorry, Reid," she murmured, her voice just as ravaged as her face. "I'm going to ride in the ambulance with Declan, but they're saying you'll have to take separate transportation. I can't... Well, I have to go."

He nodded. "No problem. You do whatever you need to do."

Separating from Nora and Declan was perfect for his purposes, actually. He watched the EMTs load the still-unconscious boy onto the gurney and then roll it into the back of the waiting ambulance. He helped Nora into the cavernous space and squeezed her hand one final time before the driver shut the door. Then the ambulance drove away, taking with it the only people who had managed to coax a smile out of Reid in a very long time.

The oil slick in his soul bubbled up, crowding out all the good waking up with Nora this morning had done. He shouldn't have come here and allowed the darkness that lived inside him to harm others. And he surely shouldn't have bribed Nora with a private plane ride here in order to stay in her orbit. Because he selfishly wanted a family without giving anything of himself.

Easily fixed. He'd just leave his pilot and plane here and fly back to Chicago some other way. The trick would be not letting on to Nora how much it hurt to not be the man she deserved and the father Declan deserved.

Reid hadn't come to the hospital and Nora had a pretty good idea why. Exhausted, Nora pushed open the front door of her house with one hand and shifted a sleeping Declan higher against her hip, making sure she didn't jostle his brand-new stitches.

"Reid," she called softly and shook her head when he didn't answer. The man was a big, fat scaredy-cat and he needed to see with his own two eyes that Declan was fine. Which wouldn't happen if he kept hiding away from the frightening parts of life.

It was a step back. A small one. Slowly but surely, Reid had been coming around to the idea that kids weren't all that bad and then this had to happen. A bump on the head that would heal in time. Like all wounds. She'd thought maybe Reid had gotten to a place where he believed that. Where they could really talk to each other about their fears and setbacks, and yeah, maybe share in the triumphs.

She could have used his strong shoulder at the hospital. She was a little upset that he hadn't realized that.

First things first. She got Declan undressed and in his crib with his stuffed giraffe, then covered him with his frog blanket. The boy didn't stir, likely a combination of the late hour and the activity at the hospital. Then she went in search of Reid.

The house was dark and silent. Reid wasn't here.

Frowning, she glanced around her bedroom and immediately noted his suitcases were gone. In the kitchen, she found a handwritten note, folded, with her name on the outside.

Her stomach sank as she picked up the page. The flowing script blurred as she took in the contents. Apparently, it didn't take many lines to rip her heart out.

One, two, three... She let the pain take over until she reached ten. Then she cut it off.

He was gone. Without explanation. "It's my fault Declan was hurt. It's better we end things now before something worse happens," was *not* an explanation.

Anger bloomed, hot and fierce. That...*man*. How dare he leave her when she needed him most? She'd kept her panic and tears under control while watching the doctor stitch up her baby, but only because she'd had to. It didn't stop her from wishing Reid had been there to hold her in the hallway while she crumbled. She was so tired of not being able to crumble, of not having someone strong enough to catch her.

Why did she always have to fall for men who were determined to leave? First she'd fallen for a man with such deep wanderlust, he'd enlisted in the army to satisfy it. And he'd paid the ultimate price with his life. She didn't begrudge Sean his choices, nor blame him for dying, but she did wish she'd had an opportunity to say goodbye. It was her biggest unresolvable regret.

As for Reid, she could blame him all day long for his choices. Jetting off and leaving her a note. That was... unforgivable. And all at once, she didn't plan to stand for it. Sean had left her to go to a place she couldn't follow. But Reid hadn't.

The note indicated that Reid had left his plane at

the private airstrip not far from Silver Falls, which was available for her use to return to Chicago whenever she deemed it necessary.

It looked as though that time was now.

In the morning, she threw the load of laundry from the dryer back into the same suitcases the clothes had come from yesterday and zipped them up. Declan was a bit harder to herd as he was still tired and cranky from the bump on his head. But she prevailed and Reid's pilot took off for Chicago before lunchtime.

After an uneventful flight where Nora passed the time fuming over Reid's cowardice, she made a quick call to Grace, who dropped everything in order to take Declan. This was one showdown that didn't need an additional audience member.

Finally, Nora walked through the door of the Metropol business office and faced down Reid's admin. "I'm here to see Mr. Chamberlain. He's expecting me."

It wasn't a lie. He should be expecting her. If he thought she was going to take that BS note at face value, he had another think coming.

"Oh." Reid's admin's eyes rounded. "Yes, you should definitely go right in."

Nora was all too happy to comply, but when she stormed into Reid's office, the genuine shock on his face when he looked up from his desk brought her up short.

The force of his presence slammed into her, far more powerfully than it had the first time she'd come here. His brown eyes were full of secret pain and even more secret longing. His body, as she knew firsthand, was full of heat and tenderness. And her heart was full of him.

They'd come full circle. A few weeks ago, she'd been looking for an old friend. Today, she was looking for the man she'd fallen in love with. And had only just realized that was the root of her anger.

She loved Reid. How dare he treat that so casually? Didn't he realize how hard it was for her to open her heart again? How afraid she was of loss?

Her legs started shaking but she shrugged her nervousness off, marching forward to yank the phone out of Reid's hand.

"He'll have to call you back," she said and ended the call, tossing the phone over her shoulder. "You left. That note? Not going to cut it. Tell me to my face that we're through and I might believe you. But I don't think you can do it. Because you know we're not even close to finished."

"Nora." Reid's gaze swept over her hungrily, weakening her already-shaking legs. "What are you doing here? Is Declan okay? Or is it your father?"

"No, nothing's changed with my father's health and Declan is fine. I just told you why I'm here." Something broke inside as he stood, circling the desk to invade her space, drawing close, so close. But not close enough. There was an invisible barrier between them that she ached to destroy but first, she had to understand. "I deserve to hear from you personally what's going on in your head. We're not just sleeping together. We're involved, whether you like it or not. I thought…"

All at once, as his expression darkened with something she had no idea how to interpret, she faltered. What *had* she thought? That Reid accompanying her to Colorado meant something different from what it had? That he'd turned into someone who wanted a woman with a kid? His refusal to entertain the idea of ever becoming a father couldn't have been clearer. When she'd gently tried to help him see that he'd surely be a better father than most, he hadn't agreed with her. And he hadn't come to the hospital because that was too much for him to handle.

She'd run all the way back to Chicago to confront a man who wanted out from their affair. She should have left well enough alone.

"You thought what?" His voice dipped dangerously low. "That something was happening between us? That I might have developed feelings for you?"

"Yes." She couldn't look away. Couldn't lie. Even though she knew it was the wrong tactic, the absolute worst thing to admit to a man who had run away from her as fast as he could. The facts spoke for themselves after all. "Tell me I'm wrong. Say it. Out loud."

"You're not." The phrase reverberated in the air, settling across her skin. Raising goose bumps as his eyes bored into her. "That's why I left. Because I care about you too much to hurt you."

"What are you saying?" she whispered as everything inside her slid off a cliff. "You…left because you developed feelings for me?"

"I can't…" He shook his head. "That's why I left the note. It was supposed to keep you in Colorado. Where you were safe. Not drag you back to Chicago. Go home. I'm not good for you."

"Reid." His name bubbled up on a sob as she fought back tears. "That's ridiculous. You're the best thing that's happened to me in a long, dark couple of years. I need you. And you left. *That's* what hurt."

His gaze was raw as he nearly closed the gap between them. But didn't. "I'm sorry. I was trying to protect Declan. And you. I've caused enough pain."

"Protect us from what? You?" She tried to laugh it off but the sound got caught in her throat. "Declan is fine. Kids get hurt. They're not as fragile as you seem to think. But I don't buy that as the reason for all of this. I think you ran because of what's happening between us."

To her shock, he nodded. "Yes. Because it's the right thing to do. I never expected to fall for you and never expected to have to make the difficult choice to walk away."

She nearly groaned at the irony. The one time he'd elected to make an adult decision, and it was the wrong one. "Then don't walk away. Seize the moment. And the next one. For the next fifty or sixty years, let's be crazy together. I love you and I'm not leaving until you say yes."

To emphasize the point, she plopped down on his desk, crossing her arms. Nora Winchester O'Malley charted her own destiny and she wanted this man, with all his glorious complexities.

She wasn't leaving without his heart.

He hesitated for an eternity and then his fingers slid around her elbows, pulling her to her feet. For a half second, she thought he was going to throw her out. But then he swept her into his arms, kissing her with an intensity she could scarcely take in.

His essence swirled into her soul, joining them in a connection that couldn't be explained but didn't have to be. Because they both felt it. Both yearned for it. Both accepted it, despite all their objections to the contrary.

When he finally let her surface long enough to gulp in some much-needed oxygen, he murmured, "I'm sorry. I shouldn't have done that. It's not fair to keep drawing you back in. You should leave."

"No." She scowled. "And I'm not letting you make this decision for me. I want you in my life. And in Declan's. We both need you."

He pierced her with his deep, soulful eyes. "I don't know how to be a father. What if there's something wrong with me that I can't overcome? You're taking too big of a chance with your son on what's essentially a work in progress."

Even now, he was trying so hard to do the right thing and couldn't see that she accepted him as he was. "Since we're on the subject, I'm a work in progress, too. I know everything about being a mom of a one-year-old. But I've never been the mom of a two-year-old. It's a lot harder. I'm making all new mistakes. That's where you come in. Be there for me. As my sounding board. As my lover, to help the bad parts of the day melt away. As my partner. That, you know how to do."

Because he'd been doing it all along. And she'd been too blind to see that she needed to encourage it, nurture their blossoming relationship by telling him every moment how important he was to her.

"Guess we know where Declan gets his stubbornness from. Seems like his mom latches on to an idea and never lets go, either."

"I don't know what you're talking about," she countered primly, her pulse racing to keep up with all the things going on inside. "I'm not stubborn. I just know what I want. And you, Reid Chamberlain, are it."

He shook his head and her heart froze. But then he smiled, the real genuine one that made her feel like she'd won the Reid Chamberlain sweepstakes and everything was going to be all right.

"What if I just want to be friends?" he asked, even as his arms slid around her, possessively, intimately, drawing her so close there was nothing between them.

Everything inside yearned for this man. "Too bad.

You better get used to the idea of being lovers *and* friends. And one last thing. No more notes."

His lips toyed with hers, not quite completing the connection. "Not even 'I love you' scrawled in the steam on the bathroom mirror?"

She pretended to contemplate it but the thought of sharing a bathroom with Reid for the rest of her life made her a little giddy. "That one might be okay. But only if you promise to follow it up verbally."

"I do."

The sweetest words in the English language. "Then so do I."

Epilogue

Nora hid a smile as Reid picked up Declan and hoisted him to his shoulders, then galloped around the living area of his Metropol penthouse. The neighing noises Reid was making were her favorite. It was the kind of thing Reid did frequently without thought and Nora fell a little more in love with the man every time he came up with a new game to play with her son.

And soon, Declan would be Reid's son, too. They'd already filed adoption papers.

Reid had put Chamberlain Group on the back burner in favor of learning everything he could about being a father, claiming he had to catch up fast. Before it became official. He didn't seem to understand it had been official since the moment Declan had picked Reid as his "Daadee."

Nora's phone rang and she scooped it up when she saw Grace's name on the screen.

"Everything okay?" Nora asked anxiously. Every phone call from a family member could be the one where she got word that her father had died. When Dr. Wilde had given Sutton Winchester until New Year's to live, it didn't necessarily mean he'd make it until then.

Before Reid and Nora had gotten married, they'd agreed to split their time between Chicago and Silver Falls, at least until the first of the year. Eventually, they hoped to buy a bigger house higher up in the foothills of the Rockies, one that would accommodate the brood of children they both wanted. But for now, Chicago was where Nora needed to be.

"No, everything is not okay," Grace said. Nora could hear the scowl in her sister's voice. "You are not going to believe what those Newport scum have done now."

The call wasn't about her father. Nora breathed a sigh of relief and wandered into the kitchen to sit at the island. "Brooks and Graham? What have they done?"

More inheritance drama. But that came part and parcel with being a Winchester. Nora's patience with it had grown the longer she had Reid to lean on.

And when leaning on his strong shoulder wasn't enough, he just took her to bed and made love to her until she forgot about everything outside of the two of them.

Grace made a very uncomplimentary noise. "They hired a private investigator to work with that lawyer, Josh Calhoun."

"They went ahead with involving their friend in this?" Nora's stomach sank. The Newport twins were fired up about getting Carson his share of the Winchester fortune and honestly, she didn't get their passion for the quest. "I don't understand what a private investigator is going to add to the mix other than making more of a mess."

"Yeah. They want to find their real father, and I guess

a private investigator is supposed to help with that. But I didn't tell you the worst part. The PI is Roman Slater." Grace nearly spat out the name. "My ex."

"Oh, Grace." Nora still remembered how her sister had cried for the six months following her breakup with Roman. "I can't believe they would stoop to working with someone so underhanded."

The twins were obviously trouble waiting to happen, and must have been deliberately involving people they thought were going to put the screws to the Winchesters. It was unforgivable.

"Well, Dad is being so closemouthed about their parentage. I'm even starting to believe he knows something."

Nora secretly agreed. Since moving into Reid's penthouse, she'd tried to spend at least three days a week at the hospital and really talk to her father. Amazingly, her dad had completely reversed his stance on Reid with no explanation, only stating—very gruffly—that he'd heard Reid had appointed Nash as the interim CEO of Chamberlain Group while he spent time with his new family. Sutton approved.

None of it made up for the years of not having a father. But Nora was slowly letting go of her disappointment and grief. Reid's love helped with that, too. When her father finally passed, she felt more confident than ever that she would be at peace with it.

"I'm glad you're here, Nora," Gracie admitted. "I have a feeling this whole thing is going to get uglier before long."

"Yeah, me, too. Sorry. Let me know what I can do to help."

Nora disconnected the call and returned to the living room to find Reid and Declan in the middle of the floor, laughing so hard, neither of them could breathe. Her soul filled with the sound. How had she gotten so lucky to find a man who could love her son as much as she did?

"What's all of this?" Nora demanded. "Having fun without me?"

"Never," Reid said, his gorgeous grin spreading across his face. "Care to join us, Ms. O'Malley?"

He smiled all the time these days and she delighted in taking full credit for it.

"That's Mrs. Chamberlain to you, buddy," she corrected and the sound of her new name thrilled her. She'd sworn to never change her name again, but that was before she found it vitally necessary to be joined with this man in every way possible.

He was her friend. Her lover. Her husband. Soon to be the legal father of her child. And she would never let him go.

* * * * *

Don't miss a single installment of
DYNASTIES: THE NEWPORTS
*Passion and chaos consume a
Chicago real estate empire*

*SAYING YES TO THE BOSS by Andrea Laurence
AN HEIR FOR THE BILLIONAIRE by Kat Cantrell
CLAIMED BY THE COWBOY by Sarah M. Anderson
HIS SECRET BABY BOMBSHELL by Jules Bennett
BACK IN THE ENEMY'S BED by Michelle Celmer
THE TEXAN'S ONE NIGHT STAND-OFF
by Charlene Sands*

Available now from Mills & Boon Desire!

She approached him and reached out to touch his scar, running her index finger along the pale line.

She was painstakingly gentle, and it made him want to kiss her. They were standing so close he could've leaned forward and captured her mouth with his. But he didn't take the liberty. They stared at each other instead, steeped in a strange kind of intimacy.

"I'm glad you survived the accident," Carol said, smoothing his hair across his brow.

"So am I." But before things got unbearably awkward, Jake stepped back, trying to restrain the tenderness between them. "After the crash, I used to pray to Uncta, a deity from Choctaw mythology who steals fire from the sun. I was the only one who was rescued from the car before it went up in flames."

"Did you think Uncta had saved you?"

"No, but I wanted to steal fire, too. To have his powers."

But that wasn't going to help Jake now. He'd already jumped straight from the frying pan and into the flame, feeling things for Carol that he wished he didn't feel. He still wanted to kiss her, as hot and passionately as he could.

* * *

Waking up with the Boss is part of
the **Billionaire Brothers Club** trilogy—
Three foster brothers grow up, get rich…
and find the perfect woman.

WAKING UP WITH
THE BOSS

BY
SHERI WHITEFEATHER

First Published in Great Britain 2016
By Mills & Boon, an imprint of HarperCollins*Publishers*
1 London Bridge Street, London, SE1 9GF

© 2016 Sheree Henry-Whitefeather

ISBN: 978-0-263-91872-4

51-0816

Our policy is to use papers that are natural, renewable and recyclable products and made from wood grown in sustainable forests. The logging and manufacturing processes conform to the legal environmental regulations of the country of origin.

Printed and bound in Spain
by CPI, Barcelona

Sheri WhiteFeather is an award-winning, bestselling author. She writes a variety of romance novels for Mills & Boon and is known for incorporating Native American elements into her stories. She has two grown children who are tribally enrolled members of the Muscogee Creek Nation. She lives in California and enjoys shopping in vintage stores and visiting art galleries and museums. Sheri loves to hear from her readers at www.sheriwhitefeather.com.

One

Carol Lawrence stood in her boss's luxurious high-rise office, with a zillion things running through her mind. Being Jake Waters's personal assistant was a demanding job, with most of her duties centered on organizing his social life. No doubt about it, the jet-setting real estate mogul kept her on her toes. Not only did he travel for work, purchasing properties all over the globe, he was the consummate party boy, dashing off to exotic locations with models and actresses and whoever else struck his rich-guy fancy.

Jake sat on the corner of his desk and flung his jacket over his unused chair. As always, his shirtsleeves were rolled up, exposing the colorful tattoos on his arms, and his dark brown hair was in sexy disarray. With his disheveled good looks and need for speed, he reminded her of James Dean, except that Jake was half-Choctaw, his mixed-blood heritage lending his features an uncommon beauty.

He certainly wasn't the type of man she should be attracted to. He was too wild for a practical girl like her. Carol spent her free time on a nice, quiet quilting hobby, whereas Jake raced sports cars as his outlet. To her that seemed like an especially reckless thing for him to do, given that his entire family had been killed in a car crash, sending him into foster care as a child. Carol had also lost her family and become a foster kid, as well. But they didn't know each other back then, and the tragedies they'd both suffered didn't make for good bedfellows.

Still, she often wondered what taming a man like Jake would involve. *Yeah, right.* If the glamorous beauties he dated couldn't pin him down, then a simple gal with tidy blond hair and a sensible nature would never fit the bill. Jake was a thirty-one-year-old billionaire who'd even made some crazy internet "Beefcake Bachelor" list as one of the sexiest single men in Southern California. Women chased him with a vengeance. Of course, some of them kept trying to fix him, with the assumption that he was damaged from the loss of his family, using his free-spirited lifestyle to hide the pain. Carol didn't doubt that was true. She knew the anguish that being orphaned could cause. But her coping mechanism was much gentler than his. Someday she longed to get married and have children of her own, recapturing the home and hearth she'd lost.

Jake glanced up and caught her gaze, and a fluttery sensation erupted in her stomach, something that happened far too often when she was in his presence.

Determined to maintain her composure, Carol focused on her job. "So," she said, "are you going to attend Lena's birthday celebration?" Lena was a pop star with a penchant for partying who ran in the same live-for-the-moment circle as Jake.

"Damn straight I'm going to go. She's my bud. I

wouldn't miss her thirtieth bash." He laughed a little. "She'll probably be half-naked and dancing on tabletops."

"No doubt." Lena was known for her antics. Carol was the same age as Lena, but she couldn't imagine behaving that way. "Who will be attending the party with you?"

"Now that's where I'm having a bit of a problem. I don't have a date."

"I thought you were seeing Susanne Monroe." A long, leggy brunette who was recently divorced from a famous baseball player. Carol had seen her strutting around the office a few times in her tight-as-sin dresses, her stilettos clicking as she walked.

"We're not together anymore."

It was over already? "Who ended it?"

"She did." He shrugged off the breakup. "But I was just a rebound for her, anyway."

Carol shook her head, then glanced out the bank of floor-to-ceiling windows, where a view of Wilshire Boulevard, with its busy Los Angeles cityscape, was spread out before them. She'd worked for Jake for two years, but she still hadn't gotten used to the parade of women who came in and out of his life.

She turned back to face him. "I'm sure you'll find a date for Lena's soiree. But for now, do you want me to RSVP for you and a plus-one? And notify your pilot to be on standby for that weekend?" The party was being held on a private island in the southeastern Caribbean Sea. Lena was pulling out all the stops, away from the prying eyes of the paparazzi.

"Yeah. Thanks. It's a couples-only theme, so I'm going to have to bring someone. Lena's latest song is called 'Couples Only,' and she always creates parties around her songs." Jake paused, then looked at Carol as if he'd just solved a strange little puzzle. "Here's an idea. You can be my plus-one. That would save me the trouble of finding another companion, and it would give you a great getaway."

Oh, my God. Carol white-knuckled her iPad, holding it against her chest. He was suggesting that she fly off to a tropical island to drink and dance and be merry with him? Sure, she traveled with him when it was necessary, but she'd never been expected to fill in as one of his dates. "You can't be serious."

"Of course I am. Or I wouldn't have said it."

"But I'm not part of your crowd. I wouldn't fit in."

"Yes, you would. You already know a lot of them."

"I know them in a professional sense."

"So now you can socialize with them, too."

The nervous sensation in her stomach swirled. "I can't." There was no way she could spend a weekend with Jake and his friends. "And with you being my employer, it wouldn't be proper."

"Really, Carol? You're going to use that as an excuse? I'm not proposing that we have a mad, passionate affair. The couples-only theme doesn't mean that we have to be a real couple. It's just a party."

"On a private island," she defended herself. "And I didn't think you were proposing anything." She knew better than to assume he was interested in her, and even if by some off chance he was, she wasn't foolish enough to jeopardize her job over it. "It doesn't seem right for us to go away together. It would be different if it was a business trip."

"So we'll call it a business trip."

Who was he trying to kid? "A party hosted by Lena Kent is more like monkey business."

He laughed. "That's true. But Lena isn't that bad. She donates a lot of money to my charity."

"I know how generous she is." Carol also knew how important the nonprofit organization he and his foster brothers had founded was to him. "But this isn't a charity gig. It's one of her nutty parties."

"Yeah, but just think of what a smashing time you'll have, sipping the most expensive champagne in the world and eating the most delicious food imaginable. Not to mention lounging around in your bathing suit, with the sea at your beck and call. We'll probably go crabbing, too. I'll bet you've never done that before." He stood, coming to his full height. "This would give you the opportunity to expand your horizons and experience new things. It's crazy how reluctant you are to let down your guard and have a good time."

"I'm not afraid of enjoying myself." She wasn't the bore he was making her out to be. "I hang out with my girlfriends. I haven't had a boyfriend in a while, but I go on online dates." So far none of them had worked out, but she was still trying to meet someone. "I'm just cautious, that's all."

"Of what? People like me? Come on, Miss Proper Employee, spend a recreational weekend with your big, bad boss and his spoiled band of misfits."

"Are you actually daring me?"

"Hell, yes." He poured on the charm, being as insistent as ever. "So what do you say? Are you game?"

She wished that his foster brothers were going to be there. She felt safe around Garrett and Max, with how cautious they always seemed, preferring to lead more private lives. They'd grown up with Jake in the same foster home and remained as close to him as anyone could be. But they didn't socialize with Jake's party crowd.

He moved forward and put his hands on her shoulders. "Come on, just do it. Jump headfirst and see where you land."

Carol squeezed her eyes shut, as if she really were diving off a cliff. *One...two...three.* She counted the breaths that left her lungs, then opened her eyes and looked straight into his, intending to decline the invitation. But somewhere in the insanity of the moment, of standing just inches from him, of absorbing the warmth of his touch, she heard herself say, "Okay, I'll do it. I'll go with you."

"That's my girl." Jake removed his hands from her shoulders and stepped back, leaving a silent gap between them.

Heaven help her. Had she actually agreed to this?

A sense of panic hit her, in more ways than one. Not only was she going to be stranded on a tropical island with her big, bad boss and his spoiled band of misfits, she was going to have to fuss over her clothes.

"I have no idea what I'm supposed to wear to the party," she said. She wore professional ensembles to work and comfy threads on her days off, but this was a whole other ball game.

He waved away her concern. "Just call Millie and have her bring a bunch of stuff to your house. Then pick whatever you want and have her bill me for it."

Millie was his stylist, a woman who also worked with celebrity clients. "You don't have to do that."

"I want to. Besides, you wouldn't be able to afford this type of couture on your own." He shot her a playful grin. "I'd have to give you a ridiculously huge raise."

She returned his smile. "Heaven forbid." In actuality, he already paid her a generous salary. But if he said the clothes were out of her price range, then she believed him. "I'll call her later today and see what her schedule is like." The party was less than a month away, and

Carol wanted to be prepared. She never did anything last minute. "At least Millie already knows that I'm not a model or actress or Beverly Hills type. I could never wear anything straight off the runway. I have too much meat on my bones."

Automatically, his gaze traveled the length of her. "There's nothing wrong with having curves."

She could have kicked herself for drawing his attention to her shape. "I didn't mean it that way." She'd already learned to accept her fuller figure and stop trying to be skinnier than her body type allowed.

He kept checking her out, not overtly, but still looking, still being a guy. "Be sure to tell Millie to include beachwear," he said. "Just so you'll have a complete weekend wardrobe."

"That's fine." At this point, Carol wanted to hightail it out of his office. But she couldn't run off without wrapping things up. She hurriedly asked, "What sort of accommodations do they have on the island?"

"It's a mansion that Lena is renting. There are caretakers who live on the property, but she'll be hiring a full staff to run it like a hotel while we're there. When you RSVP, make sure to let her assistant know that we need two rooms. Otherwise, he'll assume that my plusone will be staying with me."

"Yes, of course. I'll take care of it." After a beat of anxious energy, she said, "I better get back to work."

"You *are* working."

"I meant on something other than the arrangements for Lena's party. You have other commitments besides that." His calendar was filled with business dinners and charity events and city council meetings.

"I don't know what I'd do without you. You're good at keeping me organized."

"I'm just doing my job." But even so, this discussion seemed oddly personal. She hoped that she wasn't making a mistake by going to the Caribbean with him. How was she going sit beside him on the beach, wearing nothing but a swimsuit?

Just as she thought about the part of their trip when they'd be scantily clad, the sun shifted in the sky and the light from the windows spilled into the room, brighter than before.

He stood there for a moment, in the afternoon glare, looking as gorgeous as ever, before he picked up the remote from his desk and closed the blinds.

"I'll talk to you later," she said, telling herself not to worry, even if she could feel him watching her, much too closely, as she walked out the door.

Jake pulled his Gullwing Mercedes coupe, one of the many classic sports cars in his collection, into a guest parking spot at Carol's apartment. He didn't believe in letting his cars sit around, all pretty and polished and untouched. It didn't matter how rare or pricey they were, he drove the hell out of them. He treated women with the same reverence and vigor. But Carol wasn't his lover, and he had no business being here. Still, he'd decided to stop by because he knew that she was meeting with the stylist today. He figured the appointment was over by now. Of course, he'd timed it that way on purpose. He was curious to see what Carol had chosen.

He was curious about all sorts of things about her. Jake had been having some crazy fantasies about his assistant.

Carol was a fascinating woman, with a sinful body and modest values. An enigma, if there ever was one. And damn if her good-girl nature didn't turn him on. It was weird, too, because proper girls weren't his usual type.

He'd never had the urge to pull someone into the fray, not the way he was doing with her.

Maybe it was because they shared similar backgrounds. Maybe that was why he was daring her to let down her guard and have a good time. Whatever the reason, he needed to curb his desire. He couldn't seduce her when they were on their trip. He absolutely, positively couldn't, no matter how tempting the thought was. Jake knew better than to cross that line with a woman who worked for him. Besides, she prided herself on being well-behaved and corrupting her would be wrong.

He glanced toward Carol's apartment. He'd never actually been inside her place before; he didn't make a habit of visiting his employees at their homes. He did own this building, though. It was one of his favorite properties. He gave her a discount on the rent, a perk that came with her job. But regardless of the deal they'd worked out, he wasn't her landlord, at least not directly. A management company ran the day-to-day operations and collected the rent.

Jake got out of the car and strode to Carol's door. She lived in a unit on the ground floor surrounded by foliage. Built in the 1930s, the complex boasted Spanish-style architecture and was within walking distance to restaurants, shopping centers and farmers' markets.

He rang the bell, and she answered the summons with a surprised expression.

"Jake? What are you doing here?"

"I just thought I'd check on how the fashion meeting unfolded." He gestured jokingly to his ensemble. "Not that I'm the epitome of style today." He was attired in a plain white T-shirt, jeans and scuffed leather boots. "These are snazzy, though." He removed his sunglasses. They were the pair she'd given him last Christmas, similar to the kind James Dean used to wear. They were even trademarked with the actor's name.

She looked him over. "In that getup, you really could be him."

"Oh, sure." He mocked the comparison, even if he was flattered by it. "Maybe I should get a Porsche like his, the one he smashed himself up in."

She sucked in her breath, as if the wind had just been knocked out of her. "You shouldn't say things like that."

"I was just goofing around." And being stupid, he supposed. He should've known that she wouldn't think his comment was funny. "It was a great car, a 550 Spyder that he was driving on his way to a race. That's a pretty good reason for me to get one."

She stared at him, unmoving, unblinking. "I'd prefer that you didn't."

He leaned against the doorjamb, trying to ease the tension.

"Are you going to invite me in to see your clothes?" For now, she was wearing shorts and a loose-fitting khaki shirt, with her strawberry blond hair fastened into a ponytail at her nape. He imagined undoing the clip and running his hands through it. She had the silkiest-looking hair, with each piece always falling into place. Not that he should be thinking about messing up her hair. He was supposed to be keeping those types of thoughts in check.

"Yes, come on in." She stepped back to allow him entrance. The brightly lit interior featured hardwood floors and attractive window treatments. She'd decorated with art deco furnishings from the era of the building, mixed with crafty doodads. He noticed a patchwork quilt draped over the sofa. He knew she liked to sew. Sometimes she gave the quilts she made to the other women in the office, for birthdays and whatnot.

"You've done a nice job with the place," he said.

"Thank you." She had yet to relax. She still seemed bothered by what he'd said earlier.

Now he wished he could take it back. Not his interest in the Porsche, but the way he'd joked about it. He hooked his sunglasses into the V of his shirt, and she frowned at him.

"Do you race cars because you have a death wish?" she asked, rather pointedly.

Cripes, he thought. She had it all wrong. "I do it to feel alive." Everything he did was for that reason. "I don't want to look back and regret anything."

"I hope that's the case."

"Believe me, it is." After waiting for the smoke to clear, he gestured to the quilt. "When I was a kid, we had one sort of like that hanging on our living room wall that my paternal grandmother made."

Carol inched closer to him. "You did?"

He nodded. "She died before I was born, but the design was associated with her clan."

"Do you still have it, tucked away somewhere?"

He shook his head. "It disappeared when I went into foster care. It was sold, I suppose. Or given away, or whatever else happened to my family's belongings." He glanced at the fireplace mantel, where he spotted a framed photograph of what he assumed was her family: three towheaded girls and a forty-something mom and dad, posing in a park.

He picked up the picture and quietly asked, "Are you in this?"

"Yes," she replied, just as softly. "I'm the older sister. I was about ten there."

He studied the image. Everyone looked happy. Normal. Like his family had been. But he didn't keep photos around. He couldn't bear to see them every day.

Jake was lucky that he'd bonded with Garrett and Max. They'd been a trio of troubled boys in foster care who'd formed a pact, vowing to get powerfully rich and help one another along the way. The goal had ultimately allowed them to become the successful men they were today. Without Garrett and Max, Jake would've wanted to die, for sure.

He wondered if anyone had helped Carol get through her grief or if she'd done it on her own. They rarely talked about their pasts. Jake didn't like revisiting old ghosts, his or anyone else's, but he was doing it with her now.

"It's a nice picture," he said, placing it back on the mantel. "It must have been a good day."

"It definitely was. It was taken at my dad's company picnic." Her voice remained soft, loving. "We all had a great time that day, especially my sisters. They were only a year apart and were really close. Sometimes people mistook them for twins, and they always got a kick out of that."

"I had two sisters, too. Only, they were older. I was their pesky little brother."

Her light green eyes locked on to his. "How old were you when…?"

"Twelve. How old were you?"

She let out her breath. "Eleven."

His heart dropped to his stomach. He knew that her family had died from carbon monoxide poisoning from a faulty appliance in their home. But he didn't know the details. "How did you survive when the rest of them didn't?"

"I wasn't there. I was at a neighbor's house. It was my first slumber party. I was younger than some of the other girls, so my parents were hesitant to let me go, but I begged them, so they gave in." She breathed a little deeper. "Not being home that night saved my life."

"It was different for me. I was in the car when it crashed. The impact was fast, brutally quick, but I remember it in slow motion." It had been like an out of body experience that never ended. "I have a scar." He pushed back the pieces of hair that fell across his forehead. "Here, just below my hairline. It was noticeable when I was young, but it's faded over the years."

She approached him and reached out to touch the scar, running her index finger along the pale line. She was painstakingly gentle, and it made him want to kiss her. They were standing so close he could've leaned forward and captured her mouth with his. But he didn't take the liberty. They stared at each other instead, steeped in a strange kind of intimacy.

"I'm glad you survived the accident," Carol said, smoothing his hair across his brow.

"So am I." But before things got unbearably awkward, Jake stepped back, trying to restrain the tenderness between them. "After the crash, I used to pray to Uncta, a deity from Choctaw mythology who steals fire from the sun. I was the only one who was rescued from the car before it went up in flames."

"Did you think Uncta had saved you?"

"No, but I wanted to steal fire, too. To have his powers."

But that wasn't going to help Jake now. He'd already jumped straight from the frying pan and into the flame, feeling things for Carol that he wished he didn't feel. He still wanted to kiss her, as passionately as he could.

Two

Carol wondered what had gotten into her, touching Jake the way she had. She shouldn't have traced his scar or tried to subdue the unruly strands of his hair. Those types of things were reserved for lovers, not your boss.

But she wasn't going to apologize. That would only draw attention to what she'd done. She could already feel the discomfort it had caused.

Breaking the silence, she said, "I'll go get my new clothes so you can see them." It was the purpose of his visit, after all. But she wasn't going to offer to model them for him. That would be way too weird.

Carol dashed into her room and grabbed the garments.

She returned to the living room and laid them out on her couch. She went back for the accessories, and then lined them up on the coffee table.

"That's a cool bounty," he said.

Yes, it was, with at least two different outfits per day,

along with shoes, purses and beach bags to match. "I have you to thank for it."

"As long as you're happy with everything." He reached for a hanger with a flowing fabric draped around it. "What's this?"

"That's my party dress. It's a sarong." It was made from the finest silk in the world, decorated with a hand-painted design and trimmed in shiny glass beads.

"The material is beautiful, but how does it work?"

"There are lots of different ways to wrap it. Millie showed me how she thinks it will best suit me. This goes with it." She grabbed a big sheer scarf and swished it back and forth. "It's called a body veil. It goes around the dress for a fluttery effect."

"A body veil." He spoke softly. "That even sounds pretty."

She forged ahead. "Both pieces are from a Brazilian designer who just exploded onto the scene." She'd already memorized his name in case anyone at the party asked who she was wearing. "Millie said that they don't use beach towels in Rio. Instead, they lay a sarong in the sand and the women use them as cover-ups, too. But you probably already know that since you go there every year for Carnival."

Before she envisioned him doing wicked things in the streets of Rio, she quickly added, "My outfit was created as an evening gown and is much fancier than the sarongs they use at the beach. It's from the designer's most recent collection and hasn't even hit the stores yet. So I was wrong about not wearing something straight off the runway."

Jake put down the dress, treating it gently. "It has a romantic quality."

She supposed it did, especially with the inclusion of

the body veil, but dang if she could come up with an appropriate response.

Was Jake as attracted to her as she was to him? Was that even possible? It was sure starting to feel like it.

He was now eyeing her new bikini. It wasn't an itty-bitty, stringy thing, but the design was nonetheless sexy. Millie had talked her into it, saying that the low-cut top and high-waist bottoms showed off her curves. Thankfully, Carol already had a bit of a tan from hanging out at the pool. It wasn't summer yet. It was still spring, when the Southern California weather varied from day to day, so sometimes she cheated and used a tanning bed at the salon, preparing for the hotter months ahead. However, she was cautious about not overdoing any type of UV exposure. She never did anything in excess.

Jake did, though. He was the king of indulgences. She couldn't imagine two people being more opposite, aside from the loss of their families, which had been their tie from the beginning. She'd first met him when she'd applied for a job at his Caring for Fosters Foundation, the organization he, Garrett and Max had created that provided financial and emotional support to foster children. She hadn't gotten the job, as her experience in nonprofits was limited. But Jake had made it up to her, offering to hire her as his personal assistant, a position that was also up for grabs at the time. And now, here she was, two years later, trapped in feelings she couldn't quite define.

"I should put everything back," she said. She wanted that bathing suit out of sight, out of mind. Which was foolish, she knew, considering that eventually he was going to see her in it.

"I can help."

"That's okay, you don't have to."

"Really, I don't mind."

"All right." Carol gave in. Otherwise, letting him handle her belongings might seem like a bigger deal than it was, even if it was making her nervous.

With both of their arms full, he followed her down the hall. They entered her room, and she placed her load on the bed.

He followed suit, then said, "It's girlie in here."

"I guess it is, to some degree." Along with textured wood furnishings, the decor consisted of dried flowers, lacy pillows and a tufted headboard upholstered in blue velvet. "But what can I say?" She made a goofy joke. "I hit like a girl, too. So you better watch out."

He laughed. "There's no such thing as hitting like a girl. My sisters used to pummel the crap out of me. But most of the time, I had it coming."

She teased him. "You were a troublemaker even then?"

"I used to embarrass them in front of their dates, telling the guys stupid things about them."

She kept up the banter. "Remind me not to have you around when I go on my next date."

His expression sobered. "I wouldn't do that to you, Carol. I'm not a kid anymore."

Boy, didn't she know it. He was about as grown-up as a man could get, tall and strong, with the deepest, darkest brown eyes. When he smiled, they twinkled, but when he was being serious, like now, those eyes could pierce a part of your soul.

Anxious to get him out of her room and back to neutral ground, she said, "I never even offered you anything."

He raised his eyebrows. "Anything?"

"A refreshment." She knew that he favored seltzer water, with ice and a twist of lemon. She did, too, a habit she'd picked up from him.

"A refreshment? Who says things like that?" A smile

returned to his face. "Except for those old TV sitcom housewives. All you need is a ruffled apron to complete the picture."

"Smarty." She shrugged it off. "Maybe I was born in the wrong era."

"Maybe I was, too. Only, I would be a greaser." He slipped on his sunglasses, peering at her from beneath the tinted glass like a rabble-rouser. "Me and my fast cars."

She'd never been to one of his races, but she'd gotten used to knowing where he went, who he socialized with, even which women he took to bed.

Was it any wonder she was antsy about him being in her room? She'd spent far too much time beneath her covers thinking about the hot and sexy things his lovers sometimes said about him. One overzealous starlet had even blogged about her naughty escapades with him. Of course, he wasn't the only playboy who'd rung this woman's bell or who'd been mentioned in the blog. But he was the only one Carol cared about.

"So, do you want something to drink?" she asked.

He removed the glasses. "Sure."

They went into the kitchen, and she poured the drinks. When they returned to the living room, she was still fighting her wayward thoughts.

She just hoped that she was able to relax and enjoy herself on their trip, without her fantasies going wild. Because there was nothing tame about the battle raging inside her or how badly she needed to contain it.

Time went by in a busy blur, and now Jake was sitting beside Carol on his private jet, en route to the Caribbean. Normally he slept on long flights, shutting out the boredom, but he was wide-awake on this journey, fascinated by every move his traveling companion made.

With her reddish blond hair falling against her summer-white blouse, she looked soft and pretty, framed by the intermittent clouds billowing past her window. She'd been peering out the glass for a while, gazing at the ocean.

Finally, she turned back to him. She wasn't a frantic flyer. But she wasn't as comfortable in the air as he was, either. The aircraft was too big to land on the private island where they were going, so they'd be landing on another island, then taking a helicopter to their final destination.

"I researched the Caribbean," she said.

"You did?" He leaned a little closer, getting a deeper whiff of the fragrance she wore. It smelled crisp and fresh, like grapefruit, mixed with summer greens. "For what kind of information?"

"All kinds." She exaggerated a shiver. "You should have seen the snakes and spiders and scorpions I uncovered. Luckily our island doesn't have any of those things, at least not poisonous ones. No crocodiles, either."

He shifted in his seat. "Did you think Lena would choose a location with all that?"

"I just wanted to be sure. I didn't want to get bitten by some scary creature."

If he could get away with sinking his teeth into her, he would do it. "We're going to be fine."

"I packed a first-aid kit, just in case. We still need to watch out for jellyfish and things like that."

The only safety precaution Jake ever packed was condoms. Of course he'd skipped them this trip since it wasn't going to be a romantic adventure. Then again, he probably had some stored away in the side zipper compartment of his luggage, where he normally kept them. But none of that mattered since he and Carol weren't going to be together. Nor should he even be thinking about it.

"Speaking of scary creatures," she said.

He snapped back to attention. "What?"

"You have lots of strange beings on you."

He glanced down. Clearly she was talking about his tattoos.

She gestured to his right arm, which was the one closest to her. "What's the spidery-looking thing in the middle?"

"That's a depiction of Uncta."

"The deity who steals fire?"

Jake nodded. "And he is a spider, of sorts. He was able to appear in both human form and as a giant bronze spider. In his human form, he would entertain in his big fancy lair and offer advice to his guests. He told prophecies, too."

She gave Uncta's image a tentative touch, using the very tips of her nails. "I wonder what advice he would give you." She followed the lines of the drawing. "Or prophecies."

"I don't know." Jake wished her fingers on his flesh didn't feel so damned good. He imagined her clawing his back with those neatly manicured nails.

She moved on to another one of his tattoos: a beautiful young woman draped in a white gown, her long black hair blowing in the wind. "Is she a deity, too?"

"Yes." He tried to focus on his answer, instead of how Carol was making him feel. "Her father is the god of the sun and her mother is the goddess of the moon."

"And what's her specialty?"

"She introduced corn to the people, providing the first seeds that led to the first harvest. Even today, she still wanders through cornfields, blessing the crops, looking like an angel from above. Or so the legend goes."

"And who is this?" Another question. Another touch.

One by one, he explained who each of the deities on his arms were. The two gigantic birds that created lightning and thunder. The hunting god who taught wolves how to howl. The female ruler of the swamplands who provided vegetation that was safe to use for medicine. Overall, he had ten mythical beings tattooed on his body, each with their own purpose. Carol seemed particularly fascinated with the human grasshopper goddess who ruled a subterranean world known as an earth-womb.

"She's the mother of the unliving," Jake said. "Not the dead, but the spirits who are waiting to be born."

"What's her name?"

"Eskeilay."

Carol repeated it, using the same rhythmic inflection he'd used. Then she asked, "Do you think your future children are with her, waiting to emerge?"

Jake shot her an incredulous look. "Seriously? Can you see me being a dad? There's no way I'm ever having kids."

"I suppose it was a silly question." She smiled like an imp. "But it seems like a waste of Eskeilay's powers, to just sit there on your arm in her bendy grasshopper pose, with her antennae poking out of her head, with no little Jacob Waters babies floating around."

"Listen to you, being funny." He rubbed the spot where Eskeilay was. It was starting to tingle, almost as if the goddess was coming to life. "It wasn't like that in the beginning. The first spirits waiting to be born weren't babies. They were just people, living in Eskeilay's world. But when it got too overcrowded, they evacuated, and on their way to earth, they accidentally trampled some grasshoppers, including Eskeilay's own mother. Needless to say, she was pissed. So the opening to earth was blocked, and the rest of the people trapped underground were turned into ants."

"Oh, that's just great. Now whenever I see an ant, I'm going to think of that."

"Sorry. But you know how mythology is. Something disturbing always happens. But in this case, it also explains how ants came to be and why they live in holes in the ground," he explained. "These stories are based on what I was told. There are other Choctaw myths that don't coincide with what I was taught. But that's common with folklore. Stories are apt to change, depending on who tells them, and my dad liked to put his own spin on them. Sometimes my mom even got in on it, adding little details." He paused in remembrance. "Mom was a blue-eyed blonde with French and English ancestry, but she used to joke around and say that was she part Choctaw. Or that she had been for nine months when she was pregnant with us kids. And that's what gave her the right to horn in on those stories."

Carol smiled. "That's cute."

"My dad thought so, too. They were this ridiculously happy couple. I used to think I was lucky because they didn't scream and fight like some of my friends' parents. Or they weren't getting divorced or whatever. Then they ended up gone in the worst possible way."

"I know just how you feel." She fell silent, her gaze locking on to his. Then she said, "Except that I want to get married and have children someday. That's really important to me."

"I figured as much." She struck him as the wifely sort. "You seem like you need all that homeyness. But I don't. For me, it's easier to be unencumbered."

"Yes, I can tell."

He glanced away, his thoughts slipping back in time

once again. "My sisters used to talk about the kinds of weddings they wanted to have." He frowned, his dead siblings' broken dreams burrowing uncomfortably in his brain. "They went on and on about how romantic it was going to be. But I suppose it's common for teenage girls to do that."

She heaved a heavy breath. "I can't even tell you how many times I thought about it when I was young, even before I was a teenager."

He envisioned her, a lonely little girl in foster care, longing for the big day. It made him want to comfort her, to make the child she'd once been feel better. But it made him want to pull away from her, too.

But even so, he asked, "What kind of men do you date?"

She sat a little more upright. "What type do you think?"

"Oh, I don't know." He turned cavalier. "Big hairy bikers?"

She rolled her eyes. "Come on, Jake. I'm being serious."

In spite of his joke, he wasn't feeling particularly humorous, either. "Okay, then how about nice, proper guys who would make good husbands?"

She folded her hands on her lap. All she needed was a pair of tidy white gloves to complete the ladylike picture.

"Exactly," she said.

Yes, he thought. *Exactly.* He already knew the answer before he'd posed the question. And now that she was being so prim and marriage-minded, all he wanted to do was get to the island and sweep her into the debauchery that had become his life.

Where nice, proper guys didn't exist.

Three

It was breathtaking, Carol thought. The mansion where she and Jake and the rest of the partygoers were staying was a sprawling French Colonial–style estate, amid a gorgeous sandy white beach.

The caretakers, an older couple local to the area, escorted Carol and Jake to their rooms. Lena had brought the rest of the staff over from the States, along with a beauty team to provide in-room makeup, hair and nail services to her guests. Massage therapists could be had, as well.

No one had seen Lena yet. She wouldn't be making an appearance until the party. But she was the type who liked to make a grand entrance, so Carol wasn't surprised.

Carol's and Jake's rooms were located on the second floor and were next to each other, with adjoining doors in the center. For now they were open, making it one huge suite.

"We're going to have to lock those as soon as we get settled in," she said.

"We will," he replied, going onto his veranda.

Carol's balcony had the same view. But she joined him on his, standing beside him on the airy structure. Beyond the oasis-style pool was the ocean. In another direction, she spotted a mountainous terrain, surrounding a lush green glimpse of rain forest.

She thought it would be a wonderful setting for a destination wedding. The caretakers had already given them a bit of history on the custom-built mansion, which could be rented out for weddings. Not that she should be thinking about that. But after the discussion she and Jake had had on the plane, her mind was still immersed in marriage.

"It's beautiful here," she said as a breeze stirred between them.

Jake turned toward her. "You're not afraid of getting bitten by something scary anymore?"

"I already told you they don't have superscary things on this island." Except for him, she thought. The look in his soul-stealing eyes was filled with danger. Or lust. Or something she was too chicken to identify. He was actually giving her goose bumps.

He kept staring at her, and she crossed her arms to ward off the sexy chill.

Trying to stay focused on their schedule, she told him, "The caretakers said that the chef was making seafood for dinner, with lots of vegan dishes on the side for the people who prefer that." Their meals would be served in their rooms. After that, they could rest before they got ready for the party, which was scheduled for later that night.

He kept looking at her. "I'm getting a little hungry. Are you?"

She nodded. She definitely wanted to keep her mouth

busy. But she didn't have to wait for the meal. Baskets of fruit and nuts and other snacks had already been provided, along with fully stocked portable bars. A glass of wine sounded good about now. But Carol would be indulging in alcohol at the party, so she figured it was best to wait until then.

"Before I forget, I have something for you," he said. "I'll go get it."

She remained on the veranda while he rummaged through his luggage. He returned with a trim white box.

She lifted the lid and uncovered an elegant gold bangle encrusted with round-cut diamonds surrounded by multicolored stones. There was also a pair of starfish-shaped earrings, also glittering with diamonds.

Her pulse quickened. "They're magnificent, Jake." The pieces were going to look stunning with her dress. "Are they on loan?" She knew that jewelers sometimes let their rich and famous clients borrow from their inventory.

"No. I paid for them."

Oh, my. "You shouldn't have done that."

"I wanted to. Besides, I checked with Millie to see if you'd gotten any jewelry to go with your outfit, and she said that you hadn't."

"I didn't want to go overboard and spend more than was necessary." She gazed at the gems. "But this is way too much. I should return them to you after the party."

"Seriously? That doesn't make any sense. They were purchased to complement your wardrobe, and you're keeping the clothes. So why would you give the earrings and bracelet back? They're just part of the mix."

She studied each piece again. "They really are amazing."

"Don't be too impressed. I had Millie tell me what to get. I'm not good at giving women gifts."

That was true. Sometimes he even relied on Carol to decide on what type of flowers to send to his lovers. But she shouldn't have used that as a comparison, not with the way he was making her feel.

Had she made a mistake, coming on this trip with him? It was certainly the most impetuous thing she'd ever done.

She closed the box and held it against her chest, where her heart was thumping much too madly. She liked being in his company, far more than she should.

"So it's settled then?" he asked. "You're keeping the jewelry?"

"Yes, thank you. I'll accept it." What good would it do to argue the point, when she was already losing ground?

"I should go unpack now," she said.

He gestured to the pool. "Maybe I'll go for a quick swim before the food gets here."

She didn't want to think about him diving into the water in nothing but a bathing suit, but her imagination went haywire just the same. No doubt his naturally bronzed body would be a sight to behold.

Attempting to make a graceful exit, she said, "I'll see you when it's time for the party."

"I'll see you, too."

He didn't turn away and neither did she. They just stood there, immersed in each other. So much for a graceful exit.

Finally, she ended the connection and headed to her room, closing and locking the door on her side that separated their living quarters. She heard him close the door on his side, too, and turn the bolt.

Carol breathed a heavy sigh of relief, then glanced around at the glamorous antique furnishings and four-poster bed. Jake's room more or less mimicked hers, which didn't make it any easier, knowing he was on the other end of those adjoining doors.

She warned herself to stay away from her veranda in case he did go for a swim. Fantasizing about him was bad enough. She didn't need to watch him and become a voyeur, too.

As the evening progressed, Jake was more than ready to blow off some steam. After his swim, he'd eaten dinner. Then he'd fallen asleep, rumpled and naked. From there, he'd dragged his ass out of bed and taken a long, hot shower.

And now he was standing in front of the mirror in a designer suit, his hair styled in its usual way.

If he knew Carol, she'd probably been ready for hours. His assistant was an early bird, whereas Jake waited right up to the end to dash off to wherever he was going.

As if on cue, his phone beeped with a text. No doubt it was Carol, telling him it was time to leave. She always sent him reminders for everything.

He checked. Sure enough it was her. They agreed to meet in the hallway, outside their rooms.

She got there first, and as soon as Jake saw her, he marveled at her beauty. Her dress was wrapped in a stylish yet sultry way, complementing her voluptuous figure. It wouldn't take much to untie the sarong, either. A pull here, a tug there. The body veil that went with it was incorporated into the design, flowing softly, making her ensemble even sexier.

Her makeup was light and elegant, and her shoulder-length, blunt-cut hair was straight and shiny. The starfish earrings twinkled next to her face, and the bracelet shone at her wrist. Her skin had just the slightest hint of shimmer, too, especially around the swell of her cleavage. Or maybe that was where he noticed it most. He assumed it was from some sort of glittery lotion. Her strappy evening bag was small and delicate—the kind women carried when they danced.

"You look hot," he said. He stepped back to take another admiring glance. "Seriously, you could be a siren who roams the island, tempting guys like me to come out to play."

She flushed accordingly. "Thank you. But I'm not trying to tempt anyone, and you're always ready to play with some pretty young thing."

Not the way he wanted to play with her. "Don't worry. Tonight I'm going to be good."

Her gaze roamed over him. "Then I guess it's all right to tell you that you look rather hot yourself?"

Hell, yes, it was all right. He liked being in her sights, even if nothing was going to happen between them. "Millie brought a bunch of stuff to my house, too, and this is what I picked." Suddenly he realized his shirt was the same minty green color as Carol's eyes. He hadn't chosen it for that reason, at least not deliberately. But who knew what tricks his attraction to her was playing on his subconscious?

"Are you ready?" he asked.

"As ready as I'm ever going to be."

Was she still worried about fitting in with his crowd?

"Just hold on tight and have a good time."

"Hold on to what?"

"Me." He took her hand. "It's a couples-only theme, remember?"

She threaded her fingers through his. "I still can't believe I agreed to come here with you."

"It's too late to back out." He squeezed her hand. For now she was his plus-one, and he wasn't letting her go.

They took the staircase to the main ballroom on the first floor. Already, they could hear the thumping base of music from a DJ's turntable.

The white-pillared ballroom exploded with color and flair. The couples-only theme was expressed in enormous paintings and life-size statues that had been commissioned specifically for the party, with depictions of legendary lovers, throughout the ages, entwined in a variety of emotional embraces.

A huge flat-screen monitor projected images that complemented the music, and scattered throughout the marble dance floor were gilded cages big enough for two, where couples could go inside and dance with each other. Jake thought it was intriguing. He didn't know if Carol would agree to do that with him, but it wouldn't hurt to ask when the moment felt right. It was just a bit of fun, after all. They were supposed to enjoy the festivities, and those cages were part of it.

The birthday girl wasn't there yet. Clearly, Lena wasn't quite ready to splash onto the scene and make her debut. Most of the guests had arrived and were partaking of food, drink and dance. A gourmet buffet offered lavish hors d'oeuvres and frothy desserts. Although Jake was still full from dinner, the pastries sure looked good.

"Good grief," Carol said. "This is something else."

Jake continued to hold her hand, giving her time to settle into the environment. A three-tiered fountain filled with ice was large enough to bathe in, with pink lemonade spilling from the spigots. Champagne was being served as well, delivered by waitstaff garbed in French Colonial attire to match the mansion. There was a huge aquarium bar, too, stocked with angelfish and tended by bikini-clad bartenders wearing blue wigs and fluffy white wings. Indoor and outdoor tables were available, with figurine candles shaped into historic couples as the centerpieces. The party was an eclectic mix of whatever appealed to Lena's imagination.

After Jake and Carol took the champagne that was offered to them, she said, "I don't know where to begin."

"Anywhere you want."

She sipped her drink. "I think I'd like a pastry to go with this."

"That sounds good to me." He escorted her to the buffet and grabbed a treat for himself, too.

She wanted to eat outside, so they went onto the courtyard and sat with a few other couples who'd also decided to start their evening off outdoors. Jake introduced Carol to them. He knew most of the people in attendance.

While Carol chatted with Lena's songwriting partner and his wife, Jake studied the Napoleon and Josephine matchbooks that were on the table. The candle was a likeness of them, too, with their names scrolled across the bottom of the stand. He went ahead and struck a match and lit the wick. The wax emitted a rose scent.

Carol turned toward him, and they watched it burn together. Then she said, "Did you know that Josephine's birth name was Marie-Josèphe-Rose? And that she went by Rose until Napoleon started calling her Josephine?"

"No, I wasn't aware of that." But the rose scent was making a bigger impact now, getting stronger as the candle burned.

"She was born in the Caribbean on the island of Martinique. I came across references to that area when I was researching the islands around here, too."

He smiled. "And now we're sitting at Napoleon and Josephine's table, with you sharing your research with me."

She returned his smile. "Sometimes I overdo things like that."

"Yes, but what an interesting conversation it's turning out to be." He was fascinated by the details she'd provided. She looked beautiful in the candlelight, too, against the backdrop of sand and surf on the other side of the courtyard.

The songwriter interrupted, announcing to the entire group, "We should all go inside now. Lena will be appearing shortly."

"Do you know how she'll be making her entrance?" Jake asked.

"Yes, but she'd kill me if I spilled the beans." The other man took his wife's arm. "We'll see you in there."

"Sure." Jake wished he could stay where he was. He was enjoying being out here with Carol.

"I guess we better head in, too," she said after everyone else was gone.

"Yeah. I guess we better." They'd lingered long enough.

"Should we blow out Napoleon and Josephine?" she asked.

"You can do it."

She pursed her lips, and he watched her extinguish the flame, the candle's floral scent still drifting softly through the air.

Word got around that Lena was due to arrive, and the party buzzed with anticipation. Carol compared it to waiting for the stroke of midnight on New Year's Eve. Or a fireworks show on the Fourth of July.

Speaking of fireworks…

Jake stood beside her, his arm just barely grazing hers. She wanted to reach for his hand and hold it the way she'd done earlier, letting the excitement of touching him course through her veins. But she refrained.

Suddenly the blinds were closed on the French doors.

A moment later, the chandeliers went out, the ballroom going pitch-black. Carol moved closer to Jake, not wanting to lose him in the dark.

When the lights returned, it was in the form of spinning strobes and black lights, creating shimmering effects and completely changing the atmosphere.

The DJ's clothing and equipment shone brightly. Clearly, he was part of the show. Carol held her breath as one of the cages began to ascend from the dance floor, its cylindrical base rising on a hydraulic platform above the crowd. A man and woman were inside it, standing like statues. Their skintight jumpsuits glowed with graffiti-type artwork. They also had fluorescent streaks in their hair and makeup that illuminated their faces.

The DJ announced the caged duo, and the crowd cheered and clapped. It was Lena and her current boyfriend, Mark, who was one of her backup dancers.

Lena's "Couples Only" song began to play, and more cheers and clapping erupted.

Lena and Mark danced, moving rhythmically in a magical performance. Along with everyone else, Carol was riveted by the way they interacted with each other. Jake stared up at them, too.

As the song ended, the cage was lowered back down to the ground. The door swung open and Lena and Mark emerged, rushing into the crowd, where they were greeted with hugs and kisses.

The DJ played another of Lena's songs and everyone was encouraged to dance, with the black lights and strobes remaining on. Jake swung Carol into his arms, pulling her into the heat and passion of the dance.

She'd never experienced anything like this before. Her heart pounded in time to the music. The lyrics of the song were sexy, the beat feverish, with Jake's big broad body bumping against hers.

This was his world. This was the kind of fast-paced party he was used to attending. She felt like a newly sprouted flower that was about to be crushed. But God help her, she liked it, too.

Because of how much she liked Jake. Everything about him thrilled her. Scared her.

Jake was singing to the song while he danced.

She shouldn't have come here. She shouldn't be swaying like the siren he'd accused her of being.

Holy island hell. Some of the couples on the dance floor were kissing, tongues and all—mimicking Lena and Mark, who were making a rowdy spectacle of themselves.

Carol's skin went hot. She hoped that Jake didn't notice the sensual activity.

Unfortunately, he did. She could tell the very moment he became aware of what was happening. He stopped singing and actually bit down on his bottom lip. Carol was doing that, too, fighting the urge to join in and press herself against Jake and kiss the living hell out of him.

Finally, the provocative song ended. The next one wasn't so bad, even if the beat was still quick and thumping.

Carol didn't know how long they danced. They didn't stop until the lights returned to normal and the ballroom settled down a bit. Guests headed for the buffet or outside to catch some air.

Jake and Carol got two frosty glasses and filled them with lemonade from the fountain. She desperately needed to quench her thirst. So did Jake apparently. He practically guzzled his.

"We should go say hello to Lena," he said.

"Yes, of course." They hadn't wished her a happy birthday yet. "Where is she?"

"I think she and Mark are over there." He motioned toward the bar.

Yep, that's where Lena and her boyfriend were. As soon as Jake and Carol approached them, Lena dived straight into Jake's arms and gave him a sisterly hug. Mark, with his fluorescent-streaked blond hair and colorfully lined eyes, grinned at Carol and said hello. Up close, she saw that he was younger than Lena, by about five years or so. Lena was blonde as well, with a long, leggy figure and doll-like features, her eyes wide and her lips bowed. She came from a showbiz family. Her parents were well-known movie stars, albeit divorced now. Even her grandmother had been a go-go dancer in the sixties, which was where the cage inspiration had probably come from.

The pop star released Jake and shifted her attention to Carol. "Do I know you?" she asked. "You seem really familiar."

"We've met briefly a few times. I'm Carol Lawrence, Jake's assistant."

"Oh, that's right. Wow. You look spectacular."

"Thank you." Carol appreciated the compliment and how genuine it sounded. "So do you. It's a wonderful party, and your entrance was magnificent."

"It was fun. A girl only turns thirty once."

Carol nodded, and after a second of silence, Lena tugged her away from the earshot of the men. But by now, the guys were already engaged in conversation, so it didn't seem to matter, anyway.

"When did you and Jake start seeing each other?" Lena asked.

Carol quickly clarified, "We're not dating."

"Yet he brought you here? On a couples-only weekend?" Lena made a curious face. "Oh, come on. Who's
he trying to kid?"

"Really, it's no big deal." Carol downplayed her answer, especially with how badly she'd wanted to kiss him
on the dance floor. "He needed a date for the party, and
I was accessible because I work for him."

"Mark works for me, too. And now we're messing
around."

Carol didn't know what to say. The comparison was
making her terribly nervous. So she settled on, "Things
happen."

"Do they ever." Lena leaned in close. "I am rather
crazy about Mark. But who knows how long it will last?
I do have a reputation for being fickle."

Carol wagged her finger, a little playfully, a little seriously. "So I've heard."

The birthday girl laughed, making no apologies. "Life
is too short not to go after what you want. So whatever
you do, just have a good time this weekend. You might
even end up being crazy about Jake, too."

It was already too late for that. But still, Carol needed
to be careful not to go overboard. She didn't live by
Lena's free-spirited standards.

Their private discussion ended, and Lena went back
to her beau. Carol returned to Jake and he asked her to
dance again. Only now, the music was a little slower, a
little softer.

And more tempting than ever.

Four

As Jake led Carol toward the dance floor, he said, "How about if we go into one of the cages this time?" He wanted to give it a whirl.

She blinked at him. "You want to dance inside of one of those?"

"Sure. Why not? The cage Lena and Mark were in is free."

"I guess that would be okay." Carol sounded intrigued but tentative. "As long as it doesn't elevate like when they performed."

"That was just part of a show. They won't do that to us." He took her hand as they neared the cage. "But just in case, you're not afraid of heights, are you?"

"No, but you better be kidding about the 'just in case' part."

"I was." He shot her a teasing smile. He couldn't seem to get enough of her this evening.

When they reached the cage, she entered first, and

he held back to study her. She looked like an exotic bird who'd just been captured, the beads on her dress winking in the light.

"What are you waiting for?" she asked.

"Nothing." He joined her inside and closed the gate.

Now that they were in there together, the space seemed tighter than he'd expected. Or maybe it just felt that way. But since the song was a ballad, it made sense for them to stand so close.

Jake took Carol in his arms, and they moved in unison, naturally compatible. They had chemistry, he thought. On and off the dance floor. In and out of the cage. She fit perfectly against him, making him want to hold her even closer.

He glanced at the big flat-screen monitor. Carol's gaze flickered to it, too. The video was a montage of movie star couples, from early Hollywood until now.

"It's funny how most of them didn't stay together," he said.

"Some of them lasted a lifetime," she replied, without missing a beat.

The lights in the ballroom went low. Even the images on the screen turned gentler, with famous wedding photos. Big frothy cakes. Long white dresses. Elegant brides and dashing grooms.

"This is beautiful," Carol said.

Was it? Jake wasn't sure. But in an oddly disturbing way, he was intrigued by the stimuli, too. It was exciting to feel what she was feeling, even if he didn't understand it.

"Maybe we shouldn't stay in here for too long," he said. The cage was starting to feel like a romantic prison, with no release in sight.

"Maybe you're right. This is getting…"

Her words drifted off, but he knew what she meant. By now, their bodies were so close they were plastered together like animals who were about to mate.

But worse yet was how the video had begun to change, morphing into film clips of love scenes, some sweet and pure, some iconic and classic, some offbeat and erotic.

"Yikes," Carol said as a bondage scene appeared.

Yeah, Jake thought. *Yikes.* It actually involved a cage. And blindfolds and all sorts of unexpected things. Trust Lena, he thought, to toss something kinky into the lovey-dovey mix.

"Let's go," he said.

Carol avoided the video, looking straight at him instead. "Where to?"

"Anywhere but here." He pushed open the gate, and they dashed out of their shiny gold confinement. They kept moving until they were outside breathing the cool night air.

But once they were in the courtyard, they both just stood there, trapped within their own private hell.

"Now what do we do?" she asked.

"I don't know." He paused to think about it. "Maybe we could go for a walk on the beach. I could really use some time away from the party."

"So could I."

He got another idea. "How about this? We can grab some food and drinks to take with us."

"That sounds nice. But how are we going to haul everything out to the beach?"

"I'll tip a waiter to pack it up for us. I'll ask him to supply a blanket or some towels or something, too." He flashed a silly grin. "Then again, maybe we can just use your dress."

She smacked his shoulder, and they both burst out

laughing. It felt good to laugh. It felt good to be preparing for a picnic, too. Even if it was at night. On a tropical island.

With no one else around.

Carol walked along the beach, carrying her shoes and enjoying the sand between her toes. She looked over at Jake. His pant legs were rolled up, and he was carrying his shoes and a big square basket, filled to the brim. The waiter had even tossed in a candle from one of the tables.

"How far out are we going to go?" she asked.

"How about here?" Jake chose a spot on the other side of the estate, close enough to provide light from the mansion, but still far enough away so that the party didn't interfere.

"It's perfect." Being around so many other people, with all of that sexy activity, had been taking its toll. She was grateful for the reprieve.

Jake spread out a big fluffy beach towel and placed the basket beside it. He removed the candle, stuck it in the sand and lit the wick.

Carol sat on the towel. He joined her and handed her a champagne glass. He uncorked the Dom Pérignon and poured it.

"To peace and quiet," he said.

"The solitude is wonderful." She sipped her drink and glanced at the wax figurines. "Who was that candle fashioned after?"

"I don't know, but it smells like vanilla."

"Yes, I noticed that, too." It was a nice, pleasant aroma, mixed with the sea.

"Let's find out who they are." He lifted it up and squinted at the names across the bottom of it. "Oh, here we go. It's Robert Browning and Elizabeth Barrett Browning. I don't know much about them, do you?"

"Not really. Other than he was a playwright and they were both poets. Oh, and that they were married. I think they met through letters they exchanged."

"That's more than I knew."

"I took an English literature class in college, and I guess some of it stuck with me." Carol had a business degree from a state college that she'd funded with student loans. "It was weird, being a foster kid and trying to figure out my education. As soon as I turned eighteen, I didn't even have a place to live. But thank goodness the laws are changing now and some kids are able to stay in their foster homes until they're twenty-one."

"That's definitely a change that needed to happen. But it only involves a handful of states. Lots of foster youth are still homeless at eighteen. But I was lucky in that I was able to crash on Garrett's couch. He was back with his mom by then."

Carol nodded. Garrett wasn't orphaned like her and Jake. He'd bounced in and out of foster care because his single mother had gotten terribly ill from an infectious disease and wasn't able to care for him. At the time, she'd already been struggling with an autoimmune disorder. Although she recovered from the infection, the chronic illness continued to plague her, even now.

Jake added, "Without Garrett and his mom, I would have been totally displaced, graduating from high school with nowhere to go."

"Where was Max?"

"He was still in foster care."

"Oh, that's right. He's a little younger than you and Garrett. But you've all come a long way."

"That's for sure. Max made it first, though, being the nerd that he is."

Carol smiled, amused by Jake's description of his foster brother. Max was a self-taught software designer and internet entrepreneur who'd become a billionaire in his early twenties. But even so, she thought he was too handsome to be called a nerd. Then again, he did seem a bit socially awkward at times.

Jake said, "Max loaned Garrett and me the money to get our businesses off the ground. We couldn't have done it without him."

"The bond between the three of you is amazing." Max's childhood had been especially troubling, from what she understood. "Where is he? I haven't seen him around lately."

"He went on a long holiday or sabbatical or whatever he's choosing to call it. I guess he needed some time alone. He can be elusive when he wants to be."

Unlike Jake, she thought, who lived his life out in the open.

"Are you cold?" he asked as a breeze kicked up. "I can give you my jacket."

She wasn't freezing by any means, but there was a bit of a chill in the air. "That would be great. Thank you."

He removed the garment and draped it around her shoulders.

Then he unpacked the food and made up a plate for her. "This looks good, doesn't it?"

"Yes, it does." She balanced the china on her lap, feeling warm and cozy with his jacket against her body.

Jake filled his plate, too, and they nibbled on an assortment of fancy appetizers and decadent desserts.

"It's a yummy combination," she said.

He met her gaze. "And we couldn't ask for a nicer

setting, surrounded by the moon and the stars. You sure look pretty out here. But you've looked pretty all night."

"Even when I was a nervous wreck in the cage?"

"Yes, even then. I shouldn't have suggested that we dance in there."

"It's okay. You didn't know how it would turn out." She polished off her champagne. She had no intention of getting drunk, but a little buzz wouldn't hurt, especially with the way Jake was staring at her. She was curious to know more about him. Things she shouldn't want to know. Things she shouldn't ask. But she questioned him, anyway. "Do you do that type of stuff?"

He put his plate aside. "What stuff?"

"Like what was in the video." She refilled her glass, waiting to see what he would say. She'd heard that he was wild in bed, but no one had ever said just *how* wild. Not even the starlet who'd blogged about him had included those types of details.

"Bondage? No, I'm not into that." Without taking his eyes off her, he added, "Why…are you a secret dominatrix or something?"

If she wasn't so enraptured with him, she would have laughed. "Are you kidding? Me being a secret anything is preposterous. I just like regular sex."

"Truthfully, I was kidding. But I like it regular, too. Only, I think they call it vanilla in that lifestyle." He gestured to the vanilla-scented candle. "Like that."

Had she actually started this conversation? She put down her champagne and reached for a scone that was glazed with white icing. "This is vanilla."

Jake shifted on the towel, moving a little closer to her. "I don't think I got one of those."

"I can share it with you." She held it out to him, caught in a trap of her own making.

He took it from her, his fingertips touching hers, creating a soft stream of electricity between them.

While he bit into the pastry, she watched him, anxious to have it back, to put her mouth where his had been.

"It's good," he said.

Too good, she thought when her turn came. They continued to pass it back and forth. Carol couldn't deny that it felt like foreplay.

"What are we doing?" he asked when she finished the last bite.

"Something we shouldn't be doing," she replied. But it felt too incredible to stop.

As he leaned in to kiss her, she was thrilled, hungry for the taste of him. Their mouths came together in a burst of passion, their tongues meeting and mating.

When they stopped to catch their breaths, the candle flickered, its vanilla scent swirling around them. He took her plate off her lap, put it next to his and then moved in for the kill, nudging her down.

Again, she was too enthralled to stop him. She wanted him as close to her as possible.

He laid down on top of her, and they kissed like forbidden fiends, the sound of the ocean roaring in the distance. Carol's dress fanned out beneath her, the body veil twisting up with the towel. Jake's jacket was beneath her, too, where it had fallen off her shoulders.

He tasted like the pastry they'd shared. She probably tasted that way to him, too—sweet, sugary, filled with warmth and flavor.

She loved the weight of his body against hers, the hardness pressing down on her. Needing more, she wrapped her arms around him, trailing her hands along his spine, feeling the fabric of his shirt.

"I have fantasies about you clawing my back," he said.

"I've imagined all sorts of erotic things. Even biting you."
He nibbled at her ear, tugging on her lobe with his teeth.
"I shouldn't want you like this, but I do."

"I shouldn't want you, either." She knew better. She
was his employee. His assistant. The woman who was
supposed to be so proper and composed.

His breath rushed out. "I'm so turned on right now."

"So am I." She could barely think straight.

Jake kissed her again, all rough and sexy and dark,
his lips ravishing hers. Then he lifted his head and stared
at her. Carol stared at him, too, her heart threatening to
jump out of her skin.

Neither of them moved. If they kept going, they would
end up naked in the sand, tearing each other apart.

Hot vanilla sex.

She wanted to be with him, but she couldn't let it
continue, not like this. She needed to catch her breath,
to clear her mind, to behave like the rational person she
was.

"We need to stop," she said. Beneath her dress, her
nipples were tingling, and her panties were sticking to
her skin.

He sat up, his voice raspy. "I'm sorry. I didn't mean
to—"

"It wasn't your fault." Carol sat forward as well, and
grabbed his jacket from where it had fallen. She put it
on, needing to cover up. "We both got carried away."

He frowned in the candlelight. "We should go."

She cuffed the too-long sleeves, trying to make the
jacket fit her a little better. "Go where?"

"Back to our rooms. To call it a night." His frown
deepened. "Unless you want to return to the party."

She cleared her plate and wrapped the uneaten food.
"Goodness, no. I'd rather try to get some sleep."

"Yeah, it's probably getting late, anyway." Jake dumped out the rest of the champagne and put the empty bottle back in the basket.

Together, they cleared the evidence of their picnic, but the memory of their kisses remained, warm and wild on her lips.

He squelched the flame on the candle, pressing it between his thumb and forefinger. A moment later, he tucked the Victorian poets next to the empty bottle.

They trailed across the sand, heading for the mansion.

Once they reached the main entrance, they put on their shoes and made their way to the second floor.

As they stood in the hallway outside their rooms, she said, "We're here." It was better than saying nothing.

He set the basket on the ground, but he didn't respond.

In the silence, she attempted to smooth her mussed hair. She could still feel the excitement of lying beneath him. Was she an idiot for having stopped it?

"My key is in my jacket," he said.

"Oh, I'm sorry." She removed the garment and handed it to him, hating to let it go. She liked being snuggled up in something that belonged to him.

"Thanks."

"You're welcome." Carol's key was in her purse. She tried for a smile. "It was quite a night."

He smiled, too. "It was, wasn't it?"

She nodded, quietly confused. "I've never really had an affair," she found herself saying. "I've only been with men I was involved with."

"You don't have to explain. I understand. That wasn't even supposed to be an issue."

"I know. But we still have two more days of hanging out together, and I don't want it to be awkward."

"I should have considered the couples-only thing a

little more carefully. But I guess I just wanted to spend some time with you."

She'd had a crush on him for a long time. If she slept with him, would it get better or worse? She honestly didn't know. "I need to go." Before she did something crazy.

He waited while she unlocked her door. The key wasn't the electric card kind. It was the old-fashioned, fit-in-the-hole type. She struggled to make it work, but only because her hands were shaking.

"Do you need help?" he asked.

"No, I've got it." She finally managed. "Good night, Jake."

"Night, Carol."

She went into her room and closed the door, her pulse skittering, her emotions hanging in the balance. She flipped on the light, feeling more alone than ever.

And wishing that he was there with her.

Five

Carol didn't get ready for bed. She didn't get undressed. She didn't do anything, except battle her hunger for Jake.

Was Lena right in what she'd said? Was life too short not to go after what you wanted? Carol was beginning to think so. Or her libido certainly was.

But could she actually go through with it? And what about Jake—was he still willing? Or had he come to his senses?

She touched a finger to her lips, recalling the taste of his kisses. Should she text Jake to see how he was faring? And if she did, what should she say?

Something honest, she decided. Something to remind him that she was on the other side of those double doors.

Right. As if he was likely to forget.

She retrieved her phone and typed, Can't stop thinking about you. Then, with her heart in her throat, she hit the send button. At least she was facing her feelings.

She waited, hoping he was near his phone and hoping she'd done the right thing. She didn't have to wait long.

He answered, Me, too. About u.

Bubbling up inside, she felt like a teenager conversing with her longtime crush. She hastily wrote, Don't know what to do about it.

He replied, Are u in bed?

No. Still in my clothes.

So am I. Except my shirt.

Carol imagined how he looked, bare-chested and tousled from the beach, tapping out intimate little things to her.

This is weird, she texted him.

I know. Really weird. But I like it.

Me, too. Sort of seems like we're sexting.

Yeah, it does. A second later, he asked, If I invited u to my room, would u come over?

Her pulse jumped. But just to be sure that he meant what he said, she inquired, Do you want me to come over for real? Or are we only fantasizing about it?

He popped off a quick, Yes, I want u to come over. For real.

She released the breath in her lungs and replied, Give me a few minutes.

To think about it?

To come over. She didn't want to keep thinking about it. She just wanted to be with him.

He wrote, Excited to see u.

She was excited, too. And she wanted to look refreshed, to comb her hair and reapply her lipstick.

Before this went any further, she asked, Do you have what we'll need? They couldn't do this without protection.

Yes, he told her. It's not a problem.

Then I'll be there soon, she wrote.

I'll be waiting, he replied.

Unlock the door on your side, she reminded him.

I will came his reply.

If Carol was the brazen sort, she would untie the front of her dress, take a seductive selfie and send it to him. But she wasn't that kind of girl. Already, she was stepping outside of her comfort zone. But she wasn't going to back out. She was going through with this, no matter how nervous she was.

She went into the bathroom to freshen up, warning herself to relax. Not that it would change anything. Calm or nervous. Shy or bold. She was going to make love with her boss.

And she needed to be with Jake tonight. She needed to finish what they'd started at the beach, to feel his aroused body next to hers, to kiss him with unbridled lust, to rake her nails down his back.

Once she looked presentable, Carol walked over to the doors that divided them. A few breathless beats later, she crossed the threshold.

Jake was waiting for her, just as he said he would be. He looked tall and dark and stunning: wearing no shirt, no shoes, just his trousers. By now, she was barefoot, too.

Their gazes met, and he smiled, as if he was about to commit a secret little crime.

But he was, wasn't he?

Mesmerized, she moved closer. There were so many facets to that smile, so many ways in which it defined him.

"What kind of trouble did you get into?" she asked, reaching out to skim his jaw, her fingers igniting from the feeling.

He leaned into her touch. "What are you talking about?"

"When you were young," she explained.

He shrugged, lifting his shoulders, as if he were knocking the weight of her curiosity off them. "The usual."

To her, there was nothing usual about getting into trouble. She'd done everything in her power to toe the line, to be the kind of kid who didn't make waves. "Did you ever do anything really bad?"

"What do you mean? Like break the law?"

She nodded and waited for him to reply. She couldn't begin to guess if he had a juvenile record. At the moment, all she knew was how dangerous he still seemed, all grown-up.

"Yes," he said. "I got caught once."

"Doing what?"

"It isn't important now."

"It is to me." To understand the boy he once was, to make love with the sexually charged man he'd become.

He took her in his arms. "We can talk about it later."

He was right. This wasn't the time to discuss it. She closed her eyes, losing herself in the sweet flutter of letting him hold her.

Then Jake ruggedly whispered, "I want to strip you. Tell me I can. Tell me to do it."

With a jolt of excitement, she opened her eyes and looked into his. "Yes, do it. As fast as you want."

He didn't hurry, even if she'd just given him permission. Ever so gently, he removed the body veil that was draped around her dress. The fabric fell away, drifting to the floor. He continued his quest, untying the sarong. As he unwrapped the dress, she struggled to steady herself.

"It's okay," he said. "You won't fall. I've got you."

She was already falling, tumbling into a highly forbidden zone. He tossed her sarong over a chair, and Carol did her darnedest not to feel self-conscious, even if she was wearing nothing but a pair of beige silk panties.

Jake took her hand and led her straight to his bed. Her skin pulsed as she prepared for what came next.

As she lay there, amid his rumpled sheets, he said, "You're incredible."

So was he. Too incredible for words. She could barely believe that she was in his company, with him climbing on top of her.

He zeroed in on her nipples, teasing each one, going back and forth, moving his tongue in sexy little swirls. She thought she might die from the thrill of it.

He lifted his head and smiled. "Should I do it some more?"

Put his mouth on her breasts? "Yes, please."

"You're so polite. Such a good girl."

She didn't deny his claim, and this time, when he resumed the activity, she tunneled her fingers through his hair.

She sighed as he ran his hand along the waistband of her panties, teasing her, making her limbs quaver.

The lights were on, shining as bright as the sun. Only, it was dark outside, with stars dancing in the night.

He peeled her panties all the way off, and now she was naked, except for the earrings and bracelet he'd given her.

"What about these?" she asked about the jewels. "Should they come off, too?"

"No. I like how you look in them."

"I'm trying not to worry."

"About what? Keeping the jewelry? It's just a few little baubles."

"I was talking about how we're going to feel in the morning." She didn't want to regret what they were doing. But she feared there would be repercussions.

"Tomorrow doesn't matter. All that matters is tonight."

He gestured to the condoms he'd scattered on the nightstand. "I didn't pack these purposely. But am I ever glad that they were in my luggage."

She put her hands against his chest, where she could feel the strong steady beats of his heart. "They just happened to be there?"

He nodded. "From the last time I traveled. I even thought about it when we were on the plane. But I didn't think I'd be using them."

She trailed her fingers down his body. No doubt about it, there was going to be hell to pay later on. Anything this exciting would have consequences.

Once she reached his stomach, she followed the ripple of muscle along his abs. She was familiar with his workout routine and how disciplined he was about it. He'd built an employee gym at the office for everyone to use, himself included. He had a weight room at home, too. His main residence was a glittering estate in the Hollywood Hills, with a tennis court and a poolside view of the city. Carol had been there a number of times, either running errands for him or dropping off urgent documents for him to sign. And now she was exploring his half-naked body, with a different kind of urgency coiling inside her.

He unzipped his pants, but he didn't remove them. Nonetheless, she noticed that he wasn't wearing underwear. But she wasn't surprised. He seemed like a commando guy.

He said, "There are so many things I want to do to you."

Delicious things, she thought. He put his fingers between her legs, rubbing that one little spot, making her moan from the pleasure. Everything was warm and sexy, including the sheets beneath her skin. She moaned again, trying to contain herself.

He shifted his weight, his big, broad body casting a shadow over hers. Then he took the foreplay a step further, going down on her with his mouth.

She couldn't stop touching him while he did it: the breadth of his shoulders, the messiness of his hair, the handsome angles of his face. She even touched herself, where his tongue made contact. There were no bounds, no limits, just heat and primal hunger, shooting straight to her core, making her unbearably wet.

As the orgasm built, her nerve endings electrified. She was steeped in so many sensations, so many hungers, all at once.

Jake didn't stop until the last spasm racked her body, dragging her under his spell.

He kissed her afterward, barely giving her time to recover. But she didn't care. He took off his pants, and she saw that he was desperately aroused. She lowered her hand, closing it around him.

While she stroked him, he kissed her once again, heightening the passion. She tightened her grip, wanting to make him feel extra good. But all too soon, he reached for a condom. He was leaking at the tip.

When he extended the packet to her, she widened her eyes. "Why are you...?"

"Because I want to watch you put it on me."

"No one has ever asked me to do that before. Whenever I've been with someone, the guy always..."

"You know how, don't you?"

"Yes, of course. But you'd be better at it, I'm sure. Quicker. More efficient."

"It's not a contest, Carol." He smiled naughtily. "It's just a little fun between lovers."

She opened the packet, feeling as if she was all thumbs. But it was only because she was so darned anxious to be with him. By the time she managed to put the condom in place, he was harder than hard and sexier than hell.

And just like that, he nudged her legs apart and thrust into her, stealing what was left of her breath and making her want him even more.

Jake marveled at this moment, taking a second to process it. He was inside of Carol. His marriage-minded assistant. How crazy was that?

He thrust deeper, and she gasped, closing around him in hot, slick pleasure. This was sex at its most fundamental level, boiled down to raw need.

Need. The word punched him like a fist. Jake didn't know what was wrong with him, not having been able to control his hunger for her. She was right about tomorrow. They would have to figure things out. Normally he didn't concern himself with incidentals. But he was in bed with a woman who worked for him. That wasn't something that could be ignored.

But for now, morning was a ways away.

Taking what he wanted, what he craved, he kissed his newfound lover with heat and vigor. Twin moans escaped their lips. She wrapped her legs around him, and he moved his mouth to her neck and bared his teeth, nipping her skin.

Euphoria surged through him, so right, so wrong, so hot and pulsing. Was this how addicts felt when they slammed drugs into their veins?

Jake rolled over so Carol could straddle him. While she rode him, he touched her, cupping her breasts and thumbing her nipples. He liked how pink and pretty and pebbled they were.

She braced her hands on his shoulders, digging her nails into his flesh.

"Harder," he said.

With those neat lady's nails still sharply in place, she rode him deeper, doubling the euphoria. As she rocked forward, setting an erotic pace, a breeze from the window stirred the ghostly white curtains, sweeping air through the room.

Jake imagined that the sea was rising, crashing in orgasmic waves, coming closer and closer to the moonlit shore.

Caribbean fever, he thought. He had it bad.

"I promised myself that I wasn't going to seduce you this weekend," he said. "And now I am."

Her hair fell forward, soft and shiny around her face. "Yes, you definitely are. But I had a hand in it, too."

"Yeah, you did." She had sent him that text urging him to be with her. He switched positions again, gulping frantic breaths in between numerous kisses.

Once he was on top, he pounded her harder and faster. By now, she was clawing his back.

Was she leaving long, sexy scratch marks? Telltale

signs of passion? He hoped so. He wanted to be marred by her, to have every aspect of his fantasy fulfilled.

His skin was filled with fire, tattoos and all. Uncta was going into shape-shifting mode, and Eskeilay was hopping through the grass in her earth-womb.

"Don't stop," she said.

As if he could. He was on autopilot, moving like a sex machine, desperate to come.

So was Carol apparently. She met him stroke for stroke, maneuvering her body in ways that maximized the pleasure. Only, she seemed to be doing it naturally, unaware that she was so sexy. Jake actually envied the Goody Two-shoes who married her, simply because the lucky stiff would get to be with her every night.

"You're a hellcat in bed," he said.

Her voice went husky. "I'm not, not usually…"

"So I just bring it out in you?"

"I don't know." She clawed the crap out of him again. "Probably."

He gazed into her glowing green eyes. Was this how she would behave on her wedding night? Sweet and sensual and animalistic? "Your future husband can thank me later."

She writhed beneath him. "You're cocky, Jake."

He glanced down at where their bodies were joined. "So I am."

She followed his line of sight. "That isn't what I meant."

"Then why are you enjoying the view?"

"For the same reason you are."

Because being together was exciting. Because they both wanted to remember how it felt. How it looked.

Jake shifted his hips, making the moment hotter.

In. Out. Deep. Deeper.

Carol gasped, and a haze of hunger enveloped him, his body jerking, his erection pulsing, his vision glazing till he could barely see at all. She was falling, too, his orgasm triggering hers. Or maybe hers had jump-started his? He was too far gone to know.

Sensations slammed between them, and she clung to him, making breathy sounds in his ear. His personal assistant.

His *very* personal assistant, he amended.

When it was over Jake was beaded with sweat. He withdrew and dropped down on top of Carol, needing to drag as much air into his lungs as he could get. But what he got was the scent of sex, mingled with her citrus perfume.

She skimmed her fingers down his spine. Gone were her claws. There was just softness now.

"Am I hurting you?" he asked.

She nuzzled his shoulder. "Isn't it a little late to be asking me that?"

He grinned in spite of himself. "I meant, am I too heavy?"

"No, you're good." She traced his tailbone. "I'm not an itty-bitty breakable thing. I can take it."

He could have stayed there all night, luxuriating in her curves, except that he needed to get rid of the condom. "I'll be right back."

Jake got up and went into the bathroom to do his thing. When he returned, she was sitting forward in bed, with the sheet partially covering her.

"I should take a picture of you," he said. Beside her, the ghostly curtains were billowing again.

She tugged the sheet closer. "You better not."

It was tempting, to say the least. "You just look so

pretty, that's all." Mussed up and wearing the jewelry he'd given her.

"Thank you, but we don't need that kind of evidence from this night." She patted the space next to her. "Now, come back to bed."

"Yes, ma'am." He hopped into the spot she offered. "So what kind do we need?"

"What kind of what?"

"Evidence from this night?"

She butted her shoulder against his. "Smart aleck."

He shrugged, smiled, got closer to her. For the heck of it, he gave her a noisy kiss, and they slid down onto the pillows together.

"I'm not much of a cuddler," he said.

"Then you're doing a good job, considering."

He was trying. "You seem like the type who would like it."

She sighed. "I am. I do."

I do. He frowned at her choice of words, feeling the weight of them. Someday, she was going to find a nice, proper guy. Someday, she would become someone's honeymoon bride.

But for now she was in bed with Jake, snuggling against him, all warm and cozy, where they both knew she didn't belong.

Six

Carol awakened early. The room was bathed in soft morning hues. She noticed that the window was still open, but there was less of a breeze.

She'd slept soundly beside her lover. Too soundly, she decided. And now she was anything but calm.

She glanced over at Jake. Sometime during the night, he must have shifted onto his side because they weren't facing each other anymore. His back was turned and he was sprawled out, one leg inside the covers, the other one exposed, along with a portion of his naked butt.

Heaven almighty. What had she done?

A foolish question, if there ever was one. She knew darn well what she'd done. She'd gone into this with her eyes wide open.

She sat up and steadied her breath. She needed coffee, but first she was going to wash the remnants of makeup off her face, tame her hair and brush her teeth. Rather than trudge off to her bathroom without any clothes, she located her sarong and wrapped it around herself.

Just as she was preparing to slip away, Jake rolled over, nearly giving her a heart attack. She'd assumed he was dead asleep.

"Hey," he said with a graveled voice and a half smile.

"Hi." Did he have to look so good, so handsome and wild, with a bit of overnight beard stubble? "I'm going to freshen up, then make coffee. Want some?"

"Sure." He sat forward, dragged a hand through his hair and squinted into the hazy patch of sunlight that spilled over him. "I need to hit the head, too."

"Okay. I'll see you in a few."

As he climbed out of bed, Carol darted off and practically stumbled over her body veil. She picked it up, but she didn't take the time to look for her panties. Uncertain of what Jake had done with them after he'd peeled them off her, she would search for them later.

She continued to her room, and once she was standing at her bathroom mirror, she removed her bracelet. She'd actually slept in it. The earrings, too, so she took those off, as well.

Then, after she was fresh and somewhat tidy, with her sarong tied a little tighter, she prepared the coffee in the single-serve machine in her room, making each cup separately. She added sugar to Jake's, the way he liked it. This wasn't the first time she'd sweetened his coffee and it probably wouldn't be the last. But it felt different from before.

Everything did.

Because she'd had sex with her boss. Wild, delicious, sheet-tumbling, tongue-kissing, body-scorching sex.

She brought the coffee to his room, trying to keep her hands from shaking. Jake was back in bed, looking as if he'd splashed a bit of water on his face, too. He certainly seemed more awake. She handed him his cup, and he thanked her.

Instead of joining him in bed, Carol opted for a nearby chair. He was still naked, except that he had a pillow on his lap, to protect himself from the hot beverage, she assumed.

Struggling to stay focused, she sipped her coffee, a perfect brew for a nervous day—strong and rich and aromatic.

"Are you concerned about last night?" he asked.

Lying would get her nowhere. Besides, her emotions were probably written all over her face. "It definitely feels weird now that it's over."

"Yeah, it does. But we knew what we were getting into when we did it."

"That's for sure." They couldn't behave as if they weren't aware of their actions. "Morning was bound to come."

Falling silent, he let his gaze roam over her, his eyes dark and intense. Then he said, "I don't think it should end like this."

She blinked, not quite catching his drift. "What?"

"Us. The sex. We should keep doing it all weekend."

Confused, Carol debated what to say. She glanced at the nightstand, where the rest of the condoms were. "You want to do it some more, even though you agreed that it seems weird?"

"Ending it so quickly will make it even weirder. We might as well make the most of this couples-only thing. And there's no denying how hot we are together."

No, there was no denying it. She could still feel the forbidden thrill of their union. The warm, slick foreplay. The hard-driving rhythm. The orgasmic shivers.

Every moment was embedded in her brain. In her body. Even in parts of her soul. It had been the most exciting night of her life. But the most irresponsible, too.

Dare she repeat it over the next few days? "Are you sure we shouldn't just cut our losses now?"

"And do what for the rest of the time that we're here? Hang out at the beach and pretend it didn't happen? Better to embrace it, I think."

Her pulse jumped. "By getting naked again?"

"I'm already bare. And under that pretty dress of yours, so are you." He set his coffee aside. "Aren't you?"

"Yes." Her voice all but quavered. She hadn't put any underwear on this morning. She still had no idea where her panties from last night were, either. Maybe stuck in the bedcovers somewhere?

"So what's it going hurt?" he asked. "A weekend of fun, sun and great sex. Things could be worse."

"What about the other guests here? Are we going to try to hide it from them?"

"I don't see why we should. Besides, most of them probably already assumed that we were a couple, anyway."

She thought about her conversation with Lena and how it had influenced her to sleep with Jake to begin with. "Lena predicted it."

"She did?"

"When we talked at the party. But we can't let anyone figure it out when we get home. I can't handle people at work knowing."

"I agree. It'll be over as soon as we leave the island. We won't ever do it again, and no one at the office will be the wiser. It'll be our secret. But for now, I think we should enjoy each other's company." He held out his hand, beckoning her. "Come on, Carol. Indulge me."

Sweet mercy, she thought. He was just too charm-
ing to resist. As she left her chair and came forward, he
pulled her into his arms and kissed the living daylights
out of her.

She rolled over the bed with him, letting him untie
her sarong. He put his hands all over her naked body.
She did the same thing to him, exploring that gorgeous
golden-brown skin and those strong, sculpted muscles.
She couldn't stop touching him.

They'd both staked their claims, and now it was official. They were having a fling. A weekend rendezvous.
A mind-spinning affair.

"Take a shower with me," he said. "I want to get wet
with you."

She circled her arms around him, pressing her body
closer to his. "You're already making me wet."

He lowered his hand, spreading her, testing her, teasing her. "That goes with the territory."

She moaned from the pressure building between her
thighs. "A shower sounds amazing."

"Then let's go." He withdrew his fingers. "We can
finish this in there."

Carol wanted him to finish her, as many times as he
could. They sat up, and he removed a condom from the
nightstand.

She took stock of the inventory. "Do you have any
more of those in your luggage?"

He fisted the packet. "No, just these."

"There will only be three left after we use that one."

He smiled, then jerked his head, his hair falling across
his forehead. "That's not enough for two more days?"

She smiled, too, anxious to climb into the shower with
him. "I don't know. Is it?"

"I guess we're going to have to pace ourselves."

So far, they weren't doing a particularly good job of that. It wasn't even noon yet, and already they were gearing up for water-drenched sex.

They entered his bathroom, where the contents from his shaving kit were strewn about the counter. He'd left his toothbrush and toothpaste out, too, with the tube uncapped. Carol never did that.

Of course Jake had a housekeeper who came to his house at least once a week. He had a chef who put healthy meals in his fridge, too. He'd become accustomed to people looking after his needs.

But not always, Carol reflected. He was an orphaned child, just like her, a kid who knew what it was like to be alone, with barely anyone to care.

He turned on the shower, and as soon as it was warm enough, they stepped into the clear glass enclosure. The luxuriously designed stall was big enough for two, fitting them comfortably.

They took turns under the spray, and he helped her shampoo her hair. She'd never had a man do that for her before, and it felt wonderful. He soaped down her body, too.

Slow and sudsy.

Carol washed him as well, working her way down, until she was on her knees, rinsing him clean.

"Damn," he said, tangling his fingers through her wet hair.

She took him in her mouth. He was big and hard and getting harder with every stroke. She wasn't normally this bold, but she wasn't going to waste a second of their time together.

He moved with her, watching her, keeping his hands in her hair. But he didn't let her bring him to completion.

"My turn," he told her, changing places with her.

When Jake dropped to his knees, Carol shivered from head to toe. He was determined to make her come, and she was more than happy to let him do whatever he wanted.

Her boss had become her undoing, her vice, her craving, her full-blown, take-me, have-me, I'm-yours hunger. She didn't want to think about how difficult it was going to be when they went home, when it was over for good, so she tried to block that from her mind.

He used his hands and his mouth. He satisfied every yearning she had, being the beautifully skilled lover that he was.

The climax he gave her rocked her to the core. She shook and shuddered and gulped the steam that was rising.

Jake stood up and tore into the condom wrapper. He put on the protection hastily and slammed into her.

Carol was going to relive this encounter for the rest of her supposedly proper life. It would never fade into oblivion, not even in a million years. She memorized everything: the hammering motion, the pounding spray from the showerhead, the bar of soap that had fallen and was spinning around the drain.

"I've got you where I want you," he said, rasping the words, breathing heavily.

"I've got you, too." She raked her nails over every part of him she could reach, and he rewarded her with a rough groan, proving how much he liked it.

They kissed in wild desperation. They even clanked their teeth, making frantic love, their hips thrusting to a powerful rhythm.

Then he said, "I'm not usually a morning person."

She smiled, laughed, gazed at him through the thickness of the steam. "You could have fooled me."

He laughed, too, looking wild and boyish, yet warm and protective. He held her tighter, and she stopped clawing him, using her fingertips to soothe the places she'd scratched.

They kissed again, only not quite so brutally this time.

Somewhere in the middle of the mania was friendship. The knowledge, she supposed, that they shared a childhood bond. That they'd lost everything, and now they had one crazy weekend, wrapped up together in bouts of guilty pleasure.

His release was strong and convulsive, and Carol absorbed the friction when he came, taking everything he was, everything about him, into her body. Until there was nothing left but the sound of running water.

After the shower, Carol and Jake ordered breakfast and had it delivered to Jake's room. Carol was grateful that Lena had hired a staff that could be trusted, who wouldn't sell tidbits to the tabloids or take unauthorized pictures.

Of course, Jake wasn't a big-time celebrity. His "Beefcake Bachelor" status wasn't enough to make him a star. No one followed him around, the way they did Lena and some of her other guests. But thank goodness this weekend was private, either way.

"Do you want to eat outside?" he asked.

"Sure. Why not?" Carol thought it sounded nice and relaxing.

He carried the tray onto the veranda, and they sat across from each other at a glass-topped table. She gazed out at the view. The pool area was vacant, almost eerily quiet.

"I wonder if anyone else is even up yet," he said.

"Some of them are probably hungover from the party." She cut into her eggs. She'd chosen poached, topped with cheese, tomatoes and pesto. "And the rest of them might just be lazing around like we are."

"Yeah." He was eating a sausage and egg scramble. "We haven't even gotten dressed yet."

She nodded. Both of them were in their robes, and her towel-dried hair was still slightly damp. She'd combed it straight down, though. He'd only run his fingers through his, barely taming his thick dark locks. But his unkempt look was a part of who he was.

"So," she said, still curious to know about his youthful rebellions, "what did you get caught doing when you were young?"

He made a face. "I stole things. Mostly video games and DVDs and stuff like that. Sometimes I would nab a bottle of booze, just for the hell of it." He frowned at his food. "But my biggest thrill was lifting trinkets for the girls I liked. I'd have them show me what they wanted, then I'd go back on my own to steal it. That's what I got popped for. Taking this little diamond necklace from a department store."

She studied him in the balcony light, the way the shade played over his face. "The store pressed charges?"

"Yep. I was arrested for shoplifting."

"And now you buy women pricey gifts to make amends for what you did?"

He glanced up from his plate. "I never really thought about it that way, but I suppose I do." He paused, fork in hand. "Or maybe it just makes me feel good, being able to afford to give them pretty things."

Like the jewelry he'd given her, she thought.

"I started stealing about six months after my family died," he said. "I was so freaked out in foster care I could barely stand it. I needed something that made me feel alive. That gave me a sense of purpose, even if I knew it was wrong. I was fifteen when I got busted, so it had been going on for a while before I got caught."

Carol questioned him further, piecing his past together in her mind. "Did Garrett and Max know what you were doing?"

"Yes, but they didn't say anything to me about it. They had enough problems of their own."

"What happened after you got arrested?"

"I was put on probation. But I stopped stealing. Not because I got busted, but because my caseworker said that if I didn't get my act together, I would be moved to a group home, where the setting would be much more restrictive. And I didn't want to go someplace where I would be separated from Garrett and Max."

She sipped her orange juice. "So in a sense, they saved you? Just by being there?"

"They definitely did. We had our heritage in common, too, which also helped us stay together. We were placed in Native American foster homes, and there weren't all that many, compared to nonnative ones. The only way we were likely to be separated or never see each other again was if I screwed up and went to a group home." Jake had a thoughtful expression. "Soon after that, Max came up with the idea for us to band together. To work toward becoming megarich someday."

Carol considered the situation. "Max came from a really poor environment, didn't he?"

"Poor. Abusive. The works. He had all kinds of motivation to want to be rich and respected. So did Garrett, with how badly he wanted to keep a roof over his mother's head and keep her well. But me…? There was nothing I wanted, except my family back. But then I figured there was nothing wrong with having fancy houses and fast cars." He looked directly across the table at her, flirtation alive in his eyes. "And beautiful women, of course."

Heat unfurled in her loins. "Yes, of course."

"Sex was always an outlet for me. I was fifteen the first time it happened."

"The same year you got caught shoplifting?"

He nodded. "I was already sleeping with the girl I nabbed the necklace for. She was my first. What a rush that was, having a girl want me like that."

Carol wasn't surprised that he was having sex at such a young age. She had waited until college, with her first serious boyfriend. "And you've had lots of lovers since."

"Being rich helps."

"Your money doesn't matter to me," she told him. "That's not why I'm here with you."

"I know. But mostly women want to date me because I'm rich, even the ones who are trying to heal me. But you won't try to do that because you're already broken, too."

She didn't know whether to be offended by his assessment of her or impressed that he knew enough to call himself broken. To combat her uncertainty, she said, "You and I aren't going to be together long enough for me to try to do anything, except get through this weekend without those condoms running out."

He grinned and topped off his orange juice. "Touché, Miss Lawrence." When she furrowed her brow, he stopped smiling, the abrupt change hardening his handsome features. "Come on, Carol. Don't be upset because I said you were messed up, too."

"Did I say I was upset?"

"No, but I can tell it bothered you."

She gazed out at the pool. It was still vacant, the water rippling on its own, the chaise longues and chairs empty.

Suddenly the entire island seemed lonely, even the parts she couldn't see. "Your opinion of me is confusing."

"Why? Because you think that you're handling being orphaned better than I am? No one gets by unscathed. No one," he reiterated softy. "Not even you."

Seven

Later that day, Carol and Jake gathered on the beach with Lena and Mark and a slew of other couples. Lena had suggested that everyone pitch in to build a sandcastle, which had morphed into a whimsical fortress, surrounded by sculptures of dragons and dolphins and mermaids. So far, the results were spectacular, but this was a creative crowd. Some of the attendees were set designers and special effects artists, and they were spearheading the project, offering help where it was needed.

Jake and Carol were on one of the mermaid teams, sitting off by themselves, shaping the sand. Their mermaid wasn't half-bad. In fact, she was rather pretty, with her curvy figure and flowing hair.

Jake glanced up at Carol, but she averted her gaze. He was molding the mermaid's breasts, and she was working on the tail, giving it texture. She was also thinking about what he'd said about her being broken. No matter how hard she tried, she just couldn't seem to forget his unsettling opinion of her.

"What's wrong?" he asked.

"Nothing," she replied.

"You seem preoccupied."

"I'm just trying to focus on this."

"Are you sure that's all it is?"

She decided to come clean. Otherwise, it would keep affecting her mood. "Do you really think I'm messed up?"

He stopped molding the mermaid and sat back on his haunches. "I didn't mean it in an offensive way, Carol."

"Then how did you mean it?"

"I was just saying how losing your family was as traumatic for you as it was for me." He squinted at her, the sun shining in his eyes. "It's unfortunate, too, that neither of us had any extended family who could take us in. Or I assume that you didn't or you wouldn't have been placed in the system."

"You're right. There was no one. Both of my parents were raised by single moms, and they were gone by then. Well, actually, my dad's mom was still around, but she had cancer and was too sick to step in and help. She died about a year later." Carol sighed, pushing away the tightness in her chest. "I also had an uncle on my dad's side, but he was a young man in the military, so he couldn't raise me. He used to write me letters after my parents died, keeping a connection going, but then he was killed in Iraq." Another death that had destroyed her all over again. "But I managed to get through it, just as I got through losing everyone else."

"How? By being overly good and proper? How is that any better than me running wild?"

Irked by the comparison, she defended herself. "I'm

not being overly good and proper now. I'm here with you, on this island, sharing your damned bed."

"My *damned* bed, huh?" he mimicked her, a slow and sexy smile spreading across his face. "Is this our first fight?"

She rolled her eyes. She even smiled a little. It was silly to make a fuss over it. But that didn't stop her from being caught up in the past. It didn't stop Jake, either, apparently.

He said, "I had Garrett and Max to help me through it. I had Garrett's mom, too. But who did you have, Carol, especially after your uncle was gone?"

She kept her response light, determined to stay strong, rather than dredge up all of that old pain. "Some of my foster parents were really nice people. Of course, some were indifferent, too. So mostly I just learned to do it on my own, to not rely too heavily on anyone else."

He wiped his hands on his swim trunks. "Yes, but how?"

"By doing everything that I thought was right. By studying in school and getting good grades. By being respectful to my elders. By being as responsible as I could." She stared straight at him. "I wanted to do the kinds of things that would make my parents proud. I wanted them to be looking down on me from heaven, saying, 'Look how far she's come.'"

"That's nice. Really, truly it is. But it sounds lonely, too. Didn't you ever want to rebel? To scream and rage?"

"No. Staying calm kept me sane."

"That would have made me crazy."

There were plenty of times that she'd cried herself to sleep. But she'd refused to take her grief out on the world, the way he had. "What's the deal with your extended family? Why wasn't there anyone who could raise you?"

He returned to the mermaid, absently running his fingers over the areas he'd already shaped. "My dad was an only child, and his parents died before I was born, so that ruled them out." He spoke slowly, as if he were plucking the memories from his mind. "My maternal grandfather was still around, though, and so was my mom's sister. Grandpa lived in Ohio, where my mom was originally from, and my aunt was in Arizona, where she'd relocated years before. But at the time of the accident, she was going through a divorce, and the last thing she needed was another kid. She already had two little boys of her own and was struggling to raise them. One of them was a baby, three, maybe four months old, and the other one was a toddler, just barely out of diapers."

"What about your grandfather?"

"He said that he couldn't afford to accommodate me. Granted, he was just a working-class guy, but it was more than a money issue. He just didn't want to get saddled with one of his grandkids. He'd already raised his daughters by himself."

"When your grandmother died?" she asked, curious about the rest of the story.

A muscle ticked in Jake's jaw. "She didn't die. She left him for another man, abandoning him and their daughters when the girls were still pretty young. It tore everyone apart. Grandpa resented being left with the kids, and my mom and my aunt bore the brunt of his anger. They suffered from their mother leaving, too, of course. They were crushed by what she'd done."

"That's awful." Carol couldn't fathom a woman walking out on her children.

"Needless to say, they weren't a tight-knit family. Even when my mom was still alive, Grandpa rarely came to see to us. We hardly ever visited him, either. He remained distant with my aunt and her kids, too. He didn't help them when they needed it."

"Where is he now?"

"He has Alzheimer's, so he doesn't remember any of this, anyway. He's in a treatment center that looks after him. He's too far gone to be on his own."

"Who pays for that?"

"I do."

She figured as much. Jake didn't seem like the type of person to turn his back on someone, even if they'd turned their back on him. "So your mom and your aunt weren't close, either?"

"No. But my mom made up for her upbringing with how loving she was with us. With me and my dad and my sisters," he clarified.

Carol knew what he meant. "How did your aunt react when your mom died?"

"She was devastated, and guilty, I think, because they hadn't kept in better touch. She apologized at the time for not being able to take me in. But I understood how bad things were for her. She could barely feed her own children."

"How is she now?"

"She's doing fine. I encouraged her to get a real estate license, and now she works for an associate of mine who flips houses in Arizona. I'm putting my cousins through college, too, so they'll have a chance for a promising future, without being burdened by student loans."

Carol was still paying on her loans, but she had a good job and a generous boss who provided a discount on her rent. Without Jake, she wouldn't be making it as easily as she was. "That's nice of you."

"Thanks. My aunt appreciates everything I've done for her and her kids. But we haven't bonded, not in a way that feels like blood." He shrugged it off. "Maybe some-day we will. But what matters most to me is my foster brothers. They're my true family."

Carol nodded. After hearing the whole story, she understood more about his loyalty to them.

"I still can't relate to how you handled being or-phaned," he said, bringing the discussion back to her.

She took a moment to think about her response, to delve deeper into her history. "Being responsible is in my nature." She couldn't change that about herself, nor did she want to. "But being creative helped, too. I felt better when I learned to quilt. One of my foster mothers and her neighbors used to make quilts, and they showed me how to do it, too. The first one I worked on with them was a scrap quilt, made from fabrics they traded with one an-other. Some quilters collect scraps like trading cards." She paused, then added, "But the main reason quilting became so therapeutic for me is when I started making them by myself I would choose fabrics that reminded me of my family. It was like piecing together my memories and keeping them alive."

Jake watched her work on the mermaid, almost as if he were imagining watching her sew. "Did you make a quilt that represented your hopes and dreams, too? Did you put fabrics together that embodied your future hus-band and the kids you were going to have?"

Stunned by how spot-on he was, Carol met his gaze. He was keeping a close eye on her. So close it made her feel like a ladybug under a microscope. "What makes you think I did that?"

"It just seems like something you would've done, with how you used to fantasize about your wedding."

"You're right. I did make a quilt like that." She wasn't going to pretend otherwise. "I used a fancy white fabric to symbolize my dress. To showcase my kids, I used baby prints—pink teddy bears for a girl and blue dinosaurs for a boy."

"What about for your husband? What did you use to represent him?"

"A shiny black tuxedo material." She'd never really pictured what her groom would look like, other than that he would be dressed in formal wear. "I used a red rose pattern, too, because those are the flowers I envisioned in the ceremony."

"Do you still have it?"

"Yes. I saved all of my old quilts." She had them tucked away in her room. They were an important part of her childhood, of her heart, of the person she'd become. "Do you still think I'm broken?"

"Yes, but in a really sweet way." He sent her a teasing smile, even if he was still watching her just as closely as before.

"Okay, Mr. Juvenile Delinquent." She reached into the sand, dug around and found a shell, intending to throw it at him. But she held on to it instead, thinking how pretty it was. "You and your stolen jewelry."

"Thank goodness I got caught, huh? Or I might have become a cat burglar instead of the privileged playboy that I am today."

Privileged indeed. He'd carved out quite a life for himself. "Someday my dreams are going to come true, too."

His expression changed, his smile fading, his tone much more serious. "For a big white wedding?"

She glanced at the shell. She was still holding it, the chevron shape fitting delicately into her hand. "I want a family. I always have."

"Just be happy, no matter what you do."

· "I will." She placed the shell in the mermaid's hair, using it as decoration.

"That looks nice," Jake said. "Should we collect more of those?"

Carol nodded, and they both sifted through the sand, together yet somehow still alone.

At dusk the guests had dinner on the beach, prepared by the chef and his team. Although vegetable skewers and salads were available, the main dish was a seafood boil, lightly seasoned and served with a traditional tartar sauce or a spicy salsa, if you preferred your food with a bit of a kick.

Tons of fires had been built, either for large groups of people who wanted to socialize or for couples who preferred to be by themselves, which was what Jake and Carol had chosen.

While they ate, they sat on a big fluffy blanket at their own cozy little fire. He couldn't think of a nicer way to spend the evening, especially with how mesmerized Carol seemed.

"Look how enchanted everything is," she said, gazing out into the distance.

He followed her line of sight. The completed sandcastle had been decorated with hundreds of candles, creating an otherworldly effect. The majestic architecture presented soaring pillars, domed archways and flying buttresses. The detail was magnificent, even from across the beach.

She spoke softly, reverently. "I can see our mermaid from here."

"I see her, too." Their sculpture was surrounded by twinkling lights.

"I feel so protective of her. The way she's beckoning the sea with her beauty."

Jake turned to look at Carol, impressed with how beautiful she was, too. She wore a shiny mesh cover-up over her bikini, and her hair was pinned loosely on top of her head, a few silky strands falling about her face. "Don't worry. She can handle her own."

"Not when the tide comes in. Everything will be gone then."

"That's part of the magic. Nothing is supposed to last forever."

"Like this weekend?" she asked with a faraway sound in her voice.

"Yes, like this trip." As he admired Carol's profile, he realized that he'd neglected to share an important part of his past with her. "You're never going to believe what I forgot to tell you."

"What?" she asked, finally turning toward him.

"The Choctaw mermaid legend." Of all things to forget, he thought, after they'd spent half the day making one.

She shifted on the blanket, like an eager child settling in for a ghost story, her food half-eaten. "You can tell me now."

Jake collected his thoughts, recalling the story as it had been told to him. "They're called 'white people of the water' because they have pale, trout-like skin. They live in the bayou, in the deepest part of the water. But where it's clear, too. They aren't murky creatures."

Firelight shone in her eyes. "Are they beautiful, like our mermaid?"

"I don't know, exactly. But I'd like to think that they are. Thing is, though, that if you accidentally fall into the water, they'll capture you and take you to their world." He paused for effect. "And if you're there for more than three days, you can never return to land again."

"Why?" she asked, prodding him to finish the tale.

"Because they'll turn you into what they are, and you'll live in the water, becoming one of them."

She sighed, a bit dreamily. "Wouldn't it be cool if they were real, if you could really be transformed?"

"I went to Louisiana once with my parents, and when we visited the bayou, where my dad's ancestors were originally from, I kept wondering if the mermaids were there, watching us from below the water."

"I'll bet they were."

"I would've had to fall into the water to know for sure."

She moved closer to him. "I'm glad that you didn't or you wouldn't be here with me now."

He moved closer, as well. "Then I'm glad, too."

In the next bout of silence, they gazed at each other as if they were the only two people on the island. At the moment, that was how it felt.

They finished their food, taking their final bites and putting their plates aside. For dessert, the guests would be making their own s'mores, and Jake was looking forward to watching Carol lick the chocolate and marshmallow off her lips.

"I think we should give her a name," she said.

"What?" He didn't have a clue what she was talking about. He was still thinking about her lips.

"The mermaid," she told him. "The one we made. She needs an identity before she gets washed away. Just to make her seem more real."

"Then you can choose one."

"It should probably be a French name since this area has so many French influences." She turned her attention to the sea. "Do you know how to say *ocean* in French?"

"It's *océan*." He pronounced it o-say-AHN. To the best of his knowledge, that was right. He wasn't an expert on the language, but he'd dated a French actress for a few whirlwind months. "I think that's actually a woman's name, too."

"Then it's perfect. She'll be Océan."

He smiled. "It definitely works."

"Yes, it does. When she's washed into the sea, she'll be dissolving into her name."

"What's the origin of your name?" This woman who was fueling his fantasies, he thought. His temporary lover.

"It's a song or a hymn."

"Oh, of course. That makes sense." He analyzed his own name. "Jacob means *supplanter* because, in the Bible, Jacob was born holding his twin brother's heel."

"I've never heard of that word."

"A supplanter takes the place of someone or something else."

"Really? Hmm. Who are you taking over for?"

"How about the kinds of guys you normally date?" He touched her cheek, skimming his finger across her skin.

Her breathing grew quiet. "That's a clever analogy. With how different you are from them."

He thought about how she sewed pieces of material together to document her life. "Are you going to make a quilt to mark this weekend?"

Her lashes fluttered. "Do you think I should?"

He nodded. "You can use fabrics with beachy things on them. An island, a mermaid, a sandcastle."

"What should I use to represent us?" she asked.

He trailed his hand down, following the line of her collarbone. "You could steal the sheets off my bed and cut them into little squares."

"Jake." She admonished him, but she shivered from his touch, too. "I'll figure something else out."

"Does that mean you're going to make the quilt?"

"I don't know." She seemed to be considering the idea, contemplating the design. "Maybe."

"You could give it to me as a gift."

"Really? You'd want it?"

"Sure." He toyed with the mesh on her cover-up, poking at the holes. "It can be a part of our secret after we get home. Something for us to remember being together."

She leaned toward him. "Wouldn't it be better for us to try to forget?"

In lieu of a response, he kissed her. For now, he didn't want to forget. She reacted favorably, her lips warm and pliable against his. After they separated, they sat back to watch the fire.

Jake glanced over and saw that the ingredients for the s'mores were being passed around. "Are you ready for dessert?"

She nodded, and soon they were engaged in making the sticky treats. He took the liberty of watching her eat hers, just as he'd wanted to do.

"Everyone is supposed to go crabbing later," he said. "If they want to," he added. No one had to do anything that didn't appeal to them.

"Tonight?" She didn't just lick the goo from her lips. She licked it from her fingers, too. "I thought we'd be doing that tomorrow morning on a boat."

"No. This is a nighttime activity. They're giant land crabs, so we'll be searching for them, going into the brush, along the inland trails, armed with flashlights. But we have to be quick and quiet, so we'll be splitting into separate groups once everyone gets the gist of it. So, do you want to join in?"

She nodded. "I'll give it a try. But it sounds sort of scary, being out there in the dark."

"I promise I'll protect you." He watched while she made herself another s'more. "We'll have to put on some warmer clothes. They'll be giving us gloves and buckets and whatever else we'll need. The caretakers of the house are going to be our guides."

"That's good." She focused on her task, placing her marshmallows just so. "But I'm going to stay close to you, for sure."

"That's not a problem." He wanted to keep her as close as possible. "I don't know how many we'll catch, but the island is supposed to be filled with them this time of year. The chef is going to incorporate our catch into the breakfast menu."

"I wish tomorrow wasn't our last day."

"Me, too." They would be flying out, just before sunset, and going back to their regular lives. But for now, they were still here, immersed in the romance that had become their affair.

Eight

This was it, Carol thought as she stood on her veranda, breathing in the tropical air. Soon, she and Jake would be leaving the Caribbean.

Already feeling nostalgic, she smiled, remembering last night's crabbing expedition. She'd squealed like a child when she'd nabbed her first giant blue crustacean. Jake had been right by her side, as promised, making the experience sweet and fun and romantic. Nonetheless, hunting and gathering wasn't her forte.

Eating was, though. She'd enjoyed the crab-stuffed crepes they'd had for breakfast. For lunch, they'd had French cuisine, served in the dining room, where everyone had gathered for their final meal, talking and laughing, before they'd parted ways.

Some guests were already gone by now and others, like Carol and Jake, were preparing to depart.

She returned to her room, where her suitcase sat, carefully packed. After Jake finished jamming his belongings into his, they would head out for the helipad. When they got to the other island where they'd originally landed, they would board the jet that would take them home.

She checked on Jake to see how he was coming along and found him looking as handsome as ever, dressed in blue jeans and a loose cotton shirt, with a shiny packet in his hand.

Carol gaped at him. "Where you did get that?" As far as she knew, they'd used the final condom last night, after they'd come back from crabbing and climbed in the tub together, taking a long sensual bath.

"It was in my luggage, but in a different compartment from where I usually keep them. It was lodged in the corner, so the edges are bent. But other than that…"

She caught her breath. "Do we have time to use it?"

"We'll make time." With lightning speed, he swept her into his arms. They kissed like crazy, tongue-to-tongue, instantly hungry for the forbidden taste of each other.

He backed her against a nightstand, and she opened his zipper and pushed her hand inside. His eyes went glassy as he pressed into her palm, letting her feel him up.

After a few anxious heartbeats, he went after her, lifting the hem of her soft summer dress and removing her panties. In the next frantic second, he shoved his jeans down and donned the protection.

Carol sat on the edge of the nightstand, and as he thrust into her, she locked her legs around him, pulling him closer.

"I like that you don't wear underwear," she told him.

"You should stop wearing it, too."

She couldn't fathom it, not in her daily life. "I'm too proper for that."

He nipped at her chin with his teeth, gently, wildly.

"Yes, you should see how proper you look right now, with your dress hiked up around your hips."

Her bottom was getting sore from the friction of the wood beneath her, but she didn't care. "I couldn't find my panties on that first morning-after." But later she'd uncovered them, on the floor, with Jake's discarded clothes. Or more precisely, his pants, since that was the only thing he'd been wearing.

He pushed deeper, harder. "I should have kept them as a memento."

"So I could sew them into the quilt?"

He didn't stop the driving rhythm, not for an instant. "Patchwork panties. That works for me."

She still hadn't decided if she was going to make him a quilt. For now, all that mattered was being with him one more time.

He kissed her again, making the back of her throat hum. With her arms looped around his neck, she dug her nails into his shirt and arched her body toward his, taking as much of him as he was willing give.

Jake gave her everything. Rough and fast. Hot and sexy. Dark flashes of pleasure zinged through her blood. She closed her eyes, wanting this desperate moment to last forever, yet knowing it couldn't.

He used his fingers, rubbing her, intensifying the sensation. She was spiraling into sexual oblivion, lost in the fury. He ravished her relentlessly, lifting her into a fiery abyss.

Carol came in a burst of heat, in a sea of molten wetness. The air was thick, her breaths choppy.

He emitted a gritty groan, and all she could think was how beautiful he was, how powerfully male. His climax exploded just seconds after hers, expelling energy and lust.

She untangled her legs from around his waist, and he put his forehead against hers. In the aftermath, she clung to the feeling, her heart beating a crazy cadence.

When they separated, she wanted to pull him back into her arms. But she knew that wouldn't change anything. So she let him go.

While he went into the bathroom to clean up, she made a beeline to her own bathroom, grabbing her panties along the way. This time, she wasn't going to lose them in the shuffle.

Carol returned with her dress smooth and tidy, her underwear in place. Jake came back with his shirt tucked in and his fly neatly zipped.

Fighting a bout of sadness, she glanced down at her feet. She was wearing sandals decorated with little sparkling gems. The other jewels, the real ones Jake had given her, were packed. She didn't know if she would ever put them on again.

"Ready?" he asked.

She looked up at him. "To go home and act as if nothing happened?"

He nodded.

She searched his gaze, but all she saw, all she felt, were her own scattered emotions staring back at her. "I think I will make you a quilt, with all of the Caribbean trimmings."

"Promise?"

"Yes." She wanted Jake to remember that she'd once been his lover, even years from now, when she was happily married to someone else. "Just so you'll have it."

"Thanks. But we better go now." He took charge of the luggage, his and hers. "Should we ask the caretakers for a ride to the helipad or do you want to walk?"

"We can walk." It was a paved path, with stairs leading

to the raised platform. "But I'd like to go the beach first, to the area where the sandcastle was. Or might still be." Even if it was in ruins, she wanted to see the remnants.

"Okay." He agreed to take her there.

They went downstairs, left their suitcases on the front porch and ventured onto the beach. But there was nothing to see. Everything was gone, including their beloved mermaid.

"We're too late," he said.

"Did the candles get washed away, too?" she asked, trying not to feel empty inside.

"I think someone removed them. I doubt Lena would have allowed them to pollute the ocean."

"That's good." Carol turned to look at him as a salty breeze skimmed the shore. "It's so quiet."

He captured a strand of her billowing hair. "Lena told me at lunch that she really likes you."

Carol leaned closer. "I like her, too." She'd gotten to know the pop star a little better. During the course of the weekend, they'd chatted here and there. But mostly Lena just smiled whenever she saw Jake and Carol together, saluting Carol for taking a sexy chance on him.

He released her hair, sliding it through his fingers. "And you were worried about fitting in with my friends."

"But I misbehaved like them instead?"

"Much to my pleasure." He kissed her, soft and slow, surrounded by the tropical paradise that helped inspire their affair.

Their last kiss, she thought. Their last moment. She slipped her arms around him, holding him as if it was never going to end. Only, they both knew it was coming to a close.

But still, she deepened the kiss, savoring the taste of him for as long as she could.

* * *

A little over a month had passed since the island trip, and now Jake was meeting Garrett for a drink at the LA-area resort Garrett owned. The main building was a grand hotel, with a view of the Pacific Ocean. To the west of it, along the boardwalk, were private condos. Guests could stay at either type of accommodation, depending on their needs.

On this crisp, clear afternoon, a group of people were horseback riding along the shore. Garrett was a horseman who'd built a fancy stable on the property for himself as much as for his guests. In fact, he lived on the premises, near the stables, in a custom-built house on a cliff above the beach.

Jake entered the hotel, his thoughts scattered. He was supposed to be concentrating on a fund-raiser that was in the works for their foundation, but he kept thinking about Carol instead.

She'd called in sick four times this week. That wasn't like her. She rarely, if ever, missed work. She did seem ill, though. The last time he'd seen her, she looked tired and pale. But Jake wasn't sure if it was physical or emotional.

Being around each other was becoming increasingly difficult, even with the amount of time that had passed since Lena's party. They did the best they could, but it was awkward, with both of them overcompensating for the heat that still sizzled between them. He wasn't sure what was worse: being alone at the office with her or having other people around. Either way, he was feeling the pressure, and so was she.

Was it the stress that was making her sick? He wouldn't be surprised if it was. But at this point he didn't know what to do about it other than urge her to see a doctor, if she hadn't done that already.

He was concerned that if it continued for much longer she was going to find herself another job, one that didn't include an ex-lover as her boss.

Then what would he do? How would he replace her? Carol was an asset to his company…and to him. She understood him. She knew what made him tick. But maybe it would be better if she left, if they didn't have to see each other every day. No, he thought. He didn't want to lose her, not like this.

"Hey! Where are you going?"

Jake spun around and saw that he'd just walked right past Garrett in the front lobby bar. Cripes, he didn't even realize what he was doing.

"Sorry. I just—" Rather than try to explain, Jake finished with, "Need a beer."

"Me, too." Garrett motioned to a table that had been reserved for them.

They sat down, and a spunky little blonde came by to take their orders. They both chose bottled Mexican beer. Normally, Jake would have checked out the waitress or at least smiled at her in his usual flirtatious way, but he was too preoccupied with thoughts of Carol to behave like his old self. Garrett seemed the same as usual, except maybe a bit more uptight.

Not that he was a stick in the mud. Garrett Snow was a great guy, just in a strong-willed way. He didn't take any crap from anyone, and he didn't party or play the field the way Jake did, either. Garrett had always been a one-woman kind of man. He was also organized and focused. He preferred to do things himself, barely needing a secretary or assistant. Jake couldn't fathom it. Carol was the most important person in his employ.

The beers arrived and Jake swigged his first. He glanced around, taking in the decor, with its rich, dark woods, painted details and Native American accents. Garrett was a mixed-blood from the Cheyenne Nation, sired by an Anglo father he'd never known.

"You look like you have a lot on your mind," Garrett said, reaching for his beer.

"Yeah, I do. I don't know if I'm going to be much good today, finalizing the fund-raiser stuff."

Garrett sat back in his chair. He was tall and broad, with deep-set eyes, short black hair and hard-edged features. He squinted a lot, just as he was doing now. "We can work on it another day."

"Really?" Jake was surprised. His foster brother rarely pushed business aside. "You'd be cool with that?"

"I have things on my mind, too."

Curious, Jake leaned forward. "Like what?"

Garrett didn't respond. He didn't alter his posture, either. He remained as he was, seated far back in his chair, his eyes narrowed. He looked like the hero of an old Western B movie, a half-breed cowboy, preparing to fight the bad guys and clean up the town.

Finally he said, "The woman who ripped us off will be coming up for parole this year."

Ah, so that was it, Jake thought. Garrett had Meagan Quinn on his mind. The seemingly nice girl who'd embezzled money from them. She used to work for the accounting firm that Garrett, Max and Jake used, gaining access to their financial records and dipping her hands into the pie.

Jake was the most forgiving, of course. He knew what it was like to steal. "She's serving her time. She's paying her debt to society."

"Yes, but she still has to pay her debt to us."

That was true. As a stipulation of her sentence, Meagan had been ordered to pay restitution to her victims.

The money she'd taken wasn't an astronomical amount, at least not by their standards. But it was still a crime. And it had still pissed them off, especially Garrett, maybe even more than it should have.

Jake took another swig of his beer. "Doesn't she have to get a verified job offer before she can get paroled? Isn't that one of the terms of her release?"

"Yeah, and my do-gooder mother wants me to offer her a job, here at the resort."

Holy cow. If Jake hadn't been so shocked, he might've laughed. Regardless, he still cracked a joke. "Doing what? Working the front desk so she can get your guests' credit card numbers and go on a shopping spree?"

"That isn't funny."

"Yes, it is. I mean, seriously, what the hell is your mom thinking?"

"She's thinking that I'll be able to give an ex-con a fresh start at a new life. Of course, the parole commission would have to approve her working for me, but since the restitution she owes would be going to our foundation, they'd probably agree to it."

Jake nodded. An arrangement had already been made with the court for the money to be donated to their charity, instead of being paid to them. Garrett had taken care of that when he'd attended Meagan's sentencing. Neither Jake nor Max had made an appearance. They'd trusted Garrett to represent them.

"Mom's got it in her head that I *need* to do this, as much for the thief as myself."

"A little forgiveness wouldn't hurt."

"Yeah, well, we'll see." Garrett chugged his drink, then set the bottle down with a thud. After a moment of silence, he asked, "So what's going on with you?"

Well, shit. Now Jake had to spill his guts, too. Only,

he couldn't admit that he'd slept with Carol. He'd promised to keep their affair on the down-low once they got
home, and that included not blabbing to his foster brothers about it.

"I'm just worried about Carol," he said.

Garrett's expression softened. "Your assistant? How
so?"

"She's been sick this week."

A frown appeared on Garrett's face. "How sick?"

"I don't know. She just seems run-down, I guess."

"Then give her some time to recover."

"Maybe I should stop by her place to check on her."

"Sure, you could do that. But you should probably
call first."

"Or text," Jake said, recalling the texts that had led to
their first night together. "I just want to know that she's
going to be okay."

"You're really reliant on her, aren't you?"

"She's good at her job." Hot and sexy in bed, too, he
thought. And warm and sweet. Everything he wasn't supposed to be thinking about. But he couldn't seem to let
those images go, no matter how hard he tried. "I'll text
her after I finish my beer."

"I'm getting another one." Garrett lifted his empty
bottle and signaled the waitress.

Jake wasn't having another drink. He wanted to keep
a clear head for when he saw Carol.

Jake rang Carol's doorbell and shifted the bag in his
hand. In his text, he'd offered to bring her some soup. It
was as good an excuse as any to con his way over here.
Besides, he knew how much she loved the matzo ball
soup from a nearby deli.

She answered the door, looking even more exhausted

than the last time he'd seen her at work. Dang, he thought. He'd hoped that her condition would be improving, not worsening.

After she invited him inside, he held up the soup. "Do you want this now?"

"Maybe a little. Thank you." Carol took the bag and went into the kitchen. Jake waited at the entrance of the kitchen, watching her move about. She opened the container and poured some of the broth into a mug, then spooned a matzo ball into it. "There's a lot here. Do you want a cup, too?"

"No, thanks." Jake studied her more closely. She was wearing sweatpants and a blousy shirt, and her typically tidy hair was pulled up into a rooster-style ponytail, the ends poking out at feathery angles. In a more relaxed situation, the chaotic style would have amused him. But he was in no mood to smile.

She motioned to the living room, and he followed her to the sofa, where he sat beside her.

She tasted the soup. "It's really good. Thank you again."

"You're welcome." He paused before he continued, giving her time to eat a bit more of the soup. Then he asked, "Have you seen a doctor yet?"

She shook her head. "I wanted to wait until…"

Jake frowned. "Until what?"

"I was ready."

That made absolutely no sense to him. "You've been sick for almost a week."

"I'll make an appointment if I need to."

"I think you need to now."

She put her mug on the coffee table. "Let me handle my own business, Jake."

"I'm just worried is all."

"I'll be fine."

She didn't look fine. Not in the least. He'd never seen her in such a fragile state before.

"I started on the quilt I promised to make for you," she said, changing the subject. "But it's slow going."

"You've been sewing?"

"No. But I cut the squares from the different fabrics. Or most of them. I still need to order a few more." She glanced toward a basket in the corner of the room where the fabrics were. "You can look at what's there so far, if you want."

He went ahead and checked it out, curious to see what patterns she'd chosen. But that didn't mean he was going to let her get away with ignoring her health issues. He intended to work their conversation back to that. But first, he retrieved the basket and brought it over to the sofa.

He looked through the squares. There were a variety of fabrics, most of them containing the beach themes he'd suggested, with depictions of mermaids, sandcastles and islands on them. She'd even tossed in some printed with blue crabs. There was also a multicolored print that had the same jewel tones as the bracelet he'd given her. She'd included a shiny starfish pattern for the earrings, too. He noticed a geometric Native American print as well, that he assumed was meant to represent him and his heritage. He kept looking and uncovered a stack of squares with grasshoppers on them.

"For Eskeilay," she said. Then softly added, "The mother of the earth-womb."

"You did a beautiful job with what you chose." He wished that he could touch her, hold her, make her feel better, but he figured the last thing she wanted was for him to take her in his arms.

"I plan to include something for Uncta, too. A fire

print of some sort, something with a golden hue. That's one of the fabrics I still have to order."

"I appreciate your attention to detail." To the memories they'd created, even if neither of them had spoken of that weekend since.

"I don't know when I'll finish it."

To him, it sounded as if she had mixed feelings about whether to complete it at all. She'd probably only brought it up as a diversion to keep him from bugging her about going to the doctor.

Jake put the basket aside, refusing to let her off the hook. He asked, "Are you ill because of me?"

She had a worried expression. "What?"

He clarified his question. "Is being around me too stressful?"

She twisted her hands on her lap. "Sort of, I guess. Not wanting to face you is part of the reason I've been calling in sick."

"You're facing me now. You agreed to let me come over."

"I knew I couldn't avoid you forever. And it is a little easier seeing you here than at the office. But I still don't want to talk about it. Not until I see a doctor, and I already told you, I'm not ready to do that."

He pushed the issue, determined to get answers. "Please, Carol, just tell me what's going on."

"It's too soon to tell you."

"Too soon for what?" He noticed that she was still wringing her hands. "I'm not leaving here until you level with me."

Her breath rushed out. "Okay, but it's going to freak you out." She looked directly at him, her voice quavering. "I'm scared, Jake. Scared to death that I might be pregnant."

Nine

Carol waited for Jake to respond. But he just sat there staring at her. Was he struggling to grasp what she'd just told him? Or was he simply too stunned to move? To blink? To talk?

After what seemed like forever, he said, "That's impossible."

"In what way?" she asked, prodding him to explain what he was thinking and feeling.

"We used protection." He spoke robotically, like a computer stating a fact. Or someone who refused to believe what he was hearing.

"Condoms sometimes fail." She'd checked the failure rates and the numbers were staggering. "Mostly from them breaking or slipping off."

"But that didn't happen to us."

"No, but I might have damaged the first one. With as much as I fumbled with it, I could have poked a tiny hole in it. Or the failure could have come from the last one we used. Remember how the edges of the packet were bent from the way it had been stuck in your suitcase? The condom itself could have been compromised without us even knowing it."

Jake stood and stepped away from the sofa, pressing his back against the fireplace mantel. He was beginning to look like a caged animal. Carol knew exactly how he felt.

"Then I guess it is possible," he said.

"Yes, it is." Her voice vibrated with every breath she took. She'd never expected to be in this position, possibly impregnated by a man who didn't want children. "Last week, I thought I had my period, but it was weird. First of all, it was early and that's never happened to me before." Normally her cycles were like clockwork. "And it only lasted a few hours, which was even weirder." She hated to share all of the clinical details, but considering how crucial this was, it seemed necessary. "It was more like spotting than a full period."

"I'm confused." His voice was shaky, too. He even cleared his throat, as if it might help. "That isn't an early sign of pregnancy, is it?"

"Actually, it is. But I wasn't aware of it until I looked up my symptoms online. At first I thought I was getting a virus based on how run-down I was feeling. Then when my period seemed irregular, I got a little worried and researched what could've caused that. And that's when I came across something called implantation bleeding. It's just like what I had. It's a result of the fertilized egg attaching itself to the wall of the uterus. It typically happens two to seven days before the beginning of what would be your regular menstrual cycle. In my case, it's been about six days. My period is due tomorrow."

He looked relieved—not completely, but at least his body language wasn't quite as tense. "Then maybe it'll start and everything will be okay. Maybe you'll begin to feel better, too."

"That's what I'm hoping. That's why I didn't want to take a pregnancy test or go to a doctor yet, either."

He wrinkled his forehead. "Can a test even be taken this early?"

Carol nodded. "Yes, but I wanted to wait, just to see if my period comes first. Besides, early tests aren't always accurate." She reached for her soup, needing fuel, so she cut into the matzo ball and ate a portion of that. "I haven't been queasy, so that's a good sign. Mostly my symptoms are lack of energy and light-headedness. It might just be stress. Sometimes women's menstrual cycles can get disrupted by that."

He relaxed a bit more, moving away from the mantel. "Then that's probably what it is. It seems the most likely culprit. Even I figured that's what was wrong with you and why you're not feeling well. That's why I came over here to question you about it."

"I appreciate your concern." She hadn't wanted to see him until after she knew for sure, but she was glad that she'd gotten it over with. "If my cycle starts tomorrow, we're in the clear. But if it doesn't…"

He tugged at his hair, hard enough to create a grimace. "Pregnancy never even occurred to me."

"Me, neither, until all of this blew up in my face." She wanted to pull her hair out, too.

"If you don't start your period, how long are you going to wait before you take a test?"

"I don't know. A few days, maybe. I don't want to sit around on pins and needles, but I don't want to get a false reading, either." She was just hoping and praying that her cycle showed up. "I could go to the doctor to get a blood test. Those give you an earlier reading. But it takes longer to get the results than a urine test, so I'd have to wait, either way. I doubt my doctor would rush the results of a blood test for me."

"Will you call me tomorrow and let me know how you're doing and if anything happens?"

"Of course I will." Now that he was part of the equation, she would keep him well informed. "But if you hadn't come over today, I wouldn't have told you any of this, not until enough time passed for me to be sure." She blinked, fighting back tears. "I didn't want to worry you if it turned out to be nothing." She put down her soup, leaving the spoon inside the mug. "I'm so scared, Jake."

"Me, too." He resumed his seat on the sofa, looking at her as if she might break. "But it'll be okay."

She wished that she could believe him. But what if she was pregnant? He was the last man on earth she should be having a baby with. "You can't know it's going to be okay."

"I'm just trying to comfort you. To say what I'm supposed to say." Clearly, he was struggling with his role in this. "Would you rather be alone now? Do you want me to leave?"

She looked into the vastness of his eyes. "Do you want to go?"

He gazed back at her. "I asked you first."

They sounded like kids, debating a silly subject. But that wasn't the case. This was a serious discussion between two anxiety-ridden adults.

She took the undecided road. "It's up to you."

"Please, Carol. Either ask me to stay or tell me to leave. Don't make me choose."

"Then maybe you should go." If he stayed, she might

fall prey to the temptation of those big broad shoulders and put her head on one of them. She might even cry in his arms, and that wouldn't do either of them any good.

"All right." He wiped his hands on his pants, as if his palms had turned clammy. "We'll just keep in touch by phone."

She walked him to the door, where they both stood outside. The air felt good, so she breathed in as much of it as she could.

"Take care of yourself," he said.

"I will." She hadn't been sleeping. She'd barely even been eating. "Thanks again for the soup."

"If you need anything else, just let me know."

What she needed was to *not* be pregnant. "Hopefully you'll get good news from me tomorrow."

"I'll be waiting." He gazed empathetically at her. "I'm sorry our weekend together is messing up your life."

"Nothing is messed up yet." It was only on the verge of disaster.

His breathing turned choppy. "God, Carol. How are we going to handle this if it's true?"

"I don't know. But you need to go." She couldn't cope with his panic. She had enough of her own.

"You're right. I'm sorry. I'm supposed to be leaving."

Thankfully, he didn't embrace her or do anything to stir up more emotion. There was nothing but a softly spoken goodbye before he turned and left.

She noticed that he was driving his Corvette, a ragtop convertible that he favored on warmer days. She could see the shiny red sports car from where she stood. She watched him climb behind the wheel and fire up the high-powered engine.

Carol tried to picture him in a minivan with a baby carrier strapped in the backseat, but it was a ludicrous image.

She shook her head, afraid, so damned afraid, that if tomorrow didn't bring an end to this, her wild-spirited boss could actually be the father of her unborn child.

Nearly a week later, Jake was at home stressing about the predicament he'd gotten himself into. Carol hadn't returned to work yet, but by now a doctor had confirmed what the home test had also revealed. She was pregnant. With his kid, Jake thought. His flesh and blood. He was going to be someone's dad.

Carol had already told him over the phone that she was keeping it, but he'd figured as much. He couldn't see her terminating her pregnancy under any circumstances, not with how badly she wanted a family.

But how did Jake fit into all of this? He didn't know how to be part of a family, not since he'd lost his own. Nor did he want to be part of one, either.

Carol was coming over later so they could try to figure things out. But even now, as he looked at himself in the mirrored wall of his gym, he wanted to ram his head against it.

He'd worked out like mad, making his muscles ache, making his body sweat. He'd pushed himself harder than he ever had before, trying to block the truth from his mind.

But it hadn't been the least bit effective.

What the hell was he going to do? How was he going to cope with being a father? Jake didn't even have a dog. Or a cat. Or a fish. He'd never been responsible for anyone or anything except himself.

He entered the bathroom that was attached to the gym and climbed into the shower. He turned on the spigot and let the icy cold water pummel him. But it didn't help.

Nothing did. Still, he remained under the freezing spray for as long as he could stand it.

After he toweled off, he dragged a T-shirt over his head and zipped into a pair of holey jeans. He liked wearing old clothes around the house. For him, it took the pretentious edge off living in a mansion. Not that he was complaining. His place was amazingly cool, an ultramodern estate perched in the Hollywood Hills, with the kinds of amenities only high-dollar real estate could offer.

At least Jake could buy his son or daughter everything the child needed. That was his only comfort, the only part of this that made him feel grounded.

Over the years, he'd learned to hide behind his money. But if he hadn't gotten rich, he would be hiding behind something else. There would be a barrier either way. On the day Jake's family had burned to death in that car, he'd put up his defenses, using his grief as a shield. There was no going back, no changing it. He was what he was.

He went into the living room to wait for Carol, anxiety building with each second that passed. He couldn't marry her; he couldn't be the nice normal guy she dreamed about. But she wouldn't expect him to. Would she?

He scrubbed his hand across his jaw, feeling trapped within the walls of his big glass house.

Finally, Carol arrived. He invited her inside, and they sat across from each other in his sunken living room, decorated with red leather furniture and sleek gray tables. The floors were high-glossed wood, the artwork bold and masculine. The windows offered panoramic views, with Hollywood and all its glorious sins stretched out before them. This wasn't a home designed for a wife and child. He'd bought it as a place to party, to entertain, to live and let live.

"Can I get you anything?" he asked. "Water? Iced

tea? Wine?" He stalled, made a face. Had he just offered a pregnant woman a drink? "Sorry. Scratch the wine."

"That's okay. I don't want anything, anyway."

Carol looked prim and pretty, with her oxford blouse all buttoned up. But she seemed tired, too. As fatigued as before.

"Has the nausea started?" he asked.

She shook her head. "No. My symptoms are the same."

"Maybe you won't get sick like that."

She smiled a little. "I probably will, but it would be nice to bypass that part."

"I don't know anything about having kids, Carol."

"I'm not an expert, either."

"Yeah, but it's in your DNA. You're going to make a great mom."

"Thank you. This wasn't how I envisioned becoming a parent, but I'm not going to let that stop me from loving this baby with all of my heart."

At that moment, Jake's heart was beating uncomfortably in his chest, crushing down on his lungs. "I'll give you both whatever you need. Neither of you will go without. But I can't marry you, Carol. I hope you understand that."

"Of course I do. I didn't come over here hoping for a proposal. I could never marry you, either."

He should have been satisfied with her response. It was what he wanted to hear, after all. But instead, it made him hurt for the child they'd created. Oddly enough, he hurt for himself and Carol, too.

"I'll buy you a house," he said. "Around here somewhere. Then at least we can live close enough for me to see the kid regularly, too. I can come over and tuck it into bed or whatever."

She bit down on her bottom lip. "Oh, wow. Jake."

He frowned. "Oh, wow, what?"

Her eyes turned a little misty. "You're already starting to sound like a dad."

"I am?" He didn't feel like one. All he felt was sad and scared and confused. Not knowing what else to say, he went silent, hoping she didn't go into a full-blown cry.

Thankfully, she cleared the mistiness, blinking it away. Then she said, "I appreciate your offer. But you don't have to buy me a house."

"I'm in real estate. Investing in property is what I do." So why wouldn't he want to make an investment for her, too? "Besides, you can't stay in the apartment. It's too small for you and the baby."

"Okay, but maybe you can keep the house in your name, instead of gifting it to me. I want to be my own person and taking too much from you doesn't feel right."

He wasn't going to argue with her, not in her condition. He would abide by her wishes for now. "You can at least pick out the kind of place you like."

"I don't want it to be too big." She glanced around at his enormous digs. "I'd prefer something a little homier, you know?"

"That's fine." There were plenty of bungalows in the hills, with the warmth and charm of a family dwelling, which was what he figured she was after. "We'll find something that suits you."

"There's no rush. I can stay at my apartment until closer to when the baby comes." She placed a hand on her stomach, splaying her fingers across it, making him reflect on the little life that grew there. "We still have a long time to go."

"There's no point in waiting until the end." Jake considered how the tables had turned. Normally Carol insisted on getting things done ahead of time, but now he was the one trying to make early arrangements. He didn't know what had come over him, jumping into this the way he was. Maybe it was because she seemed so lost?

"What are we going to do about my job?" she asked.

"What do you mean?"

"Am I supposed to keep working for you? And when are we going to tell the people at the office?"

"Of course you can keep working for me." He'd already been worried about losing her before he even knew she was pregnant. He most certainly didn't want her to leave him now. "And we can arrange a meeting at the office and tell everyone at the same time. We'll just say it, plain and simple."

"It makes me nervous."

"I know." His stomach was in knots. "But it's better to just get it over with." He didn't want anyone figuring things out on their own or spreading gossip. "We'll control it ourselves, if we can."

"Will you handle that? I don't think I have the strength to stand in a room in front of my peers and admit that I slept with you."

"Yes, I'll handle it. And don't worry. I'm not going to go into the specifics. This is about the baby, not about what we did."

She kept her hand on her stomach. "Kristen is going to be concerned about me. You know how she is."

Kristen was the receptionist, a pixie-haired brunette in her early twenties who followed Carol around like a puppy. Jake had never really bonded with the girl. It was Carol she was loyal to. Kristen was filling in for Carol while she was out sick, doing what she could to assist Jake and make Carol proud. "She admires you."

"I know. I like her, too. But I never expected to be in this position. It seems so surreal."

"We'll get through it," he said, even if he didn't have a clue how they were going to manage having a child together for the rest of their lives. "As soon as you're ready to return to the office, I'll call that meeting."

"I'll come back on Friday."

That was two days away. "Then that's when it'll happen." When Jake would announce that he and Carol were having a baby. When the news would be official. When their mixed-up future would begin.

The Friday meeting was awkward, but at least it was over. Carol wasn't going to have to lie about why she wasn't feeling well. Or hide her baby bump when it started to appear. Or stress about when to tell everyone at work. As of this morning, they already knew.

Jake had handled it like the boss he was, stating only the facts. He'd made it clear that he and Carol weren't in a relationship. He explained that they would raise their child in separate households. He also pointed out that she would continue to work for him, so it would be business as usual.

Yeah, right, Carol thought. As if it was just that easy.

After the meeting ended, the other employees disbursed, silence looming in the air as they filed out of the conference room. Carol understood their discomfort. She was feeling out of sorts, too. But she suspected that Kristen was going to approach her privately, as soon as the eager receptionist was able to swing it.

Jake went to his office, and Carol headed to hers, glad to escape. She sat at her desk, trying to pull herself into work mode.

About an hour later, a light knock sounded at her open doorway. Sure enough, it was Kristen, with her trendy clothes, short, cutesy hair and big hoop earrings. Carol gestured for her to come inside.

Kristen entered the room and closed the door behind her. Then she widened her eyes and said, "Oh, my freaking God. You're going to be Jake's baby mama. You! The nicest, most normal woman on the planet. I can't believe it."

Carol could hardly believe it, either. "Things happen."

"I'll say." Kristen sighed. "I always wondered if you had feelings for him, though."

"You did?" And here Carol thought that she'd hidden her crush on Jake without anyone figuring it out.

The brunette nodded. She was a petite young woman who'd played Peter Pan in a community play. She toyed around with acting, but lots of people in LA dabbled in the arts. Kristen wasn't overly ambitious about it. Mostly she was just a flighty girl who'd gone from one bad boyfriend to another. Carol had helped her through her last horrific relationship.

"At least Jake has lots of money," Kristen said. "At least he can take care of the baby that way. But dang, it's hard to envision him being an actual dad."

Carol thought about what Jake had said about tucking the child in at night and how emotional it had made her feel. "I think he's going to try to do his best."

"That's good. My parents weren't married or anything, either. I hardly ever saw my dad when I was kid. I see him even less now."

"I'm sorry your dad hasn't taken a more active role in your life." No doubt it had factored into Kristen's terrible taste in men, too. "That wasn't fair to you."

"What happened to you and Jake when you were kids wasn't fair, either. At least my parents are still alive. But it's still so weird, with you and Jake having a baby together."

"He offered to put me up in a house near his to make it easier for him to get involved. But this isn't how I ever imagined raising a child."

"I'm just glad it's you and not one of his hoity-toity ex-girlfriends having his kid. You're a genuine person, and you'll be a great mom."

"Thank you. Jake said the same thing."

"About you being a good mom?"

"Yes. He thinks it's in my DNA." But regardless of what a natural mom she was going to be, Carol couldn't bear the thought of Jake being with other women. Yet once the dust settled, she suspected that he would dive back into his playboy ways. He was making a commitment to their child, not to her. "I just hope I don't break down before the baby is born."

"You won't. You're too strong to fall apart."

"I haven't cried yet." She'd gotten close, but she'd managed to keep from bursting into tears. "I'm trying to hold on."

"Don't worry. You'll make it." The receptionist sent her an encouraging smile. "But I better get back to work now."

"Thank you for the support."

"Sure. Should I leave the door open when I leave?"

Carol nodded, and once she was alone, she struggled to maintain her composure. Then she glanced up and saw Jake looming in the doorway. The hits just kept on coming, she thought.

"Are you okay?" he asked. "I noticed that Kristen was just here." He moved forward and closed the door, just as Kristen had done.

She tried to reassure him. "Everything is fine. She just wanted to talk."

"Did it help?"

Yes and no, Carol thought. Kristen's belief in her felt good, but thinking about Jake with other women had only heightened her duress.

"It was fine," she said again.

He didn't look convinced. "You can go home early if you need to."

"I'd rather stay." She didn't want to appear cowardly, skipping out on the first day.

Jake nodded and loosened his tie. He'd worn a proper suit to the meeting. His jacket was already gone, though. But he never remained in professional attire for too long, routinely discarding what he considered the stuffy portions of his wardrobe. Only, at the moment, his restless nature seemed even more pronounced.

He said, "No one has come to me to talk about it."

"Why would they? You're the boss."

"Who knocked up his assistant? I'll bet they think I took full advantage of you." He frowned. "I didn't do that, did I, Carol?"

The guilt in his eyes unnerved her. "No, you didn't, and me getting pregnant doesn't change the facts. I wanted you as badly as you wanted me." She'd made him well aware of that when they were in the midst of it, and she wasn't going to let him twist things up now. "Even Kristen said that she suspected I was attracted to you."

"Really? I guess women are observant that way. Of course, with the way she admires you, she would notice, I guess." He removed his tie and crammed it in his pants pocket. "I'm glad you're back. I missed having you around here."

"You're probably going to be seeing a lot of me out-side of the office, too."

"Yeah." He smiled a little. "I've been trying to pic-ture you months from now." He made a big-belly motion. "I've never touched a pregnant woman's stomach before."

Would he be touching hers? The thought made her weak. "I have. Lots of my girlfriends have kids."

"Have you told any of them yet?"

She shook her head. "I wanted to wait until everyone at work knew. I wanted to get that over with first." She questioned him. "Have you told Garrett or Max?"

"No. Max is still backpacking all over the country or whatever the hell he's doing. And since he's trying to stay off the grid, I'm going to wait to call him until the time feels right. But I'm going to tell Garrett this week-end. I already told him that you were sick, so now I can clarify why."

"I wonder what he'll think."

"After he gets over the initial shock, he'll probably want to kick my ass for not being more careful."

"It could have happened to anyone."

"Yeah, but it happened to me. The guy who plays around. That won't go over well." He shoved the tie deeper into his pocket. "Are you nervous about telling your friends?"

"Yes." She couldn't deny that her news was going to worry them, too. "They're not going to like the idea of me being a single mom, not with how marriage-minded I've always been."

"I'm sorry, Carol."

For insisting that he couldn't marry her? "It's not a problem." She'd agreed with his reasoning from the be-ginning. "I know better than to think that having a baby is going to turn us into a lifelong couple."

"I wonder if it's going to be a boy or a girl."

"It's too early to tell. But we can find out during a mid-pregnancy ultrasound, if we want to know. They can't always tell for sure, though. It depends on the position the baby is in."

He kept looking at her, almost as if she was still his warm and willing lover. "I guess we'll cross that bridge when we come to it."

She shuffled a stack of papers on her desk, wishing he would stop intensifying their chemistry, especially when she was struggling to ignore it. "We have a lot of bridges to cross."

"Too many," he said, before he moved toward the door. "Do you want me to grab you some lunch later?"

Normally she got his lunch, if he wasn't dining out with clients. "No, thanks. But it was nice of you to ask."

"Okay, well…I'll see you."

"You, too." Was it crazy for her to wish that they were right for each other? That he was a different type of man than he was? Probably. But she couldn't help it.

Somewhere in the pit of her dreamy soul, Carol wished that they were meant to be together like expectant parents should be.

Ten

Jake met with Garrett on the boardwalk located near the resort. They sat on a bright white bench, in front of a gourmet coffee shop that faced the ocean.

With as much strength as Jake could muster, he told his foster brother about the baby. As expected, the conversation wasn't going in his favor.

"It just happened," Jake said in his own defense.

"Earthquakes just happen. Tidal waves just happen." Garrett gestured to the water as if it was going to rise up like a monster and swallow them whole. "But getting your assistant pregnant? That could've been prevented."

Jake used the only excuse he could think of. "The condoms failed."

"You know that wasn't what I meant."

"Yeah, I know." Clearly, Garrett was suggesting that he should've never taken Carol to bed. "But I'm already a mess over it. So I'd prefer not to have you jumping all over me, too."

"I'm sorry, bro. I don't want to make this more difficult for you. But it's just that you got yourself into something major here. And Carol is a nice girl who shouldn't be left holding the bag."

"I'm trying to do right by her and the baby. I'm going to set them up in a place in my neighborhood and be there when they need me." Jake watched a family playing on the beach. The youngest kid was a fair-haired toddler, a rough-and-tumble boy squirming in his mom's arms. "I don't really know how, though. To be there, I mean."

"Just give it some time. You'll learn."

"I hope so. I want to keep her and the baby safe." He kept watching the family. The older kids were running toward the shore with their paddleboards, and the little one remained on his mom's lap; only now, he was playing with a red plastic bucket his dad had given him.

Garrett said, "Life takes some strange turns."

"Boy, does it ever." Being at the beach was making Jake miss the romance he'd had with Carol. But getting reinvolved with her in that way would only complicate things further. "I wonder if I should invite her to stay with me until we find her a house. Not as my lover or anything," he clarified. "But just so I can get more familiar with her pregnancy. So I can be part of it, too."

Garrett encouraged him. "That sounds like a solid idea to me."

"Maybe I'll take her on a picnic or something tomorrow and we can talk about it then." Unless she had plans on Sunday. He didn't have a clue what Carol did with her free time. "It's hard to say how she'll feel about it, though."

As Jake contemplated his all-too-grown-up life, a group of teenage girls walked by, checking out a cluster of boys who were seated on a brick wall. Typical of this generation, the girls were tapping away on their phones, probably announcing their flirtations on social media and sneaking in pictures of the boys, who were on their phones, too.

"So have you figured out what to do?" he asked Garrett.

"About what?"

"Offering Meagan Quinn a job."

"No, I haven't." Garrett seemed oblivious to the teen antics. Or maybe he just didn't care to notice them. "But there's plenty of time to decide. Her parole eligibility date is still months away. Then once that rolls around, there'll be a hearing. After that, her case will go into review. Her release isn't going to happen overnight."

"If she doesn't have a job lined up, she won't be released. The parole commission isn't going to let that slide."

"I know. I'm considering how much weight an offer from me would hold." Garrett frowned. "Meagan has a child. A daughter, who'll be around two by the time Meagan gets out."

"She has a kid that age?" Jake was flabbergasted. "How is that even possible? She's been behind bars longer than that."

"She discovered that she was pregnant soon after she went to prison, by a guy who'd already walked out on her. She gave birth while she was incarcerated, and one of her brothers took care of the baby so it didn't have to go into foster care."

Jake hadn't been aware of Meagan's plight. "Have you been keeping tabs on her all this time?"

"No. I haven't paid her any mind while she's been locked up. I didn't even know that she'd had a kid until Mom told me, just recently. She just found out, too, when she took an interest in Meagan's parole."

"Damn. Your mother is really vested in this thing." Jake considered the circumstances. "I can't imagine someone having a baby in prison." The thought twisted his stomach, especially now that Carol was carrying his child.

Garrett squinted in the sun. "You know what else Mom discovered from poking around into Meagan's life? That she and Meagan's mother used to belong to the same Native American women's group. It was a long time ago, and their paths only crossed for a short period, but there's still a connection. Of course Mom thinks it's a sign, even if she barely knew the other woman."

"What happened to Meagan's mom?"

"She died before any of this went down."

"So she never saw her daughter get locked up? That's good, I guess. But it's sad, too, that she's dead." Jake knew what losing family was like. "Your resort would be a good place for Meagan to work, especially with the day care you built for your employees."

"Are you suggesting I should hire her because of that? Her child isn't my responsibility."

No, but from the tone in Garret's voice, Jake could tell that he was concerned about the kid. "With everything Meagan has been through, she may have been reformed."

"And maybe she hasn't changed a bit. She could be the same greedy little thief who ripped us off."

"You won't know unless you give her a chance. Besides, you don't really know what prompted her to take the money."

"Is there a good reason to steal?"

"No, but sometimes it's not about being greedy. I started stealing to try to fill the hole where my heart used to be. Then later, I did it to impress the girls I was with. You remember how messed up I was then."

"Yes, I remember. We were all a mess in those days." Garrett blew out a breath. "I still don't know what I'm going to do. But at least I have some time to think about it."

"I've got a lot to think about, too." Jake shifted his attention back to the family on the beach, where the toddler had been handed over to his dad, so his mom could pour apple juice in his tippy cup or sippy cup or whatever it was called.

Jake was definitely going to ask Carol to stay with him for a while and try to figure things out. But whether or not she accepted the invitation was a whole other matter.

On Sunday, Carol met with Jake at a park in her neighborhood. When he'd called to ask her to join him for a picnic, he'd told her that he wanted to discuss another aspect of the baby arrangement. She wasn't sure what that meant exactly. But she understood that there was still plenty to talk about. So here she was, waiting to see what he had to say.

They shared a blanket beneath a big, shady tree, with a cooler of food that Jake's chef had prepared.

"So what's on your mind?" she asked.

He filled his plate. "Maybe we can relax a bit before we get into the specifics?"

"All right." She allowed him the luxury he'd requested, even if she was impatient to know what had triggered this meeting. "It's a nice park. I've never been here before."

"Me, neither." He glanced around. "It's busy today."

Carol nodded. There was even a group who'd gathered for a family reunion, with homemade signs leading to their get-together. "Lots of people are barbecuing."

"My family used to grill in our backyard. The whole suburban weekend thing."

"Did your dad do the cooking?"

"Yes. But Mom always got everything ready ahead of time, and then he would get credit for how good it was."

Carol turned nostalgic. "It was like that at our house, too." It was also the type of lifestyle she'd always envisioned having. But this wasn't the time to think about that, not while she was pregnant with Jake's baby.

He said, "I don't like doing things my family used to do. It just makes me miss them more."

She sighed. "It helps me to remember mine."

"You and I are different in that way."

"We're different in lots of ways." They'd known it from the day they'd met, and now they were bringing a child into the world.

He ate a handful of grapes. "How often are you supposed to see the doctor?"

She spread a dollop of Brie cheese on a sliced pear. "Once a month, until I'm further along. Then it'll be every two weeks. After that, it'll be every week until the baby comes."

"I wonder if you'll have any food cravings."

She savored the pear. "If I do, I hope it's for stuff like this. But knowing me, it'll be a weird combination."

"Like matzo balls dipped in chocolate or something?"

Carol summoned a smile. She even laughed a little. "Gosh, I hope not."

He laughed, too. "I should warn my chef, just in case."

She turned serious. "Why would your chef be making the food I crave?"

Jake went somber. "Because I was thinking that you could move in with me for a while. That's what I wanted to talk to you about. There's plenty of room. You can have one of the guest wings all to yourself."

Moving into his mansion was the last thing she'd expected him to suggest. "How long is a while?"

"I don't know. Maybe five or six months. That'll give us time to shop for a house where you and the baby can live later on, and it'll give me the opportunity to be part of the pregnancy while you're staying at my place."

"But won't that cramp your style, with me waddling around your big, glitzy bachelor pad in maternity dresses?"

"You make it sound like I live at the Playboy Mansion." He made a tight face. "Or something equivalent to it."

"It's pretty darn close."

"It is not. And even if it was, I'm going to have to clean up my act when the kid is around."

"I know, but the baby isn't even born yet."

"You're twisting this all up, Carol."

Because she was afraid of moving in with him, of letting herself get that close. "I don't see why I can't stay at my apartment."

"I already told you why. I want to be part of the pregnancy. I want to get comfortable with it. And quite frankly, it bothers me to think of you being alone in the apartment. What if something happens?"

"Everything will be fine."

"But what if it isn't? We both know that bad things can happen. At least if you're staying with me, I can keep an eye on you. In fact, maybe you should just live at my house until the baby is born. That would be safer."

He sounded wonderfully protective, like the kind of man she'd always wanted to have children with. Except for him being a wild-spirited billionaire, she reminded herself.

Could he really clean up his act? Or would he succumb to his old ways, even with her living there?

"I don't know, Jake." She just couldn't fathom it. "I agree that becoming a parent is something you'll have to get used to. But me being at your house until the baby is born? That isn't necessary." She tried to make him see things a little more clearly, to recognize the problems that could arise. "Having me around 24/7 might make you feel trapped." She tore at her napkin, shredding the sides of it.

He watched her. "Looks to me like you're the one feeling trapped."

Yes, but she was also the one who might get attached, who might long for more than he was able to give. "I just don't want to jump the gun."

"Come on, give it a try. Let me keep you safe." He motioned to her still-flat stomach. "You've got my blood in you now."

His blood. His life force. "I couldn't handle you dating anyone while I was living there." She pushed it a step further, being as brutally honest as she could. "Or bringing women home to your bed."

"Is that what you think I'd do? With everything that's going on, that's the last thing on my mind." He crinkled his forehead. "Are you going to go back to online dating?"

"Now?" How could he even ask her such a ridiculous question? "Of course not. I'm having a baby."

He stared her down. "So am I."

"But you're not the one who's pregnant."

"So just imagine that I am."

She almost laughed at the image he presented. Yet she was touched by his daddy-like determination, too. Heaven help her, but she wanted him to keep her and their child safe, to be warm and attentive.

"Okay, then, we'll try it," she said, warning her fluttery heart to be still. "But if it gets too complicated, I need the option of moving out before the baby comes."

"Deal." He softened his voice. The look in his eyes gentled, too. "Only, it's already complicated, Carol."

"I know." But with how romantic he was making her feel, she was concerned that it could get much, much worse.

Carol should have listened to Jake and allowed him to hire the movers to pack for her. But she'd insisted that she was perfectly capable of boxing up her own belongings.

Of course Jake had offered to help, and he'd been watching her like a hawk, squawking every time he thought she was lifting something too heavy. She'd packed everything extralight, but that wasn't the problem. Carol was battling waves of nausea, and she didn't want Jake to know.

She glanced across the kitchen at him. He was wrapping glassware in paper, just as she was.

He looked up at her and frowned. "Are you all right?"

"I'm fine," she lied.

"You're as white as a sheet."

"I'm okay."

"Then why do you look like you're about to topple over?" He abandoned the glassware and came over to her. "You need to get off your feet."

"Maybe for a few minutes." She let him escort her to the couch, where she sat down and admitted the truth. "I'm dizzy, but I've got morning sickness, too."

He looked confused. "But it's afternoon."

"It can happen at any hour. The queasiness just started, about ten minutes ago. For the very first time."

"Damn. Do you want a cup of water or anything?"

"Soda sounds good." Hopefully it would settle her stomach. "There's lemon-lime pop in the fridge."

He headed to the kitchen, returning with the drink she'd requested. Carol gripped the can, appreciating how cold it was. She flipped the top and took a small sip.

"Thank you," she said after she swallowed it.

"You're welcome, but you still look like hell."

"Gee, thanks."

He sat beside her. "I didn't mean it like that."

She sipped a bit more of the soda, afraid she might faint, falling headfirst onto his lap. "If I pass out, don't panic."

"Oh, crap. Really? Tell me what to do."

She didn't have a clue. She'd never lost consciousness before. "Nothing."

"Nothing?" He sounded on the verge of panic already. "Maybe you should put your head between your knees. I always heard that's what someone should do. But maybe not in your condition." Clearly, he was clueless, too. "Do you want to lie down?"

"Yes, I think I should." She handed him the soda, and he moved off the couch, giving her room to stretch out. Between the wooziness and the nausea, she wasn't doing well.

Carol reclined, and Jake towered over her, peering down at her face. This had to be miserable for him.

"I'm sorry," she said.

"It's not your fault." He blew out a ragged breath. "I can finish packing. There isn't that much left to do."

"You're so helpful." She teased him, trying to ease the tension. "Are you going to change diapers when the baby is born, too?"

"I guess I'm going to have to learn. But I also think I should hire a nanny to go back and forth between your place and mine. I can turn the second guest wing in my house into the nanny's quarters. Then she can stay there whenever the baby sleeps at my place."

As opposed to him coming over to Carol's house to tuck their child in at night, like he'd originally planned? "I just wish that feeling lousy wasn't part of this. Being queasy is the worst."

"I hope I don't get queasy when I have to change a dirty diaper. I used to gag when I was kid and I had to pick up dog poop."

She squinted up at him. This was a weird conversation, but at least it was helping her focus on something besides being sick. "You had a dog?"

"No. But my sisters and I used to pet-sit for a neighbor. I was terrible at it. I wonder if we should get our kid a puppy, though."

"That's sweet. But maybe we'll stick to stuffed animals at first." She sat up and reached for the soda, taking it from him. "I'm starting to feel better now."

His gaze locked on to hers. "Are you sure?"

"Yes." She brought the can to her lips. But a second later, the queasiness came back tenfold.

When her stomach roiled, she knew she was going to throw up. She just hoped that she made it to the bathroom in time. Leaping forward, she thrust the soda at him, but he wasn't expecting it, and the drink fell between them and spilled to the floor. That didn't stop Carol from dashing off down the hall.

Thank goodness she managed to get to the bathroom in time to empty the contents of her stomach into the toilet.

Afterward, she flushed the handle. On wobbly legs, she stood and rinsed her mouth, then turned around and realized that she'd left the door open. And much to her mortification, Jake was standing there. Had he been there the whole time?

"Let me help," he said as he removed a washcloth from the towel rack and ran it under the tap.

He handed her the cool cloth so she could dampen her skin. She thanked him and sank back to the floor, sitting beside the commode. He got onto the floor with her.

"I feel like I have a hangover," she said.

He smiled. "I'll bet you've never been *that* drunk in your life."

"That's true. But it's what I imagine it must feel like." Less embarrassed, she was glad he was here. "I'll bet you've been *that* drunk."

"Hell, yes. I've prayed to the porcelain more times than you ever will."

"I just might beat your record if this keeps up." She lifted the washcloth from her forehead and set it on her lap. "But I'm all right now."

"You said that right before you ran in here."

"I know, but I mean it this time. I'm actually getting kind of hungry."

"Really?" He seemed relieved. "For what?"

A treat instantly came to mind. "A steamed artichoke. Doesn't that sound good?"

"Not particularly." He gave her a perplexed look. "Who wants an artichoke after they throw up?"

She did apparently. And they'd never even been her favorite food. She liked them, sure. But they sounded heavenly right now. "Will you go the store and get me one? Actually, you better make it two, in case one isn't enough."

He looked dumbfounded. "Do they sell them already steamed?"

"Of course not. I'll have to cook them. Go on." She

pushed at his shoulder. "You can go to the farmer's market down the street. They'll be fresher there."

"Oh, wow," he said. "This is a craving, isn't it?" His dark eyes lit up. "You're having your first craving."

"I guess I am." And it was mighty powerful, too. But she was going to think of it as her second craving. Because the first one was for Jake himself on those forbidden nights that she'd climbed into bed with him.

Like a dutiful father-to-be, he left to get the artichokes, mumbling about how clever their kid was, already figuring out ways to control them.

While he was gone, she went into the living room to wipe up the spilled soda, with their brilliant little baby in tow.

Eleven

Carol had been living at Jake's house for three weeks. She still was queasy, on and off, but none of the morning sickness medications worked, so she handled it the old-fashioned way, keeping crackers in her desk at work. At home, she relaxed as much as she could.

The guest wing that had become her temporary residence was as big as her apartment, if not a little bigger. Bright and beautiful, with modern furnishings, it offered all sorts of luxuries, including a private patio surrounded by natural landscape.

Since her quarters also had a kitchen, she was able to cook for herself. She was still eating the devil out of steamed artichokes, along with whatever else she was in the mood for. The chef made special things for her, too, in the main kitchen, spoiling her with his culinary genius. His name was Raymond, and he was a charmingly robust man, old enough to be her grandfather.

Raymond didn't live at the mansion. He came and

went, providing meals, per Jake's request. Typically, Jake fixed his own breakfast, which consisted of a protein shake his trainer had designed for him. He only ate bacon and eggs and things like that when he traveled. Otherwise, he stuck to his regular routine. Carol wouldn't drink one of those awful-looking shakes if you paid her.

As for Jake's maid, she didn't live on the property, either. She arrived every Monday, like clockwork, and cleaned his private suite. Another set of housekeepers were scheduled on Mondays, too; they tidied up the rest of the mansion. Carol never left a mess for them in her wing. She'd already gotten into the habit of cleaning on Sundays before they came.

On this quiet day off, she didn't know what to do with herself. At noon, she was wandering around her wing, still dressed in her pajamas.

She didn't have any sewing left to do. Last week she'd completed the Caribbean quilt for Jake, and he'd been thrilled to receive it. He'd draped it on the wall in the room that was going to be the nursery. He thought the quilt was even more special since their child had been conceived that weekend. For a man who'd never wanted children, he was doing what he could to embrace fatherhood.

Suddenly, her phone beeped, signaling a text. When she saw it was from Jake, her heart skipped a girlish beat.

The message read, Garrett wants to stop by and bring you something. Is that all right?

Yes. Of course, she replied.

Come to the living room and we'll wait for him.

She typed out, Be there in a few.

He ended the conversation with a simple, OK.

Carol set down her phone and went to her closet, removing a casual sundress to wear. Living in a house this big was crazy. And so was her emotional attraction to Jake. She'd been having way too many dreamy thoughts about him, and his tenderness over the baby was compounding her feelings.

But Jake was still wild at heart. She could see it every time she looked into his eyes. Becoming a parent wasn't curbing his restless spirit. If anything, the responsibility that had been thrust upon him was intensifying it.

Carol headed to the living room and spotted Jake standing at a big picture window, gazing out at the view.

She didn't disturb him or alert him that she was there. Instead, she took the time to study him: the familiarity of his body, the width of his shoulders, the way his T-shirt stretched across the muscles in his back, his long denim-clad legs.

A moment later, his posture changed, as if he'd just sensed her presence. He turned around, and she braced herself for the impact he was sure to cause.

"There you are," he said.

"Yes." There she was, struggling with her attraction to him.

"How's Artichoke?" he asked.

Carol smiled. That had become his nickname for the baby. "Fine. It's behaving."

"So you're doing okay today, too?"

She nodded. As well as an uncomfortably smitten woman could be.

Jake remained near the window. Since she'd moved into his mansion, they'd been keeping a deliberate physical distance from each other. It didn't diminish the electricity in the air. Their chemistry buzzed like honeybees pumped up on nectar. Carol could almost taste the sexy sweetness.

Before things got too quiet, she asked, "When will Garrett be here?"

"Soon." He finally took a step forward.

But not close enough to make a difference, she thought. "Did Garrett say what he's bringing me?"

"No, but it's not from him. It's from his mom. He told her about us, so the gift probably has something to do with the baby. She would have come with him, but she isn't feeling well today."

Although Carol had met Shirley Snow a few times over the years, she didn't really know her very well. "I'm sorry to hear that."

"She's always had her ups and downs."

Carol nodded. She was aware of the older woman's health issues and how her symptoms were worse at times than others. "It was nice of her to think of me."

"Yeah, she's a sweet lady. She's got Garrett twisted up about the girl who embezzled from us, though."

Jake explained what was going on, filling Carol in about Meagan needing a job in order to get paroled. Since the crime had been committed before Carol had worked for Jake, she barely knew anything about it. When he brought up the part about Meagan having a daughter, Carol thought about the child in her own womb.

She said, "I wonder if she would have stolen the money and taken the chance of going to prison if she'd known ahead of time that she was pregnant."

"I doubt she would have risked it." He hesitated. "But it's tough to know for sure. I keep trying to give her the benefit of the doubt because of the things I did when I was young."

"It's terrible that her daughter was born under those circumstances."

"It bothers me, too, especially now that we're having a kid." Jake lowered his gaze to her stomach. "Would it be all right if I put my hand there? Just to see if it feels different from before?"

Carol didn't know what to say. If he touched her, she feared that she might like it, far more than she should. "It's too early. I'm not even showing yet."

"I know, but the baby is still in there. Of course I won't do it if you don't want me to."

"No, it's okay. You can," she offered foolishly. Refusing didn't seem like an option.

He walked up to her and placed his palm against the waist of her dress. His touch was warm and tender, affecting her in a dreamy way. She could have been floating, like their mermaid, out to sea.

But all too soon, the memory of making love with him hit her like a heap of crumbled sand. If he stripped her naked, here and now, would she fall willingly at his feet?

He kept his hand painstakingly still. But when she looked up at him and their gazes met, he wrapped his arms around her, pulling her toward him.

They stared at each other, poised for a kiss.

The doorbell rang, jarring both of them to their senses. Jake jumped back, and Carol smoothed her dress.

"Ready?" he asked.

She nodded and followed him to the front door to greet their guest. Garrett came inside, but he told them that he couldn't stay long, so they stood in the foyer, dwarfed by its museum-height ceiling and stylish staircase.

Garrett was dressed in business attire, as if he'd just come from the hotel. He was as polished as ever, with his slicked-back hair and impeccable posture. He was holding Carol's gift, wrapped in plain white tissue paper.

"Hey there," he said to her.

"Hey yourself." She'd always liked him. But they had similar personalities, with practical natures. Of course, the exception was when Carol had gone wild on that weekend with Jake, playing around and getting pregnant.

As the father of her child stepped back, Garrett handed Carol the package. Even before she opened it, he said, "It's a medicine bag that my mom made for you. She gave one to Jake when he was younger, and to Max, too. And me, of course. And now that you're becoming part of our little ragtag group, she wanted you to have one, as well."

Carol nearly cried on the spot. She wanted to belong to them. She removed the tissue paper and unveiled the leather bag. It was exquisitely beaded, from top to bottom.

"It's beautiful," she said, her voice catching. "So incredibly beautiful. Please thank your mother for me, and tell her that I'll come see her when she's well enough for company."

"She'd like that." Garrett gestured to the bag. "It's bigger than the one Mom gave us guys, but she made it so you could include things for the baby, too. In fact, she already put some stones inside of it to get you started."

"Really?" Carol lifted the flap and peered into the bag. Sure enough, she saw pretty little rocks.

"They're easy to identify," Garrett said. "I can tell you what's there and what they mean."

"Okay, then tell me." She desperately wanted to know.

"All right. The red one promotes fetal growth, the green one aids child development and the pink one stimulates a bonding between an infant and its mother."

She loved the sentiment already. "What are the names of each of those stones?"

"Red jasper, green aventurine and pink calcite."

"That is easy." She noticed a multicolored crystal stone that he hadn't mentioned. "What about this last one?"

"That's angel aura quartz. Jake told me that he was concerned about keeping you and the baby safe, and when I mentioned that to Mom, she thought it would help. To bring angels to you."

Feeling far too emotional, Carol glanced at Jake. He was looking at her in the same way, as if both of their hearts had just gotten stuck in their throats.

After she and Jake broke eye contact, Garrett said, "You can put anything in the bag that feels special to you. There are no rules about what goes inside."

"It's a perfect gift," she replied. "I'm going to hang it beside my bed."

"I'm glad you like it." Garrett straightened his tie out of what seemed like habit. "But I better head out now. I've got a meeting."

"Thank you again. And please give your mom a hug from us."

The hotel magnate smiled, his rugged features softening. "From you and the baby?"

"Yes." She returned his smile. She and the little one in her womb were a package deal.

Garrett turned to Jake and said goodbye to him, too. Jake clapped him on the back, and they embraced, both of them appearing strong and brotherly.

Once they separated, Garrett exited the mansion, leaving Jake and Carol alone.

After Garrett was gone, Jake and Carol remained in the foyer. He couldn't stop looking at her, no matter how hard he tried. He was mesmerized by how reverently she was handling the medicine bag. Everything about her drew his attention.

"You were right about that being the perfect gift," he said.

"I'll have to think about what I'm going to put in it. But I love how Shirley included the stones already."

"It's interesting that you're going to keep it beside your bed. That's where I keep mine."

"You do? I never noticed yours there." She quickly amended, "But I haven't spent time in your suite."

And especially not in the vicinity of his bed, he thought. "It's hanging with a dream catcher Shirley also made for me."

"I always wondered about those, with the netting and the feathers and how popular they've become."

"They're supposed to protect you while you're sleeping. The bad dreams get caught in the net and break apart by morning. But the good ones slip through the hole in the center and glide down to the feathers, allowing you to keep those dreams."

She met his gaze. "Do you have bad dreams, Jake?"

"I used to, after I lost my family. I dreamed about the crash. And the fire. I would see the car burning in my nightmares, with demons rising up out of the ashes." He glanced at his arm, where the image of the fire god was. Uncta was his first tattoo. He'd had to wait until he'd turned eighteen to get it. His ink had been a long time coming.

She shifted her feet. "I had bad dreams when I first lost my family, too. But I can't recall them now. Not the details, anyway. But I do remember that I used to wake up crying in the middle of the night." She pressed the medicine bag closer to her body. "Then I would be afraid to go back to sleep."

"That's understandable." He thought about how her family had died, asleep in their beds, poisoned by a deadly gas while she was at a slumber party. "What happened that morning, Carol? Who found them?" This wasn't a conversation he'd intended to have. But for whatever reason, he needed to know. "It wasn't you, was it?"

"No." She tightened her hold on the bag. "But it became apparent, rather quickly, that something was wrong. My mom was supposed to come get me that morning and take me home. It was only a few blocks from our house, but Mom didn't want me coming back by myself. Of course she never showed up. She didn't answer the phone when I called, either, so my friend's mother drove me home."

"The mom who was hosting the slumber party?"

"Yes. Mrs. Reynolds. Later, I found out that her first name was Nancy. Anyway, when we got there, the front door was locked, but our garage had a little window. Nancy peered into it and saw that both cars were there."

"You didn't have a key?"

She shook her head. "My parents didn't allow us kids to be home by ourselves so there was no reason for me to have a key. They were waiting until I was a little older to give me that kind of responsibility. They were overprotective. It's just who they were." She paused, took a breath. "Nancy brought me back to her house and called the police. They're the ones who found my family."

And everything changed for her, Jake thought. Just the way it had changed for him. "I'm probably going to be overly protective with our child." He was already having concerns about keeping the baby safe in Carol's womb.

"I understand how you feel, after everything we've both been through. What happened to us shaped who we are."

"They say that time heals all wounds. But that's a false statement. The wound is still there, maybe not as fresh, but it's still there."

After a second of silence, she asked, "Was there a service for your family?"

"No. There was nothing. My grandfather said he couldn't afford to pay for it. And my aunt certainly couldn't, not with how broke she was. So I just said some prayers for them in my mind. What about yours?"

"My parents had a burial plan, so it was prepaid. But my sisters weren't included in the plan. They hadn't bought plots for us kids. No one thinks their kids are going to die. Our church took up a collection, so my sisters could be buried with my parents."

"What was it like for you, attending the service?" In some ways, Jake was glad that he didn't have to stand at a grave site, looking like the broken orphan that he was.

"It was surreal. Like a bad dream. Except that when you wake up, you know it's real."

His heart hurt for her, and for himself, too. "Maybe I'll ask Shirley to make our baby a couple of dream catchers." He wanted their son or daughter to dream well. "One for the nursery here and one for the nursery at your place, after we get you settled into your new home."

She smiled. "That's nice, Jake. Maybe she can attach some of the angel crystals to them. For extra protection."

"I like that idea." He liked her being at his house, too, even if it was far more intense than it should be. "You were right. It was too early for me to feel the baby inside you." All he'd felt was his hunger for her and the kiss it had almost triggered. "But that should get easier when your tummy gets bigger."

"Hopefully it will, especially if the baby is moving

around." She lowered her voice. "Otherwise, it just seems like you and me doing something we shouldn't be doing."

"It was my fault for pulling you toward me. I shouldn't have done that. In the future, I'll be careful not to do anything to stir those types of feelings again."

"I appreciate that. But I'm going to go and hang this up." She lifted the medicine bag. "So I'll see you later."

"Sure. See you." He assumed that hanging up the medicine bag was just an excuse to get away from him and the emotion it caused. But he let her go. He couldn't keep her in his clutches, not when he'd just promised to be careful. Even if, in spite of it all, he still wanted to kiss her something fierce.

Twelve

As Carol's pregnancy progressed, so did her friendship with Garrett's mother. Over the past few months, they'd formed a nice bond, spending time together whenever it was possible. Today Shirley had invited her over for a cup of tea.

While they sipped spiced chai and chatted, Carol spotted a delicately painted statuette that she hadn't noticed before. "You got a unicorn."

"I found it online. You know me. I like to collect magical things, even if it's just a mishmash of stuff. When Garrett first bought this resort, he offered to build me a house on the property, like he did for himself, but I enjoy living at the hotel."

Carol nodded. Shirley resided in one of the penthouses, with a spectacular view of the beach.

"I like knowing that there's activity around me, and when I'm feeling well enough to get out, all I have to do is go down to the lobby. I can dine in the restaurant of my choice and get my hair and nails done in the salon. Sometimes I even hang out with the concierge and talk to the guests."

"Hotel living at its finest."

"Indeed, it is. I used to be a hotel maid. That's what I did when Garrett was growing up. Of course I was sick a lot and kept losing jobs. But he grew up in this type of environment."

"I didn't know that." But it made sense that Garrett had become an hotelier.

"I'm blessed now. My son's success has spoiled me."

"You must be really proud of him."

Shirley sighed. "I am, more than I can say. He provides everything I need—the best food, the best medical care, everything I didn't have before. I probably wouldn't be alive today if it wasn't for him."

Carol studied her companion. She appeared older than her fifty years, but she was still pretty, with graying black hair, strong-boned features and deep brown eyes. Carol's mother would have turned fifty-three this year, if she'd lived.

"What's wrong?" Shirley asked. "Did I say something that made you feel sad?"

"No. I was just thinking about my mom."

"Oh, I'm sorry. I can only imagine how much you miss her. I'll bet if she was here, she would be thrilled about the baby. Look how cute that little bump of yours is."

Feeling better already, Carol glanced down at her tummy. "It is, isn't it?" Jake certainly thought so. He was always eager to touch it, even if their attraction still sparked like a lightning rod between them. Somehow, though, she managed to get through those heart-skittering moments, difficult as they were. "Odd as it sounds, I actually like being pregnant."

"There's nothing odd about that. You're glowing, like an expectant mother should be."

"I'm at eighteen weeks already. Oh, and tomorrow is our second ultrasound, the midpregnancy one, where we might be able to find out if it's a boy or a girl. The first one was too early to tell."

Shirley clapped her hands together. "That is exciting. Do you have an intuition about what it might be?"

"No. But Jake and I both decided that we want to know. He's certainly been anxious about everything associated with having a baby. Sometimes he can barely sit still. He's been going to the track a lot lately, racing those cars of his."

"He's always been like that. Running with the wind. When they were boys, I used to worry about his influence on Garrett and Max. That he would pull them into trouble, too. But he never did. I think in some ways, Jake is the gentlest of all of them, even with how rebellious he is. At one time he had a healthy, happy family. He knows what stability is. He understands it."

"He's going to be a wonderful father." Carol appreciated how attentive he was to her pregnancy. "He adores the baby already."

"That must make you happy."

"Yes, of course." But it also intensified her feelings for him, the attachment she'd been battling. Being alone at night was the worst. She longed to sleep beside Jake so he could hold her. Yet if she shared his bed, she wouldn't be able to resist him. She desired him in other ways, too.

"Have you started looking at homes?" Shirley asked.

"For my permanent residence? Not yet. We will once the time gets closer. I'm just surprised we've been able to live in the same house for this long. But it's almost like having separate places, with how big the mansion is."

"Jake likes to do things on a grand scale. I'm surprised he doesn't have the nursery all ready to go."

"He's waiting to find out what we're having. Then he plans to bring his decorator in to get started."

"Be sure to let me know how the ultrasound goes." Shirley reached over to pat her arm. "Your parents would be proud of you, Carol. You're a good girl."

A good girl having a baby with a notoriously bad boy. "I'm trying to stay true to myself." Just as Jake was being true to himself, as much as either of them could in the situation they were in.

"That's all a person can do. Oh, I forgot to tell you. The job thing is finally in the works."

"You mean with Garrett and Meagan?" The last Carol heard, Garrett was still dragging his feet, trying to decide what to do. "He went through with it?"

Shirley nodded. "He offered her a position as a stable hand, maintaining and cleaning the stables. He submitted it in writing."

"Did she accept it?"

"Yes. She responded to his note and thanked him. But they haven't seen each other in person or spoken on the phone about it. Garrett doesn't want to have any further contact with her. He wants to wait to see if the parole board approves the offer and releases her."

"Do you think they will?"

"I don't see why not. From my understanding, she's been a model prisoner."

Carol couldn't imagine being in Meagan's predicament, but she wouldn't have gotten herself into that kind of trouble in the first place, either. "I wonder if it will be awkward having Garrett as her boss."

Shirley sipped her tea. "She won't be working directly for him. Her boss will be the man who manages the barn.

Garrett does spend a lot of time at the stables, though. He keeps his own horses there and rides as often as he can."

Curious, Carol asked, "What made him choose that position for her?"

"She comes from an equestrian family. Both of her brothers are in the horse industry." Shirley paused. "I know it seems strange that I got my son involved in this, but I think it will help him get over it. He was insanely angry when he first found out. Ragingly mad. I've never seen him like that before."

"Jake told me that Garrett took it personally."

"A bit too personally, if you ask me. And that's why I think it needs to get resolved."

"Why do you think it affected him so badly?"

"He won't talk about it. But I have my theories. I think he might've befriended Meagan before it happened, and what she did blindsided him. Garrett has been hurt by people he trusted before. But whatever it was with Meagan, I don't want him carrying that kind of bitterness around in his heart."

Carol glanced at the unicorn. It was surrounded by fairies and gnomes and dragons. There were mermaids in the mix, too. "I agree. It needs to get resolved."

"Meagan apologized at the sentencing, but I don't think Garrett believed that she was sorry. I did, though. I went with him just to see what sort of person this young woman was, and she seemed terribly fragile to me."

"Is that part of why you took an interest in her when her parole came up?"

"Yes, and then when I learned that she'd had a baby in prison and the child's father abandoned her before it was even born, I empathized with her even more. Garrett's daddy walked out on me when I was pregnant, so I know what that feels like. But the clincher was when

I discovered that I was once acquainted with Meagan's mother. That seemed like a message from above."

"All of that makes sense to me. To Jake, too. He and I both feel bad about Meagan giving birth like that."

"And now you're well on your way to becoming parents yourselves."

"We definitely are." And tomorrow, they would be one step closer to knowing more about the ever-growing child in Carol's womb.

They were having a girl, Jake marveled, a wondrous little being with a strong and steady heartbeat. He'd attended the ultrasound with Carol. He'd sat beside her earlier that day and watched the technician slide the transducer over the gel on her stomach. He'd watched the monitor. He'd seen their daughter.

They'd been given pictures and a video of her, too. It was the most thrilling day of Jake's life, even more exciting than the first ultrasound. Last time, their unborn child had looked like an itty-bitty alien. This time, he could totally tell it was a baby. He'd already watched the video a zillion times, studying every detail, imagining how it was going to feel to hold their newborn in his arms.

"What an amazing experience," he said to Carol. He sat across from her in a patio chair beside his pool, moonlight reflecting off the water.

"I know," she replied, cradling her stomach. "It was wonderful."

He never wanted it to end. But he knew Carol would probably be headed to bed soon. Jake had no idea how he was going to sleep. He was far too wired.

"We should start coming up with names," he said. "Making a list of ones we both like."

"Sure, we can do that." She smiled at him. "You look crazy excited."

"I am. Just think of what a miracle this is. You and me. Two orphaned people, creating a little person like that. I mean, really, how beautiful is our daughter?"

Her smile turned even brighter. "She's perfect."

"I know, right?" He gazed at the mother of his child, thinking how enchanting she looked, with her hair stirring in the evening breeze, her tummy swollen from the seed he'd planted. "I can't wait for the next ultrasound, so we can see her again."

"Maybe we can give her a name that represents both of our families. You can come up with a Choctaw name, and I'll work on some Irish names."

"You're Irish?" After all of this time, how did he not know that about her?

She nodded. "From my mother's side. Both of my maternal great-grandparents were originally from Ireland."

"Whereabouts?"

"A place in East Cork called Middleton."

Jake's pulse jumped. "That's where your mother's ancestors are from? That's amazing."

"Why? Have you been there?"

"No. But the Irish built a monument honoring the Choctaw Nation, and that's where it's located."

She blinked at him. "Are you sure you're not mixing it up with something else?"

"No, I'm positive. During the Great Famine, the Choctaw Nation donated money to Ireland. Their gift was especially generous, because the Choctaw were still having struggles of their own. Prior to that, they walked the Trail of Tears, where most of them were forced to leave their ancestral homelands in what's now the southeastern US and relocate to Oklahoma. There were other tribes forced to make the journey, too, but the Choctaw were the first, with many of them dying along the way."

She seemed riveted by his story, by the past that bound his ancestors to hers. "So, later, when the Choctaw heard about how many people were dying in Ireland from the potato famine, they sent them money?"

"Yes, that's exactly it. And since then, there's been a kinship between the two. The monument is called *Kindred Spirits*. I'm not sure why they chose to put it in Middleton, though. It might have something to do with the artist."

"What does it look like?" she asked.

"It's a huge sculpture, with nine steel eagle feathers arranged in the shape of an empty bowl. The bowl represents the Great Famine, and the feathers are symbolic of the Choctaw. I've seen pictures of it online, but I'd love to see it in person sometime."

"Me, too." She cradled her stomach even more closely. "What a beautiful legacy this is for our daughter."

"We'll take her there, for sure. To visit the monument, but also to learn about the town where your mother's family was from. It will be a trip all of us can take together."

As soon as the word *together* was out of his mouth, a sense of fear punched his gut. Not at the prospect of traveling together, but at the future that would also separate them.

What was going to happen as time marched on, when Carol and their child were living in a different house from Jake? When both he and Carol started dating other people again?

He considered the possibility of Carol finding the husband she always wanted, a man who would become a stepfather to Jake's daughter. Just thinking about it twisted him up inside. The baby in Carol's womb belonged to him, not to an outsider honing in on Jake's territory.

Should he offer to marry Carol, securing his place in her life? Clearly, it would be the right thing to do. And the fear of another man taking his place was far worse than Jake buckling down and making a commitment to Carol.

Wasn't it?

Yes, he told himself. He didn't want Carol going off with someone else, no matter how scary the prospect of marrying her was to him.

"I'm getting sleepy," she said, jarring him back to the moment.

He looked into her eyes, this woman he was considering as his wife. By now, his heart was thudding in his ears. "I figured you'd want to turn in early."

She stood and smoothed her blouse over her tummy. "I'll see you in the morning."

He came to his feet, too. "I can walk you to your wing."

"That's all right. I can manage."

"I know, but I want to."

"Really, it's okay."

"Can I at least say good-night to the baby?"

"Of course." She invited him to come closer.

Immersed in myriad emotions, he put his hand on her stomach, spreading his fingers across the tiny bump that was their child. Then he glanced up and said, "Sleep well," to Carol.

"I will. It's been a nice day, but a long one, too."

She ended the connection, and he watched her walk away, the night embracing her just before she disappeared into the house.

Jake remained by the pool with a life-altering decision on his mind.

* * *

Carol got ready for the office, expecting to carpool with Jake. They rode together when their schedules meshed, and today was one of those days. But when she went into the main kitchen to meet up with him, she saw that he hadn't gotten suited up for work yet. He was a wearing a T-shirt and sweat shorts.

"Are you going in late?" she asked.

He shook his head. "I'm not going in at all. I've got too much going on in my head."

"Did something happen? Is something wrong?" Now that she took a closer look at him, she noticed how frazzled he seemed, as if he'd been up all night. He hadn't even had his breakfast yet. His protein shake was still in the blender.

Everything else was in order, though. His state-of-the-art kitchen gleamed, the stainless-steel appliances shining like mirrors. Of course, the cleaning crew was just there yesterday.

"What's going on, Jake?"

He pulled a hand through his hair. "I think you and I should get married."

Oh, my God. Carol felt as if the refrigerator had just opened up and sucked her inside, closing off the air to her lungs.

"What do you think?" he asked.

Needing to get off her feet, she sat on a bar stool at the center island counter. "Did you say married?" She repeated his strange proposal, making sure she'd heard him correctly.

"Yeah, you know…" He made walking motions with his fingers, using both hands, mimicking a couple going down the aisle.

Carol couldn't have been more confused. "Why?"

she asked. "Why do you want to get married all of a sudden?"

"For our daughter."

"That's the only reason?"

He frowned at her. "Isn't that enough?"

"No." She couldn't pretend that it was, no matter how badly she'd always ached to be a wife. "People who get married should be in love."

"But we love our child," he countered. "And she deserves to have both of her parents in the same house, living as a couple."

"Just being in the same house with a piece of paper between us isn't going to make us a family. You know that as much as I do. You and I were both raised by parents who loved each other, as well as their kids. That's the kind of family I want."

"But our baby girl needs us to be together."

He wasn't listening, she thought. "I'm not talking about our daughter. I'm talking about us."

"But I don't want you to marry someone else."

She blinked at him. "What?"

He poured his foamy green shake into a glass and took a swig. "If you don't marry me, then someday you'll marry some other dude and our poor kid will be shifted back and forth, between him and me."

"So that's what this is all about? You being jealous of a man who doesn't even exist yet?"

"What's so wrong with that? Me not wanting him to hone in on my child? Or my woman?"

She narrowed her eyes at him. "I'm not your woman."

"You could be, if you married me. I'd give you everything, Carol. You'd want for nothing."

"Except love?" Her heart hurt from the thought of it.

"You're not in love with me, either, so what difference does that make?"

"It matters. It's the dream I've always had."

"Of being with a guy who is nothing like me? Well, excuse me for offering to marry you and ruining your picture-perfect dream."

"That isn't fair." Even now, as she gazed into his deep dark eyes, she knew that she was capable of loving him. That maybe she was already well on her way. But God help her, she wasn't about to say it. Just thinking it could be true, just realizing that it might be happening, made her want to cry.

"Please, Carol. Say yes."

"I can't." She couldn't put herself in a position that might result in her loving a man who might never feel the same way about her. Already she could feel her soul being crushed.

He persisted. "Just think of how beautiful the wedding could be. We could get married on the beach. And we could have a big, sweeping reception and feed each other cake and do all of the things brides and grooms are supposed to do."

Damn him for making it sound so idyllic, for putting those images in her head. "Yes, the ceremony would be beautiful. But that's just a party. A fancy event." Something Jake excelled at. "It wouldn't be our day-to-day lives."

"I think having you as my wife would be sexy." He put down his drink. "I'd carry you to bed right now, if you'd let me."

She shook her head, fighting the urges rising inside her. She couldn't let him tempt her, no matter how hot he made her feel. "It would never work."

He stared across the counter at her. "We'd be good together, Carol, and you damn well know it."

Good. Bad. Right. Wrong. They would be all of those things. But without the possibility of him loving her, she couldn't break down and marry him. "My answer is still no."

"Refuse all you want, but this isn't over yet." With a rough catch in his voice, he stuck to his misguided plan. "I'm the father of your child and come hell or high water, I'm going to be your husband, too."

Thirteen

Jake worked on Carol over the next two weeks, trying to charm her into accepting his proposal. But he struck out.

He wasn't discouraged. He was going to keep at it. In fact, he had a ring in his pocket that he hoped would eventually sway her.

This was the perfect night to present it to her, as they were going to a black-tie charity event for his foundation. Jake was already dressed in his tuxedo.

He figured that, by now, she was ready, too. He knocked on the main door to her quarters, and she answered his summons.

"I just need to put on my shoes and grab my purse," she said. "Then we can go."

"No problem. We've got time." He checked her out. She was attired in a classic black gown with a beaded neckline. Her baby bump was evident, and oh-so-sweet. He was glad there was no mistaking it. Her hair, he noticed, was swept up into an elegant twist, the strawberry blond color shimmering beneath the overhead light. "You look gorgeous," he told her.

"Thank you." She stepped into a pair of low-heeled pumps. "You're rather dapper yourself."

"Thanks. I think I look like a groom."

She didn't reply, but he suspected that his comment made an impact, just as he'd intended. No doubt, it would cross her mind throughout the night.

He said, "Before we go, there's something I want you to have." He wasn't going to waste any time in turning the ring over to her. He reached into his pocket and removed the case.

"Jake." She started to protest before he even gave it to her. Clearly, she had an inkling as to what it was, based on the box.

"Just indulge me, okay?" He flipped it open and showed it to her. The gold ring had two hands holding a heart-shaped stone, with a crown at the top. The heart itself was a flawless, six-carat, fancy vivid pink diamond. "I researched Irish rings and read about Claddagh styles, so that's what this is. I had it custom made. I discussed the specifics with the jeweler, of course, but this is the first time I've ever bought a gift on my own, where I didn't ask my stylist for help." He paused to collect his thoughts. "Claddagh rings have been around for thousands of years, but jewelry experts disagree about their exact origin, so they're shrouded in mystery, even today. According to what I uncovered, there is a right and wrong way to wear to them. There are four options—single, in a relationship, engaged and married. If you wear it on your right hand, with the crown pointing toward you it means single, away from you on that hand means you're in a relationship. If you wear it on the left hand with the crown toward you, it means engaged, away from you shows that you're married."

"Oh, my." She removed the ring from the box. "The detail is exquisite. I've never seen anything like it."

"The band is shaped like an eagle feather so that part is different from traditional Claddagh rings. I did that to represent my and our baby's Choctaw blood. I got the idea from the *Kindred Spirits* monument and the style of feathers used for that." He softly added, "I wanted this to be special between us. For now, you can wear it on your right hand with the crown toward you to show that you're single. Later, when you decide that you want to marry me, you can switch it to show that we're engaged."

She inspected the design, turning it, looking at the band from every angle. "The story behind it is fascinating."

Did that mean he was making headway? "I chose a pink diamond because they're rare. I considered a bigger diamond, but that one complements the shape and size of the ring."

"Are you kidding? It's huge already. It's absolutely breathtaking."

"When we get married, I'm going to have the same type of ring designed for myself. Men can wear them, too. But I won't put a stone in mine. It will just be made of gold."

Her voice cracked a little. "I already told you that I can't marry you, Jake."

He reiterated the point he'd made earlier. "You can wear it in the single position." He just wanted to make sure the ring was in her possession. "That's all I'm asking for now."

Her breath rushed out. "Okay. I'll accept it under those conditions." She placed it on her right hand with the crown pointing toward her. "Thank you for thinking of me and the baby. I'm touched by all of the time and care you put into it. Really, truly, it's overwhelming."

Her praise and appreciation gave him hope. "Just remember that someday you *are* going to be my wife. I can't let another man be involved in raising our child."

"Don't talk about that. Let's just go out and have a nice time."

"All right." He glanced at the glittering jewel on her finger, wishing he could hold her. And kiss her. And make her marry him. But for now, this was a start.

The casino-themed party was being held at a renovated 1930s mansion that Jake owned. Typically, he rented it out for private events, but tonight it was being used for his charity. Carol thought the place was spectacular. Mostly, though, her mind was on the ring he'd given her. The color and clarity of the diamond was stunning. The cultural history associated with the ring was beautiful, too. Problem was, the design included a heart, yet Jake's proposal didn't involve loving her. He was still making his case about not wanting her to marry someone else or separate their child from him. In that regard, nothing had changed.

Nonetheless, she'd accepted the ring. Of course, she was wearing it in a way that defined her as single.

Painfully single, she thought.

Even with how hard she'd been trying to fight her feelings, Carol couldn't deny that she'd fallen in love with Jake. And for her, it didn't get any worse than that. She'd never envisioned unrequited love as being part of her future. But what woman did? That wasn't the fairy tale of which dreams were made.

"Can I get you anything?" Jake asked as they moved deeper into the mansion.

"No, thanks. I'll grab something later." There was plenty of food and drink available; the buffet was over-flowing with gourmet goodies. "You don't have to babysit me. This is your party, and you need to make the rounds."

He frowned. "I don't want to leave you unattended."

"Don't worry. I'll be fine. I might even play roulette for a while."

"Okay. But in case you need to rest, take this." He pressed a key into her hand. "It's for one of the private suites. It's the first door at the top of the stairs."

"Thank you. That's very thoughtful of you."

"I just want you to be able to get off your feet. If you'd rather go home early, you can do that, too. You can take the car, and I'll catch a ride with Garrett. Either way, I know how tired you get these days, and it's probably going to be a late night."

She opened her bag and dropped the key inside. "I'll use the room if I need to." She didn't want to leave the party without him.

He angled his head. "What do your friends think, Carol?"

She gave him a perplexed look. "About what?"

"Me wanting to marry you. You've told them, haven't you?"

"Yes. And they think I should accept your offer." She'd hoped that at least one of them would see it her way, but none of them had. "They don't understand why I would refuse to marry a rich and handsome man who also happens to be the father of my child."

His gaze locked on to hers. "So they're not buying into your love theory, either?"

"Your billionaire status cancels that out, I guess. Most

people are swayed by money." And once they saw the ring, they would be even more impressed.

He shrugged. "I've gotten used to that. Besides, I'd rather have them on my side, no matter what their reasoning."

"You better get going." He was standing too close for comfort, making her feel too much. "You need to tend to your guests."

"Yeah, I suppose I do. I need to find Garrett, too. He's somewhere around here. I'll check on you later, okay? I have a key to the room as well, so I can let myself in if you're up there."

She nodded and watched him walk away. He was right about his tuxedo. It did make him look like a groom.

Carol went in the opposite direction. There were makeshift casinos on both sides of the mansion, with most of the ground floor having been converted into a gambling den.

She found a roulette table with an open spot. She played badly, but it didn't matter if she won or lost. All of this was to benefit foster kids. If anyone knew how important that was, it was her and Jake and Garrett. And Max, too, of course, but he was still traveling. He'd been informed about the baby by now, though. Jake had finally called and told him.

"Well, hello there," Carol heard a woman say from beside her. She glanced over and saw Lena Kent.

"Oh, wow," Carol responded. She hadn't crossed paths with the pop star since the private island party. Lena looked like the celebrity she was, with her platinum blond hair and feline eyes. She wore a slim gold dress, slit up the front, with a white feather boa draped around her neck.

"I heard that you're having Jake's baby, and it appears

the rumors are true." Lena grinned at Carol's belly. "Is that from the Caribbean?"

"Yes. Your couples-only weekend was the culprit."

Lena struck a dramatic pose, giving her feather wrap a quick toss. "So glad I could be part of it." She was still smiling. "You better make me an honorary relative."

"Absolutely. You can be her eccentric aunt."

"Her? It's a girl? Well, that settles it. I'm going to take her shopping and spoil her with all kinds of bling. Speaking of…" Lena gestured to Carol's ring. "Check out the rock on your finger. Is it from Jake?"

"He just gave it to me tonight."

Lena grabbed her hand to get a closer look. "Damn, that's nice. It's so regal with the crown, too. Perfect for you and how classy you are."

"Thank you." Carol explained the meaning behind the ring and why she was wearing it on her right hand. "I'm just not ready to marry him."

"I can see why you have your reservations. I never pictured Jake as the marrying kind. But I think it's kind of cool that he wants to settle down and try to be a husband. I'll give him points for that." Lena straightened her boa. "By the way, I'm not with Mark anymore. We stopped seeing each other soon after my birthday."

"Oh, I'm sorry. I thought you made a great pair."

"It was fun while it lasted. But I have someone new."

"Already?"

Lena laughed. "It's been a while."

Yes, of course. Carol's pregnancy was proof of that. "Does Mark still work for you?"

"No. It got too awkward. I hired another dancer to replace him." Lena nodded toward the other side of the room. "Just to make you aware, there's a hot brunette over there who's been staring at us."

"Maybe she's a fan of yours."

"I get the feeling it's you she's been watching."

Carol glanced over her shoulder. A hot brunette indeed, all decked out in red, glitzy from head to toe. "That's Susanne Monroe. She used to go out with Jake. They broke up right before he took me to the Caribbean."

"Well, that explains it, then. Because she sure seems interested in you."

"I don't know why she would care about me and my situation with Jake. Her former husband is Kenny Monroe, the pitcher, and she only dated Jake on the rebound, when she was smarting over the divorce. She and Jake weren't even together for very long."

"Maybe so, but I saw them talking earlier."

Carol frowned, fighting a stab of jealousy. "She's a guest. He has to engage with her."

Lena sighed. "Just protect what's yours, okay?"

"He isn't mine, not in the way you mean."

"The heck he isn't. He proposed to you, didn't he? That gives you a right to keep an eye on a woman who might be trying to restake her claim."

Carol didn't want to believe that Susanne was after Jake, so as the evening progressed, she tried to shut it out of her mind. It wasn't as if Susanne had become a nuisance. In fact, she left the event early. Carol saw Susanne walk out the door with a posse of other Beverly Hills socialites. Still, Lena's concern niggled at her.

Finally, when Carol needed a break from the festivities, she went upstairs to her private room.

Later, Jake appeared, like a mirage, standing beside the bed. She had no idea how much time had passed, until he told her that the party was over. She'd only closed her eyes, intending to rest, but had fallen asleep instead.

As she gazed up at him, he reminded her of a prince,

come to claim his princess, his bride. She even fantasized about him leaning over to kiss her.

She didn't say anything to him about Susanne. It seemed petty now that he was here, taking her home, this beautiful man who wanted to marry her.

While at work late Monday afternoon, Carol kept gazing at her ring, wondering how it would look on her left hand.

Should she accept Jake's proposal and create a life with him?

She couldn't deny that every moment she spent with him, every instant that he was near her, felt so good, so right.

Jake was kind and protective and attentive. Wonderfully romantic. Everything she believed a husband should be. And he was trying so hard to win her over and make her his wife. Was it possible that he was falling in love with her, too? A bit too dreamy, she studied her ring again, imagining what marrying him would be like.

A second later, Carol glanced up and saw that Kristen was poking her head in the doorway. The receptionist seemed anxious.

"What's going on?" Carol asked her.

"Can I come in and talk to you?"

"Sure." She invited the fidgety girl into her office, wondering if she was having boyfriend problems again.

Kristen entered the room and closed the door. She pulled a chair closer to Carol's desk and sat on the edge of it.

Then she said, "I know you haven't agreed to marry Jake or anything. But everyone at the office knows that he asked you. He's made that pretty clear around here."

Yes, Jake had spilled the beans, professing his intentions. "Are you here to try to talk me into marrying him? Because I've already been—"

Kristen cut her off. "I'm sorry, but that's not why I'm here. It's just the opposite. I saw him today with another woman."

Carol's heart nearly jumped out of her chest. "What?"

"I went to get some food at the taco place where a lot of us go, and when I was waiting for my take-out order, I saw Jake and one of his old girlfriends having lunch, with margaritas and everything. They looked pretty cozy to me. She was even reaching across the table to touch his hand."

Carol felt sick, a wave of nausea roiling through her body. "Was it Susanne Monroe? The baseball player's ex?"

"Yep. That's who it was, the one who used to parade around here like a Kardashian." Kristen frowned. "What made you assume it was her?"

"She was at the charity event on Saturday, and Lena told me I should be wary of her. But I brushed it off. I ignored the way Susanne had been staring at me."

"I'm so sorry, Carol. I hated to even tell you that I saw Jake with her. But I don't want to see you get hurt."

She was already hurt, torn up inside. "You were right to tell me. Did he know that you saw him?"

"No. They were in a booth and his back was to me." Kristen scooted her chair a little closer. "Do you think it's possible that I misinterpreted what was going on?"

Carol looked into the younger woman's eyes. Now she was backpedaling, after everything she'd said? "Do *you* think that's possible?"

"I don't know. I just hate to be the one to ruin things for you. And since Lena warned you first, I guess what I saw was real. It's just hard to believe that Jake would go off with another woman, not with how much he wants to marry you."

"It's hard for me to fathom, too." Especially in light of how kind and protective he'd been. "I'll get Jake's side of it, and if he has a reasonable explanation, I'll take what he says into consideration." And pray, with all of her heart, that it wasn't what it seemed.

"What if he is messing around with Susanne?"

"Then I'm going to pack my belongings and leave. There's no way I could keep staying at his house with him."

"Would you quit being his assistant, too?"

"Yes, I would stop working here." Seeing Jake every day would destroy her. She would need to separate her life from his, at least the best she could. But either way, they were still having a baby together.

"I don't think I could fill in for you, not like I did when you were sick. I'd be too mad at Jake to help him out like that."

"Don't worry, I'd find another replacement. I wouldn't expect you to pick up the pieces." Carol would have to do that all on her own.

Jake sat across from Carol in his sunken living room, with his heart sinking, too. How could everyone think so badly of him?

"I wasn't having a romantic lunch with Susanne," he said, responding to the accusation that had been thrust upon him. "And her interest in you at the party wasn't sinister. She wasn't giving you the evil eye or trying to get back together with me. She was just curious about you."

Carol didn't reply. Apparently she was waiting for him to expound further.

So he continued by saying, "When she saw you and

Lena, she wanted to come over and talk to you, but then she got nervous, so she just stayed away."

Carol folded her arms across her stomach. "Why would Susanne even care about me?"

"Because when I spoke to her at the party, I told her about you and the baby, and she thought it was romantic that you tamed a guy like me. It made her want to get to know you a little better." Jake reached for the ice water in front of him and took a swig. "Susanne is mixed up about her own life. She's still not over her ex. That's why she texted me today and asked me to lunch. She wanted to talk to me about how she can win Kenny back."

Carol raised her eyebrows. "She wanted advice from you? About relationships?"

"I know. Crazy, huh? She assumed that you and I were a couple. I didn't give her all the sordid details at the party. I just told her that I was planning on marrying you. So when she invited me to lunch today, I figured that I'd set her straight about us and tell her that I wasn't qualified to help her with Kenny."

"Kristen said that Susanne was reaching across the table for your hand."

"That's true. She did that. But it was only after I admitted that you've been refusing to marry me."

Carol unfolded her arms. "I'm sorry, Jake, that everyone jumped to conclusions."

"So you believe me?"

"Yes, I do. And I'm sorry that Susanne is still hurting over Kenny. But we aren't the role models for her happiness."

"I wish we were." He got up and sat beside her. "I still don't understand why you won't marry me."

"I was thinking about it, before Kristen came to my office and threw me for a loop."

"Really?" His mood brightened. "You were?"

"Yes, but I was thinking about love, too."

Damn. Did that she mean was still going to hold out for another guy? "What if you never find the love of your life? Or what if you think you found him and he turns out to be a jerk. Will you marry me then? Or am I never going to measure up to your dream?"

"Oh, Jake." She sighed. "If only you knew."

Now he was really confused. "If I only knew what?"

Her voice jittered. "That I already met the man I love. That he's already part of my life."

Suddenly he felt as though the world was caving in on him. "There's someone else? How is that even possible? The only person you've been spending time with is me."

She just stared at him. *Really* stared at him.

Holy hell. Realization dawned in his stupid male brain. "So it's me?" He even tapped his chest, identifying himself. "I'm the one?"

She nodded briskly, shakily.

"You actually love me? Like *love* me, *love* me?"

"Yes," she replied, leaning closer to him.

This should have been good news. He should have rejoiced in her admission. But Jake panicked instead. He didn't know anything about that kind of love. He'd done everything in his power to avoid those types of feelings.

He stood and moved toward the window. And as soon he turned back around, facing Carol once again, he panicked even more. Her eyes were filled with pain.

"I'm sorry," he said. "I wasn't expecting…"

"I have to go," she said. "I have to pack."

"You're leaving? What? No." His freak-out was getting worse. "Stay and we'll figure this out."

"There's nothing to figure. I can't live here anymore. I can't handle this."

He wasn't handling it, either. But he couldn't bear to lose her. "Please, I still want to marry you. I still want to create a life for our child."

She looked at him as if he'd just lost his mind. "How can you marry me when you won't even sit next to me? What kind of example is that going to set for our daughter?"

As much as he wanted to prove that he could still be a good husband and father, he couldn't bring himself to return to her side. He was struggling to breathe, forcing air in and out of his lungs. Maybe she was right. Maybe he was losing his mind. "I just need a minute."

"Take all the time you need, but I have to get out of here."

She got up from the sofa, and when she left the room, Jake was still standing with his back to the window, his feet frozen to the floor.

Fourteen

Carol moved swiftly, getting her suitcase ready, needing to escape. She hadn't intended to tell Jake that she loved him, and now that she had, it was the worst day of her adult life.

In the middle of her packing, Jake entered the room, invading her space, torturing her heart.

"You didn't have to follow me in here," she said.

"Yes, I did. It just took me a minute to get my feet moving."

Right. The minute he'd needed to get his emotions together. Thing was, he didn't look any less stressed. Even now, he was pulling a hand through that messy hair of his. The troubled rebel, she thought. The man who'd burrowed his way into her soul.

"I wish I hadn't fallen for you," she said.

"No one has ever been in love with me before. I don't know what to do with it, Carol."

"You're supposed to accept it and return the feeling.

It's funny, because when I was contemplating marrying you, I wondered if you were falling in love with me, too. But I was just being silly and dreamy." And wrong, she thought, so very wrong.

He lowered his hand from his hair. "I'd rather just keep things simple."

"And marry someone you don't love?" That was far from simple to her. "That isn't how marriage is supposed to work."

"Not traditionally, but it can be whatever people decide to make it." He shifted his stance. "And maybe in time I'll get used to…"

She studied him from beneath her lashes. "Get used to what, a one-sided relationship where I love you but you don't love me?"

"I'm just trying to hold on to what we have."

"What we have is a wreck." Carol took an audible breath, the sound engulfing the room. "I'm going to call Shirley and ask if I can stay there for a few days." She didn't want to be alone, and she knew that Garrett's mother would comfort her more than any of her other friends could. "I'm not taking everything with me today. I'll come back for the rest of my belongings, but you won't see me at the office again. I can't work for you, Jake. I'll call a temp agency and arrange for my replacement, then you can hire someone permanently when you're ready to tackle that."

He glanced at the hastily folded clothes she'd placed on the bed. "I don't want you to do this."

"I know. You still want me to marry you. Do you know how crazy that sounds?"

"I can't help it. In my mind, you're still meant to be my wife." He glanced at her stomach. "You and me and our daughter. We're supposed to be together."

She disagreed. "Not like this we aren't."

"There's nothing I can say or do to keep you here?"

"No." She couldn't force him to love her, to feel things he didn't feel. Still, he looked so lost, so confused, that she wanted to wrap her arms around him. But what good would that do? She was just as lost and confused as he was. "It's better for us to live separate lives and share custody of the baby, like we'd planned to do originally."

When she reached down to remove her ring and return it to him, he held up his hands, like a gunslinger who was about to be shot.

"Don't you dare give that back." He lifted his hands a little higher. "I refuse to take it."

"Jake, please."

"No. No way." He shook his head, as stubborn as a man could be. "Besides, what does it matter if you keep wearing it? It still says that you're single."

"It's different now." Single or not, wearing it was hurtful. The ring represented everything she loved about him. His warmth. His generosity. The kind and caring father he'd become. The *Kindred Spirits* legacy they shared.

After she removed it from her finger, she placed it in its original box. Then she put the box inside her medicine bag and packed it. With Jake's refusal to take the diamond back, it was the best she could do. Just leaving the ring behind would seem unkind, and she couldn't bear to create more pain between them.

She said, "When I thought something might be going on between you and Susanne, I was prepared to walk away. But I never thought I'd be leaving under these circumstances."

"I never imagined it ending at all." Jake cleared his throat. "On the night of the fund-raiser when I came into the room to check on you, and you opened your eyes and looked at me, it seemed like we were already married."

"I felt like a bride when I woke up and saw you. A princess, waiting for her groom. I even fantasized about you kissing me."

He stepped a little closer. "I wish I would have."

She backed away from him. "It wouldn't have mattered, not now."

He didn't move forward again or try to close the gap between them. He conceded, allowing her the distance she needed, but it didn't help ease her pain. She hurt just the same.

"I'll let you finish packing," he said. "Just let me know when you're ready to go, and I'll put your luggage in your car for you."

"Thank you." She didn't know what else to say. "It's just the one bag."

"You still shouldn't lift it."

He exited the room, and she fought the urge to cry. Carol dreaded the future, afraid that no matter how many years went by or how separate their lives became, she would never stop loving him.

Jake spent the next two days holed up in his house. His big, hollow mansion. He hadn't felt this alone since his family died. He missed Carol something awful.

He understood why she left. But he couldn't bear not having her here with him. He wanted nothing more than to make her his wife. And not just because of the baby.

It was the joy of being with Carol.

The same type of joy that had been snuffed out when his family's car had crashed and burned.

Was that the reason he'd been unable to return Carol's love? Yes, he thought, it was. Creating a family, *a true family,* like the one he'd lost was frightening to him. So he'd offered her a half-assed marriage instead.

What was he going to do about it? Sit here and wallow in his mistake, in the heartache of being an idiot? Letting Carol go made no sense, none whatsoever.

Still, he was scared. Since she'd been gone, he'd been dreaming about the crash, his childhood nightmares returning with a fiery vengeance. The dream catcher beside his bed hadn't saved him from reliving the pain. Nothing would, except facing his fears.

Determined to conquer them, Jake went out to the garage and climbed into the SUV he'd bought to accommodate the baby. Only, his daughter wasn't arriving today. Today he was going back to his own youth, to the house where he'd grown up.

For him, that was as close as it got to his family having a grave site. If their spirits were anywhere, it would be at the home where all of them had lived.

Lived and loved, he thought.

Jake drove to the San Fernando Valley, heading toward his old neighborhood. His parents didn't own the home where they'd raised him and his siblings. It was a well-maintained rental, a house that had belonged to a corporation, much like the company Jake owned now.

Was that why he'd started buying properties? To give other people nice, safe places to live? He'd never really analyzed the emotional impact of his investments.

He turned onto his long-ago street and parked in front of the ranch-style house. It looked different yet somehow the same. The paint was changed, the windows trimmed in blue instead of red. The lawn was less green, a result, most likely, of water conservation associated with the current California drought. The tree that graced the yard was bigger, though, its branches reaching toward the sky.

When Jake was small, he used to offer to help with the yard work. Then later, it became a chore that had been expected of him. Sometimes he'd complained, but mostly he'd enjoyed spending time alone with his dad.

Reflective, Jake sat back in his seat. Since he didn't want to intrude on the new residents, he stayed in the car. He couldn't tell if they had kids. There were no outward signs of children, not like when he used to leave his bike in the walkway.

It felt good to be here, to think about the sweetness from his youth. He wanted to provide that kind of family for his daughter. He wanted it for himself and Carol, too. Being afraid to love her was wrong. He needed to give her his heart, openly, fully.

He understood his feelings now. They were so clear, so obvious. But was he ready to do this, to admit that he loved her?

Yes, he thought. He was ready, willing and able.

Should he text Carol ahead of time or just show up unannounced? He opted for the phone, giving her a chance to prepare. He typed, A lot going on. Need to talk.

After he sent the message, he waited. Then waited some more.

He tried not to panic about Carol not responding. She might not be in the vicinity of her phone. It didn't mean that she was ignoring him.

Trying to keep from going stir-crazy, he shifted his attention to the tree that had grown so big. Sometimes his sisters used to sit beneath it, surrounded by their friends, paging through fashion magazines and yapping about the styles they liked. He also remembered when a neighbor's cat had gotten caught in the tree. Nobody called the fire department the way they did on TV. Jake's bold and beautiful mother had climbed up there, via a ladder, and coaxed the cat down. The frightened little tabby went home to its owner, only to run away another time and never be seen or heard from again.

Jake frowned, disturbed that the story didn't end well. But that didn't change the purpose of coming back to his family, of seeking them out. It didn't change how he felt about Carol, either. If anything, it was a reminder that life was neither good nor bad. It was simply what you made of it, and he wanted it to be good and happy and whole.

When his phone pinged, he grappled with the device and nearly dropped it.

Carol's response was What's going on?

Sitting in front of my old house.

What old house?

From when I was a kid.

I don't understand.

Will explain in person. Things are different with me now. Can I come over?

She agreed with a simple Yes.

But that was all the encouragement Jake needed.

Grateful for a second chance, he took one final look at the house. He was wrong about his family's spirits being here. They'd moved on a long time ago. What Jake had encountered was his own spirit, the boy he once was, growing into the man he'd become.

Carol was anxious to know what Jake meant when he'd texted that things were different now. But she was nervous about seeing him, too. Overall, she was a mess, inside and out.

Before she'd seen his text, she'd been watching TV, mindlessly, in her pajamas, without a stitch of makeup. So now, she rushed to get herself together, applying lip gloss and mascara and putting on a maternity blouse and leggings.

She hadn't told Shirley that Jake was coming over. The older woman was napping in her room.

As soon as a knock sounded on the door, Carol tried to center herself with a calming breath. But it didn't do any good. She was still nervous.

She opened the door, and there he was. The father of her child. The man she loved with every troubled, aching beat of her heart.

He looked strong and beautifully wild, much as he always did. Yet something about him *did* seem different. It was his eyes, she thought. She saw a sense of calmness beneath the wild, as if the restlessness that normally drove him was gone. So what did that mean? How did that affect what was happening between them?

Carol gestured to her surroundings. "Come in."

"Thanks."

He entered the suite, and they stood in the living room. She longed to touch him, to put her hand against his jaw and feel the slight bristle of beard stubble there, but she fussed with the hem of her blouse instead.

"Where's Shirley?" he asked.

"She's resting. Do you want to go to the guest room where I'm staying?" She didn't want to have a private discussion out in the open, in case Shirley got up.

"Sure. That would be good."

She led him down a short hallway, and they went into

the colorfully decorated room and closed the door, silence streaming between them.

Then he said, "I'm sorry I hurt you, Carol."

"I'm sorry I hurt you, too." She'd never meant to cause him pain. "I still don't understand why you're here, though, and how going to your old house factors into it."

"I was searching for my family, hoping to feel their spirits and find a sense of peace. Since you left me, I've been having nightmares again, like I did after they first died."

"Did it work? Did you connect with your family?"

"No. But I connected with myself and the reason I couldn't commit fully to you. It was because I was afraid that if I loved you the way my parents loved each other, something would go wrong. But if I only went halfway, loving our child but keeping you at arm's length, everything would be okay."

Now she wanted to touch him even more. But she listened to him instead, letting him get all of his thoughts out.

He said, "After you got pregnant, and I started worrying about you finding another husband and involving him in our daughter's life, I didn't even stop to consider that I might be falling in love with you. Or that you were on the verge of falling for me." He moved closer to her. "So when you finally told me how you felt, I panicked and pushed you away. But I do love you, Carol, and I want to marry you for all the right reasons."

Tears rushed to her eyes, and she reached out to skim his jaw, allowing herself the touch she craved. Beneath her fingers, his skin was warm, his beard stubble rough. She ran her hands over his entire face, smoothing back his hair to trace his childhood scar.

"I would be honored to marry you. For all the right

reasons," she added. What she'd seen in his eyes when he'd first arrived, the change in them, was love. She knew that now. "I missed wearing the ring you gave me."

"Wear it now."

"I'll wear it forever." She removed it from her medicine bag and placed it on her left hand, putting it in the engaged position and sealing their future with a diamond heart, an Irish crown and a Choctaw feather.

He leaned in to kiss her, and she reveled in the life they would be building together. Carol couldn't imagine a more beautiful moment. This was the proposal she'd always longed for—a dream come true.

Jake and Carol waited for Shirley to awaken from her nap to tell her the news. She was thrilled, of course, hugging them like there was no tomorrow.

But there would be plenty of tomorrows, Jake thought. He and Carol had the rest of their lives to be together.

He took his new fiancée back to his house, and as soon as they entered the mansion, he said, "I can sell this place and we can get something homier. Like what I was going to buy for you and the baby. Only, all of us can live there together."

She cocked her head. "Really? Are you sure you want to relocate?"

"I'd rather start fresh with a home that complements both of us. But it still needs to be big enough for more kids."

Her eyelids fluttered. They were standing in the foyer, with a chandelier shining above them. "More kids? Are you expecting the condoms to fail again?"

"No. I'm thinking we could actually plan to expand our family. We don't want Artichoke to be an only child, do we?"

"You're right." She smiled like the dickens. "We should give her some siblings."

"We can have three altogether." There had been three kids in his family, just as there had been in hers. "We'll make that our lucky number." Jake put his hand on Carol's tummy. "But first we need to bring this one safely into the world."

"We will. Our little girl is going to be just fine."

"Yes, everything will be okay." He'd found his peace, his life, his woman. "My parents would have adored you."

"Mine would have been crazy about you, too. They'd be so happy for me right now."

"When we get resettled, we can display all of our pictures, old and new." He studied her, thinking how amazing she was. "I have a bunch of photos stored away from when I was kid. But now I want to bring them out in the open."

"Pictures of my family have always given me comfort. But I've never been back to the house where they died. Maybe I should go there, like you did with your old house, just to come full circle, too." She studied him with the same kind of admiration he felt for her. "You were right when you said that I overcompensated after I lost them, that I was trying to be so good. I didn't let myself grieve the way I should have. I even felt guilty and weak when I used to cry in the middle of the night. I wanted to be stronger than that."

"You are strong. So am I. But we're stronger as a couple than we are apart." He took her in his arms. "Come lie down with me, Carol. I want to hold you."

She nuzzled against him. "I want to hold you, too."

They proceeded to his room. After removing their shoes, they climbed into bed. Sunlight streamed into the room, slipping through the blinds.

"I've missed being with you," he said.

"You're with me now, and you always will be." She leaned onto her side to face him. "I'm so happy that you love me. I feel like I'm dreaming."

"But you aren't. We're both wide-awake." He unbuttoned the first few buttons of her blouse to get a peek at her bra. He noticed that it was made of cotton and bits of lace. "Look how pretty you are." He toyed with the lace. "Pretty and pregnant."

"I like being pregnant. Shirley told me that I glow."

"You do. So do you want to get married at the beach?"

She nodded. "With you in a tuxedo and me in a long, breezy white dress. I can carry a red rose bouquet since that's the type of flower I always envisioned in my wedding."

Jake remembered her telling him that before. She'd even put a red rose pattern on the quilt she'd made herself when she was younger, with patches of material that represented her future. A future that was now coming true. "We can have the wedding at Garrett's resort. Lots of people get married there, along the shore."

Her eyes lit up. "That would be perfect. I want Shirley to be part of the ceremony. She's as close to a mother as either of us has now. Oh, and maybe we can hire Lena to perform at the reception."

Jake teased her, thinking about the party that had started it all. "Yeah, and we can have our first dance inside of a cage."

She laughed. "We can make 'Couples Only' our wedding song."

"Sure. Why not? But we need to set Lena straight about Susanne."

"Of course, and we'll clear it up with Kristen, too.

You should introduce me to Susanne so we can invite her to be a guest."

"I'm sure she would be glad to attend."

"Good. I don't want there to be any bad feelings or gossip. I want our wedding to be as joyous as we feel."

"I'm going to ask both of my foster brothers to be my best men. Max will be back from his sabbatical soon, so we can set the date anytime. First, we'll have to talk to Garrett about his schedule and when he can make the resort available to us. He has an event planner on staff that can help us, too."

She untucked Jake's T-shirt from his jeans, lifted the material and skimmed her fingers along his abs. "The honeymoon is going to be sexy, that's for sure. I won't be able to stop touching my groom."

"Likewise, with my bride." He pushed his hand into the waistband of her leggings and past her panties. He rubbed her in hot little circles, just the way he knew she liked it.

She gasped, and he kissed her, sweet and slow. They hadn't made love since they'd made their baby, and it felt damned good to be together again. The citrus perfume she routinely wore was a welcoming scent. Everything about her worked like an aphrodisiac.

They took turns undressing each other, and he explored the changes in her body. The bump in her tummy was beautifully round, and her breasts were bigger, her nipples and areolas a darker shade of pink.

Jake moved lower, putting his mouth between her legs. He used his tongue, and he didn't stop until she was arching toward him, coming with dizzying pleasure.

"What are you doing to me?" she asked.

"Making you feel good." Making her shake and shiver and tug at the sheets.

In the afterglow, she sat forward, dewy from her orgasm, her body flushed. "I want you inside me."

Heavens, yes. He was already fully aroused from having touched her in such an intimate way. "Climb on top of me."

Carol went for it, straddling him, moaning as she impaled herself, taking him deep. She rode him, stealing his breath from his lungs. He watched her with adoration.

Sleek and warm, she moved up and down, flesh-to-flesh. They clasped hands and looked into each other's eyes. Hers were a shade of green that could've stemmed from the sea.

She was his mermaid. His lady. His future wife.

He said, "We can get married at dusk with a sandcastle as the backdrop, decorated with hundreds of candles, like how it was in the Caribbean."

"I'm so glad I took that trip with you." She leaned forward to kiss him, brushing her lips against his. "What happened between us was meant to be."

And it would be this way forever, he thought. Together they were friends, lovers, parents…

A family in every way.

* * * * *

Look for more
BILLIONAIRE BROTHERS CLUB *books,*
coming soon from Mills & Boon Desire!
Garrett Snow's story is next!

And if you liked this novel, pick up these
other sexy reads from
Sheri WhiteFeather

A KEPT WOMAN
APACHE NIGHTS
EXPECTING THUNDER'S BABY
MARRIAGE OF REVENGE
THE MORNING-AFTER PROPOSAL

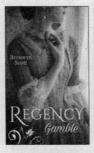

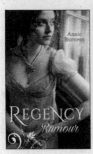

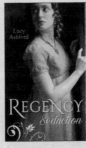

Commissioning Editor: *Alison Ashmore*
Project Development Manager: *Belinda Henry*
Project Manager: *Cheryl Brant*
Design Manager: *Jayne Jones*